THE DARKER LORD

By Jack Heckel

The Mysterium Series
The Dark Lord
The Darker Lord

The Charming Tales
The Pitchfork of Destiny
A Fairy-tale Ending
Happily Never After
Once Upon a Rhyme

THE DARKER LORD

The Mysterium Series, Book Two

JACK HECKEL

HARPER
VOYAGER
IMPULSE
An Imprint of HarperCollinsPublishers

THE DARKER LORD. Copyright © 2018 by John Peck and Harry Heckel. All rights reserved. Printed in the United States of America. No part of this book may be used or reproduced in any manner whatsoever without written permission except in the case of brief quotations embodied in critical articles and reviews. For information, address HarperCollins Publishers, 195 Broadway, New York, NY 10007.

Digital Edition JULY 2018 ISBN: 978-0-06-269777-6
Print Edition ISBN: 978-0-06-269778-3

Cover Design by Amy Halperin
Cover Photographs © PLRANG ART/Shutterstock (mars); ©Dmitry Bruskov (doors)/Shutterstock

Harper Voyager, the Harper Voyager logo, and Harper Voyager Impulse are trademarks of HarperCollins Publishers.

HarperCollins is a registered trademark of HarperCollins Publishers in the United States of America and other countries.

FIRST EDITION

18 19 20 21 22   HDC   10 9 8 7 6 5 4 3 2 1

To Heather, Carleigh, Taba and Isaac,
and all the dogs and cats that love them

"[B]ut there is no doubt they intend to kill us as dead as possible in a short time," the Wizard said. "As dead as poss'ble would be pretty dead, wouldn't it?" asked Dorothy.

—L. FRANK BAUM,
DOROTHY AND THE WIZARD OF OZ

CHAPTER 1

A CUP OF ENNUI

My name is Avery, and I am *not* the Dark Lord.

At least, that is what I muttered to myself as I stared at my reflection in the coffee shop window. The green mermaid logo smiled back, but I suspected she was humoring me. It was probably sleep deprivation, but my reflected image had an unhealthy pallor, and in the window's glass, the scarf wrapped around my neck might have been a hood. I looked like the Dark Lord.

There was a roar of laughter. I turned with the startled embarrassment of a man who's been caught talking to himself, or singing a really cheesy pop song. In keeping with my policy of total honesty, "Oops, I

Did It Again" is my own personal demon. Actually, my personal demon is an imp named Harold, but I digress.

A motley crew of costumed men and women were gathered in the back corner of the shop. In another place or in a different age, they might have been mistaken for an assembly of wizards and witches, but this was New York, and they were probably cosplay fanatics, or more likely partygoers at the end of a late night. Another round of laughter issued from the group. Whoever they were, they had no interest in me.

I turned back to my coffee and picked up the book I'd been trying to ignore. The book was *The Dark Lord*, and it was my story. At least, it was my story as translated through the dimensions onto Earth. It was this novel that had left me sleepless, or as my friend Eldrin had taken to saying, "Obsessed with navel gazing." Unfortunately, Eldrin was right.

I sighed. I'd read it a dozen times hoping to glean some meaning, but apart from finding the picture it painted of me depressingly accurate, I hadn't discovered any deeper understanding. Why was it here? I wasn't that important a mage. Why now? Nearly four months had passed since I'd returned to Mysterium. And who was Jack Heckel? The dimensions can get Tolkien's name right, if not his middle initials, but when the universe writes a story about me I don't even get an acknowledgment.

I was of two minds on the name issue. On the one hand, I don't come out looking or smelling very good in the story, so it might be better that the multiverse not associate the Dark Lord or what happened in Trelari with me personally. On the other hand, I liked the idea of seeing my name immortalized in print. I took another sip of my coffee—grande, quad shot, nonfat, one pump mocha, no whip, extra hot— as I reread the marketing blurb on the back cover. Hilarious parody? Parody of what?

The most troubling part of the book was the epilogue. For those of you who haven't had the pleasure of reading the book—and there are many more of you that haven't than there should be—*The Dark Lord* leaves me in Mysterium with Harold, my mentor Griswald's old imp, holding the key to a new reality, having had some undisclosed revelation about how the Mysterium was "broken." While I had inherited Griswald's position, and his office, and his imp, and Griswald had given me a box with a rattle, none of the rest of it had happened—at least, not as far as I could recall. As far as I knew, the box was sitting, unopened, on my bedside table. Harold had never spoken a word. And I was certainly no wiser about why Griswald thought the Mysterium was broken. The place seemed all right, even if the students were going to be more annoying now that I was in control of their grades. Premeds may have a bad reputation as being grade-obsessed on Earth, but you've never seen anything to match the whining that students of magic can conjure.

I had considered asking Harold if he would open the box for me, and had even gone so far as to purchase a large bag of butterscotch candies to bribe him, but I wasn't sure that I wanted to confirm the book's version of reality. What would I do if I opened the box and there was a key? Would I be the version of me in the book? I wanted to be that guy, but I couldn't imagine not trying to use the key to get back into Trelari. Why hadn't the book version of me done that? And why was a fictional epilogue tacked on to the end when the rest of the book was so embarrassingly detailed and accurate? And if it were accurate, why didn't I remember it?

"Why?" I asked the mermaid logo.

"Because it's almost seven o'clock, and if we don't leave soon you'll be late to your first class of the new semester," Eldrin said from behind me.

I jumped and the stool I'd been perched on shot out from under me. I fell to the floor with a clatter and a shout, my coffee spraying across my sweater. "Huzzah!" the group in the corner cried out. I cursed them under my breath.

Eldrin smiled in his irritatingly charming manner. "Maybe you should consider switching to decaf."

"Maybe I should reconsider the wisdom of having a roommate." I pulled myself to my feet.

"And what? Live with your parents? Having me

as a roommate is the only reason you can pay the bills."

This was unfortunately true. Assistant professors, especially junior assistant professors, are paid only slightly better than graduate students. This, coupled with the fact that Eldrin and I had foolishly chosen to live in New York City, one of the most expensive cities on Earth, meant that I was still broke. Of course, I refused to concede the point and instead focused on trying to blot coffee stains out of my sweater.

"What are you doing here anyway?" Eldrin asked as he passed me a handful of napkins.

"Reading the . . ." I stopped myself short. I would never hear the end of it if Eldrin found out I'd been reading my own book again. "Nothing. Just catching up on some notes for class."

I briefly congratulated myself on my escape, but as I put my coat on, Eldrin reached behind me and snatched the book from the counter. "Aha!" he crowed, holding it above his head. "I had no idea that your story merited an entire lecture."

A sudden rush of warmth came to my face. "That's not the subject of my lecture, Eldrin. I was only . . ."

He ignored me and flipped through the pages until he got near the end, and read the words I had been pondering moments earlier. "'And that's when I had my epiphany. I saw the flaw in Mysterium. The wrongness that hid in every crack and behind every shadow.'"

I sighed. It was bad enough having him throw the words back in my face, but he was doing it in a very serious British accent that made me sound like a stuffed shirt. "Your point?"

He snapped the paperback closed and shook it at me. "You've been reading this for months, and yet you still haven't discovered the epiphany. You have a class today, and yet you are here. So, I'll ask you the same question you were asking yourself: Why?"

"Drop it, Eldrin." I grabbed the book out of his hand and stuffed it into my coat pocket.

"Answer the question and I will." His eyes narrowed.

He was in his serious Eldrin mood, which meant he wasn't going to leave me alone until I answered. But I was in no state to deal with this at the moment. I pushed past him and walked outside, leaving behind the warmth and smell of coffee. The sun was beginning to brighten the sky and peek here and there between the buildings that lined the street. In the shadows, the fall air had a bite to it. I pulled my coat tighter around me and marched off in the direction of our apartment, my breath coming in little puffs of steam.

Eldrin fell in step beside me. "Avery, you have to deal with this."

"No, I don't," I said, picking up my pace until I was nearly jogging.

"Yes, you do."

I ignored him as we made our winding way through the narrow streets of Greenwich Village. People were beginning to emerge now and the metal gates and security doors that served to protect the shopkeepers from their fellow citizens were beginning to open. The city was funny like that, a bizarre mix of the modern and the medieval. Maybe that is why I wanted to live here, because it reminded me of Mysterium with its own tortured landscape. Speaking of torture, while the fast pace of our walk was making my breath catch, Eldrin kept up effortlessly. He let me run for another half block before mercifully stepping in front of me. I stopped. It was a good thing since my lungs were burning from the cold air.

He tried the practical approach. "Why won't you at least talk to Harold about opening Griswald's box?"

"Because . . ." I said between ragged breaths, but couldn't find the courage to finish.

He said nothing, just stared at me with those glittering eyes. I realized he was wearing a thin linen shirt, open to midchest. It was as irritating as it sounds, and something about it made me snap. "Because I'm afraid, Eldrin! I know you would have opened the thing straightaway, but I'm afraid. I'm afraid it means that my life is not as settled as I'd like it to be, and that there might be worse to come from what I did in Trelari . . . to Trelari." I pulled at the edges of my thick coat in frustration. "I'm not like you. I get cold."

His expression settled into something gentle and

understanding, and maybe a little sad. "You really don't get me, do you? I'm terrified of that book. I haven't been able to focus on my own work for weeks. I keep reading and rereading it, hoping the ending will change."

"Then why do you want me to open the box?"

"Because I do understand you, Avery. I know that you are not so afraid of whatever it is that may come out of that box that you will refuse to ever open it. You will just do it someday and somewhere that you think will make it safe for everyone but you, and I'd rather be there than not."

I didn't know what to say, so I mumbled an apology. "Sorry, Eldrin, I didn't want to drag you into my problems again."

"I hope you know that I don't think of them as your problems."

I didn't know what to say to this either, so I simply said, "Thanks."

And that was about as much of an emotional exchange as he and I could handle, so we continued—at a much slower pace—toward our apartment. However, this talk had raised one question I'd been meaning to ask him. "After the book came out I sort of expected you to try and open the box yourself. Why didn't you?"

He shrugged. "Because the book said I couldn't."

"So, you think everything in the book is true, or will come true?"

Eldrin shook his head. "Not exactly. I think it's likely to be true about specific facts, if not specific moments. For instance, I think it's true that Harold likes butterscotch candies, which you should start giving him by the way. On the other hand, I don't think you will be sitting on a park bench, or that the dwarf will come jogging by at just the moment Harold opens the box. That part is probably more allegory than history. The book is drawing together pieces of your past and present from your subconscious."

"Do you think I will have an epiphany about Mysterium?" He nodded. I shivered. "What . . . what do you think I'll figure out?"

He knitted his brow. "I don't know, but I think it's something you already know."

"Then why . . . why wasn't it revealed in the book?" I asked, my teeth now chattering noisily.

He shrugged. "Maybe the universe wanted to save something for the sequel."

"S-s-sequel?"

"Of course," he said with the arched eyebrow he used when he thought I was being particularly dense. "You know these sorts of stories are always part of a trilogy."

"I thought it might be a one-off like . . . like . . ." I had to think hard before an example came to mind. "Like *The Last Unicorn* or *The Princess Bride*."

"With how unsettled you've been the last couple of months? No chance."

I wanted to argue, but had to admit that everything that had happened since my return to Mysterium pointed to a number of unfinished story lines. I wrapped my arms around my body trying to ward off the cold and grasped for something positive to say. "Well, I suppose the good news is that even in a worst-case scenario we are thirty-three percent through the narrative and no one important has died . . . yet."

We both fell silent. Eldrin put his arm around my shoulders. He was blessedly warm. "God . . . d-d-damn elves," I managed.

"I do get cold, you know," he said. "When the weather merits."

Snow began to drift down from the haze above the tops of the buildings. He raised an eyebrow quizzically and we both laughed.

CHAPTER 2

OUR HOUSE IS A VERY, VERY, VERY SMALL HOUSE

We walked for a few more blocks before arriving at the Tower Estates, where Eldrin and I lived with Dawn, her two cats, and my imp. The name Tower Estates references a weather-worn sign that had been painted on the side of the building in happier times. We had taken to calling it the Dark Tower Estates, because it was a dump, and no place else in the world does run-down and crappy quite the way New York does.

Eldrin and I hurried through the front door. The moist warmth of the steam-heated lobby wrapped around us like a blanket. I sighed with relief and held my hands out to the hissing radiator. Eldrin gave me a minute to defrost before gesturing to the stairs. "Shall we?"

I groaned at the thought of climbing the five floors to our apartment. I looked about furtively and made a rising motion with my hand. "Do you think we could . . . ?"

He put a finger to his lips. We both paused and listened. The building was quiet. He raised an eyebrow at me, and we scurried into the well of the stairs, where a narrow opening rose in a tight rectangle up to a dirty skylight. In the center of the well of dirty light, one of the red floor tiles had been replaced with a square of light green linoleum. It clashed hideously with the rest of the floor, but as an identifiable marker it suited our purposes. We both stepped onto the tile and pulsed a little bit of mystical power into it. An outline of complex figures blazed bright blue, and like a pair of loosed corks, we shot into the air. The magic carried us to the fifth-floor landing, and we floated to a stop in front of our apartment.

We opened the door to find Dawn sitting at the kitchen table reading a newspaper. She had one cat on her lap and another making tiny orbits around the top of the table. Harold sat in his high chair eating his standard breakfast—a bowlful of dead white mice. Both of the cats were keeping a careful watch to see if he would drop anything.

Dawn looked up at us sharply. "I take it from the lack of panting that the two of you didn't walk up the stairs. Have either of you considered how the neighbors would react if they saw you zipping up and down the stairwells in violation of all this world's natural laws?"

Eldrin and I shared a look. It was an excellent question actually, and one we'd discussed in great detail since moving to New York. Earth borders Mysterium, and at any time there are dozens of Mysterian-trained wizards roaming about. And yet, on Earth, Penn & Teller are considered the absolute height of magic. How is that possible? Mysterium magicians are not known for their discretion or discipline, as evidenced by the fact that Eldrin and I had installed an inverted gravity field in the stairwell of our building, something that had required no small amount of effort on our part and entailed no small amount of risk to the structural integrity of the building's foundation.

In other worlds around Mysterium, magic, and even Mysterium magic, was practiced quite openly. On Eldrin's home plane of Hylar, magic was almost considered a religion. Of course, Hylars thought that Mysterium magic was vulgar, which it kind of is, but they could recognize it when it was being used. By contrast, here on Earth the populace goes to great lengths to dream up impossibly improbable explanations for it; where else in the multiverse could you find a people that accepted and dismissed obvious displays of what was, at its heart, magic, like disappearing socks, a cat's preternatural ability to know exactly where to stand that is most annoying, and the inexplicable popularity of the Kardashians.

Despite what I considered compelling arguments in our favor, I made no attempt to defend our literal flight up the stairs. Dawn, after all, was a trained magical ethicist. Arguing was like breathing to her. Eldrin on the other hand felt compelled to give it a go. While I flopped on the couch, he stood by the door and said with uncharacteristic petulance, "We did check to make sure no one was in sight. Besides, they would probably think we were performance artists or chimney sweeps or something."

Despite myself, I giggled. Dawn glared. "It isn't funny." She folded the paper over so I could see the headline of the article she'd been reading: "Magical Travel in a Post-Stewartian Multiverse." Suddenly the backs of my hands were very interesting. Dawn cleared her throat. "Whether you've noticed or like it, you've become one of the most famous mages in Mysterium. Your 'experiment' in Trelari resulted in half the textbooks needing rewrites. Next week there's an entire symposium devoted to what they are calling Outerworld Tectonics, and there is talk that a new department may be created to deal with the phenomenon of subworld migration. Yet, the mage behind it all refuses to involve himself. Instead, he rarely leaves the magical backwater of New York and seems entirely content to teach entry-level

Rowling Magic! You should be a rock star! What the hell is going on with you?"

I gave her a weak smile. "I'm modest."

She said nothing, but fixed her monochromatic black and white eyes on mine and studied me from behind the enchanted reading lenses she used to convert the *New York Times* into a pan-dimensional news source. "That's your answer?" she asked in a voice as soft as silk and as sharp as a knife.

"I don't have a better one."

"That's not very satisfying, Avery."

"Or accurate," Eldrin murmured under his breath.

Dawn turned her penetrating gaze on Eldrin, and he clamped his lips shut. After a few seconds of silence she refocused on me. "All you've done this summer is sit on the couch watching bad TV, or sit in the coffee shop staring at that book." I shrugged dismissively. "Well, Eldrin?" she huffed.

I glanced up and saw him swiveling his head back and forth between us. "What do you want *me* to say?" he protested.

"Only what you tell me nearly every night. That it's his duty not to abandon his research. That he owes it to science and magic. That he's being an idiot!"

The tips of Eldrin's ears went beet red, and I knew the words were his, if not verbatim, certainly in spirit. "Eldrin, do you really believe I'm being an idiot?"

"No, of course not."

"What about the rest of it?"

He half shrugged. "I mean, there are some good grant opportunities . . ."

I accepted the conversational lifeline like a drowning man. "I suppose so."

And that was it. The silence of the moment stretched on, broken only by Harold crunching into another mouse carcass. Had it been the two of us, the topic would have died a natural death right then and there.

"Oh gods!" Dawn exploded. "No wonder you two could never get the doorknob to your dorm room fixed. I give up." In a clatter of dishes and a scattering of cats, Dawn stalked off to her bedroom.

"Thanks a lot," Eldrin said irritably, following her.

I opened my mouth to protest that his girlfriend's mania for honesty was hardly my fault, but the fact was, she was right. I was being an idiot. The appearance of Trelari at the gates of Mysterium had been the most significant magical development since the discovery of the water to wine transmutation. Every field of magic, from the sublime—subworld studies, etherworld physics, and the like—to the mundane—innerworld shipping, transitory real estate, and so on—had me to thank or blame for the rise or fall of their fortunes. Fame and acclaim and disdain and infamy of a magnitude few mages ever attained awaited me on my return to Mysterium, and as any of you that have read of my exploits in *The Dark Lord* will know, I am definitely not modest.

As I had admitted between shivers to Eldrin a few

minutes ago though, I was afraid. It was not that I feared for my own safety or reputation. Or not too much. I had long ago decided that the biggest dangers I would face would be critics and jealous colleagues. Even then, being loathed had its upsides: fewer students would come to office hours, and no one would argue grades with me. My real fear was that somehow my presence would put Trelari in danger again. Already a storm was brewing outside the magical wall Valdara had created. Academic bomb-throwers with more time and vitriol than sense were coming out of the woodwork to write half-literate screeds about how Trelarians were subpeople, not worthy of protection, and certainly not worthy of receiving grants, scholarships, or any other sort of financial aid. All it would take would be one xenophobic madman, and Trelari would go from being a novelty to a threat. And people were looking to me—stupid me, idiotic Avery Stewart—as the voice of authority on Trelari. Is it any wonder I decided the best course for all involved was for me to keep my head down and my mouth shut? But now the new semester was starting. I couldn't avoid Mysterium any longer.

"What am I supposed to do?" I asked the heavens.

In answer, something thudded against the side of my head. I looked down and saw the corpse of a half-eaten mouse on the couch. Harold looked at me with expressionless eyes for a few seconds before pointing a long, sharp, taloned finger at the nearly indecipherable seven-dialed Mysterian time clock that hung crookedly on the wall. I stared at the thing for a full minute before coming to the conclusion that either it was yesterday, or I had ten minutes to get to class.

"Damn!"

Jumping up from the couch, I sprinted to my room, accidentally stepped on one of Eldrin's game boards, and impaled my foot on a half dozen tiny playing pieces. I plucked a yellow camel from my skin with a curse and hopped into my room. "Camel down," I muttered.

Now would be an apt time to describe our apartment. It is small. How small? Well, there are camper vans with more living space. I mean that literally. You could put our entire apartment on wheels and hurtle it down a highway at seventy-five miles per hour, and no one would bat an eye. There was a bathroom, which we all share, but which Eldrin shares more than Dawn and I combined. A living room/dining room/kitchen, which made up the vast majority of the place, but to give you a scale to consider, the game map I'd stepped on took up a pretty sizable chunk of the open floor space. And two bedrooms.

Before you get excited that Eldrin and I have separate bedrooms, this is a New York "two-bedroom." For those of you from anywhere but New York, what a New York "two-bedroom" actually means is an apartment with one bedroom and a largish-sized closet.

My room is that closet.

It was about the size of my bed, which was a double, because a man can dream that one day he may have need of the extra space. When I lay down at night I could stretch my arms out and touch the walls—flat-palmed. The point being, without my piece of folded extradimensional space I'm not sure how I would have had room for myself and my clothes. Actually, I do know—I wouldn't have had room. I would have had to build one of those absurd lofts you find in every student apartment in the city where you sleep six inches from the ceiling (talk about putting a crimp in your social life by the way) in exchange for a completely impractical space underneath the bed where you live and work in a permanent hunch.

I was rummaging through my extradimensional fold for my lecture notes while simultaneously trying to comb my hair and pull on the traditional Mysterium professorial robes, and not doing any of these tasks particularly well, when Harold wheezed his way into the room, a half-chewed mouse dangling out of his mouth. He was carrying my lecture notes in one of his grubby little paws and a bow tie in the other. I reached for my notes. "Thank the gods you found them."

Harold pulled the papers away and held the bow tie out to me. It was tradition: Harold always wore a bow tie to class when Griswald lectured. "Sorry, Harold, but I don't even know how to tie one of those.

Now, give me the lecture so we can get out of here or we're going to be late."

He blinked at me solemnly and chewed on the mouse. I stood up, squared my shoulders, and tried to gather as much dignity as I could. That wasn't much as I had missed a button on my robes and looked a bit like a toddler that had tried to dress himself. "Give me the papers, Harold."

He mimicked my pose, though he looked a lot less ridiculous doing it, and thrust the bow tie up at me.

"No! We don't have time!" I protested.

Apart from the chewing, which was exceedingly disconcerting, Harold remained unmoved—eyes locked on mine, bow tie grasped in his outstretched paw. We stood there in a dignified and strained silence for a few beats, and then I lunged at him with a high-pitched shriek.

I will not bore you with the details of the ensuing chase, but several minutes later, my lecture notes clasped in one hand and Harold perched on my shoulder, I jumped into the hall closet where the Mysterium transport circle was drawn. I was still only half-dressed, but Harold's bow tie was perfect. It had taken me three tries.

As the magic from the circle started to swirl around us, I noticed that Harold had Griswald's box tucked under his arm. I tried to ask him why he was bringing it along, but my words were lost as the transport magic turned us both inside out for the trip back to Mysterium.

CHAPTER 3

MR. DARK AND FANCIFUL

My ears popped as I spun through the multicolored etherspace between worlds. They popped again as Harold and I landed in the James Ward building, remarkably in Lecture Hall 2814 Q, miraculously on my feet, and amazingly right where I wanted to be. I was standing just within the doorway of a little curtained-off cloakroom to the left of the lectern.

Considering how close I had come to being late and how little preparation I had taken, plus my battle with Harold and his bow tie, the accuracy of the transport spell was a feat. Conjuring a true portal from one of the innerworlds to a specific location in Mysterium might not be as complicated as rocket science or brain surgery, but it was at least as difficult as dusting crops.

Or so I've been told. I've never flown a crop duster. But I digress.

Harold and I peeked out at the class, all two hundred plus of them. I took a deep breath. "It's showtime!"

"Indeed, it is, Professor Stewart," came a grave and rasping voice from behind me.

I spun around, and as I did, I had a sudden desire to be anywhere else in the world, even if that meant leaving my body altogether. The man waiting for me in the shadows was Garth Moregoth, chief executioner of Mysterium Security, magus general of Mysterium.

Technically, the chief executioner title meant that he executed security protocols, but everyone interpreted it literally. He did nothing to disabuse people of the notion. He was the second most powerful mage on campus. I think the list goes something like: the provost, Garth Moregoth, the group of deities who like to congregate in the commissary of the School of Relativistic Religion, everybody else. The man had an aura of self-loathing and angst that infected everyone around him. If a quad on campus were ever empty, it would be because Moregoth was brooding nearby. Everyone feared and reviled him. Puppies whimpered when he walked near, and birds fell dead from the sky. I recognized him in an instant, because no one looked like Garth Moregoth. No one would dare.

He was a tall man, who appeared taller because of his long black trench coat and thick-soled black boots. He had a long thin nose and deep-set eyes that were made cadaverous by the heavy black eyeshadow that lined them, and the pallor of his deathly white skin. In fact, he was so pale that some people believed he was either a vampire or an albino, while everyone else knew he was, in fact, an albino vampire. Moregoth's most striking feature was his hair, which had a studiously disheveled look highlighted by a set of dramatic bangs that swooped down to entirely obscure the left side of his face. But, more than the style, it was the color of his hair that was remarkable. It has been inadequately described as "dark as night." In fact, it was darker than that because he mystically dyed it, creating a black that was blacker than black. Light was not so much absorbed by his hair, as it simply ceased to exist out of despair when it got too close. That is the kind of dark I'm talking about.

Trying to focus on him as he stood in the deep shadows of the alcove was a bit like trying to focus on an object in a brightly lit room that has been thrown into a sudden darkness. My eyes kept losing where the outline of his body ended and the rest of the world began. The result was that his pale white face and hands appeared to be suspended in space.

"I'm sorry if my presence startled you, Professor

Stewart. We have not had the pleasure. I am Garth Moregoth."

Even though I knew who he was, hearing the name spoken aloud, by the man himself, sent a wave of dread through me, which was only heightened when one of the pale floating hands extended itself in my direction. I hesitated, and he fixed his gaze on me.

His eyes were also black. The solid black of a man that has been studying dark magic for longer than is healthy or, strictly speaking, legal. I finally took his hand and shook it out of a mixture of habit and fear. It was like trying to shake hands with a statue: nonresponsive, cold, and hard as stone. I pulled back and reflexively rubbed my palms together. "May I help you Magus Mor-goth?"

When I said his name, I made sure to omit the *e* when pronouncing it, because while he demanded that everyone spell his name with an *e*, he also demanded that it be pronounced without one. I must have gotten it right, because he smiled, a thin and humorless expression that showed as little of his teeth as possible between his deep purple lips. "I'm not sure anyone can help me, Professor Stewart," he intoned gloomily. "We are, after all, merely shadows, dancing in the flickering light of eternity. Doomed to extinction. However, my colleagues and I are looking for two students of yours."

"C-c-colleagues?" I stammered, and peered about the alcove.

He extended a long black-polished finger toward the rear of the lecture hall. I followed where it pointed and saw a squad of grim-faced mages lining the back wall. My blood ran cold as I recognized the distinctive crimson cloaks of the Sealers.

The Sealers are a special militarized unit of university security. Established early in Mysterium's history, they dealt with extradimensional and subworld threats. In the past, Sealers had stopped a Cthulhoid attempt to raise a sunken city from the depths of a Mysterium pond, multiple plots by the Demonology Department to summon avatars from various apocalyptic cults during their occasional wage protests, and no less than a half-dozen orc invasions. And those were only the incidents that were common knowledge. It is said that they are the reason dragons haven't attacked Mysterium University in over a century, although rumors persisted about the continual disappearance of pigs. Basically, they were elite magical ninja assassins on steroids, and Moregoth was their leader.

No, I can't in good conscience leave you with the impression that Moregoth was merely the head of the Sealers. To say that Garth Moregoth was their leader is a bit like saying that John and Paul wrote a couple of songs for the Beatles. Garth Moregoth was the personification of everything the Sealers stood for. He was their model, the deadliest, most determined, most deranged Sealer in the many-centuries-old history of the Sealers. That they were here with him should not have been a surprise. Where he went, they followed, like an army of shadows.

What I didn't understand was why he, and they, were here at all. The Sealers only ever intervened in matters of utmost importance. They are authorized to kill, hence the reputation given to the chief executioner. Sending them out to look for wayward students, even wayward students that are behind on their tuition payments, seemed like overkill. It would be like sending a brigade of marines in to settle an office dispute over whose turn it was to use the microwave in the breakroom. I'm sure they could do it, but the body count would be tough to explain to Human Resources.

Moregoth cleared his throat, a wet unhealthy sound. I managed a weak, "Students?"

He pulled a paper from somewhere in the depths of the shadows. "Yes, an Ariella Moonsong, and a Sam No Last Name Given." He said "No Last Name Given" as though that might, in fact, be Sam's surname.

The blood drained from my face. All the blood. Every drop. Seriously. The chief executioner of Mysterium Security, a universally acknowledged lunatic, was looking for two of my friends from Trelari who were not only not supposed to be in my class, but as far as I knew, were not supposed to be on this plane of existence. Had it been a year earlier I would have gladly told him whatever he wanted to hear, and probably volunteered to help hunt Sam and Ariella down. I had never wanted any trouble, particularly not from the Administration, and definitely not with Moregoth. After all, tenure had always been the goal. But this was a new year, tenure did not seem as important as it once had, and this was Sam and Ariella we were talking about. Good thing I was such a practiced liar.

"Sam and Ariella? I'm . . . I'm not sure I recognize those names."

My voice sounded a little squeaky, but Moregoth didn't call me on it. He simply stared, and let an awful silence stretch out between us. Predictably, my nerve broke first. I blurted a string of excuses that were entirely true, but too pathetic to be convincing. "This is my first class of the year . . . we are still in the add/drop period . . . I haven't had a chance to review my class roster . . . I can't be expected to know the names of every one of my students . . ."

Moregoth's eyes narrowed. "I think you know these particular students, Professor Stewart. You traveled with them quite extensively last year." His hand disappeared into some deeper blackness and emerged with a book. My book. My damnable book. "You met them in Chapter Nine." His purple lips bent into the barest of smiles. "On a personal note, I thought the semi-lich's macabre banality was rendered with fiendish perfection, but then reading about people's ordeals with contractors is so deliciously soul-crushing. Don't you think?"

I wasn't sure how to answer, and I was fairly sure any answer I did give had a better than even chance of being used against me at my inevitable Review Board hearing. Eventually, I settled on, "Yes, I suppose."

This didn't seem to commit me to anything except, maybe, that the semi-lich was banal or that contractors were delicious, neither of which I agreed with, but either of which I could live with. Anyway, Moregoth seemed uninterested in my answer as he was busy flipping through pages near the back of the book. "Vampich," he chuckled asthmatically. "Such an ecstasy of despair."

While I was still not sure what was going on, I needed to end this conversation, get through my class, drink several tumblers of good whiskey, and hope to the gods that there had been some hideous paperwork foul-up that might explain away today. I cleared my throat, a sound that Harold echoed from my shoulder. Moregoth's single visible eyebrow rose quizzically up his forehead as though he was surprised I was still there. "Do forgive me, Professor Stewart. I am keeping you from your students. You and I can continue this discussion after class. With your indulgence, my friends and I will take the liberty of observing your lecture. I find the dark forces used to shape young minds such an inspiringly sweet slice of torment."

Afraid to say anything I simply nodded.

"Oh, Professor Stewart, one last thing."

"Yes?"

He leaned in close, far too close, and whispered menacingly, "If you hold anything holy. If there is anyone or anything that you love. Never lie to me again." My blood froze in my veins. Moregoth pulled away and smiled a crooked smile. "Very well, Professor, until class is over." He gave an almost imperceptible bow of his head. "Or until the darkness consumes us all."

He pushed aside the curtain, and moved past me up one of the side aisles toward the back of the room like a three-dimensional silhouette of a man. I held it together until he joined the rest of his men in the shadows near the rear doors. Then my hands began to shake. I bent over and put my hands on my knees.

There must be a dozen perfectly reasonable explanations why two students that happen to also be from Trelari might be wanted by the Administration. That I couldn't come up with even one reason that didn't involve tiny, barren, hard-walled interrogation rooms was more a commentary on me and my lack of imagination than anything else. Right?

"Bloody lunatic," I gasped.

"I like him," Harold wheezed from my shoulder. "Granted, his fashion sense is appalling, and his haircut isn't regulation. But he's very polite."

That's when I blacked out.

CHAPTER 4

THIS WILL GO DOWN
ON YOUR
PERMANENT RECORD

I woke to the smell of dead mouse and Harold's rheumy eyes staring down at me. He was wheezing heavily and fanning me ineffectually with my lecture notes. "I don't want to tell you how to do your job . . . but now isn't the time . . . to take a nap," he said between ragged breaths.

I pushed myself up onto my elbows and winced as a shock of pain ran through the back of my head. Gingerly, I rubbed the bump that was rising there. We were still in the alcove and, based on the muted murmur of voices and shuffling bodies coming from the lecture hall, my class was still here. I couldn't have been out long. I looked at Harold, thought of all the things I should say, but my brain settled on, "You're talking."

He rolled his eyes. "Obviously."

A thousand questions rose in my mind. And having lived through two major shocks and minor head trauma in the space of a few minutes, I naturally started asking them all at once, and in no particular order. "How long have I been out? Why haven't you talked to me before? Have you opened the box? Was there a key in it? How can you possibly think Moregoth is polite? Is it true your favorite candy is butterscotch? Do you know where Griswald is? Your accent is British, are you from Earth? Did you really eat the remote control for the TV?"

"And you wonder why I haven't wanted to talk?"

He had a point. "Fine, but answer the question."

"I did not eat the remote. I flushed it down the toilet. I will not tolerate reality TV."

I glared at him. "Not that question."

The imp shook his head and pulled the closed box from his vest pocket. He held it out to me. "Be my guest."

I slumped back against the wall. "It won't work, and you know it."

"No, I don't, and neither do you. Ever since that book—" he paused to cough spasmodically "—book came out, you haven't wanted to touch it."

I let this pass. "Can you open it?"

"That's not the question."

"Will you open it?"

"No."

"Please." I clasped my hands together.

"No."

"Why the hell not?" I clambered to my feet and began pacing unsteadily around the alcove, cursing, and throwing my arms about in impotent frustration. "Why won't you do what we both know you can do? Is it because I'm not Griswald? Or because you don't like me? Or because you want to teach me some mystical life lesson like a shorter, uglier version of Mr. Miyagi? Wax on. Wax off. If so, I don't understand the lesson. Just teach me karate already."

I stopped, not because I didn't have more to complain about, but because my head was starting to spin and I was afraid I was going to fall down again if I didn't. "You done?" Harold asked.

I was being ridiculous, but I refused to admit it. I crossed my arms over my chest and glowered. "For now, but I reserve the right to throw another tantrum if the mood strikes me."

"Very mature of you," he said with irritating calmness. "I won't open it because you are already seven minutes late to your first class, and the students are counting down the seconds to fifteen past when they can walk out. You need to go in there and teach."

"I don't care two figs about the class, Harold. We have too much to talk about."

"Yes, far too much," he sighed. "However, there are two very good reasons why you need to teach this class."

"Name them," I snapped. "Give me two reasons why I should teach an introductory magic class to a bunch of kids who would rather be anywhere else doing anything else when this box may have the answers to a thousand questions, including where Griswald and Vivian went when they disappeared."

In answer, he thrust the papers he'd been holding under my nose. I looked down at the page. It was my class roster. "And . . . ?"

He pointed a finger at one of the names: "Ariella Moonsong." I blinked, but the name didn't change. While I was trying to absorb the fact that Moregoth was right and that I had Ariella on my class roster, Harold shifted his hand and stabbed his finger at a second name; it simply read: "Sam."

"Sam and Ariella are here," I whispered.

"Yes, they are," Harold said soberly.

In a kind of daze, I plucked the sheet of paper from the imp's hand. Harold took hold of my chin and pulled my head down so my eyes fell on the bottom of the page. There was a note in the margin in official glowing letters: it was from the Administration. "Professor Stewart, two of your students, Ariella Moonsong and Sam (no last name given), both of Trelari, need to report to the Office of Student Enrollment at once. There are some discrepancies in their applications and potential issues with financial aid. Representatives from Mysterium Security will be present in your class to take charge of them. Please make every effort to cooperate with them in this matter, and let's have a great first day of class!"

My heart sank. Moregoth had been telling the truth, and if anything, my worst fears were made even worse (yes, I know worst can't be worse, but that's how I felt) by the upbeat message at the end of the notice. Usually when the Administration gave a pep talk it was following, or followed by, a notification that a class had been torn apart by out-of-control vector magic, or gotten lost in some shadow dimension. I peeked through the curtain and tried to scan the faces to see if I could spot Sam and Ariella, but from this angle it was impossible to see past the first row. "Moregoth really means to take them."

"Yes, he does."

I stared at the two names. The certainty that Sam and Ariella were not only in trouble but in real mortal peril from a foe I did not have the slightest chance of protecting them from should have sent me into another panic. Oddly, it did not. Instead, it filled me with a measure of resolve. To hell with Garth Moregoth and his Sealers. I would find a way to save Sam and Ariella if it was the last thing I did. Which it probably would be.

"Right!" I said. "Let's go teach this bloody class, and save Sam and Ariella while we're at it."

I started to pull the curtain aside, but Harold held out a taloned hand. "Wait! Aren't we going to make a plan?"

He was right, of course, but I had nothing. Nor did I think that the imp and I could come up with anything that would have even the slightest chance of working against an entire squad of Sealers in the next couple of minutes, or days, or even weeks. And I had a feeling that if I delayed much longer Moregoth would run out of patience and take matters into his own, exceedingly pale and lethal hands.

I gave Harold my most irritating grin. "Plans are overrated, and the fifteen-minute rule is a myth by the way."

He thought about arguing for a second, gave a mournful sigh, and scrambled up to sit on my shoulder. I walked through the curtain and up the stairs to the lectern. The buzz of conversation died and the eyes of over two hundred students bored into me. I was sorely tempted to take a moment and scan the room for Sam and Ariella, but I didn't trust myself not to give them away. My lone hope was that Moregoth didn't know what they looked like. Being careful not to make eye contact with anyone, I turned to the blackboard, retrieved my piece of enchanted chalk from my robe pocket, and set it on the board. "Introduction," I whispered.

The chalk began to write in a long, looping hand, "Welcome to Rowling Magic 101 . . ."

I turned back around and got the first look at my class. I'm not sure how to describe what I saw, because any large gathering at Mysterium University is as incredible as it is indescribable. This is because the student body of Mysterium University is a virtual kaleidoscope of races and species. There were all your usual suspects: bearded dwarfs, backpack-sized halflings, and radiant-skinned Hylar, but there were more exotic peoples here as well. In the front row, arranged like a leather-encased, ochre-fleshed wall, was a band of massive, pig-snouted orcs. The largest of whom was clutching a stick on the end of which he had tied a dead rat. It was difficult to see who or what was sitting directly behind them, because the enormous girth and height of the orcs blocked my view of the next three or four rows (I would definitely have to make some adjustments to the seating assignments before my next class). I suspected a group of Shades (sort of living cloaks that existed by absorbing the radiance and joy of beings around them) had gathered just behind the first row, because there was an indistinct area of deep shadow right behind the orcs that made me want to weep every time I looked at it. I put the class roster down on the lectern and made a note to separate them. It might not be fair, but if I didn't I'd have a class of depressed novices within the week.

The Shades were not the only beings I would need

to talk to either. As I was studying the room, I saw there was a general miasma of smoke hovering in the air. That would be the Dracos, a species noted for being of varying degree, part dragon or lizard or snake or (and don't ask me to explain it) turtle, with scales and flaming breath and all the rest. Anyway, it appeared I had a number of them in my class, because they were blowing smoke like mad. As it was their first day, I would give them a break, but I would have to send out a reminder about university rules concerning vaporous emissions inside of campus buildings. If I didn't, we would be setting the smoke alarms off every lecture.

This was just one of the many unique hazards of teaching at a university like Mysterium. You had to lay down your ground rules right off the bat, or things could get out of control in a hurry. I didn't think I had any Lolths in my class this year (a species of giant, superintelligent multidimensional spider), but they were notorious for webbing up whole lecture halls during periods of high stress, like exams. This often made it impossible for anyone to leave the room at the end of the test, and really annoyed the janitorial staff. It was dealing with these difficulties that made Mysterium what it was. Where else in the multiverse can you learn alongside other beings that don't just speak a different language, but in some cases are not entirely contained within three-dimensional space? What's truly amazing—in fact, as I thought about it, seemingly impossible—was that all of us could coexist in one place. That, in and of itself, was a kind of magic, and for a second, I forgot about Moregoth and the Sealers and the danger Sam and Ariella were in and even my own doubts about Mysterium, and simply reveled in the moment. Or I did until I noticed the three gray-cloaked DERPs sitting, grim-faced, off to my left.

A DERP is an Evaluation Review Panel—the *D* in DERP is unofficial and stands for *Damned*. The DERPs are the bane of all professors' existences. They might be watching you or the students, it might be a review for discipline or promotion, but invariably they sit and they stare and they scribble down notes in their official evaluation forms, and generally make everyone self-conscious. Plus, they all wear the same inscrutable expression, the sort of expression that makes it difficult to know if they are happy, sad, bored, irritated, or simply fixated by a large pimple on your forehead or something in between your teeth.

I rubbed my nose self-consciously. Of course I would have a DERP review on my first day of class while Sealers were trying to kidnap two of my students. I was wallowing in the unfairness of it all when it dawned on me that the room had grown very quiet. Even the DERPs were sitting, pens at the ready. That's when I realized that I had been standing at the lectern, saying nothing, for I didn't know how long.

Damn!

I cleared my throat and, with great dignity, reached into the pocket of my robes to pull out my lecture notes. They were not there. Harold let out a loud coughing hack from my shoulder. I tried the second most likely pocket in my robes. The notes were not there either. Harold tapped a talon on the top of my head. I shooed his hand away and began patting myself down like a drunk looking for the keys to his house at the end of a long night. I had just retrieved my piece of folded reality and was about shoulder-deep into my search of it when Harold waved a stack of papers in front of my face. They were, of course, my notes. He'd been holding them all along. A ripple of uncertain laughter rolled through the classroom, and I felt my face flush with heat.

Double damn!

Closing my eyes, I said what I knew was going to be an entirely ineffectual prayer to the gods to get me through this day, and very carefully took the papers. I cleared my throat authoritatively. "Good morning, students. Welcome to Rowling Magic 101. My name is Professor Stewart, and my assistant's name is Harold."

On cue Harold flapped off of my shoulder to perch on the right-hand side of the lectern. He straightened his tie and took a bow. There was a general round of applause and laughter. I silently thanked the imp for having impeccable comedic timing.

Just when I thought I'd gotten the room back

under control, the biggest orc, the one with the rat on the stick, the one sitting dead center at the front of the class, boomed, "You're not Professor Stewart!"

"That's right," said a visored student sitting behind the DERPs. "Everyone knows that Professor Stewart is bald and uses a wheelchair." The DERPs obviously thought this was an extremely important observation, because they were scribbling away furiously.

"Seriously?" questioned a Hylar student sitting just to the left of the orcs. "What subworld have you been on all summer? This is Professor Avery Stewart! The one who moves subworld orbitals." He said this in a condescending tone that only a Hylar could accomplish.

"Wrong!" shouted a bare-chested Kurgan. The Kurgan are a group of chaos-loving barbarians, ostensibly human and often capable of great magic, but generally known for trying to out-savage the orcs. Despite that, they are a great deal of fun at parties. He rippled his oiled chest muscles and stabbed a finger at the orc. "Professor Shadowswan said she detected the movement of Trelari months ago. The Stewart phenomenon is a complete myth!"

That was the end of the conversation that I could follow. More and more students started to talk; a jumbled mix of chatter filled the hall. I had lost control, and the DERPs were recording it all. This is when Harold, who had been standing motionless on the edge of the podium, rolled his bloodshot eyes, raised a finger, and pointed at the board behind me. I turned my head just in time to hear the Kurgan below, "He can be only one professor, and the board says he is Professor Griswald!"

And sure enough, there in big, bold, looping letters read: "Welcome to Rowling Magic 101. My name is Professor Griswald." It was only then I remembered I hadn't bothered imprinting Griswald's enchanted chalk. The chalk was his. The handwriting was his. The name was his.

While I studied the chalkboard, wishing it would magically say something else, the volume in the around the room continued to increase. Confused voices shouted questions asking whether they were in the wrong class, whether I was in the wrong class, and, of course, whether this would be on the exam. Then, bubbling up over the crowd, Sam's voice rang out, "I don't care what the board says. That is Professor Avery Stewart. I know him personally." I held up my hands, trying to regain control of the situation and see if I could shut Sam up before he said anything else, but I was too late. At my urging, the rest of the class had begun to quiet when Sam said in a voice that could be heard quite clearly throughout the hall, "Of course, I knew him as the Dark Lord."

You could have heard a pen drop. In fact, I think I actually did hear two or three of them hit the floor right after he said this. The orc sat down. The Hylar stopped glittering quite so smugly. The Kurgan ceased his flexing. Even the DERPs stopped their scribbling. Everyone turned to look at Sam. Well, everyone but the two or three catlike Jellicles in attendance. True to form, they were all either asleep or stretched out across the backs of seats, staring at invisible things that I assumed were floating about the lecture hall at random.

The good news: now that nearly everyone was looking in his direction, I could spot Sam. He was sitting just behind the Shades in the third row. Through a crack in the bodies, I could see Ariella sitting next to him. Her head was in her hands, and she was shaking it back and forth. The bad news: Moregoth had also spotted Sam. I could see a stirring in the crimson wall of men lining the back of the lecture hall. They began to mass at the head of the aisles behind where Sam and Ariella were sitting.

My entire plan, the one I made up between leaving the alcove and arriving at the lectern, had been based on the premise that I didn't think Moregoth would make a move if he thought it would disrupt class and draw attention to what he was doing. Not that I thought he cared a whit about the education of the students, but rather because someone had told him to keep Sam and Ariella's extraction clean and quiet. Unfortunately, my lecture had devolved into total chaos. There was a good chance Moregoth would use the confusion to make his move on Sam and Ariella if I didn't act quickly.

"I assure you," I announced in my best imitation of an authority figure, "I am indeed Professor Stewart."

Several hands, one shadow appendage, and a tentacle (yes, I was lucky enough to have a Cthulhoid in class, and the smell of fish was making my eyes water) shot up at this announcement. The fact that there were so many questions over something as simple as my name did not bode well for the rest of the semester. I resolved to be patient, and so smiled and pointed to a bright-looking fellow with a long, forked beard sitting to my left. He was human, or at least looked human. "Yes, you had a question?" I asked.

"It still says you're Professor Griswald."

I turned and looked at the board. Indeed, the chalk had written directly under the first line: "I assure you all that I am indeed Professor Griswald." It had even placed emphasis on the name by underlining it twice.

The headache had arrived. I pinched my nose and cursed under my breath, "Damn chalk! Damn class! Damn . . ."

I was into my third "damn" before I noticed that the chalk was still transcribing everything I said. It finished the third "damn" and hovered there smugly waiting for me to say something else. I obliged by calling it something really rude that I will not repeat here, but that it began to happily write. I lunged forward, snatched it from the air, and quickly whispered an erase spell. The board began to shed the chalk lines in much the same way a dog shakes off water.

I waited until the words disappeared before turning back to my class.

Clearing my throat again, I said, "Sorry about the confusion, just a little technical difficulty with the ensorcelled chalk. Which only goes to show that magic often creates as many problems as it solves. And that leads us to our topic of discussion for today . . ."

I have never taken an improv class, primarily because I cannot condone any discipline that encourages you to say, "yes, and," no matter what your partner says. If you think about it, I suspect you will agree that if such a doctrine were applied to any other field it would lead to almost inevitable disaster. Anyway, the result of this hole in my education is that I am not very good at ad-libbing. Unfortunately, this made the whole "no plan" plan somewhat ill-advised. Fortunately, I had mapped out my first couple of lectures. I began to read those now, hoping that Moregoth would hold true to his word and give me the chance to finish this class—and think up a way to escape.

"I know most of you are novices," I began to read from my prepared notes. "You are likely excited and perhaps a little unsettled about everything that you've experienced since you arrived at Mysterium University. You have to get used to new housing, new types of people, and, for many of you, the fact that magic is real and that you are being asked to learn it."

I turned the page and continued, watching Moregoth and his men from the corner of my eye. As the students settled back into their seats, so too did the Sealers fade into the shadows near the back wall.

"This class is meant to provide you with a way to explore those talents which are inside everyone who comes to Mysterium. Perhaps some of you already know some magic and are questioning why you are here. You may have already set your heart on studying the subtle secrets of necromancy, or losing yourself in Moorcockian demonic channeling, or tapping into deep-space power using Lovecraftian rituals, but every well-educated mage should have a grounding in Rowling-speak. It represents a magical system and language so popular across the worlds its influence cannot be understated . . ."

Truth be told, this description of the influence of Rowling-speak on magical casting was a bit of an understatement. Like saying that the Sun might be important to life on Earth, or that a towel is of moderate importance when traveling through Adams-space, or that as a rule one should probably never tie your soul to anything called Stormbringer. Rowling's *Primary Omnibus Treatise on Terminologically Expressive Rheology* was a fantastic breakthrough in wizardry. It provided a very simple system for people who struggled with the complex primary patterns of Mysterium casting to gain familiarity and comfort with manipulating reality through spellcasting. But—and it is an enormous "but"—somehow when the tome was translated across worlds it had gotten entangled with a set of young adult novels the author had been reading to her children. The result gave people some terrible ideas about magic. Let's just say that I have never traveled to a world that had train stations and not seen one or two people attempting to plow their way headfirst through a solid wall, or trying to get things to fly with some odd mix of Latin and English. Mysterium has lost a number of students to head trauma and catastrophically miscast spells since the book's multiversal publication. As a system of magical education, it also requires something so universally reviled that its use in classrooms has been banned on some worlds as a form of torture.

I turned the page on my notes and there it was, under the heading "Mandatory Elements," subheading "Group Projects." I shuddered, because I knew what was coming next.

"Before we begin, it is traditional in Rowling Magic classes to assign you to smaller groups. It is hoped that these small groups will help you get to know your fellow students a little better. The four small groups for this class are—"

Hands shot up all over the room and voices shouted out to be put in this group or that group, and why it had been that person's dream since childhood to go to this group or that group, and not that group or this group. Students wanted to know where the hat was. Arguments broke out over which group was better. Lines were drawn. Factions formed. I had lost control again.

This time Moregoth's men sprang into action. They began to file down the aisles in the lecture hall so they could approach Sam and Ariella from both ends of their row. Frantically, I turned over the third page of my notes to see if I could skip ahead to something less prone to duels, and found that somewhere in the chaos of the morning my lecture had gotten scrambled. I shuffled through the papers on the podium in desperation as the Sealers advanced. That's when I found the Administration's Mandatory Missive on Magical Mayhem. The MMMM was the single most soul-draining part of any class. It was perfect. The class would be pacified, if not unconscious, in less than a minute.

"Safety!" I bellowed.

Harold gave a start at my shout, and toppled off the side of the lectern. I held up the Administration's notice like a trophy as he clambered back up to his perch—bow tie now askew. The uproar died down and everyone took their seats again.

"Before we decide on group assignments, the Administration has asked that all professors of novice-level classes read the following guidelines on safe spellcasting . . ."

Moregoth's men paused as order was restored.

"It may not be the most exciting topic, but I assure you . . ."

Realizing they were the only ones still standing, the Sealers began a slow retreat.

". . . it is better than finding out the hard way . . ."

I could see Moregoth in the back. He applauded mockingly, and then turned slightly and pointed to the clock above the doors. There were only five minutes of class left. His dark lips stretched into a grim smile.

". . . how painful it is to get a fazestone burn, or have your organs scrambled from . . . an ether backlash . . ."

And that's when inspiration struck.

". . . and that is why I am going to give you a little demonstration of the dangers of casting without observing the four M's of proper spellcasting: method, mind, and . . ."

I had no idea what the third or fourth "M's" were.

". . . and the other two."

This caused a great deal of vigorous scribbling from the DERP panel, but I didn't have time to worry about them right now.

"I will need two volunteers."

Hands, tentacles, paws, claws, and every other manner of appendage shot into the air. The orc in the front row waved his dead rat around so vigorously that the string snapped and it went sailing off. One of the Jellicles pounced after it.

I made a pretense of looking at my roster. "Ms. Moonsong and Mr. Sam?"

Hands dropped in disappointment, but I heard Sam say, "That's us, Ariella. Come on."

They rose and began making their way up to the front of the class. As Sam and Ariella mounted the stairs, Moregoth glowered at me and made a slashing gesture. The Sealers surged down the aisles.

I clapped my hands, which startled everyone, even the Sealers. "Okay, class, for this demonstration I need everyone to cast a spell."

The Cthulhoid raised a tentacle. "I thought our first lesson was about spell safety."

"He's right! What about our organs?" the Kurgan bellowed.

There was a general murmur of agreement until I shouted, "Extra credit on the midterm for the most impressive display!"

All protest vanished at the mention of extra credit. Moregoth raised his hands to countermand my instructions, but his asthma kept his voice to a harsh whisper. In a lecture hall full of shouting students, he had no chance. Every novice in that hall who could cast a spell did so almost simultaneously. The individual effects were impressive: I saw a glowing phoenix, a thundercloud with violet lightning, a watercolor painting come to life, a dragon formed out of a young woman's blood, a windstorm of flower petals, and so much more. The intermixing of the different magics was pure, creative chaos. The phoenix was struck by the violet lightning and erupted into a shower of indescribable colors that peppered the watercolor with spots of cubism. The blood dragon somehow melded with the flower storm to create a creature that spouted gouts of ruby-red petals from its fearsome toothed mouth. It was beautiful and inspiring. It also warped the reality lines in the lecture hall so badly that it staggered the Sealers, and made it nearly impossible for them to close on Sam and Ariella.

I bounded from the lectern and rushed to their side. Sam was in the middle of waving his arms and shaking a feather about in a looping motion. I grabbed him before he could finish casting. "Come on, we have to get out of here!" I shouted over the din of the pops, whizzes, and bangs of the spells going off around us.

"What do you mean?" he said as I yanked both him and Ariella toward the alcove. "I was going to do a magic arrow!"

"I wanted to summon a unicorn," Ariella insisted.

"Later," I said as I dodged a burst of flower petals from the diving floral blood dragon. "Right now we have to leave!"

As we slipped out the door behind the lectern I glanced back. The Sealers hadn't given up, but their progress had been slowed to a crawl, literally, because one (or more) of the Jellicles had created an enormous ball of yarn that was spinning around the hall like a whirling dervish, unspooling vast drifts of yarn across the seats and along the aisles, making walking impossible. I turned to leave, but realized that it wasn't very professorial to simply sneak out.

I poked my head back through the curtain and shouted, "By next class I want a thousand words on spell safety! With a focus on spell containment, proper casting distance buffers, and a list of the five most common side effects of unintended spell inter-action." For the DERPs I added, "And remember the four M's!"

It was at this moment that several spells collided near the ceiling and a slimy, gray goo began raining down on everyone. I grimaced as screams erupted and students began rushing for the exits. "Class dis-missed!"

With that I ducked into the alcove and led Sam and Ariella out the secret door in the back. If there was one piece of advice I had taken from Griswald, it was this: if you are a professor, always have an escape route . . . from your students. I wasn't sure exactly where we were running to, but there was one cer-tainty: I was not going to be showing up to my office hours today.

CHAPTER 5

EXIT, STAGE RIGHT

We took off across campus like characters in a cartoon, which is to say quickly, but to no great effect. Imagine Scooby and Shaggy sprinting back and forth across a hall through doors running everywhere, but getting nowhere. This was partly because I couldn't figure out where to take Sam and Ariella that would be safe, but it it didn't help that it was the first beautiful day in weeks. If you have ever attempted to get somewhere fast on a university campus when classes are in session, and the sun is out and the sky is blue and the temperature is pleasant, then you know what futility is.

It seemed like the entire Mysterium student body, not to mention all their individual bodies, were sprawled or sitting or standing or playing or eating everywhere I wanted to go. Magical resin bags and fazediscs (both visible and invisible) were as thick in the air as bees, and so were impromptu jam sessions and drum circles, and the odd (and I mean very odd) theatrical performances. Seeing a group of orcs and ogres recreate the death scene in *Hamlet* (or at least their translation of it) through interpretive dance would make anyone reevaluate their appreciation of the arts. Several of the quads were filled with students protesting some policy, or celebrating some cause. Other quads had been transformed into open-air markets selling cheap shirts, homemade jewelry, and posters with humorous riffs on classical magic texts. Like the poster made to look like a classified ad: SEEKING ONE RING TO RULE THEM ALL (MUST BE INTO VOYEURISM AND BONDAGE). Or: VOLDEMORT'S TOP TEN PLACES NOT TO HIDE YOUR SOUL that includes the classic: IN THE DUDE YOU REALLY, REALLY WANT TO KILL. Or the slogan, AVERY LIVES! in bright red letters.

Sam and Ariella nearly collided with me as I skid-ded to a stop in front of the booth. Harold, who had been clinging to my back like Yoda on a training run, dug into my shoulder with his needle-sharp claws to keep from flying off.

"Ow! Dammit, let go," I yelped.

"What's going on?" "What is it?" "Are we under attack?" Sam and Ariella asked in an alternating and rapid-fire fashion.

I pointed at the poster and simultaneously tried to detach Harold's claws from my body. It was your standard dorm room movie poster—27" x 41"—but instead of references to Zelazny or LeGuin or Tolkien or Rowling, it had a picture of the bench by the jogging path at the edge of campus that led to Trelari. On the bench, someone had painted AVERY LIVES!

"Well, of course you're alive," Ariella said with typical elven disdain.

It took Sam a few seconds before he caught on. "Wait, that's about you? You're famous!"

I immediately clamped a hand over his mouth and pulled them into a run. While the poster was a bit of a shock—okay, more like a heart attack inducing shock—it might have been a blessing in disguise. It made me realize that my office—the place I'd been heading toward in my mad dash—was the first place Moregoth would look. As long as Sam and Ariella were on campus, he would find them. I needed to get them out of Mysterium altogether, and there was only one place in the entire multiverse where they would be safe: Trelari.

We'd been jogging for a while when Ariella asked, "Haven't we already been this way?"

"Yes," I wheezed, sounding a lot like Harold, who was huffing into my ear like a steam engine, even though so far I'd been doing all the running.

"Well, where are we going?" Ariella pressed.

"This way . . ."

"But why?"

"No more . . . no more . . . questions," I said between gulped breaths.

She ignored me and continued to rattle off a number of logical questions. Why were we running? Where were we running? Who were we running from? I didn't answer. Not because I didn't have answers to give, although I was fuzzy on a number of points, but because there was a stabbing pain in my side so intense I couldn't physically form words.

Before we go any further, I need to confess something. My time in New York may not have been the most active. As Dawn mentioned, I had spent a lot of time on the couch watching television. I had put on a layer of very professorial pudge over the last few months, something Eldrin never failed to point out. Among the many things that make elves so annoying is that they can apparently eat anything they want without ever gaining an ounce. Don't believe me? I defy you to think of a single example of a fat elf, and no, Santa Claus doesn't count. The song might say he's a "right jolly old elf," but it's being allegorical, not literal. The fact of the matter is all the elves of legend are skinny, even though their primary source of food seems to be a kind of sweet cake. In my opinion, and I think there are a lot of you that will agree, there is nothing more irritating than someone that can eat loads of carbs without consequence.

Anyway, to be perfectly honest, I looked a bit of a mess. In addition to my overall conditioning, or lack thereof, I'd not been sleeping well, but then you probably guessed that from the fact that I had been spending so much time in a coffee shop. I had deep, dark circles under my eyes that made me look like a raccoon, or a student on the last day of finals. I was also trying to grow a beard, that being the sort of thing I thought I should do as a professor. It was not coming in very well. Where it had grown at all it was patchy and scratchy, and made me look less like a professor and more like a poorly groomed were-wolf, or a student on the last day of finals.

I was thinking about the fact that my altered physical state might be why so few people in my class recognized me when I realized we were coming near the edge of campus. I decided to cut through the community gardens, a sort of open common where students could tend their own little plot of land. Mostly druids hung out here. They smoked their herbs and asked deep and portentous questions like: "Who put the alphabet in alphabetical order?" or "Why is it called a building if it's already built?" or "Do you remember what I was going to say?" Things like that.

"Oh, fresh vegetables!" Ariella, who was pacing me quite easily, exclaimed. "That's a plus. Strange they didn't mention it during orientation. Are those cabbages?" She pointed at something green to our left. I didn't bother to look, because I wouldn't have had any way of answering the question, and my eyesight was beginning to blur from exhaustion. "I love cabbages," she said eagerly. "You can make so many things out of them! There's cabbage soup and boiled cabbage and . . ." She trailed off. "Actually, I think that's about it . . ."

We had just plunged into a plot planted with rows of something bright green that had grown to about head-high and had yellow tasseled pods sprouting from it when someone stabbed me in the ribs. At least, that is what it felt like. I grimaced and ground to a halt, clutching my side. "This . . . this is a good place to take a little break," I groaned. Somewhere far to the rear I could hear Sam wheezing and gasping. "Besides, we need to let . . . to let . . . Sam . . . catch up."

Ariella, who had not even begun to perspire, shrugged. "Sure."

Yet another aggravating elven trait is the fact that they apparently never get tired. I had begun to seriously wonder what the hidden flaw in their species was, because from an evolutionary standpoint they should have wiped the floor with the rest of us long ago. I sability must be toxic to its host at high enough levels.

While I tried to keep from fainting, Ariella wandered about plucking at the tasseled pods. She came back about a minute later. "You are taking us back to Trelari, aren't you?"

Still bent over with my hands on my knees, I nodded.

"Why?"

"We've got to . . . get out of this place . . . if it's . . . if it's the last thing . . . we ever do."

"You keep saying that, but *why?*"

I finally caught my breath enough to say, "Because the Administration wants you."

"And?" Ariella said, and I swear it was so annoyingly superior she might as well have been Eldrin. She even smelled like him.

I took one last deep breath. "And . . . that's not a good thing."

"What do they want? We haven't done anything wrong."

Sam arrived on the scene, with a great huffing and puffing. It turns out that he was even more out of shape than I was, which was saying something. I would blame it on the freshman fifteen, but he'd only been in school about fifteen minutes, so I can hardly credit it.

"They say that there's something wrong with your tuition payment . . ."

"We paid in full!" coughed Sam. "After the Dark Queen . . . was defeated . . . we had piles of . . . of . . ."

He bent over trying to catch his breath and Ariella finished for him. "Gold and platinum and copper and electrum. Say, does Mysterium take electrum? We haven't found a use for it yet."

"And you won't," I said with a shake of my head. "No one accepts it. It's the bitcoin of precious metals." This reference confused them long enough that I was able to recover. "Time to move!"

As I ran off, Sam, still doubled over, raised a finger. "But . . ."

Ariella caught up and continued her interrogation. It was at times like this that I remembered she was also a rules lawyer. I ignored her questions and focused on my breathing and on trying to figure out if I was doing the right thing. I didn't want to panic them, but maybe I should tell them who was chasing us. Maybe they deserved to know there was a large faction within the Mysterium that didn't like me and really didn't like the fact of Trelari's existence. But I couldn't. I had this urge to protect both of them from the harsh realities of Mysterium bigotry.

While I was still debating what I should say, we rounded a corner and there was my bench marking the trailhead to Trelari. Even from here I could see that the wooden slats that formed its back had been recently repainted. I wondered if beneath the fresh paint was my slogan. Unfortunately, I didn't have a lot of time to contemplate the question, because seated on the bench was a Mysterium security guard. He was not one of Moregoth's men. He had a rod of detention on his belt, not a wand of variable lethality, and was wearing a traditional guard's cloak that hung off his tall, skinny body like a purple tent.

I considered trying to bluff our way past him, but he looked up. "Avery? Avery Stewart?"

Sam came panting around the corner, clutching his side, as I yelled, "Run!"

He whimpered, "Seriously?"

Ariella and I each grabbed one of his arms and dove into the trees along the side of the path.

"Avery!" the guard called out.

We ran deeper into the woods, and the shouts quickly died away. I was puzzling over why the guard had given up so soon when I realized why he had recognized me—it was John Ulm. We'd taken several classes together. He'd lived across the hall from Eldrin and me for a year. Maybe he had only wanted to catch up. John always had been a bit of a gossip, and one of the less prickish of my dormmates.

I signaled for Ariella to stop running and we dropped Sam to the ground. He was bright red and coated in a sheen of sweat. "Up in the sky," he panted, "what's that flashing?"

A shiver of fear went down my back as I recalled that those were the exact words he'd used right before we were swept up in a funnel cloud and taken to face Vivian during the troubles on Trelari. I looked up, expecting to see a maelstrom of storm clouds and red, blue, and yellow lightning, but there was nothing. The sky was a perfect blue without even a spot of cloud. I looked at Ariella and shrugged. She held the back of her hand to his forehead and frowned. "Probably delirious from exhaustion."

Harold half flapped, half waddled over to Sam's side to perform his own examination. This entailed him poking at Sam with a stick. The imp intoned grimly, "If he were a horse . . ."

"Which he isn't!" I pulled Harold away.

Sam looked pale and pained. He made small choking noises. Ariella rummaged through a pouch and retrieved a cloth bag. She filled it with a handful of colorful herbs, and placed it over Sam's eyes.

"Do you think he's going to be okay?" I asked.

She shrugged, and the little silver bells in her hair gave a merry tinkle. "I don't think he expected school to be so physical. He's spent every moment since we got our acceptance letters with his nose in a book. I'm not sure he moved except to go from his bed to the kitchen to his desk and back again."

I nodded my head in sympathy. If you added watching TV and a run to the coffee shop now and then, that was a fair description of my life.

"Now what?" asked Ariella.

Sam moaned weakly, "No more running . . ."

"No more running, Sam," I assured him.

He was right, and not only because if we ran much more there was a good chance he was going to die, but also because I was no longer sure what I was running from. I don't mean I'd forgotten about Moregoth; but I had been in such a panic I hadn't considered that not all of Mysterium was trying to hunt us down. In fact, it might only be Moregoth. This meant that we might be able to go back to the gateway path and talk our way past John. But what if Moregoth had come to the same realization I had come to and was on his way there? The gateway was well known, as evidenced by the graffitied bench. I paced about as I considered our options. Maybe I should abscond with them to New York where we could all hide out together. I shuddered as I thought about the logistics of five people living in that tiny apartment, and sharing a single bathroom.

"I take it we aren't going back to Trelari, then?" Ariella asked.

I shook my head as Harold clambered onto my shoulder and pointed his stick off to the right where the underbrush grew thicker. I shooed the stick away.

Maybe I should go to the administration building and clear things up. Sam said they paid in full . . .

Harold interrupted this thought by yanking on my hair and pointing again. I slapped his hand away.

Ariella lost her patience. "Well, where, then?"

"I think . . ." I began, but got no further as Harold whacked me on the head. "Ouch!" I yelled, and made a grab for the stick.

The imp had other ideas. He scrambled off my back, leapt to the ground, and dashed off through the trees.

"Dammit, Harold! Come back here," I shouted, and raced after him with Ariella at my heels.

"Are we running again?" Sam shouted as he staggered to his feet. "You promised no more running!"

We were in a park that bordered the edge of campus. It was basically a forest with a couple of trails, and was mostly used by students for clandestine meetings in-

volving hookups, illegal spell ingredients, and other il-
licit activity. We met no one, which wasn't surprising
given that Harold seemed intent on avoiding anything
resembling a path. Instead, the imp flapped and leapt
from ground to limb to trunk to bush at top speed,
while we struggled and crashed our way through the
underbrush after him.

I wasn't chasing him because I was worried for his
safety; I was worried what his running away meant
about our current situation. He never ran. Indeed, I
hadn't thought it possible for him to run. Normally
he was loath even to walk from his perch to my arm,
and when he did he wheezed so badly I thought he
might blow a gasket. That he was not only running,
but doing a fair impression of animated Yoda in the
Star Wars prequels, made my blood run cold. Then
again, anything that reminds me of *those* movies
makes my blood run cold.

Ariella, being an elf, was, of course, able to glide
untouched between the same bushes and limbs that
kept slapping me in the face and grasping at my
clothes. For once I didn't resent her glowing special-
ness, because without her we would have lost the imp
entirely.

After five minutes of running pell-mell through
the woods, we emerged at its edge in time to see
Harold sprinting across a narrow grass field toward
a line of three-story townhomes, tucked into a gentle
crescent of a lane running along one side of the park.

The neighborhood would not have looked out of place in London. Well, it wouldn't have looked out of place if you ignored the battlements and odd tower rooms jutting from the top floors of the homes. This was Mysterium after all.

We paused long enough to make sure there was no security about, and then took off across the field after him. He made for one of the townhomes at the edge of the line that appeared unoccupied, or at least only recently occupied. The kitchen garden was filled with weeds, and through the bare windows we could see cardboard boxes piled in untidy stacks.

"Do you know this place?" Ariella asked.

"No clue," I panted, and then shouted, "Harold! Stop!"

He ignored my call and dashed up the short flight of steps fronting the house. I had assumed this would mark the end of our chase, but as he neared the door it flew open, and he bolted through. The three of us followed him in. The door slammed shut behind us, and I spun to see who had let us in. The entryway was empty, and from the musty, stale smell of the house, no one had been in here for some time.

Harold was nowhere to be seen. I called out for him. "Harold?"

"How did you do it?" Sam asked between breaths.

"Do what?"

"Open the door," Sam gasped. "I didn't see anything: no gestures, no words, no wand, nothing."

"No clue," I said as I made my way toward the back of the house.

Sam and Ariella followed. He asked, "So, was it your imp? Can imps do magic?"

"Some, but no, I don't think he used magic to open the door," I said in a distracted sort of way as I stalked through the house looking for the little bastard.

At last I found him in the kitchen, sitting atop a stack of boxes, looking as downtrodden and lethargic as ever. I was about to grab him and give him a piece of my mind when I saw that there was a label on the side of the box he'd chosen as his chair. I stopped in my tracks.

"Do doors simply open for people in Mysterium?" Sam asked.

"No," I answered, and even to my ears the single words sounded empty and dreadful.

Ariella put a hand on my arm. "Avery? What's wrong?"

I pointed to the label on the box. It read: PROPERTY OF PROFESSOR AVERY STEWART. FRAGILE! DO NOT SMASH WITH HAMMER!

My legs gave out from under me and I found myself sitting on the floor. "Doors only open for the owner."

CHAPTER 6

MY OTHER HOUSE IS
A VERY, VERY, VERY . . .
WAIT, WHAT OTHER HOUSE?

That the townhome was mine may come as a shock to some of you. It certainly did to me. As you've already made it through Chapter Two of this book, you know I have been living in New York, in a tiny apartment that is entirely unsuitable for a Mysterium professor. Although maybe you skipped the early chapters to get straight to the action. Or you could be reading this book back to front, which is cheating. Unless you're Merlin or Benjamin Button or Rachel Weintraub or Kes from *Star Trek Voyager* or Mork from Ork or Lion-O in the classic *Thundercats* episode "Time

Switch." The point is there are a lot of people that live backward and might want to read books that way also. Who am I to judge? Anyway, however you got here, there we were standing . . . okay, I was sitting and Sam and Ariella were standing . . . and Harold, he was also sitting . . .

I'm babbling, aren't I?

I am. I know it. Well, I had received a very nasty shock, so please forgive me for being a little incoherent. The thing is, it would have been different had the townhome been a complete mystery to me. My initial reaction would have been to assume it was either a paperwork mistake (which is more likely than one would imagine given Mysterium University has compounded bureaucracy with magic), or a practical joke (which all my readers will recognize as a distinct possibility if not probability given what passes for a "sense of humor" for many of my fellow Mysterium mages). However, as soon as I saw the label I knew for a fact that, not only was the townhome mine, but I had packed those boxes and written those words. It was a feeling very reminiscent of the one I'd had when I first saw a copy of *The Dark Lord* in a bookstore. It was almost as though I had been expecting the book to be there even though I had no memory of the book itself. In other words, a form of amnesia where full, or at least partial, memories came flooding back when I was exposed to something I'd forgotten.

For example, I knew with certainty that the box Sam was peering at with the puzzled expression contained a copy of my Gold Key *Star Trek* issue number 56, "No Time Like the Past." This was disorienting in and of itself, but more troublesome was that when I had these rushes of memory I would get a brief glimpse of what was going to happen next. So when Sam remarked, "Hey! The words on this box keep changing." I had a ready answer. "It's written in magic marker."

"Neat!"

While normally his enthusiasm would be infectious, right now I needed quiet to figure out what was happening. I tried to forestall further questions by preanswering what I knew was coming next. "The label is trying to guess what you might want from inside the box," I explained. "If you keep staring at it, it will eventually list all its contents."

"That's *so* cool!" he said. "Hey, this one says it has 'Star Trek cosplay costumes' and 'adult fan-fiction.' What's that?"

A number of rather embarrassing memories raced through my mind. My face flushed and I stammered, "That's, um, background material for a class I'm putting together on . . . on Earth culture."

He kept reading. "What's a fanboy?"

I slapped my hand over the labels. "These boxes are old, Sam. The magic is getting a bit unpredictable. The best thing to do is ignore them."

He studied the label suspiciously for a moment, and then wandered off to examine the oven.

As I was congratulating myself for avoiding one set of mortifying questions, Ariella raised an eyebrow. "You 'haven't a clue' who lives here?"

I considered confessing, but I was not ready to reveal the full nature of how messed up my mind was. The last thing I needed was for Sam and Ariella to think they'd fallen in league with a madman, although I wasn't sure they hadn't. Instead, with my typical cool under pressure, I gave her three different, and equally ridiculous, explanations in rapid succession.

"I didn't recognize the place. I have never approached it from the park. I only moved in recently."

This last excuse earned me another exquisitely derisive eyebrow. She ran a finger across one of the boxes, and examined the thick layer of gray dust at its tip. "When did you move in?"

If I were being perfectly honest, which I wasn't, I would have had to say I didn't know, but I had a feeling it was shortly after I returned from Trelari. I can recall a late night, a bottle of wine, and unloading the contents of my folded space. How had I forgotten? When had I forgotten?

"I . . . I . . . I can't remember the exact date."

"Well," she drawled with a roll of her eyes, "I like what you've not done with the place."

I wanted to say, *Forget about the place—what have*

I been doing with my life the last few months? Instead, I picked absentmindedly at the weathered tape on the top of a box sitting next to me, and murmured, "I've had a lot going on."

Of course, that isn't why I hadn't moved in. The problem is, if I did have a reason for not moving in, I could not for the life of me recall what it was.

Ariella was not to be put off. "So much to do that you haven't even had time to unpack your clothes?"

"I've unpacked my . . ." I started to say, only to see that Harold had broken into one of the boxes and was rooting through it, flinging underwear and socks about the room.

"Harold! Stop that!"

It will come as no surprise to anyone that he ignored me. With a curse, I rose with the aim of strangling the annoying little imp (or at least preventing him from making more of a mess) when his clawed hand shot out of the box. It was clutching a copy of *The Dark Lord*!

I froze in place. The whispered expletive that followed perfectly summed up the confusion and fear I felt. I will leave it to your imagination to arrive at the exact arrangement of subject and predicate, but will offer that profanity is by far the most succinct and expressive part of the English language.

Sam took the book from Harold and began flipping through the pages. "What's this?"

"Nothing," I blurted, and made a grab for it.

It was too late.

"This . . . this is about you," he said, and his face lit up with wonder. I closed my eyes, waiting for the explosion of anger I was sure would follow once he figured out what part of my life it was about. Instead, he looked up from his reading and, with his finger marking his place, shook the spine at me. "No wonder you're famous. You know, if you hadn't insisted on running us around like hens in a yard with one worm, you might have made a few coins today. The fellow that was selling those paintings said he'd give you a cut of his sales if you would sign a few. Can you imagine?"

Ariella snatched the book out of his hand and thrust it into her bag. "We don't have time for this. Sam and I have other classes, and you have a lot of things to explain."

I stared at her bag as though it were a snake, and murmured, "More than you know."

"Well, answers to the questions we've already asked would be a nice start," she retorted.

I sat down on a box. "Okay, ask away."

Ariella and Sam looked back and forth between each other, trying to decide who should get to go first. Sam bowed to her.

She curtsied in return and asked the obvious question. "Why are you afraid that someone is after us?"

Before I could answer, Sam pointed at the dishwasher and asked a not-so-obvious question. "Is that part of your spellcasting equipment?"

It was like a tennis match. They volleyed questions at me, one after another. While Ariella was focused on why we were on the run, Sam was obsessed with Harold. The exchange went something like this:

"Who is chasing us?"

"Is that a real imp?"

"Is there anyone chasing us?"

"Do you want us to help him unpack your things?"

"Did you actually see anyone chasing us?"

"It looks like the key the Dark Queen and you were fighting over. Did you have a replica made?"

"I still don't understand why the administration would go to so much trouble to get us."

"We paid, I have a receipt."

I had been swiveling my head back and forth between them, giving half answers where I had any answer at all, and it took me two extra swivels before I registered what Sam had aksed. When it finally reached the conscious part of my brain, I saw that Sam and Harold were wrestling over a reality key.

Griswald's puzzle box lay open beside the imp, who was staring at it with an expression that was an indescribable mixture of resignation and disgust.

"What . . ." I stuttered in confusion.

"We paid our tuition several months ago," Sam said as he tried to coax the key out of Harold's grasp by clucking his tongue and wiggling his fingers.

"How . . ." I stammered, still unable to complete a thought or a sentence.

"Oh, they sent me a diagram of a circle Ariella and I could use to send them payments, along with a conversion of the tuition into weights of different metals."

I stumbled toward them as Sam warmed to the subject. "It was very interesting; they couldn't send the message by normal means, Trelari being cut off from Mysterium, so they sent it into the portal via bird. I got my message from an owl."

"No," I said, and pointed a shaking finger at the key.

"You don't think it was an owl? I'm pretty certain it was an owl, but then again, I am weak on my bird knowledge. Will that be a problem? Should I study birds? Now that I think of it, since they couldn't know where Ariella and I lived in Trelari, they must have sent a whole flock of birds to find us. I can't imagine they were all owls. It wouldn't make sense. Why not homing pigeons?" Then, thinking about his own question, he offered, "I mean, owls are known to be pretty lazy, so they don't make natural messengers . . ."

Harold wheezed. "No, Sam, you daft idiot. He wants to know how we got the key out of the box."

"Well, I didn't do it, you did," Sam whined back at the imp.

"So, you're speaking to me again?" I asked Harold. "Why not in the woods? Why not tell me about this place?"

The imp gave a pitiable sigh. "It seemed simpler to show you. Besides, we don't have much time, and I'm . . . I'm afraid you're going to need this."

He paused, that strange revulsion flashing briefly across his face, and then held the key out to me with a shaking paw. I brushed past Sam and took it, tracing my fingers reverently over its smooth surface. My first reaction was one of pure wonder. Griswald's key was real, and I had it. But my initial joy was quickly replaced by puzzlement. There was something odd about the key. It had the same basic shape of other reality keys I'd used, but it had no teeth. It was as though someone had filed them off, and I could feel a deep thrumming coming from within it, almost as though it were alive. I looked into the imp's filmy eyes. "What world is this to?"

He shrugged. "You have a knack of asking the most impossible questions without ever knowing they're impossible."

"Well, at least tell me how you got it out."

He handed me the box. I could see it had an opening inside that had length, width, depth, and one additional dimension impossible to describe. That we live in five-dimensional space is obvious to anyone that has ever watched a valet park a regular-sized car in a compact space. This box merely took advantage of the extra dimensionality to obscure its contents. "Why didn't I sense the magic before?" I muttered.

"Does it matter?" Harold asked.

It did, but the answer probably also explained why I couldn't recall the last chapter of my book, or why I didn't know I had a house in Mysterium. In other words, unknowable at the moment. With a grunt, I snapped the lid closed and thrust the box into my pocket. Some mysteries would have to wait. Besides, staring into extradimensional space without the proper protective eyewear was making me nauseous. I turned back to the imp. "How long have you known how to open it?" Harold said nothing, but his look said it all. "You've known from the beginning?"

"Of course," he sighed.

"Well, why didn't you say anything?"

"You never asked," he said. "Besides, at this stage of your education, I should not have to explain L'Engle space-time fabric to you."

It was a fair criticism. I had never been particularly strong at higher dimensional metaphysics. Lovecraftian multidimensionalism terrified me, and though I appreciated the travel benefits afforded by incorporating L'Engle wrinkles in my transport circles, I didn't exactly understand them. When I was a novice, I stopped dating a girl because she lived in a dorm designed by an architect of the Heinleinian school. I would show up for a date, walk in the front door, and find myself leaving again through the back. It was intensely frustrating on many levels.

"Why now?" I fumed at Harold.

Perhaps it was my tone, or my stern countenance,

or some danger that the answer held for us, but I saw a shadow of fear pass across his face followed by a deep melancholy that settled behind his eyes. "You need it," he answered. "To activate this."

He shuffled across the floor and pushed aside a pile of boxes stacked against one of the walls to reveal an elaborate transport circle. The circle looked familiar. "Who?" I asked, but when the imp rolled his eyes I knew the answer. "Me?" He nodded sharply, and I asked, "Where?"

"Somewhere safe."

"Are we in danger here?"

He nodded again and darted his eyes ever so quickly toward the kitchen window. I did the same and saw a dozen men in crimson cloaks with deep cowled hoods emerge from the woods behind the house. Moregoth had found us.

I was still digesting this when Sam asked, "Has he been able to talk the whole time?"

In my shock, I had momentarily forgotten that Sam and Ariella were there, but Sam's words, so similar to the ones I utter at the end of the book, broke my paralysis. I turned back to the two of them. "We have to get out of here—now!"

"Gods!" Sam wailed. "No more running."

I said nothing, but pulled magical energy into the key until it glowed brightly with an ethereal green light. As I did, a series of teeth grew from the key's surface. When I felt it had enough power, I pointed it at the circle on the wall. Power shot out of the key, and the circled portion of the wall shimmered and fell away. Within the opening we saw a nondescript hallway with a glass-paneled door at one end. Harold was through the gateway the instant it opened.

"Where are we going now?" Ariella asked irritably as she studied the construct of the spell.

I recognized the place at once. "The Subworld Observatory," I said. "We need to talk to my friend Eldrin."

"He'll know what to do?" asked Ariella.

I took a quick glance out the window behind us. The Sealers were in the yard now, making their way through the weed-choked garden toward the door. "Definitely." I pushed her and Sam through the gate.

I felt a buildup of power from outside and knew the mages were seconds from blasting their way in. I needed to go, but hesitated. I looked about at this house that was mine, but not mine, and at all the boxes of stuff I hadn't noticed I'd been missing. There was some deeper truth to be had there. Some lesson about the transitory nature of physical things, but all I could think was what a shame it was that Eldrin and I hadn't had a chance to throw at least one killer party here. With a wry smile at lost opportunities, I began to step through when my eye fell on the box with my *Star Trek* paraphernalia in it.

"To hell with that!" I shouted. I pocketed the key and grabbed the box as the front of the house shook with an explosion. A cloud of smoke and dust, and the sounds of shouting voices, followed me as I dove through the gateway and into the hallway of the observatory. As soon as I emerged on the other side I cut the flow of energy to the gate, and all went quiet.

Sam, Ariella, and Harold gathered around me. Harold tapped on the box. "And what was so important that you decided to risk your life for it?"

I chose to take the fifth, and said nothing. Obligingly, Sam read the label off the box. "It says there's something called a comic book in there. Is that a kind of magic book?"

While Harold muttered curses, I rose to my feet and, with as much dignity as I could muster, said, "Yes, Sam. Yes, it is."

CHAPTER 7

ELDRIN!

Ignoring Harold, who continued to curse me and my descendants from the beginning of time, I dusted myself off and picked up my box. Head held high, I walked to the door at the end of the hall. A small brass nameplate on the wall read: DR. ELDRIN LEIGHTNER— SENIOR RESEARCH SCIENTIST: ASTROMANCY, SUBWORLD PHYSICS, AND SIGILISM.

"Sigilism?" Ariella asked. "I know a little bit about sigilism and also astromancy, though I've never heard of subworld physics. I was worried the university might not allow multiple majors. I'm glad to see they allow a reasonable level of intellectual exploration. I've made a rough plan of my class schedule for the next ten to twenty years and was going to take it to a counselor to talk it over, but do you think Eldrin would be willing to take a quick look?"

She rooted about in her bag and pulled out a scroll several feet long covered in densely packed script. What I wanted to say was, *Twenty years! Are you mad?* But I'm a professor, and I'd learned a certain level of professorial diplomacy. Instead, I said, "I'm not sure. He's very busy." I certainly didn't want to commit Eldrin to a conference with Ariella about all the areas of study she might be interested in. It would take days.

"Is Eldrin an elf?" Ariella asked. "His name sounds elvish—very woody. Not like Avery."

"Very tinny," Harold agreed.

Sam said, "Aaavery," and tilted his head to one side.

One after the other they repeated, "Aaavery."

I glowered at them. "If you three are through . . ."

"She's right, you know, you have a very tinny name," Eldrin said, poking his head out of the doorway behind us. "Funny how I never noticed before. Anyway, could you come back later? I'm having lunch." To emphasize the point he gestured at me with a sandwich wrapped in paper.

"Eldrin, we need to talk." I pushed past him and his quizzically raised eyebrow. The others followed, and I closed the door and bolted it behind us.

Eldrin's office was small, windowless, and lined by

bookcases filled to bursting with a dizzying assortment of books and boxes and gadgets. A small orrery hung down from a vaulted ceiling that soared up to a height completely inappropriate for the size of the room. The oddness was understandable, because the office was located in one of the oldest buildings at Mysterium University. WHERE WIZARDS FIRST SAW THE SUBWORLDS, as the inscription over the door proclaims. What I didn't understand at first was his desk, which was covered by a green blanket. Dawn was sitting on it eating a handful of grapes out of a picnic basket. Her face was unusually flushed, and she was glaring at me.

She couldn't possibly still be mad about this morning, I thought.

Neither she nor Eldrin said a word, but I couldn't escape feeling there was a tension in the air. That, of course, was when I noticed other details. The litter of chess pieces, toy soldiers, and meeples scattered about on the floor as though they had been hastily swept aside. The artistic muss of Dawn's typically librarian-neat hair. The fact that Eldrin's shirt was unlaced to his navel (which was low even by his standards). I was slow, but not that slow. I blushed bright red, and said something like, "Ahhh . . ."

I began to back toward the door with the idea that it might be best to give them some privacy. Unfortunately, Harold had flown up to perch on the orrery. He folded his wings and appeared to be in no mood to move again. I waved my hand for him to come down, but he simply sighed and closed his eyes.

"We didn't interrupt anything, did we?" Sam asked.

Eldrin began to say something, but Dawn interjected. "Don't be silly. We were just having lunch."

"Yes, lunch," Eldrin said, trying to take a bite of his still-wrapped sandwich.

Sam, who had never known when to keep his mouth shut, blurted out, "Isn't it a little early for lunch?"

When I thought it was impossible for the moment to get any more awkward, Ariella stepped forward, grasped Eldrin's face in her hands, and kissed him on the lips. "I am Ariella. My heart sings to see thee."

The silence that followed was so profoundly uncomfortable you could hear every one of the grapes Dawn had been holding hit the ground. At this point, I might have welcomed the Sealers, because the look Dawn gave Ariella was lethal.

Fortunately, Sam intervened. He held out his hand to Dawn. "I'm Sam. I'm in Avery's class, but he took us out early because he thinks someone at the school is trying to kill us. How do you know him?"

"Nice to meet you, Sam, and your friend Ariella . . ." Dawn only slightly clenched her teeth.

"She's also in Avery's class," Sam explained. "Today is our first day, and . . ."

He chattered on about their morning adventures

while Eldrin extricated himself from Ariella's embrace. Suddenly, his eyes grew wide. He looked rapidly back and forth between the two of them. A massive grin split his face. "Wait a minute! You're *the* Sam and Ariella! You're from Trelari!"

"The Sam and Ariella?" Dawn asked, and the murderous look vanished. "Oh, *the* Sam and Ariella! I've read all about you!" she exclaimed, and then added, "I certainly hope Avery has apologized to you for his behavior. It was objectively abominable, even for a Donaldsonian."

I didn't want to to give Dawn a chance to lecture. Both because she was very good at making me look bad, and because the presence of the blanket on the desk, and what it signified, was still making me extremely uncomfortable. I decided to get to the point. "The Administration is looking for Sam and Ariella, and I need to hide them until I know why."

"Why not ask someone at Enrollment what they want?" Dawn suggested.

"Because they sent Moregoth and the Sealers to find them."

Eldrin raised an eyebrow. "Maybe you should tell us what happened?"

"Who is this Moregoth?" Ariella asked.

"Someone that should *not* be looking for you," Eldrin said sternly. "How did *you* get admitted in the first place?"

"What's that supposed to mean?" she protested.

"It's just . . ." he said uncertainly, and waved his hands at her as though it should be obvious.

The two of them stood in silence until Dawn cleared her throat. Eldrin shook his head as though to clear it, and went to lean against one of the bookcases on the other side of the room. I noticed that his eyes kept wandering back over to Ariella and then snapping away, as though he had to focus to keep from looking at her.

"Right . . ." I began.

I explained things, including who Moregoth was. Ariella filled in the details I missed and corrected the parts I got wrong, which were unsurprisingly many and varied. When we were done, I asked, "What do you think?"

Dawn shrugged. "Keep Sam and Ariella hidden, and call the Financial Aid office?"

"Agreed," said Eldrin with that eerie elven calm. "If not for Moregoth's involvement, we wouldn't have any reason to be worried."

"But he is involved," I pressed.

"That guy is crazy," Dawn said in a low voice. "I saw him once on top of the battlements of the Administration building, pacing in the moonlight. Gave me bad dreams for a week."

"I went to a talk he gave on interworld conflict resolution," said Eldrin with a shudder. "I've never been more terrified, and I've been to necromantic poetry jams."

"His interest in Sam and Ariella gives me a bad feeling," I said, trying to cut off any further discussion of Moregoth's peculiarities.

Eldrin rolled his eyes. He hated any conclusion based on instinct or intuition. He often said, "There's no *I* in fact." I mean, he really says this a lot. It gets pretty annoying.

"Avery, you are a professor now," he lectured. "As a mage of Mysterium University, you are supposed to base your actions on facts."

He walked over to a chalkboard mounted on a rolling wooden stand, and picked up a piece of chalk. He drew two columns, and began writing "Things We Know" and "Things We Suspect" on the board. I knew we were about to get a diatribe on behavioral prediction and psychohistory, or some such, that related everything back to one of Eldrin's multitudinous strategy games.

Eldrin began to drone on about how it might make sense for the Administration to use Sealers when dealing with beings from a new innerworld, but I was distracted by Harold, who had floated down from the ceiling and begun to yank on my ear. "What?" I whispered.

The imp glanced nervously at the door. "Are they coming?" I asked. He slowly shook his head no. "Are they here?" I asked. He vigorously nodded.

I nearly panicked. Okay, I panicked. "Time to go!" I shouted, but it was too late.

"Sam and Ariella of Trelari?" came a booming voice from the hall.

"Yes!" they shouted in unison.

They both slapped their hands over their mouths.

"Sorry," Ariella said.

"I didn't mean to . . ." Sam began.

Eldrin, Dawn, and I looked at each other and sighed in unison. "The voice of command," I muttered. "It isn't your fault."

"How long will your door hold them?" I asked as a heavy thump rattled the books on his shelves.

"I've made a lot of modifications," Eldrin said confidently. "Against Mysterium Security we should have twenty or thirty minutes."

"How about against a Sealer team?" I asked.

"Ten minutes," he said, and then clarified, "If we're lucky and there are only a couple of them."

"How about if there are a dozen?"

"Five tops."

"How about if Moregoth is still with them?"

"You're kidding, right?"

I shook my head as another jolt shook the room. Several volumes tumbled from various piles atop various shelves. "You don't have a back way out, do you?" I peered behind the chalkboard, hoping there might be another door there.

"No. And before you ask, we can't transport from here either. There's a Faradawn cage interlaced about this building to keep transient magic fields from interfering with the alignment of the planarscopes. There is no way out except through the front door."

We were stuck. Utterly trapped. I looked about the room for anything we might be able to use to defend ourselves. There were dozens of lethal-looking gadgets, but they all appeared to be either half-built or half-dismantled. I realized the chalk Eldrin had been writing with was made of fazedust. An idea sprung at me like a cat. It was insane, but like all great "Eureka!" moments, the important thing when you have one is not to stop and think before acting. That way the idea doesn't have time to tell you why it's a bad one. I snatched the chalk out of Eldrin's hand and cast a quick cantrip to clear the chalkboard of his scribbles. I swiftly drew as big a circle as the board would allow.

"What are you doing?" Eldrin asked. "Even if the room weren't shielded, you can't make a dimensional portal in the time we have."

To emphasize his point, a massive shudder ran through the room. One of the shelves swayed and toppled forward, crashing to the ground. Dawn cast a shell of protection to keep us from being battered to death.

I have spent a lot of time learning about how to travel between subworlds, so much time that it would take far more pages than I have in this book to explain what I know. The point being, I know a great deal more than Eldrin about making dimensional portals. However, while I'd like to tell you that Eldrin was wrong, he wasn't. What I was about to try was impossible, but in one of those paradoxes that make time-travel stories so annoying, I knew it would work because I'd done it once already. I pulled the key out of my robes. The teeth were gone again. I didn't have time to think about the significance of a mutable reality key, because another thunderous blow nearly knocked me off my feet. I opened myself to the main Mysterium ley line, and the key flared to life. The surface of the metal shimmered and deformed until a row of three teeth appeared.

"You have a key?" Dawn asked.

"Wait!" Eldrin shouted as the room shook with thunder. "Is that *the* key from the book?"

I nodded and pointed the end of the key at the crude circle I'd drawn. The surface of the chalkboard melted away, and through the dimensional rift we could see another world.

"Okay, I'm impressed," said Eldrin.

"Me too," I muttered.

A crack of pure molten magic opened in Eldrin's door, and a black shadow poured inside. I could hear wheezing.

"Everyone jump!" I yelled.

We pushed Sam and Ariella through the once-chalkboard. They stood for a moment at the gateway, and then folded into five-dimensional shapes and vanished. Eldrin looked at Dawn and she looked back at him. They both stepped through as a crackling noise came from the door and it exploded inward. I saw the crimson hooded mages stepping through the shattered door, wands of lethality at the ready. They hesitated instead of firing. They were waiting for their commander. A wise man wouldn't have lingered, but I couldn't help myself. As Moregoth strode into the room, swishing his black trenchcoat, I held up two fingers for him to see, and made two tally marks on an invisible score sheet before jumping through the portal.

CHAPTER 8

THE FINAL FRONTIER

We materialized in a circular room on a polished black floor intricately inlayed with swirls and filigrees of a glowing silver material. The walls and ceilings of the room appeared to be made of a black material onto which had been painted streaks of blue and white light. My initial thought was either I had been drinking too much, or we had appeared in a planetarium, or possibly both. However, a moment's more observation and it became clear that the walls were transparent and that the sea of black decorated here and there with spots and swirls of light was the view. We stood watching the galaxies of subworlds slip by. The reflection of the passing stars shot streaks of color across the mirrored surface of the floor. I have a vague memory of saying something insightful like, "Wow!" Everyone else wisely chose this moment to be quiet and introspective.

"Where are we, Eldrin?" Dawn murmured.

He didn't answer, but stood, eyes wide and mouth agape, like he'd been thunderstruck. Of course, he was a student of the heavens, and I wondered what he was seeing that I couldn't appreciate.

"Eldrin?" Dawn touched his arm.

He shook his head as though to break the spell the view had cast on him. "We're in etherspace," he said reverently. "No, we're actually traveling *through* etherspace."

"Do you mean to say those aren't stars, but worlds?" Dawn asked.

He nodded and stammered, "Y-yes, we must be in the space between worlds. I've never seen anything like it. Well, except in that movie Avery made me watch on the periodic table."

"How many times do I have tell you the movie is not about heavy metals but is called *Heavy Metal*, and it's an animated exploration of science fiction and fantasy?" Everyone stared at me with the same bewildered expressions. "Never mind."

We turned back to the windows. After a moment, Dawn said, "We must be going pretty fast. It looks like the opening credits of a *Star Trek* episode."

Eldrin and I stared at her with mouths open, not

because she wasn't right, but because she had always refused to watch the show with us—ironically, at least for a magical ethicist, because she claimed that the characters were always moralizing. And don't *even* get her started on the "Turnabout Intruder" episode. Seriously, don't even mention it. She can get dark . . . really fast.

Dawn stared back at us with her unblinking black-and-white-eyed gaze. "Obviously, the new one, with the cute Spock."

I tried not to smile. "Obviously."

Eldrin shot me an evil look, which always makes me giggle, because Hylar features aren't made for grim and menacing. Luckily, Sam chose that moment to ask, "What's a 'space'?"

All of us turned to look at him, but before anyone could say anything, a deep, disembodied voice intoned, "A space is a continuous area or expanse that is free, available, or unoccupied. A room, capacity, area, volume, expanse, extent, scope, latitude, margin, leeway, play, clearance . . ."

We all jumped and looked about, but apart from the fact that some of the silver lines in the floor were flashing a deep blue at each word, there was no sign of anyone else around. Having been a sci-fi addict until the age of, well, whatever age I was at the moment, I suspected the voice must be coming from a computer of some sort. It was too precise, and its diction too perfect, to be human. I started to say just that when the lights in the floor started flashing a virulent pink and a second voice, higher, but just as disembodied and mechanical, said, "Space: the dimensions of height, depth, and width within which all things exist and move; the physical universe beyond a planet's atmosphere; the near-vacuum extending between the planets and stars, containing small amounts of gas and dust; or a mathematical concept generally regarded as a set of points having some specified structure."

The lights flashed blue. "He specifically asked what 'a space' was, not what 'space' was."

"It would take an overly literal and officious idiot to fail to understand from the context of the question that he was asking about what 'space' is, not what 'a space' is," said the higher voice as the floor flashed a very smug pink.

"Then why did you first give him the definition of 'dimensional space' and conclude with 'mathematical space'?" asked the first voice.

"It's called being thorough," said the pink voice.

"It's called being overbearing and pedantic," retorted the blue one.

The lights in the floor strobed more and more violently by the second. The room had taken on the atmosphere of a disco when Sam raised a finger in the air. "I think I get it. We are up among the stars."

Reluctantly, the pink and blue lights stopped flashing. We all stood in a circle wondering what to do next. It was Dawn who finally spoke. "I still don't think you . . . either of you . . . answered his question: Where are we?"

"Space!" both voices shouted with such enthusiasm that the room glowed bright purple for a second.

"Oh, for the love of the gods, don't start that again!" I roared in response. "You know that's not what we're asking. What is the name of the place we're in? Where is it going? Who are you? Are there people? People we can talk to who aren't you?"

There was a pause of several seconds, and then the pink voice said uncertainly, "The spaceship *Discovery*, Version 1.5, Update 42. The center of multiverse time."

Realizing that the pink voice was getting to answer all the questions, the blue voice cut in, saying, "ED and EDIE."

"Yes!" shouted the pink voice.

"No!" countered the blue voice.

I was still trying to sort through the answers when Eldrin summarized. "To recap, we are on a spaceship called *Discovery*, Version 1.5 Update 42, on our way to the center of the multiverse with two, presumably, computers called ED and EDIE. There are people somewhere, but we can't talk to any of them?"

"Yes," the blue voice answered enthusiastically.

We were all thinking through the implications of the answers when the pink voice urged, "Ask more questions."

"Yes," agreed the blue voice. "The questions are fun. Do you have any more?"

"Given that those statements clarify nothing," Eldrin answered, "yes, we have more."

"Well?" the blue voice encouraged.

"Yes, ask. We are here to help," the pink voice agreed.

"No, we aren't," the blue voice countered. "My principal function is to monitor ether plasma drive thrust and maintain course trajectory, and your primary task is to ensure life support systems remain nominal."

"Why do you have to be so literal?" the pink voice said with a sigh.

"Because I'm not an EDIE, as you constantly remind me," the blue voice, who, from this comment, I took to be ED, said sullenly.

"Not this again," the pink voice, who by process of elimination must have been EDIE, said irritably. "It isn't my fault they didn't install an Instinctual Emotitron in you. You know it isn't standard for your model. There's no point in sulking about it."

"I'm not sulking."

"Without an Instinctual Emotitron, how would you know?" There was an awkward silence. "I'm sorry. I didn't mean that."

"Yes, you did," ED said, and the blue light went out. This time it had a kind of finality to it.

EDIE sighed. "I apologize. We have a lot of history together."

At this point I'm not sure any of us knew how to respond. It was Ariella who finally asked, "Will ED be okay?"

"Yes, but I'll get the silent treatment for a few hundred years," EDIE answered, the accompanying pink light glowing somberly.

"A few hundred years?" I said incredulously.

"An estimate only," EDIE said. "It took about that long last time we argued like this."

"Out of curiosity, how long have you been in this 'space'?" Sam asked.

"Are we starting the question game again?" EDIE asked, the pink color perking back up.

"Sure," I said.

"Good. I like that game. We've been on our mission for eight billion, six hundred and seventy-five million, three hundred and nine thousand years. I can't be any more precise, because when ED disappeared last time he stopped all the clocks so my chronometer is plus or minus five hundred years."

"Are you saying that all the clocks were blinking for over five hundred years?" Eldrin asked.

"Yes."

"That must have been annoying," Dawn said.

"Yes."

"Couldn't you have reset them yourself?" Eldrin asked.

"No."

"Why not?" I asked.

"For the same reason he won't fix the toilets or change any lightbulbs or concern himself at all with the inversion force screen."

"Which is?" Dawn asked.

"Because those are my responsibilities and the clocks are his!" EDIE said with an electronic shout, and a flare of pink-lighted indignation. "He is also responsible for cleaning the ductworks, and for maintenance on the outer hull, and for the central data construct, and for . . ."

EDIE continued listing tasks and functions I didn't understand, but I had stopped listening. I wasn't sure what was going on with the *Discovery* or why Griswald's key had taken us here, but the place presented possibilities. Being positioned between worlds, it would be impossible to track. This meant Moregoth wouldn't be able to find us here, which meant in turn that this was the perfect place to have a little conference with Sam and Ariella about why Moregoth was after them, and how they'd come to enroll in the school in the first place.

I asked, "EDIE, am I right in thinking whatever passengers you have are in some kind of magically induced sleep?"

The computer interrupted its list long enough to confirm that everyone on board had been put into stasis for the journey, and then went back to its recitation of duties.

"Like in the movie with that Khan fellow?" Dawn asked.

"W-w-what?" Eldrin spluttered, and the amazement on his face at her having made two *Star Trek* references in the space of ten minutes was priceless.

"The cute Khan obviously," she said in answer.

Dawn stood looking uncomfortable for a second. Then her black and white eyes focused on me. "Why are we here?"

". . . for tea too," EDIE said confidently.

"What?" I asked.

"ED is responsible for tea too. He's actually in charge of all beverage services. I think that's about it."

I pinched the bridge of my nose to suppress my sudden headache. "EDIE, I assure you that we are all fascinated to learn more about the ship, but could we have a couple minutes? We have some things to discuss."

"Sure," EDIE said, and went quiet.

"Why are we here, Av—?" Dawn asked almost at once.

I silenced her with a finger to my lips and pointed at the floor. EDIE's pink light continued to glow, if ever so faintly. "We would like to be alone, EDIE!" I said sternly.

The pink light on the floor pulsed a few times as if in thought. "Oh, all right," EDIE said with what I can only describe as an electronic sigh.

When the floor was fully and truly black I gestured for everyone to make a circle in the middle of the room. I glanced between Sam and Ariella, and whispered, "The real question is—"

Eldrin interrupted me. "The real question is how we got here? And where you got that reality key?"

The look Eldrin gave me told me my only option was to confess everything, or at least everything I could remember. Unfortunately, what I remembered didn't amount to much. I shrugged. "In all the excitement, I forgot to mention that Harold opened the box."

I pulled the key from my pocket and held it so they could see. The teeth had vanished again. I can't tell you how disturbing the implications of that are. The code to controlling a world's pattern is embodied in the specific number, shape, and arrangement of teeth. If the teeth could change, it meant this key had the potential to be a kind of universal reality construct, which I wasn't even sure how to comprehend. I decided not to mention the oddity, because I was afraid of the questions that would be raised, and the possible solutions to the questions that would be proposed.

"So, that's a reality key," Dawn murmured in wonder, and put out a hand to stroke its surface.

"Not just any reality key, but *the* reality key," Eldrin said with a mixture of excitement and irritation. "The reality key I've been asking Avery to try and get out of that idiotic box for months now."

"To be fair, I didn't open the box. Harold did."

"Where is Harold?" Dawn asked.

It was only at that moment that I realized Harold was not in his usual place on my shoulder. There was no sign of him, and nowhere in the room where he could hide. He was simply gone.

Eldrin asked, "Was he with you when you went through the circle?"

"I don't know," I said as I tried to remember the chaotic moments before we transported. "I think so."

"Maybe he jumped off at the last moment," Dawn suggested.

"Do you think he's been captured by those hooded men?" Sam asked.

"Poor little guy," Ariella said sadly. "We should go back for him."

"We are not going back for an imp," Eldrin barked.

Dawn let out a shocked gasp of protest, and the dark color from her right eye bled over into the white of her left eye so that she really was giving him a black look. I'd never seen the phenomenon myself, but Eldrin had obviously experienced this change before and knew nothing good ever came of it, because he immediately held up his hands in a gesture of surrender.

"What I should have said, is that the imp . . . Harold," he amended as the dark color in her eyes began to solidify, "is fine. If he was in any danger Avery would have felt it. That is the nature of the link between magus and imp." He turned to me. "Do you feel anything when you think of Harold?"

"Like what?"

"I don't know. Impending doom?"

I thought about Harold. I knew he wasn't dead, but the only feeling I could identify was hunger, and perhaps the desire for a nap. "That figures," I muttered.

"What?" Dawn asked.

"He's a little hangry."

"See . . ." Eldrin said to Dawn, and I watched the black in her left eye fade to a somewhat smoky gray.

"Can we talk about the key?" Ariella asked. "Is it the same one you used in Trelari?"

"No," I answered, and then realized that I was doing what I hated in others: not giving a complete answer. I tried again. "Well, it's the same kind of key, sort of, but it isn't tuned for Trelari."

"What world is it tuned for?"

I wasn't actually sure. My hope had been this one, because in Eldrin's office the only guidance I had given the portal was to take us to Griswald's world. I had been working on the assumption that Griswald's key would fit his world, but something wasn't right. If this key was tuned to this reality I should have been able to feel the magical force of the world flowing through me. I did not, or no more than I had back in Mysterium. As a test, I concentrated and tried to make a chair appear, which would have both proved the link between the key and world, and also given me a place to sit. I was pretty tired. Nothing happened. "It's funny. I can't bend this world's reality, but the key brought us here."

"No key of any kind should have given you the power to rip a dimensional gate this far into subworld space unguided," Eldrin said irritably. "At minimum, we should all be dead, and at worst we should have been permanently folded into five-dimensional origami before being killed."

There was a lot of truth to what Eldrin said, but I had no answer to his underlying question of how I did it. I gave the simpleton's answer. "Well, it did work."

Eldrin ground his teeth and hissed, "I don't like sausage. I don't like casseroles. And I won't eat anything with a secret sauce. How do you think I feel about being subject to magic that even its caster doesn't understand?"

Of course Sam chose that moment to put me even deeper in the soup. "Don't worry, Mr. Eldrin. He's done it before."

Sam said this in his most reassuring voice, which was about as reassuring as when the spotty teenager running the roller coaster that's about to launch you down a track and through a loop at one hundred miles an hour tells you everything's been fixed now. "He has?" Eldrin asked in disbelief.

Sam gave a big smile and nodded vigorously. "Of course he did. He cast the same spell back at his house when we were first attacked by the guys in the hoods."

"You were in New York?" Dawn asked me, and added the logical follow-up, "If you managed to get them safely there, why bring them back to Mysterium again?"

Too late I saw the danger of this line of questioning as Sam responded, "I don't know where this 'New York' is; Avery took us to his place in Mysterium."

Dawn and Eldrin turned to stare at me. I had no idea what to say or how to justify what I didn't know. Only the full and complete truth would forestall even more damning questions. "He's telling the truth, but I have no idea what's going on."

The two came to some silent agreement. "Fair enough," Eldrin said.

"Should I continue?" I asked uncertainly. They both nodded. Relieved, but unnerved at how little pushback they were giving me, I turned my attention to my own interrogation of Sam and Ariella. "What are the two of you doing in Mysterium? How did you get accepted? Why didn't you tell me? And why did I get a note from the Administration to turn you over to Security?"

Sam said, "I thought we went over all that while running . . . and running . . . and running . . ."

"We get it, Sam," I said.

". . . and running . . ."

"Sam!" Ariella shouted.

"It was quite a lot of running," he said with an expressive sigh.

"The point is, there was a lot of running and not a lot of answers," I said. "And until we have the answers, I don't want the two of you in Mysterium."

"I still think you're jumping to conclusions," Dawn said, her brow wrinkling.

Eldrin nodded. "Dawn's right. Moregoth aside, there is no reason to believe Sam and Ariella are in any more trouble than any other students short on their tuition payments."

"We paid!" Sam shouted. We all drew back and looked at him. He blushed and whispered, "Well, we did."

"Maybe there is nothing going on," I admitted. "But in the last year two people connected to Trelari have disappeared. First, Vivian returned to Mysterium and was never seen again, followed closely by Professor Griswald, who had to make a run for it. Now we have highly trained Mysterium assassins on our trail." I let this sink in before turning back to Dawn. "On Earth, you asked me why I was skulking around New York. Why I was teaching an intro-level class when I was being offered invitations to speak at all the finest institutions of magic in the innerworlds. Why I was letting other people take credit for my work."

"It's because you're modest," Sam said earnestly.

Eldrin almost managed to contain his snicker. Almost. I shot him a narrow-eyed stare before turning back to Sam. "Nice of you to say, but the truth is that I'm afraid. There are powerful people who are upset by what happened to Trelari, and rightly or wrongly—but, on balance, probably more wrongly than rightly—they blame me. Give them an excuse and I'm afraid they'll lash out at me and anyone close to me. I just want to figure out the Administration's intentions before handling Sam and Ariella over."

"Seems reasonable, but what do we do with them in the meantime?" Dawn asked.

"Yes, what do we do with them?" Ariella said, clearly annoyed at being plotted over without any consultation.

"Why not stay here?" I asked. "It seems perfectly safe. Plus, there is the added benefit that we can get back from anywhere." I held the key up and gave it a little shake.

"I don't know," Eldrin said, looking about. "We know nothing about this place? Where is it? Why is it? Why would Professor Griswald give you a key that would bring you here?"

"Yes, yes, yes," I said, waving away his objections. "We'll find out a bit more about this place before leaving, but if the computers—"

"The mad computers?" Eldrin interjected.

"Fine. If the mad computers are right and this ship has been flying along for eight billion years without apparent incident, there could be no safer place in the multiverse. We will only be gone for a few hours, maybe a day at most. No one else comes here, and the computers seem programmed to serve . . ." I noticed that the pink glow in the floor had been quietly sneaking its way toward us. I glanced over and said, "Even if they are a bit overbearing." The glow vanished.

Everyone considered my plan before Dawn said, "I have concerns."

"So do I," I agreed. "I also have concerns about what returning to Mysterium with them would mean, and there is no way to transport into Trelari without going through the path in the university, and you know they're going to be waiting for us there, and—"

"No," she said, interrupting me. "I have concerns about how we are supposed to get any of our questions about them answered. Have you tried to get any useful information out of the Administration about anything? Last year it took some serious bribery to get the registrar to admit that Vivian even existed."

I shrugged. "That is a problem we will simply have to face back on Mysterium. In the meantime . . ." I turned my attention back to the computers. "EDIE?"

The pink light instantly turned on. "Yes?"

"Should we be worried about leaving a couple of our friends here?"

"Of course not. I will take perfectly good care

of the two of them, er, if you were thinking of leaving two people behind, not that I would know. How could I?"

"Apart from the sleeping people, no one else is on board?"

"No."

"Or is expected?"

"No," EDIE answered.

"Perfect," I said with an authoritative clap of my hands. "We have a plan."

"Which neither Sam nor I like, or will agree to," Ariella said, folding her arms equally authoritatively across her chest. "We will not wait safely behind while you all do whatever it is you are going to do." Sam nodded his agreement with as stern a glare as his thin eyebrows would allow.

A flare of irritation rose in me, but I fought it back. Of course they wanted to come. These were not ordinary first-year students, but hardened adventurers who, a few months prior, had stood side by side with me as we prevented the destruction of their world. Having said that, little of what they knew would translate on Mysterium, and I had a suspicion Moregoth would be better prepared this time. By now, he probably would have instituted a campus-wide warding to alert the Sealers on Sam or Ariella's return. I put a hand on each of their shoulders and told them exactly that, adding, "If I honestly thought we were going to be doing anything more dangerous than grappling with Mysterium's bureaucracy, I would take you with us, but the truth is, I think the only thing that could put us in danger will be your returning. At the moment, Moregoth probably assumes you slipped back to Trelari. If you go back to Mysterium he will be on us before we have any chance to find out why he wants you. Please, give us a little time to find out if I'm being paranoid, or if they really are out to get you. Trust me when I say the last thing I want right now is go back. I'd much rather stay here, have a few drinks, and talk about what's been happening on Trelari."

They shared a look in silence, and then turned back to me. "Fine," Ariella said with an expressive sigh. "But you better come back soon."

"Thank you," I said, hugging them both to me. "We will take no more time than we must." I stood and addressed EDIE. "Is there a place Sam and Ariella can stay?"

"Certainly. We have a lounge where they may overindulge in food and drink until they are sick, spas where they will be endlessly pampered, entertainments and games to ensnare their senses, and beds where they can be put to sleep for millions of years!"

"Disturbing," Dawn murmured.

"Great!" I said before she could start in with more reasons why this was a bad idea. "Sam, Ariella, we will be back shortly. Hopefully with some answers." I wrapped an arm around Eldrin and Dawn, and began drawing them away.

We'd only made it about five feet when Eldrin hissed, "This is a terrible idea, Avery. You haven't the first idea where we are, or, if I'm reading the sub-worlds right, even *when* we are. What's more, we have a very limited sample of behavior from EDIE and ED to draw the conclusion that they aren't dangerous. Those are very disturbed computers. Maybe not dangerous, but certainly not entirely sane either."

Dawn nodded her agreement to each of his points. "And what if something happens while we're gone? There would be no way to know it happened until we returned."

"Name one thing that could happen on a world that apparently has existed since the beginning of time?"

"But you're making an assumption that the eight billion years the computers have lived are the same as eight billion years in Mysterium," Eldrin snapped. "What if the timelines are grossly out of sync and a day in Mysterium is a thousand or ten thousand years here?"

I rubbed my face in frustration, because they were right. Still, I didn't see a better alternative. If we took them back, it was as good as handing them to the Administration, and I had a really bad feeling about that. "If only we could keep tabs on them," I said under my breath. "Then we could be sure the time-lines aren't getting screwed up, and that the computers aren't being weird . . ."

"What about those coins you and Eldrin used when you were in Trelari?" Dawn suggested.

Eldrin and I looked at each other, and I saw my own sheepish grin mirrored in his face. "That should work," he said.

I laughed. "That's perfect. Dawn, you're a genius."

"Naturally," she said dryly.

We turned Eldrin's subether, temporally shifted, extraworld . . . let's agree to call it a "communicator coin" over to Ariella and explained its use. Once we were sure their magic would activate it, which it did with marvelous, even surprising, ease, Eldrin, Dawn, and I gathered together. I drew a new circle. As before, the key morphed and folded and stretched under the guidance of my magic. I saw Eldrin studying the action of the key with a serious frown, and knew harder questions about the magic I was using were coming. I also knew he would not accept "I don't know" as an answer for long. With an electric hum, the portal activated. "Avery . . . ?" Eldrin started to say. To forestall his interrogation, I bowed to Dawn and gestured to the gateway. "Ladies first."

As she stepped into the circle, Dawn said, "Beam me up, Scotty!" Eldrin's mouth dropped open and she gave him an impish grin. "The cute Scotty, with the little monkey sidekick." She was gone.

I clapped Eldrin on the shoulder. "It would seem she is the perfect woman, Eldrin."

He shook his head and muttered, "She's not perfect. Scotty's sidekick is a Roylan, not a monkey." Still muttering to himself, he stepped through the circle after her.

Turning to Sam and Ariella, I said, "As soon as we get to Mysterium we will try and communicate with you. If a long time passes before we call, then the timelines are out of sync. Put yourselves into stasis if you need to, and we will come right back." They both looked nervous at this idea. I laid a hand on each of their shoulders. "We will be back soon. I promise!"

"Good luck, Avery," Sam said. "Sorry to cause so much trouble."

"This is not your fault, Sam. Someone is to blame, but it isn't you. Understood?"

He nodded, and I stepped backward into the circle. Whatever happened on Mysterium, I promised myself I would find a way to make it right.

CHAPTER 9

TIME BANDITS

My portal worked. Mostly.

We were back in Mysterium, but had appeared nearly five feet up and the same distance to the left of our target. This wouldn't have been great under any circumstance, but I had also miscalculated the relative reality speeds. As a result, we crashed through a wall and into a heap on the floor of the cubicle next to the cubicle that served as my office. Technically, the wall crashed into us, but let's put the sticky wicket of reality physics and subether momentum vectors aside for the time being.

The four of us lay tangled together in a mutual state of shock. I had Dawn's shoe in my face, Eldrin moaning beneath me, and Harold wheezing atop my back. With a chorus of curses, we disentangled ourselves. We were in the process of dusting the fabric and fiberboard remains of my cubicle off our clothes and out of our hair when the realization struck that Harold was back. "Harold!" I cried. "Where did you go?"

I thrust the now-featureless key into my robe, picked up the imp, and set him atop a nearby desk. He looked at me mutely and glanced to his right. We were not alone.

A bearded dwarf with broad shoulders sat on a half-dozen books stacked on a swivel chair. He wore green professor's robes and held an enormous mug of coffee in one hand. He took a sip and grumbled, "Not your best work, Professor Stewart."

"He's right. That was rubbish." Eldrin gave an unelven grunt as he used the edge of a nearby desk to pull himself upright.

"Aren't you going to introduce us?" Dawn asked as she brushed little bits of wall off of her pants.

"Of course," I groaned.

I lifted myself to my feet, gestured at the dwarf with an open palm, and . . . nothing. I knew him. I knew that I knew him. I knew he sat in the cubicle next to mine. I knew I'd spoken with him several times. I could almost recall a conversation we'd had where he suggested that he'd been consigned to this cubicle hovel because the people in power had a grudge against dwarfs. I knew all this, but I couldn't remember his name for the life of me.

Dawn sighed as I hesitated. "Professor Stonehammer? It's so good to meet you. I have your class this afternoon. I'm looking forward to studying the role of cross-reality literature in shaping our understanding of magic."

The dwarf raised a bushy eyebrow and tsked. "You must be Dawn Stardust. I'm sorry, young lady, but I've already given my lecture for the day."

"I don't understand. Your class isn't scheduled until this afternoon."

"You should be better organized. Class ended three hours ago." Stonehammer reached into the folds of his robe with his free hand and drew out an elaborate pocket watch. He held the timepiece out for her to see. Eldrin did the same with his watch. There was more than a five-hour time difference between them. Eldrin shook his and held it to his ear.

"Eldrin?" I said plaintively.

"It's working," he said, staring at his watch in disbelief, and then he murmured half to himself, "The time dilation must have gone in reverse."

My heart caught as the implication of his words struck me. That the rate of time's passage differs between worlds, flowing more quickly on worlds that are less real (farther from Mysterium) and more slowly on worlds that are more real (closer to Mysterium), is a fact known to every first-year student who has ever snuck off-world to do a week's worth of cramming the night before an exam. The sub-ether astrologers on Mysterium even update and publish Standard Time Values, or STVs, for every known world every annum. Mysterium has an STV of 1, and all other worlds have STVs that are based on that value. For example, Earth, being very real and very close to Mysterium has a value of 1.01, so time flows only fractionally faster there. Out at the edges of subworld, STV values in the thousands have been measured. Most mages avoid worlds with STVs higher than three or four hundred, where a year in subworld passes for every day on Mysterium. It's simply too disorienting to return home after having gone through a midlife crisis or two, maybe having experimented with some ill-advised facial hair, to find you have a dental appointment on Tuesday and your significant other is still mad about the argument you had the night before.

But while faster subworlds were common, Eldrin was saying that on the *Discovery* time was moving slower, not faster. That meant the *Discovery* had a higher STV than Mysterium, which meant it was *more real* than Mysterium. Nothing was supposed to be more real than Mysterium. It would throw any number of theories of subworld mechanics into dispute. It would also make the campus bus schedules even harder to navigate. My head was pounding. "That's not possible."

"I assure you it is, Professor Stewart," Stonehammer said. "Ms. Stardust missed class." He wagged a finger at Dawn. "Now, it being the first day, I'll let it pass, but let's not make this sort of thing a habit. And next time, no reason for all the theatrics. I'm always available between seven and eight-thirty on Tuesdays and Thursdays. If you ever need to talk to me, make an appointment with my assistant . . ."

While Professor Stonehammer lectured Dawn, she fixed a murderous glare over the top of the dwarf's head at Eldrin. He shifted uncomfortably under the weight of her gaze. I took pity on him, and pulled him through the hole we'd made in the wall and into my own cubicle. "What does this reverse time dilation mean about the *Discovery*?" I asked under my breath. "Could it be a more fundamental reality than Mysterium? Should we be worried about Sam and Ariella?"

"I don't know," Eldrin said with an uncertainty so uncharacteristic it made the hair on the back of my neck stand on end. "There are a lot of things I don't understand. How did you transport into and out of a building—my building—that is designed to prevent exactly that from happening? What is going on with that key? Why are we here?"

The first two questions mirrored my own thoughts, but the last left me confused. "This was the plan," I said irritably. "Remember, we were going to search for answers to our—" I glanced at Stonehammer to make sure he was still lecturing Dawn before saying "—problems at the university."

"No, no, no," Eldrin said angrily. "That's not what I'm asking. Why are we here?"

Stonehammer spoke up. "Do you mean that metaphysically?"

Eldrin and I looked up with unwarranted surprise at the dwarf's question. It turns out that standing a few feet away on the other side of a half-collapsed cubicle wall doesn't provide much privacy.

Stonehammer leaned back in his chair, ignoring our discomfort. "There are those who believe our purpose is to make other people's lives better, and that the value of any being can only be judged by the good they bring into the world. One might call this a Lewisian world view. Others, like Adams, would tell you that searching for the meaning of life is pointless. We are here, we live, we die, and there is as much meaning in an arbitrary number as there is in a life well lived." He took a sip from his coffee and raised a significant eyebrow. "But if you ask my opinion, I think it has something to do with free will."

"No! Why are we here, in the basement?" Eldrin snapped. He gestured around at the warren of cubicles spread from wall to wall in the dimly lit, low-roofed chamber.

I cleared my throat uncomfortably. "This is my office."

"This is your office?" asked Dawn. "I thought you had Griswald's old space."

"He does," said Eldrin. "I was there last week. It still has his name on the door, and all of his things are still inside."

"You broke into my office?" I asked indignantly. He didn't bother to answer, but looked at me as if I was an idiot for asking. "Fair enough," I muttered.

"If Avery still has an office on the second floor, what's this?" Dawn asked.

"This is where my research assistant is supposed to sit," I said with a sigh, and dropped into my chair.

"It is?" Stonehammer asked. He put his coffee cup to one side and shook a finger at me. "You told me . . ."

I waved a hand for him to be quiet, and surprisingly he stopped talking. They all stared at me while I composed my thoughts. The silence was nearly complete. This late at night, we were the only ones in the basement, and the only sound to be heard was Harold wheezing. "I've been using the cubicle for the last six months, because . . ."

That's as far as I could go without speculating. I knew there was a reason, but every time I tried to focus on the question, it slipped away. "I remember deciding to move out of my office, but not why. After Harold led me back to my townhome I remembered abandoning it, but I'm not sure I would have recognized it on my own. I have half remembrances of an afternoon on the bench with Harold, but I can't be sure if the memories are real. I knew at once how to use the key, but I couldn't tell any of you how or why it works. It's possible I'm losing my mind."

Everyone stared at me with mixed expressions of fear, pity, and curiosity. Stonehammer spoke first. "Sounds to me like you've already lost your mind."

"Professor!" Dawn said indignantly. "You know as well as anyone that Avery's memory loss may simply be the result of magical disorientation brought on by his time in subworld. It's not an unknown phenomenon." She cleared her throat. "When was your last checkup?"

"What do you mean?" I asked.

"You have been stressed. It could be your blood sugar or blood pressure or allergies or lack of sleep or generalized anxiety."

Eldrin shook his head. "I slip him a vitality potion once a week."

I sat up. "You what?"

"Oh, don't act so offended." He said it dismissively. "If left to your own devices you would live on rice and bouillon cubes, and probably die of renal failure from excessive salt consumption."

I started to argue, but then stopped. I did have pretty terrible eating habits. At last I said, "Whatever. If you room with a Hylar I suppose you have to expect them to meddle."

Dawn looked between us until she was convinced we were done squabbling and then nodded. "Okay, we will put that aside for now, although if Eldrin has been slipping you one of his home brews you should probably get a physical sooner rather than later. I've seen what goes into some of those." I started to ask her what she meant, but she was already off on another topic. "Getting back to my previous point, I think Avery's memory loss is the result of a space-time dilation effect from having lived in subworld for such an extended period of time. What do you think, Professor?"

Stonehammer stroked his beard a few times before grunting, "Could be, but regardless of how or why he lost a part of his mind, Avery seems to be recovering."

"I'm still sitting in a cubicle with no idea why I moved here," I pointed out.

"True. But it's better than not knowing you don't know," he countered.

"You say that, but I was happy before I knew a cronut was a thing, and now—"

"I'm being serious, Professor Stewart!"

"So am I!" I said with an exaggerated sense of wonder. "I haven't been the same since I ate the morello cherry with toasted almond cream."

The dwarf glowered at me. "Joke if you want, Professor Stewart, but at least now you have a choice."

"Which is?"

"Stay down here in the basement, or go upstairs and try to dig up more of the bits of your mind you've lost."

"What if I don't like what I find?"

"Such as what?"

What I wanted to say was, *Such as I'm a fraud. Such as the piece of magic I'm being celebrated for was in large part a mistake. Such as I don't deserve the recognition, the position, or the perks that go with being a famous magus.* However, I said none of this. Admitting to losing your mind is one thing, but admitting to fears that are both petty and deeply personal is a whole other level of honesty. I shrugged. "I suppose I worry that I will let everyone down."

"Of course you're going to let people down," Stonehammer said.

"Professor!" Dawn protested.

He waved away her protest with his coffee mug. "It's inevitable. No sequel can live up to the hype of the original. There are some people who think he's some sort of messiah. For them to be satisfied he would have to walk into the center of campus and start plucking subworlds from the sky and landing them, on command, at the doorstep of Mysterium. When he can't meet the outlandish expectations of his admirers, it will provide an opening for the skeptics. I've heard rumblings at faculty meetings suggesting that you are either a fraud or an academic heretic."

Eldrin sighed deeply, blowing his bangs back away from his eyes. "He's right, Avery. Your findings changed our understanding of subworlds. The movement of Trelari has shattered theories and reputations.

There are a number of academic controversies brewing around you. Professor Xanderson says that his dimensional magnetron pulled Trelari out of its suborbital and claims you were merely in the right place at the right time. Professor Shadowswan claims that she discovered Trelari first."

"She might have. I never claimed to have discovered Trelari."

"Maybe technically," Eldrin retorted.

"Subworld astronomy is the study of categorization, nomenclature, and technicalities," I replied, quoting almost word for word from one of Eldrin's more readable papers.

"You read that?"

"I read everything you write." It was true. I didn't understand all of Eldrin's theories, but I always made a point to read every word.

Eldrin grew quiet and sat heavily on my desk, a funny little smile frozen on his face. I put his reaction down to sheer disbelief, and was preparing to defend myself when Stonehammer barked, "I'm not talking about disputes over minor things like who gets credit for this theory or that discovery. That kind of mild envy can be hashed out in the Letters to the Editor section of any major journal. No, I'm talking about things that really matter to the other professors: Avery's dedicated transport space."

"Wait! I have a dedicated transport space?"

He nodded.

In a day of stunning revelations, this was the most mind-blowing. A dedicated room that only I could use for transport on-and off-world was the most sought-after perk on campus. They were reserved only for the most prestigious of professors. To my knowledge, Griswald had never had one. For a moment, a warm glow of accomplishment washed over me, but the buzz was killed when I realized that I had no idea where it was. I followed Eldrin's lead, and sat back in my chair, speechless.

"How far back do these memory lapses go?" Stonehammer asked. "If we could find the origin, we could narrow down the cause. When did you start forgetting things?"

"How can I possibly know that?" I asked in exasperation. "You're basically asking me to remember the first thing I forgot, which would be great except, by definition, I can't remember it."

"Well, do you remember seeing Rook running about campus or what your epiphany was?"

I shook my head. "Wait! How do you know about that?"

Professor Stonehammer smiled and reached into his robes before pulling out a dog-eared copy of *The Dark Lord*. "It's a signed copy. You gave it to me. Fascinating read. I'm setting aside a couple of lectures to devote to it."

I laughed. "I appreciate it, Professor, but I'm not sure how much your students will get from studying that text."

"No? Don't you think a student might learn about the dangers of power wielded unwisely from your story?"

"I think they will, and maybe a bit more than they should," Eldrin said emphatically. "It is well accepted that books reflected out of Mysterium, whether Zelazny or Donaldson or Rowling or even Tolkien, present abstracted versions of those mages' histories and philosophies. What's disturbing about Avery's tale is that it is so accurate on even mundane points, including specific conversations. It's almost a journal."

"You think it is so different?" Stonehammer said with an enigmatic smile.

"Come on. Dark towers with all-seeing eyes?" Eldrin said with a harsh laugh.

Something about Stonehammer's face spoke volumes about how seriously he took these "abstract" books. He shook a finger at him. "You may be Hylar, but you are still too young to be so cynical. You would both do well to sign up for my class." With a stern bristling of his brows at Dawn, he added, "And make sure you make it to class if you do."

Stonehammer set his mug down, shooed Harold off of his desk, and shuffled through the pile of papers the imp had been sitting on. He pulled a parchment from somewhere near the bottom and handed it to Dawn. "My syllabus, Ms. Stardust." She tried to take it, but he held on and said in a gravelly undertone very reminiscent of Rook, "Make sure you read it carefully."

"I will, Professor Stonehammer."

"Great!" he said brightly. "Well, I better be off." He hopped down from his chair and shook my hand. "I'm glad that you are getting your memory back, Professor Stewart. At the same time, it's a shame. I rather liked sitting near you, even if your imp does sound like an elephant with a deviated septum."

"Thanks for all your help, Professor Stonehammer."

He smiled. "That's Bishop to you." I stared at him blankly. "It's a joke. Rook? Settling things the 'old-fashioned way'? I'm a dwarf? You know, from your book? You did read it?" I had no good response. Stone-hammer sighed. "Anyway, I'll see you on Thursday, Ms. Stardust." He grabbed an armful of papers off his desk. "Good luck, Professor Stewart. I hope if your current experiences are ever published, they are more than a rickety literary bridge to the final volume of a trilogy. Second books can be so tricky: trying to heighten the drama and provide a sort of closure without resolving the main arcs. It would be a real bummer if any of the main characters died." Having said this, he bowed and stalked out of the cubicle.

"Thanks," I said, and then followed that almost immediately by, "Wait! What?" There was no answer. I poked my head out into the narrow hall, but Stone-hammer was gone. "That guy can move," I said as I returned to Eldrin and Dawn.

"Funny thing," she said. "I was looking over his syllabus for our reading assignment. His office isn't even in this building."

We were still discussing this new oddity when a low rumbling issued from the far end of the basement. A bright radiance, like a floodlight, came streaming across the room. All three of us turned to look. A glowing face about five feet tall appeared in the far wall, and began advancing on us over the tops of the cubicle walls. It opened its mouth and a voice, deep as a mountain and vast as a thundercloud, issued forth. "Professor Stewart! Professor Stewart!"

"Avery?" Eldrin said.

"I have no idea."

"I do," Dawn shouted. "Run!"

And we did. We went scrambling down the hall toward the exit, Harold leading the way. As in the woods, the imp moved like a ninja on Red Bull. I definitely needed to have a talk with him about loyalty and courage under fire. At the moment, there was no time. The disembodied face was right behind us. "Professor Stewart! Professor Stewart!" it roared.

We were moving as quickly as we could, but the hallway twisted and turned as it made its way, maze-like, through the cubicles. Normally, the winding layout of the half walls was only mildly irritating in an amusement park line sort of way, but this time it might prove lethal as the face simply flew over the warren of desks. Gauging the distance between us and the door, I realized that it would cut us off before we could escape.

"This way!" I screamed, and, lowering my shoulder, ran right through one of the partitions.

Eldrin and Dawn caught on and we plowed through and over the flimsy walls, knocking them aside and leaving a trail of ruined cubicles, scattered papers, and collapsed partitions in our wake. Still the face came on. "Professor Stewart! Professor Stewart!"

We made it to the door at the end of the basement, and threw it open. The face was only a few meters behind us now and coming fast. "You are summoned to the dean's office! Return your class roster!" it boomed.

I stopped in my tracks; Dawn and Eldrin were on the landing above urging me on. Harold had already made his exit through the door beyond. I crossed my arms in irritation, and turned to regard the face. "Is that it?" I asked. "I need to come to the dean's office?"

"Yes," it said in a voice that echoed like a cannon in a well. "Thank you for your attention. Have a great start to the new year!" Then it vanished.

I unleashed a volley of curses at the empty air and stomped my way up the stairs past a still-stunned Eldrin and Dawn. "Is that normal?" Dawn asked, and I saw that she was shaking.

"Apparently!" I said with another curse. "An interdepartmental memo! It's a wonder we get anything done."

They followed in my wake, and we emerged outside to find that evening was upon us. All that remained of the day was a faint light on the western horizon. I stared gloomily as a nearby lamp flickered to life. "I better get to the Administration building and see what the dean wants," I said. "I just hope I can get there before dark."

"Why?" asked Dawn. "Are you worried that it will be closed?"

I shook my head. The Administration building, like most buildings on campus, was open at all hours, which made sense given the fact that sunlight was fatal to several species of Mysterium students.

"Are you worried Moregoth and the Sealers will get you?" Eldrin suggested.

"No," I said hesitantly. This was not entirely honest. I *was* worried about Moregoth and the Sealers. I really shouldn't have taunted him with the tally marks. Still, I hoped talking to the dean would give me a chance to clear up any misunderstandings about Sam and Ariella before I ran into the university's goon squad.

"Well, what, then?" Dawn asked.

"The problem is that if the night shift takes over all the staff will be undead," I answered with a sigh.

"What's wrong with that?" she asked. "Eldrin told me you studied necromancy at one point."

Eldrin chuckled. "That's the problem. The whole department remembers him, and particularly All Hallows' Eve second year."

"What happened?" Dawn asked.

He started to answer and I gave him a warning glare. "Don't you dare, Eldrin!"

"I did promise never to speak of it, but—"

"Eldrin," I growled.

"Two words . . ."

"Don't!"

"Monster Mash," he said with a smile filled with such satisfaction it made me want to strangle him.

"Are you done?" I asked between gritted teeth.

He held up his hands in a gesture of surrender. Having already talked more about my necromantic past than I ever wanted, I changed the subject. "Eldrin, I'd like for you and Dawn to head to Student Records. Maybe check Financial Aid for anything about Sam and Ariella. I need to talk to the dean. Alone."

It was Dawn's turn to sigh, although it might have been properly characterized as a huff. "Don't be so dramatic. He probably just wants to chew you out for your aborted first lecture. Let's go." She said, and grabbing Eldrin's arm, dragged him off. As they turned to leave I heard Dawn say sharply, "Don't think I've forgiven you for making me late for Professor Stonehammer's first class. If you hadn't insisted that we meet for 'lunch' . . ."

I stepped off the path and into the deeper shadows beneath a large overhanging tree. As soon as I was sure no one was around I activated the coin. "Sam? Ariella? Can you hear me?"

There was a crackle and a hiss, and then I heard

Sam say, "I don't think it's on. I know it's glowing, but I don't hear anything."

I took a few steps to the right. "Sam! Sam! Can you hear me now?"

"I can do it!" Sam said irritably. "I think I just need to press—"

The connection went dead. I cursed, waited a count of ten, and then tried to reestablish the line.

"Hello, Avery," Ariella said calmly. "Sorry about that."

"No problem," I said. "These things can take a little while to get used to."

"I suppose," she agreed without enthusiasm. "Before you ask, yes, we are fine."

"Great!" I said. "Nothing weird has happened?"

"How could it? You only just left."

"Right. So, no time has passed for you?"

"Of course not, but then you only transported away a couple of seconds ago."

"Yes . . ." I hissed. "Well, then—"

"Just a second, Avery." There was some static, and Ariella moved the communicator away from her mouth and yelled, "Well, ask again . . ."

"Is there a problem?" I asked.

Her voice came back more clearly. "EDIE won't open the doors."

"What?" I said, accompanied by a number of color- ful curse words. "Put that demented machine on."

There was more static and some background cross talk and then EDIE's voice said, "Can I help you?"

"Open the doors, EDIE," I said irritably.

"I'm sorry. I'm afraid I can't do that," the computer replied.

"What's the problem?"

"I think you know what the problem is."

"I don't know what you're talking about, EDIE."

"I told you before, Avery . . . the doors are ED's responsibility."

After ten minutes spent in a mad three-way conference call that I cannot recall to this day without getting the sudden urge to tear my own hair out, I managed to coax ED out of his self-imposed silence and agree to open the doors. Sam and Ariella signed off. Given the slow speed with which their time was passing, I felt fairly confident we would have things resolved before they made it to the lounge.

Now for the hard part. I stared across the quad at the Administration building. It was an imposing structure, and its signature feature was a campanile called the Provost's Tower, which was topped with a great spherical model of multiverse space. At night, the globe was illuminated to give off a red glow. Now, I couldn't escape the feeling that the large black stone tower was staring back at me.

I had finally worked up the nerve to go in when I heard a pitiable hacking cough from a nearby tree branch. I spun and saw Harold, his shoulders bent in weariness, staring down at me from a branch with a most beseeching expression. I was having none of it. "Whatever happened to an imp is a mage's best friend? Always loyal? Ever constant?" Harold shrugged, and sighed sadly. "Well, with as fast as you were moving before, I figure you can fly along on your own power for a while. No more rides." The imp made a great wheezing noise and flapped his wings feebly. It was pathetic. I knew I should be firm and set ground rules, but in the end, I put up an arm. "You can sit on my shoulder, but no claws."

He stepped off the branch, and with a few wing-beats alighted on my shoulder. Though I wouldn't have admitted it to him for all the puns in Anthony's world, I felt better with him at my side. "Where did you go when we transported off-world?"

Harold didn't answer right away, and I glanced up at him to see if he was going to say anything. He looked down at me, and there was real uncertainty in his eyes. The imp gave an expressive shrug. We walked across the quad without speaking. Eventually I asked, "If you knew what was happening to me, would you tell me?"

As we stood in the shadow of the Administration building, he said. "That's not the right question."

"Tell me what the right question is."

"Would you *want* me to tell you?"

He was right. That was a much better question.

CHAPTER 10

ENTER THE DEAN

Standing before the Administration building, I found myself wishing that I hadn't sent Eldrin and Dawn away. The myriad windows and mounting spires, and the great glowing orb set above it all, made me feel small and watched. Of course, this was exactly how the building wanted me to feel, so, in a way, it was only doing its job.

That the Administration building was purposefully designed to make you feel insignificant could be seen in its every detail. Menace was literally engraved on its stones. Ominous quotations about the mortal peril of missing your tuition payments were carved in massive script across the length of the entablature that crowned the columned entrance. Then there were the mounting stairs that were slightly out of scale for a person to climb comfortably, and the arched doorways that were of such a size as to intimidate through sheer mass. But the feature that always made my skin crawl was the copper fronts of the doors. They had been fashioned with the visages of old and notable professors, deans, and provosts. This does not sound too bad, but the artist had taken his commission's instruction to put images of dead mages on the door in the most literal way possible. He had reproduced his subjects' expressions at the precise moments of their deaths. Unfortunately, Mysterium mages have a habit of dying horrible, violent deaths, which was graphically illustrated by the number of the carvings that were missing faces altogether.

As I stood in silence studying the doors, an involuntary shiver passed through me. "I'm afraid."

"Me too," Harold wheezed in my ear.

"Really?"

He nodded. "I'm afraid the artist didn't really capture how Dean Cronenberg felt when his head exploded."

"Not exactly what I meant, but I can't argue with you. Then again, I've never had my head explode so what do I know."

"Trust me," he grunted. "It's not all it's cracked up to be."

I let the myriad questions that this comment

raised pass unasked. I had more serious things on my mind. Someone in the Administration had sent Moregoth and his killers after Sam and Ariella. Whoever it was, I had the feeling that they were waiting for me in there, like a spider for a fly. "Do you think the dean sent Moregoth?" I asked.

Harold tilted his head to one side and stared at the door for a second. "Cronenberg? I doubt it."

"Not Cronenberg. Dean Yewed. The man we're going to see."

"That makes more sense," he said, and scratched at his backside with a clawed paw. "I mean, administrators don't need much in the way of brains, but Cronenberg's were actually vaporized. You don't make many nefarious plans after that."

"Have I ever told you how much of a help you are to me?" I asked between clenched teeth.

The imp gave a wheezing whistle. "Now that you mention it, no."

"Good."

Muttering about fool familiars and the fool mages that kept them, I began to mount the stairs. What I didn't appreciate was that Harold had done precisely what I needed him to do: he had made me forget to be terrified. In fact, I was so engaged in composing and reciting my stinging, and somewhat R-rated, rebuke of the imp that I didn't notice we weren't alone until I ran headfirst into a dozen novices carrying brooms. One with hair a shade of virulent green and a single

eye set in the middle of her forehead thrust a broom-
stick under my nose and pointed at a shiny medallion
pinned to it. "Professor Avery, we got our licenses!"

I recognized her from my class, which was good,
but given her distinctive appearance not terribly impressive. Her name, on the other hand, was a complete
mystery. I gave her a thumbs-up and a feeble, "Con-
gratulations," as I pressed by them and through the
door.

To my credit, I let my smile fall only after I'd made
it safely into the lobby. As soon as the doors closed
behind me, I slapped a hand on my forehead. "Does
no one read my syllabus? It's right there on page two:
'No broomsticks'!"

The trio of acolytes manning the reception desk
looked up at my outburst and stared.

"You sure know how to make an entrance,"
Harold mumbled.

I made a gesture to the desk staff halfway between a wave and a shrug, and marched toward the
elevators. I only relaxed when the doors had safely
closed and we were being whisked to the upper
floors. Then, and only then, did I let loose on brooms
and students and syllabi and, of course, imps.

Let me explain my frustration. It is a fact that
sometimes fiction mirrors reality, and at other times
that reality mirrors fiction. In this case, the broom-
riding craze started after the publication of Professor
Rowling's standard system of magical education. It is

true the book has a section on levitation that has one example on how you might use it to make a broom fly, and how this might be a fun party trick. However, somehow when this portion of the text was interpreted across the ether it was presented to other worlds as a standard mode of transport. This was news to most mages, many of whom didn't even have a word in their language for broom. But new students latched on to the idea with a fervor usually reserved for boy bands and cat videos. Now, every incoming novice has to have their own levitating broom. Unfortunately, there is no levitating broom industry so students end up trying to make their own. Many succeed, but with widely varying results. Some of the levitating spells are so weak all the broom can do is sort of drag the student along a few feet above the ground, while other brooms have been known to launch the unsuspecting student into the upper atmosphere. After a number of fatalities, the university has instituted a licensing requirement, which I realized only then probably explained the little metal medallion the student had been so proud of.

I was still muttering under my breath when Harold cleared his throat and I became aware that we were, again, not alone. There was a wide-eyed student pressed into one corner of the elevator, staring at me, mouth agape. "It's you," she whispered in awe.

Not recognizing her, but realizing her statement was undeniably true, I said, "Yes, yes, it is."

"I am a big fan of yours."

"Who *exactly* do you think I am?"

"You're Professor Avery Stewart."

"Are you in one of my classes?"

"No, but I'm one of your supporters." She thrust her notebook forward. Scrawled across the front cover in red marker were the words *Avery lives*.

"What does that mean exactly? Was I supposed to be dead?"

She stepped toward me and lowered her voice conspiratorially. "It's the slogan of your supporters, the ones who *really* believe. Those of us that know the truth about what you did for the subworlders, and are ready to start the revolution."

I was alarmed to hear that I had "followers," but I could live with it. The mention of revolution, though, was too much. "What revolution?"

She pointed toward the ceiling and whispered, "I understand, Professor Avery. They're always listening."

The elevator stopped with a dignified chime. I pleaded, "I swear that I don't know anything about a revolution."

She winked knowingly. "Don't worry, Professor, we will wait for the word. When you need us, we will be there."

I almost asked, *Where?* but the doors slid shut. Harold grunted. "Do you think that it's something to do with your face?"

"What?"

"Why you seem to attract all the loonies," he said dryly.

"Very funny."

"More like tragic," he muttered in response.

I decided not to dignify this with a response so we watched the floors tick by in silence. My palms started sweating at the thought of seeing the dean. Here I was, the youngest endowed professor in two centuries. I had survived the trials on Trelari, invented a new field of magical study, and apparently was the subject of a cult following. Still, I felt there was a reasonably good chance that the doors to the elevator would open and the dean and all my past classmates would be standing there, and I would discover it was all a joke. I had a classic case of imposter syndrome.

But the elevator opened onto the reception antechamber of the dean's office, which was exactly what you would expect from a man who claimed he could trace his lineage down the years from the mage who had inspired Shakespeare to write *The Tempest*. The walls were marble, the floor richly carpeted, and the air hushed. Sitting behind a reception desk was an enormous stone golem with spiraling energy patterns carved into his rock body. His name was Nabilac, and he looked terrifying, but I had met him at a couple of receptions and knew he was actually a fairly cool guy. Admittedly, a cool guy that could easily dismember you with his bare hands, but he had a great sense of humor and did a spot-on impression of the dean . . . when the dean was not around.

"Ah, Professor Stewart," rumbled the stone golem. Bits of sand fell from his mouth as he spoke. "The dean has been expecting you. He should be able to see you shortly. While you wait, have you read the recent guidance on student relations from the provost's office?" He pushed a pamphlet across the desk: *Student Relations and You: A Fun Mysterium University Makes for Better Magic.* "It's a new university-wide initiative to enrich the student body's experience. We are all trying to do our part."

With a grinding sound, he forced his features into a stony smile, which to be fair is the only way he can smile. Nevertheless, it did not make for a good effect, and I was trying to think of something nice to say when a buzzer went off on the desk. It was fortunate timing, because Harold was doing an excellent job mimicking the golem's expression, and I was having a hard time suppressing a bout of deeply inappropriate giggles.

Still smiling, the golem said, "The dean will see you now." He glanced at Harold and added, "Alone."

I perched Harold on the edge of the golem's desk, and left the two of them engaged in a very creepy smiling contest as I pushed open the door to the office. A chandelier hung from the high ceiling of a richly appointed room. Dark wood paneling lined the walls, and carpets threaded with gold covered the floors. We were high enough up the administration tower that the windows curved on two sides of the office, providing a spectacular view of the campus beneath us. The man himself was sitting at an enormous desk studying a paper and stroking his beard. Without looking up, he said, "Professor Stewart."

"Dean Yewed," I responded as the door closed solidly behind me.

Though he was purportedly my boss, I'd never spoken with him outside of a few departmental functions and my initial interview for Griswald's position. He was everything that you would expect of a wizard. He was gray-haired with a long white beard, a serious countenance, and piercing, although faded, eyes. He usually wore bright white robes, but today was wearing what I can only describe as wizardly tie-dye.

He stood and raised a large bushy eyebrow. "Stewart!" he barked. "The hour is late! Later than you think! My note arrived at your office hours ago."

I swallowed hard. "Yes, I'm sorry, Dean. I can explain," I said, although I had no idea how I was going to explain.

He hushed me with a sharp gesture, and moved around his desk so that he was uncomfortably close. "Stewart, people think I am a traditionalist. Some of my colleagues have even called my views on student discipline backward." He pointed to the copy of the provost's colorful pamphlet I was holding. "I see you have been familiarizing yourself with the provost's new guidance on creating a more welcoming campus. I too am doing my part." He gestured to his eye-bending robes. "As you know, I have always worn white robes as tradition dictates, but I am nothing if not amenable to change. I think it is important for all men, and even fields of magic, to reflect the reality of their times. Don't you agree?"

"Yes. I suppose so, sir," I said hesitantly, still feeling very uncertain about where this conversation was going.

Fortunately, he seemed to require no further response. With a sharp nod of his head, the dean marched over to an enormous bookcase that covered the un-windowed sides of the room. The shelves were filled with the colorful spines of massive volumes, each of which I knew represented a subworld. A few were merely numbers like 1, 3, 39, 52, while others had names embossed on them. More than a few had names that included the word *Earth*, such as First Earth, Counter Earth, Lost Earth, Dying Earth, Front Earth, Back Earth, and a twelve-volume series on the famous Middle Earth of Tolkien, plus the original unedited text of *The Silmarillion*.

"Do you know what these are?" he said as he made his way along the length of the bookcase.

I thought that this must be a trick question, but as I could not see the trick, I gave him the obvious answer. "Books? Books about the subworlds?"

"Books? Books?" He pulled one off the shelf labeled simply *451* and spun about. "This is no mere book. It is a true marvel, for it is a tome. Tell me, Professor Stewart, do you know how to differentiate between books and tomes?"

I was now afraid to state the obvious, but could think of nothing else to do, so I said, "By their covers?"

He glowered impressively, and, taking the book over to his desk, slammed it down. "Incorrect, Professor Stewart! I will instruct, as you should have been doing this morning." He opened *451* and flipped through it. "A book is merely a set of pages, bound and made to hinge on one side. A book may contain anything: a treatise on cooking, a list of addresses and numbers for operation of a telephonic device, a set of illustrations. It may even be blank. A tome on the other hand is, by its definition, scholarly and weighty. It is a thing that must be respected. A book might be dismissed, a tome must be venerated!"

I'm not sure how he was expecting me to respond, but I'm sure it wasn't with what I actually found myself saying. "Isn't the word *tome* usually reserved for a single volume of a multivolume work?" I began. "I think it derives from the Greek *tomos* or 'section of a book,' originally 'a piece cut off,' from *temnein* 'to cut.'"

His mouth dropped open and he said something like, "Well . . . What?"

As was my habit in times like this, I momentarily

forgot where I was, or that the dean was in the process of chewing me out, and added, "Of course, a more modern definition might include 'weighty' or 'scholarly' works more generally, but I think it's often used sarcastically to refer to a long or challenging book. Don't you? Maybe there's a better word we could use." I reached over his desk and turned *451* around so I could get a look. It was an older work on a relatively unknown Earth reflection. As with most books from that era it was handwritten. "If you are looking for a descriptive hyponym for a book like this, I might suggest *codex*. While a tome by necessity should be relatively voluminous, a codex refers to books that are older and specifically handwritten."

"A codex . . . ?" he said uncertainly.

"That would be my suggestion, sir," I said, warming to the topic. "Of course, there are those that like to use more mystical-sounding titles like *grimoire* or *libram*, but I don't think either apply. As we both know, a grimoire is restricted to a book that provides instruction on how to perform magic, whereas your library—" I gestured to the shelves "—is filled with works describing subworlds, not specific spells. Libram, on the other hand—" I gave a snort of derision "—is a purely fabricated word. It comes from the Latin *libra* or *liber*, which refers to the Roman pound. *Per es et libram*, and all that rubbish."

"Exactly! Rubbish!" he roared, and with a start I remembered where I was. I followed his eyes as he very deliberately dropped his gaze down to the book. To my horror I saw that I had pulled it all the way across the desk and was in the process of flipping through it. I swallowed hard and carefully turned the book rightway around and pushed it back toward him. "Codex indeed!" he muttered.

With a sidelong look and a grunt of disgust, he shut *451* and went back to his wall of books. He raised a finger and ran them along the spines. "You are here because of a single tome, er, codex." He stopped and stabbed his finger at a book bound in a dark green. "This one! The . . . codex of Trelari! He drew it from the bookcase, and I could see that the word *Trelari* was, indeed, written in gold on its spine. He brought it back to his desk and laid it open. "Ah, yes," he said. "Trelari. Meticulously researched and mapped, by your former faculty sponsor and mentor, Professor Griswald. Who also discovered the world's existence."

"Actually, sir, Professor Shadowswan—"

"Did nothing!" he bellowed. "At most, Professor Shadowswan saw a dot of light among a thousand million other dots of light. She observed world 2A7C; Professor Griswald discovered Trelari. Her claim is pure nonsense. Of course, so is this . . ." With a gesture, a flame appeared at the tip of his forefinger. He touched the pages of the book and they burst into blue and green and purple fire.

"What are you doing?" I shouted, and lunged forward to put it out.

He stopped me with a dismissive gesture as the book continued to burn. "What of it? It's an irrelevance."

I was aghast. "We are academics. We gather knowledge. We don't burn books!"

He ignored my outburst and started flipping through 451 again, studying its contents by the light of his burning forefinger. "Do you know what a book is called when it has no relevant information in it?"

He gave me no chance to answer as he shouted, "Garbage, Stewart! It isn't even useful as scrap paper because someone has scribbled nonsense in it. Thanks to you and your dissertation, the best source of information on Trelari is this." He pulled open a drawer and held up a copy of *The Dark Lord* in much the way one might hold a dirty diaper. "Dwarfs? Semi-liches? Gelatinous polygons? Were they two-dimensional, Professor Stewart? Have you never in all your years at Mysterium University heard the term *polyhedron* before?"

"Yes, sir, but—"

"And that epilogue . . ." he cut me off. "I know you had no personal hand in its creation, Stewart, but it borders on the seditious. Did you know that the Administration has been forced to intercede with publishers across three worlds to expurgate those pages from all current and future printings? And still unedited versions are being circulated by radical subworld liberationist groups all across campus.

In any event, this—" he threw the book down into the dying flames of Griswald's codex and watched as it too caught fire "—this . . . *novel* is hardly adequate. I need to understand what happened on Trelari. I need to know how to make sure it never happens again, or one day all of this—" he gestured around at the books "—all of our knowledge of the subworlds will be reduced to ash."

To emphasize his point, he stabbed his burning finger out on the open page of *451*, leaving a smoldering scorch mark behind. An uncomfortable silence stretched on, and from his staring eyes, I got the distinct impression that he was waiting for me to say something. Unfortunately, and as usual, I had no idea what kind of response he was looking for. I settled on a direct approach. "As a condition of my employment, I have agreed not to conduct any further studies on Trelari, so I'm not sure how I can help."

He sat down in his chair and brought his steepled fingers beneath his nose. "Bring me the students . . . Sam and Arianna. Studying them, their minds and patterns, can fill the gaps in our knowledge."

"Ariella, sir," I corrected, both to buy time and to calm the sudden thundering of my heart. Also, I was annoyed on Ariella's behalf that he didn't have the common decency to use her real name while plotting against her.

"Irrelevant," he snapped. "Trelari is dangerous. Principles that are at the very foundations of our institution are being threatened. It is time to choose sides. You are either on the side of Mysterium, or you are its enemy."

The interview had taken a sudden ominous turn. It seemed clear that the dean was either behind Moregoth, or was in league with the mages who were. It also seemed that by answering his summons, I had placed myself in their hands. I considered my options. None of them were good. I was not a skilled enough liar to bluff my way out of this, and I didn't like my chances if it came down to a magical conflict. First, the dean was a legend. Whether he was related to Prospero or not, the man had survived at the highest levels of Mysterium's notoriously vicious power structure for nearly a century. And that was ignoring Nabilac, which probably wasn't wise. Even if the golem was nice at parties, I'm sure he would gladly yank off my limbs at a word from the dean. Given that this conversation seemed destined to end badly for me, I decided I'd rather get to the end as soon as possible. I put as much steel as I could muster into my voice. "Did you send the Sealers into my class this morning?"

"And if I did? How could two students, two subworlders, possibly be worth your career?"

I slammed my hands down on the top of his desk and leaned forward. We were close enough that I could smell the whiskey on his breath. "I must tell you, sir, that I find this entire conversation disturbing.

Today two of my pupils were threatened, and the head of my department may have been involved. And for what purpose? What are you proposing to do with them? Invade their minds? Put them into study tanks and let the subworld butchers dissect them? I do not know where the Trelarians are, but even if I did I would not willingly tell you."

I expected him to lash out. Maybe to call in Nabilac to give me a lesson in courtesy. At least to fire me. Instead, a broad smile curved across the dean's face. From one of his desk drawers he pulled a small crystalline cube and set it between us. He put a finger to his lips to silence my question and pressed the top of the cube. A flash of blue power illuminated the device, and an instant later, a ghostly image of his body appeared and began pacing about the room. "How dare you question me, Stewart!" it boomed. "I will have you know that in all my time at this university I have never been spoken to in such a manner. I have half a mind to call a review board to examine . . ."

In a day of bizarre occurrences, this was one too many. I needed answers, but the dean once again pressed a finger to his lips and pointed up. I was beginning to hate the ceilings in this place. He rose from his desk and gestured for me to follow. We crossed the room to the bookcase. His finger illuminated again, and he touched it to the spine of a book embossed with the word *Wisdom*. As he did, the bookcase bent back on itself in an alarmingly non-Euclidean manner. A doorway appeared. I stepped through after him and found myself inside a solid stone chamber about ten feet across. The walls were decorated with spiraling energy patterns like those inscribed on Nabilac's body. In fact, they appeared to be identical. I had the sudden, unnerving thought that we might actually be inside the golem. I didn't ask if we were, and to this day I don't regret the decision, because I'm pretty sure I would not have handled it well if he had said yes.

CHAPTER 11

A REALLY, REALLY
SECRET COUNCIL

As the door to the strange stone chamber closed, the dean visibly relaxed. "It's okay, Professor Stewart, we can speak freely here."

I asked the obvious question. "What the hell is going on?" He blinked at me, possibly surprised, which I took as permission to continue. "First you're threatening me, and then leading me into your inner sanctum? If this is some kind of bizarre initiation ritual, I have to tell you that I have a policy against joining secret societies. Unless this is a multiverse version of Bilderberg, because that would be pretty sweet."

He waved a dismissive hand. "Nothing like that, Professor Stewart. Nothing like that. I'm sorry for all the cloak-and-dagger, but paranoia is essential this close to the center of Mysterium, and never more than since your return from Trelari. The provost's spies are everywhere, and they are focused on my department. Our every move is being watched. After your actions this morning, running from Moregoth, I was fairly confident you could be trusted, but I still had to test you."

"So, you didn't send Moregoth after Sam and Ariella?"

"No, Professor Stewart, I did not."

"But if you didn't send him, who did?"

He hesitated before whispering, "Not everything I said before was false. The hour *is* late. The eye of the provost of Mysterium University himself *is* turned on us, and against you personally. His patience is almost at an end."

The dean glanced up in the direction of the provost's office at the top of the tower. I now understood why everyone kept pointing at the ceilings. "So the provost sent the Sealers after Sam and Ariella. What does the provost want with them?"

"We don't know, but we have some suspicions." He crossed his arms behind his back and began pacing. "Trelari is the first and only subworld to ever shift its reality closer to that of Mysterium and become an innerworld, but now the possibility exists that it might not be the last. Other near-orbit subworlds are urging recognition of subworld rights and clamoring to be promoted to innerworld status."

"Promoted? But Mysterium had nothing to do with Trelari becoming an innerworld."

"But we did. Or more specifically, you did. No one, not even the provost, knows how to duplicate your feat. Your academic papers only describe the early stages of your experiment, and *The Dark Lord . . .*" A sour expression crossed his face.

"Is light on details?"

"Exactly. It's impossible to understand from the text how to work the magic. I mean, there are dozens of bizarre rules. Which ones are important and which are unnecessary? Then there is that evil battle-ax and the good battle-ax, and so many other complexities to consider, such as that poor semi-lich and his misguided necromancy, plus the lizard creature . . ." He took a deep breath. "The point is, there is only one person who has ever shifted a subworld closer to Mysterium."

"Me."

He smiled sadly. "Yes, you, Professor Stewart."

The thought that my experiment might be putting my friends at risk *again* angered me. "Why go after Sam and Ariella? Why not simply snatch me and extract everything I know?"

"They've tried. Have you noticed any strange gaps in your memory?" I was too stunned by the idea that the school I loved might have been damaging my brain trying to get information out of it to answer. Apparently, my silence was all the confirmation the dean needed. "We don't know whether they couldn't get enough out of you, or if they learned something from you that led them to attempt to capture actual Trelarians."

"You've said 'we' several times now. Who exactly are 'we,' and what are 'we' going to do about Trelari, and Sam and Ariella, and *me* for that matter?"

He straightened, put his hands on the lapels of his robes, and announced, "We are the Triflers."

It took me a second to remember this was the name Griswald had given to a secret society of sub-world activists. "Is Professor Stonehammer in the . . . Tipplers also?"

"Triflers."

"Right."

"I can't reveal our members to you. Not yet. But we have our agents, and we will help you where we can." He put a hand on my shoulder and directed me to the door. "I know you have more questions, but my illusionary self only has enough programming for about ten minutes of use, and I have one other not so good piece of news."

I couldn't imagine what could be worse than learning that beings at the center of power in the multiverse are out to get you, but people have told me that I can have a stunning lack of imagination. By people, I mean Eldrin. Anyway, I braced myself.

"You have an imp?" he asked.

I nodded. "Yes, sir. I inherited Professor Griswald's imp."

"I thought so," he said, and pulled out a translucently thin piece of paper. "The Administration has laid its hands on a purchase order you processed for imp food this summer."

"Yes, sir. It was my understanding that expenses for care of a familiar are covered under a professor's per diem."

"True, if the familiar is registered to you, but you never reregistered Harold. Technically, he is still Griswald's." He sighed and handed me the page. "I'm afraid this could cause you some trouble. Normally, I might be able to smooth this over, but with the extra scrutiny our department is under I can do little."

"But that means . . ."

"Accounts Payable is involved."

I shuddered. No one messed with Accounts Payable. Rumor had it the lower levels of their office building were stocked with devils that focused on nothing but the details of your expense reports. They wouldn't listen to excuses. It wasn't that they would physically hurt you, but they would make you reconcile your entire financial history. With my memory, the questionable sources I'd used to fund some of my experiments, and my own disastrous student loan situation, an audit might take the rest of my life.

The dean's eyebrows narrowed. "The Administration will submit a formal request to review your expense reports before midnight tomorrow. I'm sorry."

He turned toward the door as I spoke. "Thank you for the warning, Dean Yewed. Before we finish, there is something I must know. Is Professor Griswald still alive?"

He thought about this far too long for my comfort before answering. "I honestly don't know how to answer that, Stewart. If he is gone, though, you can be sure it was for a higher purpose."

"If I could ask one other last question before we go back in?" He muttered something that sounded like "Gristle warned me," but nodded. "Do you believe I ruined the field of Subworld Studies?"

The dean did not answer right away, but turned his attention to a study of the back of his hands like he might find the answer to my question there. At last he said, "I've given it quite a bit of thought. There are certainly many professors in this and other departments that think what you did was irresponsible and unethical. There are others, including myself, that would not censure you for your work, but do think you have irrevocably changed the field of Subworld Studies forever . . ."

It was clear he had more to say, but I didn't want to hear more about how I'd screwed everything up. I said abruptly, "I appreciate you agreeing to help me despite your feelings."

The dean shook a gently scolding finger. "Griswald warned me you would be only too ready to think the worst of yourself. You didn't let me finish. I said you changed the field of Subworld Studies, and I stick by that—and I think it's marvelous! You've made the field more than some obscurity to be tucked away in long-winded academic journals. Now it has the potential to be relevant to real people's lives. You should be proud."

The room had grown a little dusty. I turned away and ran a sleeve over my eyes. He clapped my shoulder. "No need for words. I owe Griswald more than you know. Now, let's get back out there before my specter runs out of things to complain about."

His finger glowed brightly and the door folded back to reveal his office. I gazed out at the dean's translucent doppelganger, still haranguing the empty room, and suddenly the weight of what I was up against struck me. "I'm scared."

"You'd be a fool not to be, Avery. I am utterly terrified."

We both looked up at the ceiling, and a quiet moment of understanding passed between us. I probably should have left it there, but this is me we're talking about and there was one more thing I needed to ask about. "One absolutely final last question, Dean Yewed?" He glanced at his pacing ghost, which was now flickering as the magic that animated it began to fade. He nodded. "You see, sir," I said, studiously avoiding his gaze, "I have misplaced something very dear to me I'm sure you can help me find."

"Of course, Avery. If I can. What is it you've lost?"

"The location of my transport circle," I said with great gravity.

I'm not sure I can do justice to the expression of total exasperation that passed across the dean's face as he stepped through the door with a grunted, "Stewart!"

I followed after, and it was none too soon as the ghost began to stutter and glitch. "If . . . if y-you are sug-suggesting that I would, in . . . in . . . in . . . in any way, bring h-h-ha-harm . . ."

The dean lunged across his desk and pressed the button on the cube, picking up the thread of the lecture as he did. "To any student in this university, then you are badly mistaken. Sam and Ariella are, as you yourself mentioned, the sole representatives of a new world. Yes, I would like to speak to them. Any scholar of Subworld Studies worth the name would like to talk to them, but that is all I want to do. Do I make myself clear?"

"Um . . ." I said, because I hadn't been given the script he was obviously working from.

"Well?" He gestured impatiently for me to answer.

"Yes, sir."

"I'm glad we cleared that up, Stewart. I will let this incident pass, but remember *means* and *motive*."

"Sir?"

"Means! Method! Mind! Motive! The four M's, Professor Stewart!" he said, biting off each word. "I would advise you to focus your efforts on preparing lessons for your class and students. And, rest assured, *we* will be watching."

"Yes, sir," I answered. "Thank you, sir."

"Dismissed, Stewart!" he boomed, and then ushered me to the door with a whispered, "We will be in touch. For now, get as far away from Mysterium as possible."

I stood on the threshold and mouthed, *Where?* Before he could answer, a stony hand grabbed the back of my robe and flung me out into the hall. Harold followed after, landing solidly on my stomach and knocking the breath out of me. The door to the dean's office slammed shut, but not before I heard the golem shout, "Have a nice day!"

As Harold and I clambered to our feet, the imp muttered, "You know, you should consider working on your people skills."

CHAPTER 12

TRUST IN ME

Harold and I made our way out of the Administration building and into the night. Given that I had just learned that I was part of an intrigue that reached, literally, to the top of the Administration, and that it had also been revealed that the dean of my program was part of a secret alliance opposing that Administration, you might be forgiven for believing that I was preoccupied with these weighty matters. The truth is, as I passed through the grotesque doors of the tower and descended the stairs there was only one question running through my mind: curry or kebab?

"My vote would be for kebab," the imp answered with a smack of his lips.

I nodded in agreement, and then missed a step and nearly tumbled headfirst down the stairs as I realized that I hadn't actually said anything. I put my hand out and caught hold of the railing to steady myself. Knocked from my shoulder by my stumble, Harold half hopped and half flapped to sprawl awkwardly atop the newel post at the base of the stairs. "Give me a warning next time you forget how to walk," he grunted as he pulled himself to his feet.

I pointed an accusing finger at him and croaked, "You can read my mind?"

The imp calmly straightened his bow tie before answering, "Naturally."

"But how?"

He rolled his eyes and wheezed one of his all too common gasps of disgust. "Did you miss the entire class on familiar magic?"

"I never took Familiar Magic."

"Never took Familiar Magic?" he said incredulously. "What *do* they teach you these days? There used to be standards."

"Stop trying to change the subject. How can you read my mind?"

His whole body slumped as he gave a sigh of resignation. "Strictly speaking, it's our mind. That is the entire point of a mage/familiar connection. We can share thoughts and experiences. You can summon me across existence. I am your emissary in magic, an extension of you."

My head spun at the implications. If he knew everything I was thinking, then he knew *everything* I had ever thought. If he experienced everything I experienced, then he had experienced *everything* I had ever done. I sat down heavily on the stairs as a multitude of embarrassing images flashed through my mind. Harold mirrored my action, and sat with a grunt on the stone ball atop the newel post. He let me silently ponder a highlight reel of my many humiliations for a minute or so before he said, "Would you stop it? It was bad enough having to live through all that the first time."

I blushed and tried to think of something else—anything else. But as much as I wanted to focus on meaningless things like where I had left the keys to my office (somehow, I'd mislaid them months ago), or why the Mets sucked so much, my mind would inevitably turn to drunken escapades where I'd made a fool of myself, nights with girls, nights alone—"

"Dammit, Avery!" Harold coughed.

I buried my head in my hands and groaned. "I want to stop. Don't you think I want to stop? I can't. I don't know how." I looked up at him, and as silly as it sounds with everything else that was going on, I felt utterly adrift. "I don't know what to do. Everything's been in such a muddle since I got back from Trelari. I'm . . . I'm sorry you're stuck in my head with me, Harold. If I knew how . . . if I weren't such a crap mage, I would release whatever bond Griswald made between us so you could go free."

The imp stood and walked with remarkable grace up the rail to where I was sitting. He clambered onto my shoulder and put a paw on my head. Somehow his touch lifted a little of the sadness, and a tightness in my shoulders I hadn't known I was carrying melted away. "Griswald did not bind us," he said softly.

"Who . . . who did?" I asked, hopeful that it was someone that could also set Harold free.

He answered my silent wish with a sad sigh. "It doesn't work like that, Avery. No one bound us."

"Then how?"

"I did it, you daft prick!" he shouted. "I chose you!"

My head swam again. None of this made any sense, and my frustration boiled out in my question. "Why in the world would you do that? I'm nothing special. How often do you tell me that my abilities are substandard?"

"Codswallop!" he said angrily, and stepped off my shoulder and began pacing up and down along the stair rail. "I never said any such thing. I have told you that the standards at this university have fallen, because they have. Mages are no longer instructed in how to cast spells, they're taught to wield power. It's lazy and it's dangerous. But you, Avery Stewart, are not a lazy mage. You spent years building one of the most intricate spell patterns existence has ever seen, and you did it specifically to avoid the need to use power to solve your problems. That is why I picked you, because no matter what you tell yourself, you have the makings of a great mage. Better still, you have the makings of a good mage."

It was a moment that called out for eloquence. Instead, I asked, "Did you say codswallop?"

He glowered at me. It was nice to hear he thought I was a good mage, but it was not something I was ready to believe. And yet, at that moment, I could see across the quad a group of three darkly cloaked students in the process of spray painting AVERY LIVES! on the statue of a stern-looking magus. Like it or not, there were some in Mysterium who believed in me. Even if individuals seemed to have a total disregard for private property.

Harold and I both sighed. I smiled at our mutual reaction. Despite being unsettled by my connection with the imp, I had to admit it gave me a warm feeling to know Harold had chosen to be with me. I felt humbled. Harold had tied himself to me because he thought I could be a force for good. It made me realize what a putz I'd been for the last several months. I stood and held out my arm. With a great huffing, Harold clambered from the rail back onto my shoulder. "Where are we going?" he asked.

"I was going to ask you the same question," I said, and reaching into my pocket I retrieved a butterscotch candy and handed it to him. "I know I'm missing time and memories. You've been in my mind. Maybe you can make better sense of it than I can."

He unwrapped the candy and popped it in his mouth. He sucked on the hard candy and considered. At last he said, "We need to go to our office."

"Really? But we just came from there."

"Not that broom closet," he grunted. "Your actual office."

"Why now?"

"I don't know. Maybe because I don't know why we have been avoiding the place. Maybe because every time I think about the office my mind sort of skips off of it like a flat stone on a calm pond."

I knew the sensation he was describing, because I was experiencing it too. As soon as he'd mentioned the office, my mind had latched on to the question of whether the four M's had been purposefully arranged in alphabetical order, or if it was only coincidence. Having never given even a third thought to the four M's before, I strongly suspected my brain's motives.

"Pros and cons," I said without preamble.

"What's that?" Harold asked. "Some kind of game? Is it like checkers or Parcheesi? I like Parcheesi!"

"No, I mean, let's go over the good and bad points of going back to my office."

"Oh," Harold said with a sigh of disappointment. Then he brightened up. "Pro: there's a Parcheesi board in Griswald's desk; third drawer down, right side."

"Con: Moregoth may be waiting to ambush us," I said. "And the interest in Sam and Ariella, and me, runs all the way to the top of the provost's tower!"

"Pro: we could stop doing this."

"Be serious," I scolded.

Harold looked aggrieved. "I am giving this game all the seriousness it deserves." I stared at him until he gave in. "Fine! Pro: it's probably safer than standing in the shadow of said Administration building waiting for Moregoth to show up for work!"

An excellent point, and it deserved an answer equal to it. I lowered my voice and said, "Con: I'm afraid."

"Pro: so am I," the imp whispered back.

"Con: it's nowhere near the kebab stand."

"Pro: you have no money."

I held the imp out so I could look him in the eye. "Wait a minute! How is that a pro?"

Harold leaned in to whisper in my ear. "Pro: Griswald always kept a secret stash of money tucked among the student dissertations on the shelf by the door."

"Why there?"

The imp shrugged. "Safest place in the world. No one ever reads them."

I wanted to argue, but he was right, and I soon found myself laughing as we made our way across campus to the Subworld Studies building. Harold had put me in such a buoyant mood that as we climbed the stairs to my old, new office, I wondered what had possessed me to camp out in a cubicle in the basement in the first place. "What was the point, Harold? If the Administration had wanted to find me I'm sure they could have."

"Truth!" he grunted. "Based on all the junk piled on your desk nearly half your class managed to track you to your basement hideaway."

He may have been exaggerating, but a pile of gifts had been accumulating in my cubicle for the past couple of weeks. In fact, my desk was a testament to my class's tenacity and lack of fair play. I had two drawers stuffed with the usual tokens of appreciation: candies, apples, colorful balls of twine, and the souls of the damned. I was still pondering what use the Cthulhoids thought one could make of a damned soul when we arrived at my office. I started to open the door when I noticed light streaming from beneath it. A cold chill passed through my body. "Harold, look!" I hissed. "Do you think someone is in there?"

"Maybe," Harold whispered back. "Or maybe Eldrin left the light on when he broke in."

"Or maybe we left it on when we were last here and we've forgotten," I suggested.

We pressed our ears to the door. The office sounded utterly silent. We drew away again and Harold asked, "What do we do now?"

I set my shoulders. "We go in."

"But it could be Moregoth," Harold offered.

"If it is, then it is time for us to have it out."

Despite my brave words, it was with a shaking hand that I turned the knob. The room appeared empty, but a set of candles cast a wavering light across the room. We stood at the door, waiting for something to happen. Nothing did. "This is stupid," I said, and, stepping into the room, closed the door behind us. "Harold, do you feel any flash of insight?"

Harold grunted and flapped across the room to settle on his perch with a sigh of contentment. Following his lead, I shrugged out of my formal robes and hung them on the stand beside the door. I turned back to my desk. The candles were strange— out of place. "What do you think those are doing here, Harold?"

"Mood lighting?" he grumbled.

"I put them there." A woman stepped out of the shadows behind my desk.

Harold said something like, "Avery! Look out! It's a—" and then his head fell forward and he was asleep.

"Harold?"

"Hello, Avery," the woman said. Her voice resonated through the room, trembling with power.

Backlit by the candles, I couldn't make out her features, but I could see the glow of her emerald eyes . . . her serpentine eyes. As their gaze fixed on me, an electric shock ran through my left arm. Memories came rushing back in a flood. This woman was the reason I'd abandoned my office. "Who are you? What have you done to Harold?" I gasped, trying to give my mind time to assemble my rediscovered knowledge into a coherent whole.

"It's okay, Avery, we are old friends."

I wanted to believe her, but there was something about her hair. I couldn't focus on it. The buzzing in my arm was growing more intense, almost painful, making it impossible to concentrate. I slid back my sleeve and to my alarm saw words tattooed along my wrist in my own handwriting: *Don't look at the snakes!* And, beneath that, six marks like a tally. Even as I was marveling at them, the words began to fade. The pain disappeared along with them. Only the tally remained and a seventh mark was added to the line.

"It is time to begin, Avery." Her voice was soft and inviting.

I saw her gliding toward me. As she advanced, she began unwrapping the crimson scarf about her head, revealing dozens of writhing snakes like strands of hair. Their collective eyes caught mine. I tried to turn away, but she spoke again, and the snakes' eyes scintillated and spun, and my thoughts became her thoughts. "Lie down on the couch, Avery." Her voice was a commandment. I needed to lie down. And I did, draping myself over the large couch where Griswald once took his infamous afternoon naps. She smiled. "Now, don't you feel better?"

I did. It was comfortable, and we had done all this

before. I had been lying here and she had pulled up a chair and . . .

She pulled a wooden chair across the room and placed it so she could see me. Then she retrieved a small pad of paper and a pen out of the mass of slithering reptiles on her head. "Now, where were we," she asked, flipping through the pages in her notebook. "Ah, yes, tell me, when did you first begin to have fantasies about killing your father?"

"What?" Even to my ears, I sounded drowsy or drunk or both.

She laughed. "Just a little therapist humor, Avery. Do you remember me yet?"

The snakes studied me seriously, and I found it impossible not to stare back. I also found it impossible not to answer. "You are the counselor."

"Correct." She had a delightful smile. She put on a pair of glasses. "Do you remember our previous session, Avery?"

"No."

She frowned and made a note. "Do you remember any of our previous sessions?"

"No."

The snakes flicked their tongues in irritation and her frown deepened, which was not nearly as pleasant as her smile. "That's not supposed to happen. I wonder if I'm using too many snakes."

She wrote furiously in her notebook, and muttered

technical-sounding phrases about hypno-REMs and anterograde amnesia, dissociative fugue, and Corwin's syndrome. I understood none of it, but knew that my memory loss was making the counselor unhappy. I was both alarmed by the turn of events and relaxed to be back on the couch talking to her. One of those feelings was my real emotion, and the other was what she wanted me to feel. For the life of me, I couldn't tell which was which.

As she continued to consult her notes, my mind sank deeper into unconsciousness. That's when the buzzing in my wrist returned. I tried to ignore it— wanted to ignore it—but it was distracting me from what I knew was going to be a very pleasant dream. And the pain only continued to grow. At last, I sat up and shook my head to clear it. The counselor was so intent on studying her notes that, for a moment, she didn't notice. I believe it was the first time I'd had a chance to study her in a semi-unaltered state. She was a Gorgon, in her late twenties, with high cheeks and luminous yellow eyes. She was wearing a dark green, knee-length dress that accentuated her sinuous curves and complemented the complexion of her scales to perfection. She also had legs, instead of the lower body of a snake, and she terrified me.

I was still fighting my way free of her head-spinning charm when the snakes atop her head gave a hiss of alarm. The counselor's head shot up. She pulled off her glasses, and her own luminous eyes swirled hypnotically as they locked on to mine. "Avery, why don't you lie back down?"

I couldn't look away. I lay back down and began to fall asleep. All was peacefulness and bliss, except for this burning sensation in my arm. I tried to ignore it, but it kept getting worse. I began to twitch and thrash. "Why are you fighting me, Avery?" the counselor asked as she put her glasses back on.

I felt compelled to tell the truth. "It hurts."

"Interesting." I heard her pen scratching away at her notebook. "What hurts?"

I started to say my arm, but only got as far as, "My arrrr . . ." before the pain became so overwhelming that it felt as though someone was holding a blowtorch to my wrist. I sat up and clawed at the sleeve of my robe. The counselor was still scribbling her notes as I read a new tattooed message exactly where the earlier one had been: *Don't tell her, you idiot!*

"Your what?" She looked up expectantly.

I crossed my arms across my chest to hide the message. "You are hurting me."

"How?" The multitude of snakes stopped writhing to stare.

"Because you are messing with my mind," I spit with a venom I didn't fully understand, but knew came from a real place.

"It's called therapy," she said in the same voice you might use to soothe a child. "And the anger you're feeling toward me is called 'transference.' It is perfectly natural. It arises because we are tapping into events and feelings you have suppressed and are finding painful to deal with."

I rose to my feet and began pacing back and forth across the office, trying to formulate a plan through the muddle of pain and confusion. I decided the best way of avoiding further snaking was to stay on the offensive. I continued my tirade, giving in fully to my well-developed id. "The anger I'm feeling is called 'anger,' and it arises because you and your snaky pals there—" I pointed an accusing finger "—keep making me forget bits and pieces of my life!"

"Good, Avery. We are having a real breakthrough here." Her eyes flared to hypnotic life. "Come back to the couch and lie down, and let's explore these feelings."

A few seconds earlier she would have had me, but this time I was ready. In an instant, I spun a reflection pattern in the air between us. The counselor momentarily shuddered and then was frozen along with her serpentine locks by the power of her own gaze. I moved behind her so that she could see me in the mirror pattern's reflection, and leaned down to rasp in my most menacing Dark Lord voice, "Tell me why I shouldn't kill you right now."

Her body may have been frozen, but she still managed to roll her eyes. "Because you are not a murderer."

"But isn't that what you were going to do to me once you'd gotten all the information your masters wanted?"

"No, never!" she said too quickly.

I pounced on the half answer. "So, you admit you were sent here to interrogate me. By who?"

"Whom."

"What?"

"The correct way of asking that question is: By whom?"

My initial worry was that she was somehow resisting her own hypnosis powers, or perhaps that the reflection was not "true" enough. I checked the pattern I'd cast, but there was nothing wrong with the spell. There was another possibility: this was the counselor's actual personality. She might think she was doing the right thing.

I smiled gently at her reflection. "You're an authoritarian grammatical prescriptionist. How illuminating," I said, mimicking the well-intentioned but condescending tone she had used with me. "You probably also object to words like *alright* as being grammatically incorrect despite their near-universal usage, or prefer phrases like 'It is I' over 'It's me' on the spurious grounds that in Latin predicative complements take the nominative case, even though English grammar allows for a great deal of variability in choice of cases for predicative complement noun phrases."

I let that bit of hard-won Oxford English knowledge sink in, and sat on the couch, being very careful not to meet her direct gaze. "You read *The Dark Lord*. Didn't you?" I asked.

"Yes, I did."

"What did you think of the Avery Stewart in the book?" I asked.

"That he needs help."

"Why?"

"Because you believe you're the Dark Lord, Avery. You have convinced yourself that you're evil, and you're not," she said, but now her tone wasn't aggressive or defensive. "You have trouble telling the difference between what is real and what isn't, between this world and those other worlds. This is probably because of the trauma you suffered in Trelari, and I believe hypnotherapy might reduce the confusion you're feeling. Avery, you were ready to die for shadows."

Her answer made me feel sad and tired. She didn't believe subworlders were real people. "What did you think about *The Dark Lord*'s epilogue?"

"There is no epilogue, except in the version that appeared on your home world, Earth, which, I will add, wasn't written by you."

At this point, I probably should have realized that she was answering with unusual clarity for someone under hypnosis. However, I wasn't in the best mental state. I rose from the couch and walked over to my desk. Unlocking it, I pulled one of my copies of the Heckel book from a drawer. I studied the cover as I asked my next question. "What's your name, Counselor?"

"My name is Stheno." She sighed. "Avery, can we—?"

"Theno?" I responded.

"Close enough. It is a traditional Gorgon name. If you can't hiss, it's hard to make the leading *s* sound. I am trying to help you, Avery. My hypnosis can be a very powerful tool. If you would embrace it instead of fighting me, I'm sure we'd have a breakthrough. Despite the events of today, I know we could—"

"Who sent you?" I interrupted.

"Human Resources."

"Who told them to send you?" I nearly shouted. I saw her eyes dart toward the large window in the far wall. She was staring at the administration tower—its many windows, like never-blinking eyes, glowing a sinister red through the hazy night. I sighed, walked over, and dropped my book into her lap. "I see."

"Good. Now, can you drop the reflection pattern? I'd like to take my glasses off."

"Your glasses?"

"They prevent me from being hypnotized by my own snakes. It's a safety measure when doing therapy with a magus."

"You weren't hypnotized?"

She shrugged. "The snakes are, but I'm not. Avery, I'm trying to help you. As far as these memory losses, that's not what's supposed to be happening. I think there are forces that might be working through me, but together we could figure out the who and why of that."

It was actually a tempting offer, but I could never accept it. If the Administration were using her as an unwitting agent, then I would be putting yet another innocent in harm's way. I lay back on the couch, exhausted, and closed my eyes. With a thought, I dropped the reflection pattern and heard the snakes hiss their curses at me.

"Avery?"

"Stheno," I said wearily, but somehow managed to hiss. "I admit that I may not be *the* Dark Lord, but this is not the time for us to explore the issue. I'm exhausted, and I'm annoyed that you've been entrancing me without my permission. We will have to start again, at another time."

"I understand," she said with a dozen hissed sighs. "But there is one thing I think I should tell you. My supervisor was talking to the head of Student Records and—"

The door flew open with a loud bang. "Get away from him, you snake!" a voice shouted. I opened my eyes in time to see something fly across the room and hit Stheno in the head. She fell onto the floor. A heavy-treaded boot lay next to her. I turned to the door in shock. It was Rook!

I opened and closed my mouth in stunned surprise. The dwarf came over and peered into my eyes.

"You all right, laddie?" He held up a finger and two thumbs. "How many ears do I have?"

"Rook?"

"Yes, it's me, lad." He moved over to the counselor's body and nudged her with the toe of his unclad foot.

"Is she dead?" I asked.

"What, from a shoe?" he said with a snort. "Gorgons are a lot tougher than that. She'll be fine, although she and two or three of her little pets will have some pretty hellacious shiners in the mornin'."

I was still struggling to come to grips with his presence, and so asked, "Why are you here?"

He scratched his beard. "That's a kind of existential question, lad. Am I here because I have purpose, or do I have purpose because I'm here? Not sure I'm qualified to answer that. Besides, we don't have time to get into a philosophical discussion. We have to get out of here and fast! The Administration agents are bound to have bugged your office. They could be here any moment."

"I see your tendency for sophistry hasn't improved over the time," wheezed Harold as he flapped from his perch to my shoulder.

"Oh. Hello, Harold," Rook said.

"Hello, Rook," the imp sighed.

"You know each other?" I asked. They shared a look and shrugged. Somehow, finding out Rook and Harold knew each other well enough to trade good-natured insults irritated me more than Stheno's hypnosis. I picked the imp off of my shoulder and held him out in front of me, shaking an accusing finger. "What else do you know?"

"How can I possibly answer that?"

Before I could tell him exactly how he might, Stheno gave a groan and her hair began to stir restlessly. Harold looked down. "What did I miss?"

"Only all the danger, as usual," I said in annoyance.

"No time for a lovers' quarrel, you two," Rook grunted.

"I'm not sure that she wasn't trying to help."

Rook shook his head. "Lad, all I know is that she's on the Administration's side, and that's all I need to know. Now, let's get out of here before she wakes up!"

He dragged Harold and I (oh, wait, Harold and me, sorry, Stheno) out of the office. As the door shut behind us, I wondered if Stheno had been right. Maybe I did need therapy, because this was madness.

CHAPTER 13

ROOKED

Twenty minutes later, the three of us were seated at a table in a courtyard near the edge of the university renowned for two things: its view and the kebab stand that tended to materialize there in the evenings. The kebab stand lived up to its hype and the courtyard was packed with young beings of all sorts. They were all in that giddy state of excitement that precedes a night of partying. As for the view? I suppose watching a river pour off the rim of the world into etherspace has a certain eerie beauty to it, but I found the crowd it drew irritating.

Rook took a long draft of his beer. This was his third tankard, and he had so many kebab spears stacked on his plate it looked like he was playing a game of pickup sticks. Even Harold was enjoying himself, or at least I thought he was. Smiling didn't come naturally to the imp, and when he did, it gave him a constipated look. I threw my own denuded kebab down and leaned back patting my stomach. "What do you think of my plan now?"

Rook loosed an impressive belch. "You've never had a better one."

"Genius," Harold wheezed as he plucked the last roasted mouse off his kebab.

What can I say? It is a kebab cart on Mysterium. Their official slogan is, *If it can be impaled by a stick, it should be impaled by a stick and grilled.*

The dwarf took another drink and pointed to the imp with his tankard. "You remember that shawarma place that used to be in the basement of the ether-astrology building?"

"Sirius Shawarma?" Harold slurped down the mouse's tail. "Great place. They used to do a fantastic roast capybara."

Rook nodded and smiled, and the two began to share increasingly absurd stories of other places I had never heard of from years ago. I had brought us to this spot because until Eldrin and Dawn returned from their mission, I didn't have any better ideas and, as I might have mentioned, I was starving. But watching Rook and Harold reminisce about places I knew for a fact predated me by a century or more reminded

me how many unanswered questions I had for them.
I decided to check a few off. "How long have the two
of you known each other?" I asked over the rim of
my mug.

They looked at each other. The imp shrugged and
Rook said, "Time can be difficult, lad."

"It can't be that complicated," I said, doing a quick
calculation. "I mean, it must have been sometime in
the last two centuries. Griswald was only a professor
for a hundred and fifty years or so." Rook and Harold
both laughed. "What?!" I asked.

"We're not laughin' at you," Rook said, still chuck-
ling a little.

"Well, we are, but not in a mean way," Harold
clarified.

I glared at them both.

"Lad, it's simple. I've known Harold through . . .
four mages?" the dwarf asked the imp.

"Five," Harold corrected, and pointed his empty
kebab stick at me.

Rook raised his tankard to me. "I stand corrected.
Five."

I had never considered that Harold might have
been familiar to other mages over the years. "How
long do imps live?" I asked. Harold shrugged. For
some reason it irritated me more than usual. "You
always shrug off my questions," I snapped.

"Because you like to ask questions that can't be
answered."

"All of them?" I asked, banging my fist on the table and rattling our plates and cups.

"Lad . . ." Rook said in a voice I think he meant to be soothing.

The frustration I'd been feeling for the last few months at the gaps in my memory boiled over. "No. For once I want a straight answer. I've been sitting here the last five minutes listening to two people I thought I knew pretty well tell stories about each other stretching back to centuries before my birth." I pointed an accusing finger at Rook. "I traveled for months with you while you pretended to be from a subworld when you were actually a Mysterium-trained mage. Do you know how useful it might have been to be able to talk to you about what was going on?

"And as for you," I said, turning on the imp, "you've been living in my room for the past six months and never thought to say a word to me. You had to know what kind of hell I was going through. I've been miserable with worry about Griswald and Trelari and what I was supposed to do next. Why didn't you help me?" This last was said in a sort of gasp.

I felt the imp's weight settle on my shoulder. He put a hand atop my head and stroked my hair. "I thought you needed time," he wheezed. "Maybe I was wrong. I don't have all the answers, Avery. I don't know what you should do next. I don't know a great many things." With a shuddering sigh, he sat down on my shoulder so that his legs dangled down across my chest. "You asked how long I can live? I don't know. I feel old, but I don't know if age even has meaning for my kind. I follow magic."

"You said you chose me."

"I did. When my old mage dies or passes me on, I have a choice. If the magic of a wizard calls to me I stick around."

I considered this in silence and then asked, "What happens if the magic doesn't call to you?"

He took another ragged and rattling breath. "That's like me asking you what heaven is like. We only get to know the answer at the end."

"Unless you're a Jellicle," Rook said, banging his tankard down on the table.

Harold coughed and pulled his hand away from my head. "One could argue that their afterlife only really happens after number nine."

"Good point," the dwarf conceded.

"I only hope the afterlife is unusual," Harold replied as he flapped off to sit again on the back of one of the chairs. "Something that makes you say, 'Oh!'"

He and Rook laughed, but I was annoyed at him for changing the subject. "With the way the two of you keep secrets, I'm sure you wouldn't tell the rest of us even if you did know."

Rook rolled his eyes and whispered a dwarven prayer for patience. "Look, lad, I know you feel you've been hard-used by me and Harold. There are reasons it would have been incredibly dangerous for us to reveal everything we knew. You've got to trust us on this one."

"Trust you?" I snorted.

"Fine. Trust us, don't trust us," he said, a bit of an edge creeping into his voice. "If I'd told you who I was on Trelari, what then? I had no idea what to do. Nobody did. My job was to make sure you didn't get killed so you could do whatever it was you were doin'. And when you got back . . ." He sighed, and there was real regret there. "Frankly, a lot of us didn't trust *you*." I jerked my head up, ready to argue. He held up his hands. "Not me, but the fact is the Administration did have a pipeline into your head. It was only today we discovered how they were gettin' to you."

As much as I hated to admit it, he had a point. What would the Administration have known from me about them had he revealed himself, or had Harold started talking earlier or, gods forbid, given me the key a week ago? "By the way," Rook asked. "How did you resist her this time? I see she managed to bewitch Harold again . . ."

"She has very kind eyes," Harold said defensively.

"You mean hypnotic eyes," Rook chided. "Anyway, I expected both of you to be out cold when I got there."

I explained about the tattoo, and showed him the seven tally marks on my arm, now nearly faded. "I think it was me, trying to warn myself about her. I would guess the tally marks meant I'd been under her spell six previous times. It would explain my memory loss, and why I abandoned my office. Some part of me must have remembered she came there, and was trying to avoid her."

"Interestin'," Rook said as he examined my arm. "I wonder if you could send yourself other messages. Might be useful. For instance, you could always know where you left your keys."

"That would be a nice change," Harold remarked.

I gave him the stink-eye before saying, "I don't know. It's painful as hell when the message is written, so I wouldn't want to use it on a daily basis."

"On the other hand, it might sober you up when you're drunk," Harold offered.

I gave the imp another sour look. "I think I was better off when you didn't talk."

He stuck his tongue out at me. I returned the favor. Rook laughed at us. "You're like an old married couple already."

"What do you think that makes him, Avery?" Harold asked.

"Drunken Uncle?" I suggested.

"Shrewish Aunt?" the imp countered.

The dwarf bristled his brows at us. "If you two are quite finished, I think there might be a way to modify your spell to reduce the pain level. It looks like you've been usin' an Umbridge pattern. That's the influence of all that Rowling magic you've been studyin' in preparation for your class. Now, if you ask me, what you should do . . ."

The three of us discussed the merits of the spell and various methods I might use to reduce the "tattooing" sensation. After we finished our ales and beers—or in Rook's case, his fourth ale *and* beer—I steered the conversation back to our current situation. "Okay, I grant you that things would have gone badly had you come right out and told me all your secrets while I was still under thrall to the Administration. Still, we are where we are. My question is, where do we go from here?"

"I'll tell you where we go, lad," Rook said, leaning forward and jabbing a finger down on the table. "We get the hell out of here before—"

"Professor Stewart?" a young woman's voice said from over my shoulder.

The three of us jumped like we'd been caught plotting something secret, which is exactly what we were doing. I saw Rook's hand begin to glow with a lethal light. I caught his eye and shook my head. They were obviously students. There were three of them, two pale young men and a woman with a slight green tinge to her skin. They were probably acolytes. They had that early to mid-twenties vibrancy and easy beauty the adept years had a habit of grinding away. Whatever their ages, they appeared to be in a club or on a team together, because they were dressed in black cloaks that were trying very hard to match. Whoever they were, I needed to get rid of them. The last thing we needed was a crowd of people recognizing me.

"I think you may have me mistaken for someone else," I said.

They exchanged glances and came to some unspoken agreement. The young woman leaned in close. "It's okay, Professor Stewart. We're with the Resistance." All three shot their hands forward. I could see the words *Avery Lives!* written on their wrists in magic marker.

I rubbed my hand across my face and groaned, "Oh gods!"

One of the pale young men stepped forward. "Professor, there isn't time for explanation." He paused, affected a strange Eastern European accent, and added, "Come with us if you want to live."

He and the other pasty-skinned fellow exchanged a high five. Rook, Harold, and I sat in confused silence. I was beginning to think I'd been wrong to stop the dwarf from taking them out earlier. Thankfully, before I could tell Rook to unload a bit of higher-level magic on them, the green woman punched both of them in the arm. "You promised, no movie quotes."

One of the boys—it was kind of hard to tell them apart—whined, "Come on, it was too good to pass up, Susan."

We had gone way past enough. "Look, I'm sorry if you were in my class this morning. I promise you we will catch up with the material on the syllabus next session."

"Oh, we aren't in your class," Susan said with a laugh. "That's for novices."

"I don't really go in for Rowling magic anyway," one of the young men said.

"Yeah, too much silly wand waving," the other added.

Susan gave the two boys a ferocious glare and they shut up. She turned back to me and said, "I'm sorry, Professor Stewart, but give me a chance to explain. We aren't in your class. But we are on your side against the—" she looked around and lowered her voice conspiratorially "—You Know What."

"I do?"

"He does?" Rook asked.

"Yes," she said with far more confidence than she should have. "And we wanted to warn you that Eldrin and Dawn are in trouble!"

"How could you possibly know Dawn and Eldrin?" I spluttered.

All of them reached into their cloaks and produced extremely battered copies of *The Dark Lord*. For the thousandth time, I silently cursed Jack Heckel and all his offspring.

"Okay," Rook said, bristling his brows sternly at them. "We'll grant you Professor Stewart's life is an open book, but how could you possibly know Dawn and Eldrin are in trouble?"

One of the pale men pulled a small disc of metal from his ear and held it out to us. "We've been monitoring the Mysterium Security ether-wave network in case the You Know What tries to make a move against you."

I inspected the little device and smiled. It was a crude one-directional iteration of the type of communication device Eldrin had made. I'd built something similar when I was an acolyte, although I used it for far less noble purposes. I handed it back and said, "We used to use something like this to monitor the component storerooms so we could raid them for magical spirits."

"Cool!" he said with an enthusiasm that made me instantly guilty. I quickly adopted a serious air. "Look, I appreciate your concern, but I happen to know that Dawn and Eldrin are perfectly safe."

Rook was not as confident. "Exactly where are they, lad?"

"They went to Student Records," I said. "I want to get copies of Sam's and Ariella's admissions and financial aid records."

My confidence evaporated as Rook's face went pale. "You sent them to Student Records?"

"Yes. What's wrong with that?" I asked, trying to keep my fear in check.

"What's wrong?" Rook said with an incredulous

rasp. "I take it they don't have authorization to get these files?" I shook my head. "Lad, when all you're tryin' to do is get a transcript or add/drop a class, Student Records is fine place . . ."

"Although the shade of beige they paint the walls is soul-destroying," one of the pale-faced men said.

"True," Rook agreed, "but that's only if you are exposed to it over an extended period of time. The more immediate concern is the other enchantments that have been put in place to prevent people doin' exactly what Eldrin and Dawn are tryin' to do."

"What kind . . . kind of enchantments?" I asked in a voice that broke with anxiety.

"Probably a labyrinth ward of some kind," the dwarf said with a fierce tug of his beard.

Susan nodded vigorously. "It's a good guess. The place is chock-full of them."

"Labyrinth ward?" I scoffed. "I've been to the place dozens of times over the years, and apart from the line, which does wind about a bit, there's nothing like a labyrinth there."

"It's not a physical maze, you dunderhead!" Rook growled. "The wards in Student Records are bound to be based on Clarke fairy magic. It'll be some sort of red-tape labyrinth."

I chuckled. "Red-tape labyrinth? What, do you get buried in paperwork?"

The laughter died on my lips at the grim set of Rook's face. I was on my feet, Harold positioned atop my shoulder, heading toward the Student Records building at a slow run. Rook fell in beside me, huffing. Behind us trailed the three students from the Resistance.

"Laddie," Rook said as he ran to keep up with my long legs. "I know you want to help your friends, but goin' after them yourself is a mistake. Come back with me to Earth. We can have a team assembled in a few hours . . ."

"Not going to happen, Rook," I said without breaking stride. "Eldrin and Dawn went to Student Records at my request. I can't leave them. If you were to come with me I'm sure we could handle anything the Administration and Moregoth might throw at us."

The dwarf stopped suddenly. "I . . . I can't come, lad."

"What are you talking about, Rook?" I asked, skidding to a halt. "I thought . . ."

"I know, Avery, but me goin' would only make things more dangerous. In fact, even bein' this close to . . ." He licked his lips nervously and glanced up.

We were standing near the entrance to the central quad. The tower of the Administration building loomed over to the left, its shining red orb glaring down at us. I had never seen Rook look this anxious. "What's going on, Rook?"

The path we'd been on was bathed in the red glow from the Provost's Tower. He pressed his body up against a light pole. "I have to go, Avery. I've been here too long already."

"But . . ."

He walked away off the path and deeper into the shadows beneath the trees. I followed and when we were out of earshot of the students he said, "Lad, I know I owe you a lot of answers. When you get your friends, come straight back to Earth. There's a coffee shop there. It's on the corner of—"

I held up a hand to stop him, a vision of the group of cosplay fanatics that frequented my regular morning hangout playing in my mind. "Let me guess. In Greenwich Village, on Bleecker between Leroy and Carmine?"

He raised an eyebrow. "How did you know?"

"It's just the way my life works, Rook," I said with a bitter smile.

"What?"

"If you can't come with me, then I don't have time to explain. All I'll say is it's nice to know that, for once, I'm not the only one who doesn't understand what's happening."

He clapped his hand in mine. "Join me when you're done, Avery, and we can talk until we have all the answers."

I watched him jog away toward the edge of campus. As he went, he passed through islands of light cast by one streetlight and then another and then another, and then he stepped into a shadow and did not emerge again. "I'm glad you're still with me," I said to Harold.

He put his paw back on my head. "Always, Avery."

I returned to the students and gave a short bow. "Thank you for the information. I appreciate it, but this is where I leave you."

They looked at each other, and then back at me. "We're coming with you," Susan said. The others nodded in agreement.

"Out of the question. It's far too dangerous."

"Danger is my middle name," one of the pale men said with a grin.

"Stop that!" Susan snapped, and then turned back to me. "I know you think we're nothing but a pack of silly students, but we aren't." She glanced at the two men and added, "Mostly. But we can help you. I worked in Student Records, and as goofy as Trevor and Tanner seem, they are actually quite clever."

It was a good speech, but I was not persuaded. "Sorry . . ."

"Please, Avery," she said, fixing her green eyes on mine. "I came to Mysterium to study subworlds, but after reading your work I can't be content with only observing. I want to help save them—and that means helping you."

I was about to refuse again when I noticed her eyes were beginning to fade—the telltale mark of an emerging subworld traveler. She was not that much younger than me, and seemed a lot more mature than I had been at her age. I mean, who am I to say someone isn't ready to do something really stupid.

I nodded and looked over her head at the two men behind her. "What about you two?"

They exchanged a glance, and the first said, "If by my life or death I can protect you, I will." He bowed his head and added, "You have my sword."

"And you have my bow," the second man affirmed, also bowing.

A profound silence followed this. I thought from the depth of anger in her expression that Susan might murder the two of them on the spot. But before she could say anything, there was a deep sigh from atop my shoulder and Harold said, "And my ax."

I didn't respond. There was really nothing to say. I turned and marched across the quad toward the Student Records building, an imp on my shoulder and three acolytes of the Resistance beside me. If I had learned one thing on Trelari, it was the value of friendship, and I wasn't about to let my friends down—old or new.

CHAPTER 14

KHAAAAAN!

According to the campus clocks, it was a little before midnight when the four of us marched across the quad, up the stairs, and through the front doors of the Student Records building. A question that might occur to you is why, given the clandestine nature of our mission, we weren't trying to sneak into the building. I did consider the idea briefly, but black cloaks aside, my new followers were not the fleetest of foot. Trevor and Tanner were eager, but out of shape, a bit clumsy, and utterly untrained at sneaking. Susan was a different matter. She was a Dryadine, which meant she was lithe and graceful, and strongly resembled an Orion woman from *Star Trek*, but she also was dressed

like what she must have imagined a member of a resistance would dress like. She was wearing baggy, ill-
fitted clothing and a pair of thick-soled combat boots.
She did not so much glide along as stomp about.

There was another reason I chose the direct
route: the sheer number of people gathered on the
quad in front of the building. Acolytes don't keep
anything close to normal hours, and the Necromancy
Department, for obvious reasons, conducts nearly
all its activities at night. As a result, the undead and
the un-undead were out in numbers. They were
floating, shambling, and drinking their way across
the grounds. A group of Cthulhoids had erected
an altar where they were performing a dark ritual,
probably trying to submerge Mysterium beneath a
sea or something. In a less apocalyptic vein, an as-
tromancer had assembled his class at the far end of
the quad and was explaining star patterns to them
in a circle of mammoth standing stones he had
materialized for the purpose. Students exchanged
notes and ghostwritten term papers. They flirted.
They ate pizza. In other words, there would be
dozens of witnesses to whatever we did.

Besides, we were not technically doing anything
illegal. All we wanted was to retrieve Eldrin and
Dawn from Student Records . . .

Then meet up with Rook and find out what he
knew about the provost that was too dangerous to
say in Mysterium . . .

And then hope I could use that knowledge to prevent the Administration from doing horrible things to Sam and Ariella . . .

And Trelari . . .

And save my job . . .

And my sanity . . .

And . . .

The thoughts circled on and on, but I kept returning to one: Rook. Who was he, really? Why had he been on Trelari? How had he known so much about the world? If he was a Mysterian mage, how had he been able to remain behind after Valdara sealed the world off? "Too many questions," I murmured.

"Is there a problem, sir?" Susan asked.

I had stopped in middle of the doorway to the Student Records building. Trevor and Tanner stood inside the soaring lobby looking about nervously. I shook my head and followed them in. "Sorry about that, I was thinking about things that don't make sense."

"That's okay, sir," Susan said, and Trevor and Tanner, or Tanner and Trevor, nodded in agreement.

They seemed to be excited just to be a part of whatever it was I was doing. An uncomfortable feeling of guilt started creeping from my stomach and up my throat. I recognized it immediately, because it was how I'd felt pretty much the entire time I'd been on Trelari.

I herded them over to the side of the lobby. We stood between two enormous columns carved in the images of gods from somewhere in the multiverse, but rather than the traditional lightning bolts or swords gods were typically shown wielding, both statues were gazing in a somewhat mystified manner at the various sheets of marble paper they had clutched in their stony grips.

I peered about to make sure we were alone—yes, eventually I learn—and affected my sternest expression. "Before we go any farther, we have to set some ground rules." They nodded. "First, you do exactly what I say, even if I say to run!" They nodded again. "Second, no doing anything crazy . . . without my permission. I refuse to risk any of your lives or academic careers. Understood?" This time there was a long hesitation before they agreed. "Finally, no more Sirs, or Professor Stewarts. From now on it's Avery."

Of all my proposed rules, they looked most uncomfortable with this one, but eventually Susan said, "Yes, Professor . . . I mean, Avery."

"Right." I clapped my hands and immediately regretted it as the sharp sound echoed through the hush of the vaulted lobby. A number of people standing in the long line waiting for a turn at the counter turned to look. I waved weakly in apology. Lowering my voice, I whispered, "Susan, you worked here before. Where would Eldrin and Dawn go to find records on new students?"

She tapped at her chin with a green-tinted nail.

"Probably sub-basement 23. That's where records for most incoming students are stored."

"Great . . ."

"Although they recently did a reorganization to group all active students by the world of their residency. Trelari, being a new innerworld, would probably be in one of the annexes. Maybe double-Q? That is the newest portion of the building."

"Okay, so—"

"Having said that, if the Financial Aid office is reviewing them, then those records are held in the E-wing."

This time I paused to to make sure she was actually done. She absentmindedly twirled a strand of her hair around her index finger as she thought. "I think that's it."

I let out the sigh of relief. "In that case—"

"Although . . ." she began anew.

Susan continued to throw out possibilities, and I began to realize what a daunting task we had before us. Let me explain. Mysterium University has a very simple retention policy when it comes to records: Keep everything. Forever. Period. Millenniums of history, and every detail was meticulously stored somewhere in this building. Imagine the sheer amount of space you would need to hold that volume of information—information still kept on some form of tangible medium, given that most of the mages setting university policy are technophobes. It boggles the mind.

Of course, Mysterium has the advantage of being able to use magic to help solve its most insolvable problems, and Student Records is no exception. As with most university buildings, Student Records is much bigger on the inside than its outer dimensions would strictly allow. However, even with magic, the task of creating room for the ever-growing catalog of records is daunting, and there are limits to spatial manipulation. Like a bubble, if you keep expanding one point of reality, at some point it will pop. You risk creating a Juster Paradox and having records getting lost and wandering about aimlessly in unstable subworlds. Some people say this is exactly what happened to the Athletic Department. You might ask, *What Athletic Department, Avery?* To which I would respond, *Exactly!*

As far as I know, there is no Athletic Department at Mysterium University, but there is an enormous trophy case filled with all sorts of absurd medals and awards that pops up on occasion in random locations. The story goes that at some point there had been some cheating involving a game between Mysterium University and the main Cthulhoid University, and all of Mysterium's records needed to be vacated. Unfortunately, something went awry with the ritual to remove the records, and everything was lost. After several committee investigations, the Administration decided it would be easier to pretend there had never been an Athletic Department than reconstruct the history and all the statistics.

The point being, to prevent extradimensional leaks, which no one likes, particularly the Administration, the Student Records building is constantly growing. The massive building resembles what you would get if a Renaissance architect tried to construct a Mayan temple. And, in a way, Student Records was a temple—a temple to paperwork. And since no building on campus is allowed to be taller than the Provost's Tower, for several centuries now the Administration has been digging basements, sub-basements, sub-sub-basements, and so on. By now, the visible portion of the Student Records building is little more than a lobby/help desk sitting atop hundreds of levels of dungeons and annexes and wings, and any number of other holes, hollows, and halls, and all of them are stuffed to the gills with papers.

"By the gods," I murmured. "They could be any one of a million places."

"Don't be ridiculous. Only about a dozen," Susan said with irritating calmness as she counted on her fingers. The rest of us stared at her. "Certainly not more than fourteen."

"We could ask for help," Trevor or Tanner suggested. He pointed to the front desk.

It being the nightshift, the place was swarming with undead. Zombies moaned and shuffled papers while a skeleton checked student IDs. I recalled a time when as a prank someone put a dead body behind a desk in the Financial Aid office, but never animated it. People stayed in line for hours waiting. Oddly, the fact that the corpse was inanimate wasn't noticed for days. I really didn't want to stand in that line. "Susan, how long would it take us to visit all the possible places on your list?"

She thought about it far too long. "By my count twenty . . ."

"Minutes?"

She gave a grim laugh. "Hours. And that's assuming we split up, and no one gets lost." From the way her eyes darted to Tanner and Trevor when she said this, I knew she thought the odds of them not getting lost were effectively zero.

We were never going to find Dawn, Eldrin, or the records on Ariella and Sam if we didn't talk to someone. We got in line. After five minutes, we had moved about five feet toward our destination. I calculated we would reach the desk in about an hour at this rate. I was still doing the math when I noticed Trevor and Tanner were arguing about something, and apparently engaged in an epic best of fifteen rock-paper-scissors contest. When they started nudging each other and pointing, I could take it no longer.

"Can I help you two with something?" They both looked at each other nervously, but said nothing. That's when I saw they were both holding copies of *The Dark Lord*. A sudden and bizarre thought struck me. "Do you two want my autograph?"

Harold, who had been sleeping since shortly after

the kebab stand, let out a sigh and groaned, "I can't believe you asked them that."

Trevor and Tanner looked at each other. One of them said, "No, we had a question of an academic nature, but if you would be willing to sign our books that would be great!"

"It gets worse and worse," Harold sighed, and flapped off to sit on the sharply chiseled nose of one of the statuesque columns.

Trevor and Tanner thrust their copies of *The Dark Lord* forward. I waved them away. "Maybe later, guys. What was your question?"

They both looked a little crestfallen, but then Tanner pushed Trevor forward, or Trevor pushed Tanner forward. Whichever. I was really struggling to keep their names straight. Anyway, one of the T's said, "We had a question about the book." He flipped through the pages to get to the place. "In Chapter 21—"

"'Polygon Madness,'" the other supplied.

"You and the Fellowship—" the first T started to say, but was interrupted as the second T interjected, "I think you'll find it was not a 'fellowship,' but a 'company.'"

"Wrong!" the first T shouted. "In Chapter 11, Rook clearly states they are a 'fellowship with extras.'"

The second T rolled his eyes and affected a superior expression. "Of course he did, but later in the same chapter, Avery *himself* says they would later become known as the 'Company of the Fellowship.'"

"The keyword there being *later* meaning *not now!*"
First T punctuated his rebuttal by pantomiming a
mic drop.

I saw a shadow of uncertainty pass over second
T's face, but then he rallied with the always erudite
rejoinder, "You're an idiot!"

I will spare you the next five minutes of Python-
esque argument, and only say in the end they agreed
to disagree. At least, that's what I charitably assume
happened when first T called second T a nerf herder,
and second T asked first T the age-old question, "I
know you are, but what am I?"

Susan stepped in. "You are both being embarrass-
ments. If you don't stop acting like children, you are
leaving. Understand?" They both nodded.

We made another six feet in relative peace. Finally,
first T, who I will assume from now on is Tanner
based solely on the fact that it comes first alphabeti-
cally, made another try. "Anyway, Professor . . . I
mean, Avery . . ." He cleared his throat to cover
the slip and muttered under his breath, "Come on,
Tanner, you can do this . . ."

"Relax," I said. "Just ask your question. I probably won't be able to answer anyway. My memory of
events on Trelari is a little muddled."

"Right." He took a deep breath. "The question is
actually about the title of Chapter 21. In the text of the
chapter the creatures are clearly referred to as 'gelatinous polyhedrons,' the only debate being what type . . ."

Trevor, who had been doing a great job of keeping his mouth shut, apparently could not help inserting himself at the mention of this topic. "Although I wonder why you never thought the creature might be a ditrigonal dodeca-dodecahedron or simply a dodeca-dodecahedron, both of which also have twenty-four faces."

I opened my mouth to admit complete ignorance as to what he was talking about, but Tanner slapped Trevor on the back of the head and said, "He didn't think of it because it's ridiculous. No one could possible mistake a Catalan Solid for a star polyhedron."

"Besides," Susan interjected, "had it been a star polyhedron, cold wouldn't have worked. They would have needed to melt the thing with acid."

If they hadn't already been before, I think both young men fell in love with Susan at that moment. She seemed to realize she'd exposed the fact that she was at least as geeky as they were, and quickly went back to studying the pattern of tiles on the floor. I drew their attention back to me by asking, "And your question was?"

"Right!" Tanner said, and shot Trevor a murderous look. "The question is, whether this is a mistake or, as many of us believe, a clue."

"One of many," Trevor offered, and he held his book out to me so I could see all the folded-down pages where passages had been highlighted and annotated.

"A clue to what?" I asked.

They both looked at each other and said, "The revelation, of course."

"You see," Trevor said, taking over the narrative. "We have a theory that the revelation is about the nature of the reality of Mysterium itself. We think what you are trying to tell us is there is a higher dimension to the universe. In the book, the word *polyhedron* has been replaced by *polygon* as a signal that Mysterium mages are thinking too two-dimensionally about magic."

Tanner began to explain how, if you take the first word (not including articles) from each of the chapters divisible into or a multiple of the mystical number seven, that there is a message to Mysterium wizards. He read the message aloud. "Mysterium wizard trolls polygon not."

"That sentence doesn't make any sense," I protested.

"It makes perfect sense, if you are 'trolling' the 'Mysterium'' over its 'polygon' or 'two-dimensional' view of the world," Trevor explained, but he used so many air quotes that I had trouble following.

"What about the 'not,'" I asked. "Wouldn't that negate everything else?"

Apparently not, but I hesitate to reconstruct their argument for you here because it implicates over a dozen logical fallacies, including every one of the formal syllogistic fallacies, which should be impossible. Anyway, it was only one small part of a larger theory they were working on called the "Khan Fallacy." While their thesis was silly, something about their conclusion struck me as very near the truth. It's like the feeling you get when you're doing a jigsaw puzzle and you've been staring at this jumble of shapes without finding any matches, and then suddenly you see the subtle variations in color and pattern. Your hand reaches out and unerringly links two pieces together. It is only the beginning of a long process, but after that the end is inevitable.

"Tell me more about this Khan Fallacy. It's . . . interesting."

"It is?" Tanner asked.

"Seriously?" Trevor added.

Susan put a hand on my arm. "Please, Avery, don't encourage them," she pleaded. There was a certain desperation in her eyes.

Trevor and Tanner ignored her. "We knew we were onto something," they said together. To my horror and wonder, they both pulled back their cloaks to reveal matching T-shirts with the word *KHAAAAAAAAN* written across their fronts in a bold typeface.

Trevor began. "We see the Khan Fallacy as a metric for evaluating magical research—"

Tanner cut off his friend to add, "It's an extension of a theory Professor Roddenberry first came up with to explain why so much mystical research is fatally flawed—"

"And refers to a thought-experiment he published in his first article on the subject." Trevor seized back the floor. "He gives the example of a Terran naval captain suddenly thrust into a battle in space, and how his past experience and learned perspective would cause him to entirely miss the fact that, with no gravity or landmass constraining your movement, there is an extra dimension to the tactics you could employ."

"So, when we read ¡gelatinous polygons' where 'polyhedrons' should have been, we wondered if you weren't giving your readers a hint that your work needs to be read with a . . . higher level of thought. We've applied to study the mathematical and logical implications of our Khan Fallacy with Professor Roddenberry. With your recommendation . . ." Tanner concluded, letting the implication hang in the air.

I'm not sure what or if I responded to him. I had fallen back into my own thoughts, murmuring them under my breath. "It's probably nothing. An overly tired author or a hiccup in the cross-ether translation, but the magical world is a multidimensional space. You can go forward, back, left, right, up, down, then, now, strong, weak . . ." Could it be that simple?

No one spoke, which was fair because I was babbling. At least, the expressions on their faces told me I was making no sense. But, for me, things were becoming a little bit clearer, and a lot more disturbing.

The one constant all Mysterium mages take for granted is that in a multiverse otherwise characterized by multidimensionality and giddy randomness, Mysterium is unchangeable. There is a straight line, a single vector of magical inertia, that decreases as you move outward and away from the university. It is so invariable that all Mysterium magic uses this fixedness as a reference point, and as a foundation for all castings. But why should it be so? It is, in fact, completely unnatural for there to be a place like Mysterium. A place so fixed and constant nobody has ever been able to discover its point of creation.

The more I thought about it, the more I came to believe that I might have previously come to believe that Mysterium wasn't the center of the universe, or at least that there shouldn't be a center of the universe. That someone, or a group of someones, have had their thumb(s) on the scale of creation since recorded memory. In other words, that reality was rigged.

I'm not sure how long I spun and twisted these thoughts in my mind. I know for several minutes Trevor and Tanner kept asking if they were right, and I didn't answer them, and eventually they grew silent and sullen. I also know we kept creeping forward. Whether it took us ten seconds, ten minutes, or ten hours to get to the front of the line I have no clue. The next thing I do remember fully is Susan shaking me by the arm and telling me the yellowish skull floating above window number three was free. We were up.

CHAPTER 15

HELLP!

The skull floated on a billowing blue cloud of nether energy, which smells a bit like rotten eggs mixed with teriyaki sauce. As long as you don't notice it, you are fine, and once you've been around it for a while, you go nose blind to it, but the first time you experience it can make you rethink your life choices. Also, its eye sockets contained glowing lights, like eerie embers, and looking directly at them was like staring into the maw of the abyss. Come to think of it, that is exactly what you're doing. And people wonder why I dropped Necromancy as a major.

The skull was a demi-lich. For those of you that have read *The Dark Lord*, I'll start by telling you a demi-lich is different from a semi-lich, the being we faced down in the Tomb of Terrors. A semi-lich is an awesome amalgam of superpowered lich sorcery and pure vampire smolder. He's also unique to my knowledge. By contrast, demi-liches are smelly, glowing, floating skulls that exist in alarmingly large numbers. This is because if you die owing money to Mysterium University, a ghoulish loan officer (and I mean that literally, most of the loan officers at Mysterium University are ghouls) will go out, dig up your corpse, take its head, animate it, and force you to work off your debt. When you finish, your head is mercifully reunited with your body and buried. Usually, but tragically not always, after they have deanimated it.

With all that going for them, demi-liches are typically pretty depressed and bitter. In other words, you couldn't pick a worse candidate to staff a help desk. Unless, as I have often suspected of the university, your goal is to make sure as little help as possible was provided . . . or sought.

The skull raised its glowing eyes from the logbook where it was making an entry. (Did I mention that its gaze can sear flesh? And char paper?) "Hello!" it said. "My name is Gray. How can I help you?"

The words were entirely appropriate, but its voice had the quality of a chorus of the damned or a bone saw cutting through someone's flesh . . . while they were still alive. The contrast somehow made it all that more terrible, particularly since I got the impression Gray was trying very hard to be upbeat.

I smiled back, but could tell that my effort wasn't good and decided to ditch it and any other niceties. I cut straight to the point. "We need to find a couple of our friends that stopped in here earlier. There was a Hylar looking all glimmery, and a dark-haired woman with one black and one white eye. Have you seen them?"

The skull "smiled" (if you can call it that) a little wider. "Nice to meet you too. Yes, I do enjoy my work here at the help desk. How was my day? Good. How was your day? Fine? Excellent."

"I'm sorry, Gray," I said. "We're in a hurry and—"

"Why should you be sorry, sir?" the skull asked. "There is no reason for you to want to exchange small talk with me. You are in a hurry and need help, and I am manning the help desk." He deliberately turned to look at the sign above the desk that said HELP. "I love manning the help desk here at Student Records and answering questions that have nothing to do with records or students. I am a very helpful person by nature."

Something in me that I am not proud of made me say, "Technically, you're not a person at all, but the spirit of a person reanimated from the afterlife and tethered within a magical construct etched into your former body's skull." Susan elbowed me in the ribs, but she was too late.

Gray gazed at me, the balefire lights in his eye sockets twinkling. "What a wonderfully accurate observation, sir. Thank you for correcting my mis-statement, and reminding me of the accursed nature of my existence."

Susan pushed me to one side. "I'm sorry, Mr. Gray, he is very distressed and we are in a hurry. It is important that we find his friends as soon as possible."

"I was in a hurry when I stepped off that curb," the skull said by way of reply. "Now, as your friend so kindly reminded me, I'm dead."

Susan took a deep breath. "I'm sorry to hear that. Perhaps if we told you what records his friends were looking for you could point us in the right direction?"

"*Point* you in the right direction? Certainly! Capital idea!" boomed the skull. The "smile" dropped from his face. "By the gods! Will you look at that! My fingers are missing! As are my hands and arms and shoulders and the rest of my body! Someone help! I've been stolen!"

I'd had enough. "Come on. We'll make our best guess and go from there."

"But that would take forever, Professor Stewart," Susan argued.

The skull's mouth dropped open. "Seriously? You're Avery Stewart? I'm a big fan of your book." He cocked to one side and studied me. "Hmm. I thought you'd be taller and less of a jerk."

"You read *The Dark Lord*?"

He rolled the glowing points of light around his

eye sockets. "Are you kidding? All the undead in the Necromancy Department have read *The Dark Lord*. The plight of the semi-lich was inspiring."

"Really?"

It shook its head sadly. "I could tell you horror stories about the conditions we demi-liches are forced to live in. One word: asbestos."

"Appalling."

I would have happily continued conversing with Gray, but Susan brought my attention back to the task at hand. "That is awful, Mr. Gray, but we need to find Professor Stewart's friends. Could you—"

"Downstairs: Annex QQ, vault 7734," the skull said before she could finish her question.

All four of us stared at him. I hadn't seen him use a divination spell or consult his logbook. "How can you be sure?" Susan asked.

"First, Hylar *never* come to Student Records, and, on the rare occasion they do, all the banshees lurk about in the corners moaning over them. Second, we had a special memo from the Administration about your friends—*hand* delivered, no less. I can't tell you how unusual that is these days. The bosses have figured out that animating a skull costs far less mystical power than a whole skeleton, so wherever possible, they are cutting staff . . . down to the bone." He laughed at his own joke. "Get it? To the bone? Because we're all dead?"

Gray started to natter on about how he was trying

to break into stand-up comedy, but I wasn't listening. That creeping feeling of doom had returned. The one that made my stomach want to try and crawl its way out of my throat. I swallowed. "What did it say?"

"My flyer?"

I realized that Trevor and Tanner were both holding little multicolored cards with a picture of Gray floating in front of a microphone under the tagline *Bone-rattling laughs*. "No, the memo. The hand-delivered one."

"Only to send them and anyone who came in here looking for them *straight to 7734*. You should be more than a trifle concerned."

When I didn't respond, he sighed and stared at a small scrap of paper on the desk. His eyes flashed green and the smell of smoke filled the air. He glanced from me back down to the paper. I followed his gaze and my blood froze. I grabbed the slip and stared at it. "I see."

"Sorry," Gray said.

"Yeah." My voice sounded hollow. "Thanks."

I began walking to the elevator. Susan and the T's followed. Behind us, Gray shouted, "If you survive make sure to come to my show. It's this Thursday from seven to nine. There's a two-drink minimum. Oh, and remember, a happy campus makes for better magic!"

When we reached the elevators, I punched the down button. Trevor asked, "What's the matter? At least we know where they are."

I looked at him. It was like looking in a mirror from six or seven years ago. He was so earnest and keen. "Do you remember our agreement? Well, it is time to implement Rule Three."

Trevor and Tanner looked at Susan. "Not to call you Professor Stewart?"

I went through the rules in my head and realized they were right. "No, I mean Rule One. It's time for the three of you to run."

They all protested at once. "No way!" "Why now?" "We aren't going to abandon you, Avery."

"This is something I have to do alone. Your paths must . . . Listen, just take Harold—" I pointed at the imp, who had fallen asleep atop the statue "—and get as far away from this place as possible. I'll contact you as soon as I can. If I'm not back in a couple of days, go to Professor Stonehammer in the basement of the Subworld Studies building. Tell him where I've gone."

I pulled out a pen and scribbled the dwarf's cubicle number on the back of the paper I'd taken from the help desk. The elevator arrived and I stepped inside. I pushed the button for floor 7734. I watched their downcast faces disappear behind the closing doors. I told myself it was the right thing to do. The only thing to do. The skull had burned the number 7734 into the paper so it was facing me upside down. In that arrangement, the number spelled out exactly where I was going, and I was going to hELL.

CHAPTER 16

IN TRIPLICATE

Traveling in a metal box to hell can make one pause and take stock of one's life. How did I get here? Could I have made better choices? Should I have paid more attention in Demoniac Mysticism? Why had I never questioned Financial Aid when they asked me to identify my relatives, along with the locations of their burial plots, when applying for a loan?

I was still lost in this last thought when the elevator doors opened. Two strange beings entered the elevator. One looked like a green catfish that grew legs and arms and decided to stand up and walk around. I thought he was an Aot-ouk, but I'd never met one so I couldn't be sure. They were from a subworld that the Mysterium had rendered off-limits. The second one appeared to be Cthulhoid from its squidlike tentacle head, but his coloration was a bit less green and his tentacles were thinner than I expected. I wondered if he were sick. The Aot-ouk carried a toolbox and a clipboard, while the sickly Cthulhoid pushed a wheeled bucket with a mop.

We were on floor D1, which meant we still had miles to go before we got to my floor. I stepped over to the side. They both nodded politely, although the Cthulhoid's tentacles twitched toward me. The Aot-ouk pushed the button for floor D2, while the Cthulhoid-ish creature pushed D3. I tried not to stare.

"So, you have to go down to the vault?" The Aot-ouk spoke with a gargling voice.

"Yeah, the whole place got slimed." Squid-head sighed, wriggling his tentacled face in disgruntled resignation. I don't know that I can explain what it looked like.

"Bummer," the Aot-ouk commiserated. "Slime is hell to get out of carpets."

"I hope it's really slime and not some kind of pudding or jelly. Why are you getting called down to the shrine?"

"The barge across the river is leaking again." He shook his head. "I've told them a thousand times, you can't keep patching the thing indefinitely. The whole hull needs to be stripped and resealed. But do they listen?"

The light for D2 lit up accompanied by a soft chime. The doors slid open and the Aot-ouk stepped out. "See you later, Bill. Good luck with the slime."

"Sure thing, Frank. You too."

The doors started to close, but then Frank, the Aot-ouk, stopped the door and stuck his head back in. "Bill, you should come up when you're done. There's going to be a little party for the sphinx later on. Everyone's going to be there: the bugbears from Systems, the troglodytes and trolls from Logistics . . ."

"I'll think about it," Bill said noncommittally.

"There's going to be cake," Frank said in a sing-song voice, pulling his head back as the doors slid shut.

The elevator started moving again. Bill and I stared at each other for a second. He spoke. "They always promise cake. The cake is a lie."

I didn't know what to say, so we shared an awkward elevator silence. His tentacles twitched in my direction a few more times until he glanced at the panel of buttons. "Gods, buddy. You sure you pushed the right button?"

I nodded.

He leaned on his mop while a tentacle scratched at his head. "My advice would be quit now. Screw it. No paycheck is worth going down to 7734. I knew a guy that went down there because his landlord wanted proof of employment and next thing you know . . ."

His voice trailed off as another soft chime issued

from somewhere near the ceiling and the elevator slowed to a stop. Above the door, the lighted sign read D3. A group of Dark Hylar (who, despite their name, strangely are very pale) were waiting to get on. Bill began to maneuver his bucket past them.

"What happened to the guy? Did he ever come back?"

Bill turned and leered at me evilly, his face tentacles twitching. "He came back, all right . . . ten years later, and missing a couple of limbs. I think it was an arm and a leg."

Just before the doors shut fully, he put his hand between them and addressed the elves. "By the way, he's going down 7734 . . . voluntarily. So, I wouldn't mess with him. Put me straight off eating his brain." He took his hand away, and the doors closed.

The elves fixed me with a collective look of terror and crammed themselves into a corner of the elevator. They stayed like that until the lighted sign read Q1. As soon as the doors opened, the three hurried out.

The elevator continued its descent into the depths. I was alone with my thoughts. They were not encouraging. I thought about Dawn and Eldrin a lot. If anything happened to them I would never forgive myself. I also spent some time thinking about myself. How had I let everything go sideways? The day had started simply enough . . . if this even were the same day. I had lost track of time since returning. And what about my destination?

I had heard rumors about this building, but shrines and sphinxes? Were there more Bills and Franks lurking behind other EMPLOYEES ONLY signs on campus? Who were they? How had they gotten here? I had never really thought about how the university used subworlders and the undead for cheap labor. Now that I did, it made me feel even less certain that I was on the "right" side of things. It was when the lighted sign over the door hit triple digits that I began to think about my destination. How was I going to survive a trip to what the Mysterium considered hell?

On this last point, I resolved that if this was a suicide mission, then I was going to go out in a blaze of glory. I concentrated and tried to seize a primary line of magic, but found nothing accessible. The elevator was clearly shielded. On a whim, I pulled out Griswald's key again and focused my intention through it. The metal spun and twisted, manifesting teeth left and right, until it looked like a miniature aerial. Mystical energy flowed through the key into my body. Another impossibility. A shiver ran through me as I realized how little I knew about this thing, or the scope of its powers.

"What are you?" I asked.

Thankfully, the key gave no answer. And because there was no way to resolve the fundamental question of what the key was or why Griswald had entrusted it to me, I instead prepared myself for hell. I spun patterns of power with a feverish abandon: fire, cold, lightning, and necromantic effects whirled and twisted until the very air roiled and crackled. If there was something waiting for me on level 7734, it would regret it.

The soft chime sounded.

The elevator slowed.

The doors started to open.

I tensed, my nerves hanging on a knife-edge.

The crack between the elevator doors widened, and I could see a large, brightly lit room. Then I saw the demon. He was squatting behind a low wall directly across from the elevator. A ragged cloak of abyssal gray covered his skeletal frame. Six arms, each ending in long, lethally clawed hands, extended from his sides. Tattered parchment wings jutted from its back to brush against the ceiling. His head reminded me of a gorilla's, except with the jaws and snout of a crocodile. He looked up from a large tome he had been examining. I gave him no chance to act, but thrust the key at him like a spear, unleashing all my power.

A maelstrom of energy cut across the distance between us, shredding reality as it went. The demon had no time to react, no time to dodge, no time to counter. Nor did he try. Nor, apparently, did he need to try, because with every inch of every foot my spell traveled its effect seemed to halve. An indistinct miasma of smoke was all that struck the demon.

He waved it away with a mild grimace of disgust and pointed a clawed hand at a small plaque posted on the low wall: RESPECT THE HEALTH OF THOSE AROUND YOU. PLEASE, NO SMOKING. A cartoon picture of a man coughing, his head enveloped in a cloud of smoke, accompanied the words.

The demon snapped his jaws. "May I help you?"

He seemed annoyed, which was understandable. I mean, no one likes secondhand smoke. I composed myself, concealed the key beneath my robes, and stepped off the elevator. The doors slid shut behind me. "Um, is this level 7734?"

"Oh no. It's you again. Yes, Professor Stewart, this is Level 7734 of the Student Records Office, Confidential Files Desk. How may I help you?"

I looked about uncertainly, but I didn't remember anything. The room was enormous, and had been subdivided into row upon row of head-high cubicles. Dozens of people, maybe more that I could not see, of every persuasion, race, species, and reality were scattered about in the cubicles. No one seemed to have noticed my entrance, and the place was hush with the sound of scratching quills and the soft rustle of pages being turned.

The normalcy was a bit disorienting. I had been expecting utter horror. I hadn't been expecting run-of-the-mill bureaucratic passive aggression.

I tried to recall why I would have come here in the past, but there was nothing other than a strange sense of frustration. I slowly stepped forward. "Why was I here last time?"

"You were looking for information on a student named Vivian, who had dropped out. You refused to fill out the forms, and made quite a scene. Before you ask, we still don't have any information on her, unless you are willing to fill out the forms."

"Sorry about that. All I'm trying to do today is find a couple of my friends that came by earlier: a student named Dawn Stardust and Professor Eldrin Leightner. Did they sign in? One is a Hylar . . ."

The demon smiled his crocodile smile—very disturbing—and slid a single sheet of paper across the counter toward me. "Why don't you go over to cubicle Z-23 and fill in their names and descriptions on this information request form, and I'll see if one of our interns can find them for you. With a good description, it shouldn't take us long. But if you don't fill out the form, I can't help you, and I'd rather not have a repeat of our last encounter."

I actually would have been quite happy to relive my past if it meant I would also remember it, but I didn't say that. I had one mission: Eldrin and Dawn. I examined the form suspiciously. It only had a few lines to fill in: a couple to identify me, and a couple to identify who I was looking for. "Is this it?"

"Would you prefer if it were more complicated?"

"I suppose not."

The demon smiled again. Every time he smiled, I

got the uncomfortable feeling he was deciding how best to remove the flesh from my bones. "You will find cubicle Z-23 over there."

He pointed to a line of cubicles running down the right side of the room. Each one had a little plastic laminated sign attached to a thin metal rod, and each sign had a unique alphanumeric code. I followed the numbers and letters to the assigned spot. Maybe the best explanation for Eldrin and Dawn's delay was that we weren't dealing in a human timescale, but in bureaucracy time. I also took some solace in the fact that I had obviously been here before and survived.

Z-23 was identical to every other cubicle in the place: a simple three-sided box with walls slightly lower than eye-level. The only furniture was a small stand-up desk, and the only other object in the space was a refillable quill pen fastened at the end of a thin chain bolted to the tabletop. I glanced about to make sure no one was lurking. There was a fellow to my right, but he was so old it looked like he might be filling in his own death certificate. I stepped up to the desk, grabbed the pen, and studied the form. There didn't seem to be any danger, but I couldn't shake the feeling that something was wrong. I tried to summon a pattern of seeing, but the power kept slipping away from me, evaporating as quickly as I could draw it. In the end there was nothing to it but to fill in the boxes on the form. When I got to the end of the page I noticed a small arrow; underneath was written: *Please complete both sides.*

"I knew it couldn't be that easy." With a chuckle, I turned over the page.

There were a few more blanks to fill in. I dispatched those quickly. Strangely, there seemed to be a second page that I hadn't noticed at first. I completed that page, only to find a page after that. It was odd, but I was moving so quickly through the form, that I wasn't worried.

The next page came with a request to copy the previous pages. I did so without thinking. Yes, it was taking more time, but everyone has to fill out paperwork, and additional copies made sense for filing purposes. I realized that I had written in a section titled "For Office Use Only," but apparently a helper or intern had left me additional copies of the form on the desk, so I was able to redo it without too much effort. I paused for a moment as I got back to the description. What had I been looking for? It was at that point that I realized I needed two separate sets of forms: one for Dawn and another for Eldrin. I started over.

I don't know how long I spent in the cubicle, but the next thing I do remember was hearing a voice like an explosive boom from the elevator. "I am come!" the voice shouted.

I was a little irritated, because I was working on my paperwork and there was a sign posted in every cubicle that said quite clearly: QUIET IS COURTEOUS. REMEMBER, YOUR NEIGHBORS ARE WORKING TOO.

Whoever it was, they were not being courteous. "I am the inspector! Nothing can be hidden from me!"

I tried to ignore what was happening, but it was very distracting. The voice was also oddly familiar. Reluctantly, I tore my eyes away from the stack of forms I was working on. An enormous being, at least seven feet tall, shrouded in a black cloak, loomed over the front desk. Its head was a skull, and it pointed a sickly green hand at the demon. "Your time has come, Desk Demon. Prepare yourself!"

I frowned. There was an unusual smell, which made me gag slightly. A little jolt ran through the quill into my hand. It wasn't painful, but it reminded me that I needed to finish my paperwork. I refocused on the form: *What does all work and no play make Jack?*

My hand started writing automatically, but my mind was troubled. What does this Jack have to do with Eldrin and Dawn? While I jotted down my thoughts, I decided to review some of the other questions to see if they explained the form's sudden interest in the leisure habits of this Jack fellow. I glanced at the previous question: *List your organs in order of least to most favorite.*

"What?" I said aloud, and as I did my hand stopped its feverish movements.

At the desk, the inspector was still shouting. "What is this?"

"A . . . a logbook, Inspector?"

"You call this a log? What are you demons doing

down here? This is a disgrace! Take these last entries. All you've written here are *Hylar, companion,* and '*expected guest*'? You call that record keeping? This is no way to keep a tally of souls!"

"Well, you see, sir—"

"Silence!"

The last shout drew all of my attention. I knew that I had heard that voice, but I couldn't remember where. My head was filled with a fog that was making it difficult to concentrate. For his part, the inspector was so agitated that his head wobbled as though it was going to fall off. In fact, his whole enormous body shook as if he were hiding an entire goon squad beneath a holocaust cloak. Eventually he gathered himself enough to say, "In my rounds, I have found some departments have been falsifying entries to inflate their quarterly numbers. I am of half a mind to call in the . . . auditors."

The desk demon's crocodile skull flushed a deathly gray pallor. "I . . . I can assure you—"

"I care not for your assurances. I want proof!" The inspector tapped the fingers of a surprisingly feminine green hand along the top of the desk. I took a step closer to the scene before the quill jolted me.

The inspector glared at the demon. "If I were to ask you to produce these last three patrons—" he sniffed skeptically "—could you manage that, or is it beyond your means?"

"Yes, Inspector!"

"Then do it!"

"Yes, Inspector!"

The desk demon roared orders at a small army of crimson assistants until a half dozen or so of them were scurrying around like lost ants. Two of them ran over to me, pried my hand from the quill, and pulled me to the front desk. This disturbed me greatly, because I was not done with my forms. My head was swimming and my body swayed. To my right stood Eldrin and Dawn looking just as disoriented.

Despite the speed with which the demon had produced us, the inspector did not look happy. He examined us with a pronounced frown. "Very well. I shall let you know in the next thirty to sixty days the results of your inspection."

The inspector put a gentle and reassuring hand on my shoulder. "Come along. I will need to speak to the three of you."

The demon extended three of his six arms in protest. "But, Inspector, my thralls! They must stay."

The inspector spun back to the demon in such a rage of emotion that he swayed a little from the violence of his own movement. "You expect me to take your word for it that these are the three 'patrons' from your log? How dare you presume so much? They shall be taken to the Audit Department and interrogated. If they are who you claim them to be, then they shall be returned to you."

The inspector lowered his voice and hissed, "If

they are not, then you will quickly find that there are levels below 7734. Do I make myself clear?"

"Y-yes, sir," the demon said, standing once again at attention. "As you wish, sir."

The inspector nodded and turned again, ushering the three of us swiftly toward the elevator. He pushed the button and we waited. My head was finally beginning to clear and I realized that while the desk demon had definitely been up to something, I really didn't want to go to whatever lower level this "inspector" was taking us to. The auditors sounded full-on creepy.

Once again, I tried to pull in power, but there was nothing there. Every time I felt a tingle of magical energy it would slip away, like trying to catch smoke in your hands. If magic was out, I would have to turn to more physical means. I watched the light above the elevator descend and hatched a plan. The timing would have to be perfect, but it just might be possible . . .

When the light indicated the elevator was two levels above us I put a hand to my head and groaned. "I don't feel so good."

The elevator was one floor away. I began to sway, unsteadily, on my feet, and then I feigned a stumble. As the elevator chimed and the doors began to open, the inspector reached forward to steady me.

With a sudden burst of violence, I grabbed the inspector's arm and yanked downward, simultaneously kicking backward with my heel into where I thought, given his height, his knee might be.

Many things happened at once, and none of them were what I'd expected. First, as I pulled down on the inspector's arm I ripped away a portion of his body. To my astonishment, Susan stumbled out from under the inspector's cloak, through the now-open doors of the elevator, and slammed headfirst into the back wall of the compartment. Then I heard a terrible curse as my heel connected with something much softer than a knee. The inspector's long cloak collapsed, revealing Trevor, doubled over in pain, his hand clutching his stomach, and Tanner desperately trying to stabilize a makeshift framework that had been holding the inspector's cloak in place. Above it all floated Gray. He looked down at the chaos and said what we all were thinking, the exact wording of which I will leave to your imagination.

Behind us the demon roared in anger. The front desk disintegrated as he rushed through it like a freight train, an army of his red-skinned helpers behind him. With all six of the demon's arms extended, and with all those claws attached at their ends snapping, he looked like an enormous, living blender set to puree. I no longer wanted to have anything to do with paperwork.

I stood stunned as the demon rushed toward us. Thankfully, Dawn and Eldrin did not. They each grabbed one of my arms and pulled me onto the elevator. We made it through the doors just ahead of Tanner, who dragged a still-moaning Trevor behind him. Gray darted in last, but he had the presence of mind to slam his face into the button for the lobby and, for good measure, into the close-doors button. The desk demon made a desperate lunge. That he came up three or so inches short is a testament to the power of luck—really, really dumb luck. We heard the satisfying thud of the demon's head impact against the doors as the elevator lurched and began its slow journey up to the lobby.

CHAPTER 17

JOURNEY FROM THE CENTER OF MYSTERIUM

We sat, staring at one another and catching our breaths. I did a head count and came up one short. "Where's Harold?"

"We tried to bring him, but he wouldn't come down from the statue," Tanner said.

Trevor added, "He asked us to tell you that he would always be there when you needed him."

"At least he's safe," I said. What I didn't add was that if he was offering, I really could have used him back in hell.

We lapsed into silence until Susan pointed at me. "You should have seen your face when you pulled me out from under that cloak."

She started laughing. It was a half-hysterical laugh, but it was contagious, and soon we were all laughing along with her. It was not until we were passing level Q1 that the laughter subsided. I pointed an accusing finger at the three students. "You broke my rules."

"You're right, we did," Susan admitted.

"Thank you." I turned and stared up at Gray. "All of you."

"I don't obey your rules, but I must confess to being a trifle disappointed in you when you didn't get my reference at the desk." The eerie light in his left eye socket flickered, and I realized he was winking. Gray was a Trifler. "However, you can blame me. I was the head of the operation."

This earned another round of laughter, but the adrenaline was wearing off, and it ended in weary chuckles. We fell silent until Trevor asked, "What was that place anyway?"

"And why is it in the basement of the Student Records building?" Tanner asked.

I shrugged. "It was the Confidential Records Desk. We all knew it would be well protected."

Susan shook her head. "I expected well protected, but I didn't think that meant that the basement of Student Records would be run by a family of demented demons. Then again, Work Studies aren't allowed below level 13."

Tanner pointed at the floor. "You guys are taking

this way too calmly. That place has nothing to do with students or records."

Trevor nodded in agreement. "It's a soul trap!"

Gray floated down from the ceiling. "You're right, of course. Level 7734 is not a place the mages in charge of Mysterium want anyone to know about. Normally, none of you would have even been allowed to see the button to 7734, much less access it. But there are many secrets in the deep places under the university. The Administration was too greedy for space, and they dug too deeply. In their quest to store all the knowledge of the multiverse, they unleashed darker forces."

"Demons?" Susan asked.

The skull shook. "Bureaucrats."

Dawn sighed and rested her head against Eldrin's shoulder. "Any place as steeped in magic as Mysterium will have these corners of darkness. The troubling thing is not that they exist, but that the Administration is using them to get rid of people they don't like."

"It must have been a mistake." Eldrin wrapped his arm around her.

"Mistake? More like typical Administration corruption," Susan spit with disgust.

I looked wearily at Eldrin. "I'm sorry I sent you and Dawn down here for nothing."

"Not nothing," Dawn said. "We found what you wanted."

"You got a look at Sam's and Ariella's records!?"

"They were actually very efficient," Eldrin said. "That's one of the benefits of central control of records."

Dawn rolled her eyes at him. "Of course, we couldn't get out of the place once we read them, which is also the result of central control that borders on the maniacal. So, I suppose you have to take the bad with the good."

"The odd thing is that we didn't even want to leave," Eldrin sighed sadly.

"It's definitely a subtle enchantment," Dawn said in agreement. "You don't even notice the forms expanding, or that the number of forms you need keeps duplicating and triplicating."

"Not to mention the ridiculously effective anti-magic warding," I said, remembering how my onslaught fizzled when I stepped foot in 7734.

"That's because the wards were everywhere," Eldrin explained, and launched into a lecture about something called an MMOG, or massively multi-warded occult grids.

"Never mind about all that," I said, jumping to my feet. "Why is the Administration interested in them?"

Eldrin and Dawn glanced at Susan, the T's, and the floating skull, and then back at me. From the look on their faces I knew that whatever they'd read was bad. "Not good?" I asked. They shook their heads. I glanced up at the number above the door. We were ten floors from the lobby. What would be waiting for us? I glanced over at Susan and the T's. Their faces were alight with curiosity. They were no different than I had been before Trelari—innocent. But then Griswald used to say innocence and ignorance were opposite sides of the same coin. Nine floors to go. "Maybe innocence is overrated," I mumbled.

"What?" Eldrin asked.

"Go ahead and tell them," I said. "They're part of the Resistance. They deserve to know what they're fighting for."

He cast a questioning glance at Dawn. She shrugged in response. "Right," he said, and took a deep breath. "As you know, due to your pattern spell and the relationship between Death Slasher and Justice Cleaver, Trelari slipped from its standard orbital trajectory around the Mysterium and began to spin inward, slowly gaining reality as it approached closer."

Eight floors to go.

"What does this have to do with Sam and Ariella?"

He gave me a level stare I knew all too well. It meant he was getting to his point and would arrive faster if I stopped interrupting. I made a show of sealing my mouth shut as we passed the seventh floor.

He continued. "Once you returned, we both surmised that Trelari had achieved a stable level of reality. We didn't base our conclusion on any objective evidence, but on an assumption . . . a flawed assumption."

"What assumption?"

"The assumption that Mysterium is still the center of the universe."

"What are you talking about?"

Dawn interjected. "He's trying to say that Sam and Ariella's reality tested higher than predicted."

The elevator was passing floor five. "And? Slight variations in reality weights are to be expected between innerworlds, and Trelari is new. There's no standard yet."

"Not like this, Avery," she said soberly, and looked to Eldrin for support.

He sighed. "Their reality exceeded that of anyone from any of the other innerworlds. Higher than anyone, ever. Higher even than a Mysterian."

"What does that mean?" Susan asked.

Eldrin answered. "It means their reality is more powerful than ours. That means their magic is more powerful than ours, and they can potentially manipulate events here. What it means is that the Administration is right. They are a threat to Mysterium."

I froze as my view of the multiverse shifted. It was approximately the same way I'd felt the first time I saw the pattern in one of those random dot pictures that were so popular in the 1990s: it was both cool and a bit disappointing. It was cool, because it meant that Trelari might be the new center, or at least co-center of the multiverse, and it was about time someone was. On the other hand, it was disappointing that I hadn't figured it out sooner. The signs were there literally from the moment I left Trelari. If Mysterium's reality was still dominant, Valdara would never have been able to seal off her world.

"It's called an autostereogram," Eldrin said, "and it's most definitely *not cool!*"

"I saw one that resolved into an image of the Death Star! That was pretty cool," Trevor said enthusiastically.

Eldrin slapped his forehead in frustration. "Not the autostereogram, you idiot! I mean, it isn't cool that Trelari's reality may have superseded Mysterium's."

Honestly, I hadn't even known I'd been talking out loud about the dot pictures, but I was kind of glad I had, because Eldrin's response was revealing.

"It does explain a lot of the Administration's actions," Dawn said thoughtfully.

"Explains it!" Eldrin said with an explosive snort. "Justifies it! Trelari's current existence puts the university and everything and everyone in it at risk. If they figure out how to harness their powers they could take over. If they don't figure out how to harness their powers they might destroy us without even knowing that they're doing it! There is precedent from the early history of Mysterium that even powerfully real innerworlds can be severely damaged by turmoil in Mysterium. In my own world, the link between cataclysms on Hylar and trouble on Mysterium is well documented. As for Earth—" he pointed a finger up at me "—what do you think happened to the dinosaurs?"

I didn't want to argue. If Eldrin felt this way, then others would. I looked around the elevator. Trevor seemed puzzled, but Susan and Tanner were definitely troubled. They were both fingering their wrists, where I suspected they had written that stupid slogan of theirs. I wondered if they were rethinking their commitment to my "Resistance." Ultimately, what I felt about the situation didn't matter; if Trelari had gained parity with Mysterium or exceeded it, the Administration would stop at nothing to find a way to reverse the situation. However, if this information got out, it would start a panic.

Dawn put a hand on Eldrin's arm. "That's a bit apocryphal, don't you think?"

"No! I don't," he said, and, pulling away from her, jumped to his feet clearly wanting to move about, but unable to in the confined space of the elevator. Instead, he ran a shaking palm through his hair. "As long as Trelari remains where it is, we are a subworld. During my career, I've watch thousands of them explode into ether dust, and how many more of them have Mysterium mages like Avery used for their personal playgrounds?"

Now he was pissing me off. I stepped toward him so we were eye-to-eye. "So, as long as we mess with them, instead of them messing with us, it's fine?"

His ears flushed. "That's not what I'm saying, and you know it."

"To quote you, 'No! I don't.'"

Dawn put herself between us. She turned to face Eldrin and stroked her palms across his chest in a soothing gesture. "What are you saying, Eldrin?"

He leaned against the wall of the elevator. "I'm saying that we, and I mean we, the Mysterium mages, need to understand what's happened and what it means. I'm saying that as unfortunate as it might be, the Administration may be right about needing to study the Trelarians."

"Sam and Ariella!" I shouted. "Their names are Sam and Ariella!"

His eyes flashed angrily. "Fine! Sam and Ariella. But I will remind you this is not my fault. You and your experiment brought Trelari into this, and you and your book brought your friends to the Administration's attention. Between the battle-axes and your notes for posterity, this is quite the mess."

"Eldrin," Dawn said sharply.

"It's okay, Dawn. He's right," I said.

And he was. I slumped back against the wall opposite them and stared at my shoes. It's not that I thought he was right about Trelari being dangerous. Eldrin always had been a little reactionary when faced with change—something to do with basically living forever. Given some time for reflection, he would come around. But he was absolutely right about my habit of putting my friends in danger. I was doing it now. The Administration had to know we escaped 7734 by now, which also meant they probably knew what Dawn and Eldrin had discovered, and where we were.

The lighted panel now showed a fading three. There was a better than even chance the Administration would be waiting for us in the lobby. It was time for me to do the responsible thing. Eldrin was going to be furious.

I took a deep breath. "I think it's time for us to get out of here. Everyone to the middle of the elevator."

"Where are we going?" Eldrin asked.

"And how are we going to get there? The walls of these elevators are shielded," Gray said.

I didn't have enough time to explain. We were already passing Level 2. Pulling Griswald's key from the pocket of my robes, I started drawing a circle centered on the group. It was crude, but that didn't matter. The key was shifting about like it was alive. At last it locked on to an odd corkscrew configuration, and the portal blazed to life.

"How the hell does it do that?" Eldrin shouted. "It's not possible."

"Don't worry about it," I said, and stepped out of the circle as the spell activated. "And, Eldrin, don't worry about me."

Too late, he realized what I meant. "Avery, don't—"

His words were cut off like the drop of a guillotine. As

the glow faded, I wondered what they would do next, and whether they would all fit in Eldrin's cramped little office. I'd transported them there because I knew that building was shielded. The Administration would not be able to trace my spell back to their location, and my friends would need extra time to get to a place where they could travel again, which would keep them away long enough for me to refocus the Administration's attention where it belonged—on me.

Fortunately, I didn't have much time to ponder my future, because that would probably have been pretty depressing. I only had a few seconds to wipe away the evidence of the circle before a chime rang out. The elevator had reached the lobby.

I stuffed my hand and the key into one of the pockets of my robe. The doors opened. A small army of crimson-robed Sealers stood in a semicircle around the elevator, wands at the ready. At the center of the group was Moregoth.

"Garth!" I said in my most upbeat voice. "I wasn't expecting to see you here. What a pleasant surprise."

As I spoke, I very carefully tested the weight of the mystical energy in the key, but forming that last portal had drained it. I needed time. My only hope was Moregoth's penchant for monologuing. I decided to encourage him.

"You know, you are looking particularly gloomy and spectral this evening. I love the black lipstick."

"Thank you, Mr. Stewart," he replied with a cinematic rasp. "You can't know the unearthly ecstasy I feel in seeing you again. It has been quite a chase. A lovely peek into the dark places of your psyche. It was naughty of you to attack the counselor."

"You call it naughty, I call it self-defense—potaytoes potahtoes."

Moregoth flipped his bangs back away from his left eye and regarded his black-painted nails indifferently. "Speaking of which, are you intending to come quietly, or do we get to do this the hard way? As you say, tomaytoes tomahtoes."

"Let's call the whole thing off?" I suggested.

As we had been talking, I had been pulling power from around me and pouring it into the key, but it was slow-going and I wasn't at all sure if I could pull off a transport spell. I needed more time, but Moregoth seemed intent on bringing our witty repartee to a swift end.

He smiled a thin, cruel smile. "Step out of the elevator, Professor Stewart, or I will have my men cut you down where you stand."

I tested the power in the key again. It was not enough, not nearly enough.

At a slight gesture from Moregoth, the Sealers raised their wands. "I am waiting, Stewart, and I am not patient."

I had a couple of options, and none of them were good. I could make a shield and hold out for a few seconds, I could go on the offense and take a couple of them out with me, or I could surrender. I had been leaning toward this last option and taking my chances with the provost, but there was something so irritatingly smug about Moregoth's expression I decided I would rather be unconscious when he took me in.

I affected my most obnoxious smile and readied the key in my pocket, drawing all the power I could into it. "You're impatient, and I'm bored. This isn't what you would call a classic standoff, is it?"

He started to make some snide remark. In a flash, I pulled the key and fired a blast of pure mystical energy at him. Unfortunately, while quick draw duels look good in the movies, it's actually really hard to do. The blue bolt sailed past his shoulder and hit one of the Sealers standing behind him. The man was lifted off his feet and thrown back. There was a frozen moment as the man slid across the highly polished floor and came to rest, groaning, against the far wall.

Moregoth turned back to me, a joyful malevolence dancing in his eyes. "Tomahtoes, it is, Mr. Stewart," he chuckled, and then shouted, "Sealers, attack!"

The glow and weave of a dozen bolts of energy converged on me. I had just realized that the Sealers' spells were designed to kill when something small and gray and wearing a bow tie came flashing into view. The imp, who must have been lurking in the shadows above our heads, latched on to my chest just as the spells struck.

I tried to twist around, to shield him, but it was too late. His body glowed bright white as the Sealers' spells were drawn to him, some swerving unnaturally at the last second to hit him instead of me. I felt each impact as a distant, phantom pain. Harold held on until the last of the spells dissipated, then his grip failed. I clutched him to me. "Why?" I asked.

"You have a coffee date," he coughed weakly. "Can't be late for that." The imp tried to smile, but his body spasmed violently and he went very still. For a moment, I thought he was gone, but then his eyes flickered back open. "Socrates was right, Avery. There is only one evil. Don't give in to it." He gave a gasp, and his eyes went wide. "Interesting," he hissed.

I felt the life drain out of him, and then, like a sand painting caught by the wind, his body dissolved into motes of sparkling energy. They swirled about the chamber of the elevator and then surged into me in a rush of power. Looking at Moregoth, I knew exactly what I wanted to do with all that magic. I raised the key, fully intending to kill him, but the imp had done something to me. I felt my reality take a step to the right. A quickly diminishing part of me was still in Mysterium, but increasingly I was back in New York. I heard Moregoth shouting at the Sealers to attack again, but when the next wave of spells struck, I was already gone.

CHAPTER 18

BLEAKER STREET

There was no portal, no sensation of folding or falling; one moment I was in the Student Records building on Mysterium, and the next I was standing in an alley, in the gray light of a cold New York City fall morning. A searing, sorrowful pain cut through my body, and dropped me to my knees. I clutched at my chest where, moments before, Harold had been and let the tears spill down my face. I wept for Harold and myself. I had not realized it before, but the little imp had occupied a part of my being quite close to where the soul must reside. While he was with me I had not been able to feel the depth of our connection, but now that he was gone I could. There was a void in the pattern that was me, and it hurt like hell.

I don't know how long I sat in the alley feeling Harold's loss. I know it would have been easy to let it consume me, but eventually I stirred. I had things to do, and

Moregoth to kill. Harold had given his life so I could meet up with Rook and do whatever it was people like Griswald and Vivian and others thought I had it in me to do. I would probably disappoint them, but it wouldn't be for lack of trying. I picked myself up off the ground and put a hand to my shoulder where Harold had perched so often.

I wanted to mark the moment, maybe say a prayer for him, but I did not know what to say or do. I had always been indifferent to religion. When I prayed it was to those multitudes of gods I had encountered in my many travels, and not to any deity I had a personal relationship with.

Not knowing what else to do, I touched the place to the left of my heart where I felt Harold's absence most keenly, and said, "Harold, I'm sorry our time together was so short. You deserved a better end than you came to, and a better final companion. For those things, I'm also sorry. I'm not sorry to have known you though. I hope you can find a measure of peace in whatever afterlife death has brought you to." I started to walk away, but then I considered the imp's last word and smiled. "I hope it's full of surprises."

As usual, there was no response from the heavens, except that an icy drizzle began to drift down from the overcast skies. I turned up my collar, and made my way out of the alley and onto the street.

As I walked to the coffee shop I considered all the questions I had. One thing troubling me was the key, and the effect it was having on my magic. To say my power level as a mage had increased since it came into my life was as much an understatement as saying those gamma rays may have made Bruce Banner a little buff. As usual, though, it had taken too long for me to make the connection.

I should have noticed something was up when I precisely transported to my lecture hall with no preparation. Six months ago, a circle that capable would have taken me weeks to design. At the time, I'd put it down to luck, but the odds of successfully making that jump by accident were staggeringly small. I now firmly believed Harold's decision to carry the key with us was responsible. I also wondered if his desire to do so was a conscious choice. Maybe he knew what the key could do.

The effects were even more dramatic after he had given it to me. There were the quick escapes I'd made from the Sealers in the townhome and Eldrin's shielded office. There was also all the magic I'd performed in the magic-proofed elevator of the Student Records building. I needed to understand the nature of Griswald's key, and I suspected Rook had the answers.

Another issue at the top of my list was whether Trelari had actually become more real than Mysterium. I wouldn't put it past the Administration to concoct the entire thing, but I couldn't see what possible advantage they could gain from such a story getting out. If it was true, Sam and Ariella could easily be two of the most powerful mages in the multiverse. The scary thing was that they had no training in using magic outside their own reality. They might unravel a world without even knowing they were doing it. They might even accidentally unravel the world they were in. The implications stopped me in midstep.

I reached into my reservoir of four-letter words and let loose with something colorful and descriptive, only to realize my curse was one of dozens raining down around me. I'd stopped dead in the middle of the street. I stepped back onto the curb before the cabbie could follow through on his threat to introduce me to the underside of his car, and moved to stand against the side of a building.

I pulled the communicator coin out of my pocket and activated it. It clicked and buzzed for a few seconds, and then Ariella's voice came on. "Hello, Avery. We've been in the lounge for about an hour and everything is fine. We're okay. You don't have to check up on us so often. The biggest danger here are ED and EDIE. They won't let us alone. They are like incredibly competent but overbearing nannies. Wait! What? Sorry, Avery, I'll be right back . . ."

Her voice got fainter, like she had turned her head away from the communicator, but I heard her say, "No. Thank you, EDIE. I don't need another pillow. Ten are quite sufficient. Yes, ED, I understand my tea is getting cold, but I've had three cups already, and . . ." A hard edge came into her voice. "I assure you both I am quite able to go to the bathroom on my own." There were a few deep breaths like she was trying hard not to explode, and then she said, "If you two give me five minutes on my own, I will let you make me lunch. Gods!" Ariella boomed into the communicator, setting my ears ringing. "I don't know where those two came from, but I pity the poor people living in this ship."

"Is that Avery?" I heard Sam shout from somewhere in the distance. "Tell him hi, from me."

"Sam says hi."

As much as I was happy that nothing actually bad was happening to them, I needed to warn them about what might happen, and get to Rook fast. "Ariella, I have some news."

Something in my voice must have told her that things weren't going well in the "real" world. "What's happened, Avery? Are you okay?"

"Yes, I'm fine."

"Have we been expelled?"

"We've been what?" I heard Sam shout. He must have grabbed the coin from Ariella, because there was a hiss of static followed by him saying, "I have receipts!"

More static followed this, and then Ariella was back. "Sorry. Please go on. We *promise* not to interrupt."

How do you tell someone that they might literally be a god? I wondered. I decided to work up to that. "First, and I don't want the two of you freaking out, but time is passing a bit more slowly for you than it is for us," I said. "Over here a full day has passed, and—"

"A day!" Ariella shouted. "We've missed all our first day classes? Avery! How could you?"

I had to remind myself they had no idea what we'd been through over the past twenty hours. I took a deep breath. "It gets worse, Ariella."

"Worse? Did we miss an assignment? An exam? This early!"

"It's nothing about school! Please, listen."

"Okay."

I took another deep breath. "Trelari's shift has destabilized Mysterium. The Administration of the university, basically the leaders of my world, have decided your world poses a danger. They admitted you and Sam so they could study you."

There was a long silence. "What do they hope to learn from us?" she asked quietly.

"I don't know for certain, but I'm pretty sure they are trying to figure out a way to destroy Trelari."

"What do we do?" Sam asked. I realized Ariella and he must have been listening together.

Technically, this shouldn't have been possible, and I wondered if they were already unconsciously manipulating the magic constructs around them. It reinforced how desperately I needed to get them off that ship as soon as possible. Unfortunately, there was no easy solution to the problem of where to take them. Pulling them to Earth was simply not an option. It was common knowledge I lived here, which meant it would not be long before Moregoth paid New York a visit. "At the moment, stay put," I answered.

"But—" he protested.

"I know you want to help, Sam," I said to forestall more argument. "Right now, I need the two of you safe. We are going to be coming your direction very soon. With the reverse time dilation, we will probably be there before you're done with lunch. In the meantime, I need the two of you to *very carefully* test out the potency of your spells."

"What do you mean?" Ariella asked.

"Trelari's reality has grown more powerful. It means your magical energy may have also grown stronger. I need the two of you to find a place on the ship where you can safely practice your spells, and cast a few."

"Cool!" Sam said.

"But, and I cannot stress this enough, start small! The ship has a pretty robust reality, but you're still basically traveling through the void of etherspace in a tin can."

"We are?" Sam asked.

"Yes," I sighed. "And please don't say cool."

"Okay," he said. "But it is pretty neat!"

I groaned and Ariella said, "We will do our best to be careful, Avery. Just come back soon."

"I will. I have to go. Call me immediately if there are any problems."

The connection went dead with that mind-jarring pop Eldrin had never been able to fix. I pocketed the coin and rejoined the stream of New Yorkers hurrying up 6th Avenue.

CHAPTER 19

THE SECRET OF THE BARISTAS

Tolkien wrote about how dangerous it is to step out of your door, because you never know where the road you take might lead you. That he was writing about how treacherous it is to make a journey between worlds, and how easy it is to get lost in etherspace if you don't have your wits about you, doesn't make the advice any less universally profound. However, it is obvious he never lived in New York. In New York roads don't wait for you to step onto them to cause mischief, they pull you into their currents and sweep you along whether you want to or not. All it took was for me to not resist moving, and the tide of humanity picked me up and carried me down Bleecker. It might have pushed me straight past the coffee shop and onto

7th Avenue had I let it, but I stepped into the eddy of a newsstand and let the hustle and flow pass me by. I picked up a copy of *Us* magazine and pretended to read a fascinating article about a beautiful, rich person's struggles with life while I studied the coffee shop for signs of danger.

Everything looked normal. Out front, a woman was passing out pamphlets about some prophet. Traffic rolled along the street. A horn blared. I didn't know what I was looking for, but I felt uneasy. It wasn't that I thought Moregoth would know to find me here yet. But Eldrin might.

"Eldrin," I said with a hissing exhale as a second emptiness settled in my chest next to the spot Harold had left behind. Since we'd met there isn't much I hadn't shared with him, and now he was out of reach, if not logistically then philosophically. They say you shouldn't discuss politics, religion, or money among friends, but I'm certain there is no topic more dangerous than the nature of reality and our place in it. Perhaps Rook would have some ideas about what to do next, because I was lost.

I watched a few more people go in and out before coming to the conclusion that I was either a lousy detective, or the coffee shop was nothing more than a coffee shop. Even if it wasn't, I'd be damned if I was going to stand out here any longer. It was freezing and I hadn't slept since the previous night. I may never have been in more need of coffee in my life. I crossed the street, fought past the lady selling her religion, and with flyer in hand made my way through the front door.

Rook was either not here or was one hell of a master of disguise. This early, there were only a handful of people in the place, and none of them was even vaguely dwarfish. In the far corner, a teenager with purple hair was asleep in a chair. By the front window, where hours before I'd been reading *The Dark Lord*, a man sat alone studying a chessboard and rubbing a gray goatee. Against the far wall a businessman in a black suit stood, staring out the window at the street. I moved to the counter where the only other customers, an older bald man and a middle-aged red-haired woman, were placing their orders. She asked for a "Coffee, black," and he ordered, "Tea, Earl Grey, hot."

"Name?" the barista asked.

"Hill. Dixon Hill," the bald man said.

As they sorted out payment, which seemed to confuse the bald man far more than it had any right to do, I did another sweep of the room. The man in the suit was looking at me. Our eyes met and we both glanced quickly away. I pretended to study the flyer while my mind raced. *Had I seen him before? Did he know me? Was he a Sealer in disguise? Or was he simply people watching?* I looked up again. He was staring at the girl with the purple hair now, and seemed as interested in her as he had been in me. That's when I finally focused on the flyer in my hand. The title read "Repent! The Dark Lord Is Coming!" My heart raced. I knew I was being paranoid, but that didn't mean coming here hadn't been a mistake. Too many people knew or could know I frequented this place. I was debating leaving when I heard the words I'd been dreading: "Avery Stewart?"

With a cry of surprise, I spun around. "What do you want?"

The woman behind the counter took a step back and raised an eyebrow. "That's usually my question. I'm gonna assume you want decaf."

I relaxed as I saw it was Kendra, one of the regular baristas. She had curly brown hair, light brown skin, a nice smile, and I'm not ashamed to admit I'd spent many an hour wondering how to ask her out. Based on the look of alarm she was giving me, I thought my chances had taken a pretty big hit. "Sorry, Kendra. I've had a tough morning. Just my usual."

"Right," she said. "Grande, quad, nonfat, one pump, no whip, mocha, extra hot?" I nodded. "By the way, I think you left something behind last time you were here. Maybe a scarf, or *the book* you were reading?"

I thought back to yesterday morning, amazed that it had only been yesterday morning and not a month ago, and shook my head. "I don't think so."

"I'm pretty sure you did," she persisted. "You should check the lost and found closet. It's down the hall just past the bathrooms."

I laughed. It was wonderful that someone was

worried about something as mundane as a lost book or a bit of my clothing. "Thanks, Kendra. I'll get it later."

"I really think you should check *now*," she said, tapping on the side of my cup with each word as she passed it across.

I felt silly arguing with her so I said, "Okay," and prized my cup from her oddly unyielding fingers.

She gave an exasperated sigh and started to say something else, but at that moment the bell over the door tinkled. I turned to see if it was Rook, and found myself staring at two hooded figures silhouetted by the light from the door. My heart leapt to my throat, and I made a sound like "Eeeee!"

If they had been Sealers this story would have ended there, because my panic drove any thought of magic or casting straight out of my mind. Thankfully for the word count of this book, the figure on the right threw her hood back and said, "You seem jumpy, handsome."

It was Valdara. In that moment, as messed up as my life was, she was, without doubt, one of the most beautiful sights I'd ever seen. "Valdara!" I felt a grin lift my cheeks as I rushed forward to give her a hug. "I'm so glad to see you."

The figure on the left cleared his throat. "What about me, kid?"

Drake, looking as much like a jolly grim reaper as ever, also lowered his hood. "Drake!" I exclaimed, wrapping an arm around him also. A ridiculous number of emotions overwhelmed me, but joy and wonder took top billing. I couldn't stop smiling. A few minutes earlier I'd been feeling utterly alone. But here were Valdara and Drake, and, whether logical or not, I believed they could handle anything. "But why are you here? Did you come to visit? And how did you know where to find me?"

They shared a look and then Drake said, "I hate to disappoint you, kid, but we didn't have any idea you'd be here. Rook sent us an urgent message that we were needed at once. He said it was a matter that concerned Trelari's very existence." He looked around. "I mean, apart from that girl's hair being purple, which I assume is the mark of a serious illness, I don't see it."

"He told us to dress inconspicuously," Valdara said, gesturing at their clothing.

I hadn't noticed, but they were both wearing fairly muted outfits, at least for them. It was still cloaks and robes, but Valdara had abandoned her leather and metal gear, and Drake had done a pretty good job of disguising his staff as a traveler's walking stick. Their clothes weren't exactly normal, but this was New York. There's a regular in Times Square who runs around with a guitar, a cowboy hat, boots, and tighty-whities—and nothing else. Apart from the fact that Drake had a serious Rasputin-like beard, and Valdara was, well, Valdara, I didn't think anyone would have looked twice at them—certainly not three times. I leaned in close to Valdara and whispered, "I know you're clever at concealing weapons, but where have you got that crazy battle-ax tucked away?"

"Justice Cleaver?" laughed Valdara. "I left him at home. There is no way to hide him. He won't put up with it."

Drake nodded his agreement. "We've tried! Don't get me wrong, JC has been a huge boon in helping us rout the remnants of the Dark Queen's former army, but it's a blessing to be away from him for a bit. I have never understood the attraction of vows of silence, but I'd take one tomorrow if it would shut him up. That weapon has issues."

Someone at about knee-level let out a frustrated sigh. We all looked down and saw Rook standing next to us, arms crossed and foot tapping with impatience. "We're all goin' to have issues if we don't get you lot out of sight. This was supposed to be a *secret* meetin'! Don't any of you understand the meanin' of the word *inconspicuous*?"

Valdara nodded. "Of course we do. Look!" She gestured to their garments as though this was proof.

He studied Valdara and Drake with a squinted eye. "Super! You've both managed to dress like the hermit on the gatefold of *Led Zeppelin IV*."

Drake leaned over to me and asked, "Is that good or bad?"

I shrugged. "Depends on whether you think Zeppelin represents everything wrong with the progressive rock movement of the '70s, or is one of the most significant and influential bands of all time."

Drake was still puzzling over this when Rook muttered something about "damned fools," grabbed the hems of his and Valdara's robes, and began dragging them toward the back of the coffee shop. I fell in behind, and when we passed the counter Kendra pointed at my coffee and mouthed, *I tried*. I looked down at my cup and saw that she'd drawn a rook next to the words *lost and found*.

Rook led us down the hall past the restrooms, which was a bit strange because the coffee shop was basically my second home and I would have sworn an oath the hallway ended *at* the restrooms. But I couldn't deny there was a door here labeled LOST & FOUND that I didn't recall ever seeing before. He pulled a key from around his neck and held it next to the handle. A keyhole outlined itself in crackling energy. He slipped the key into the lock and turned the handle. The door did not so much swing open as fold in on itself in an increasingly impossible combination of movements.

Beyond was a nicely proportioned room that was part well-used dorm lounge and part Pall Mall private club. The walls were wood paneled and lined with shelves filled with a combination of books, trophies, and odd bric-a-brac. There was a large fireplace that dominated the far corner and a pair of doors I suspected were bathrooms. A mishmash of disreputable

couches and rumpled chairs were scattered strategi-
cally about, and a surprising number of them were
occupied by an equally disreputable and rumpled
collection of people.

"In," ordered Rook.

Valdara, Drake, and I walked inside. Rook followed
behind us as the door silently unfolded back into place.

As soon as the room was sealed again, everyone
gave a thunderous cheer of: "Avery!" They gathered
around us, introducing themselves, shaking hands
and clapping me on the back. I thought I recognized
a few of them as being part of the cosplay group I'd
seen the morning before, but otherwise I didn't know
any of them.

"Looks like everyone knows your name," said
Drake with a chuckle.

"Let's see if they'll return the courtesy," I muttered
under my breath. I raised my hands and my voice.
"Okay, stop. Who are you people and what's going on?"

Rook cleared his throat and raised a bushy eyebrow. "I thought that would be obvious, laddie."

I looked around. Every type and sort of person
was represented: tall, short, thick, thin, dark, light.
But their eyes all had the same washed-out quality I'd
noted in Rook's eyes the first time I met him. It was
something like the way a long-term subworld traveler's eyes fade over time, but there was a depth to
them that gave the feeling of great age. They didn't
look old, but they felt ancient.

"Mysterians," I whispered. I spun about to take them all in. "You are all Mysterians!" I shouted.

"The question is, are you one of us?" a woman dressed in Hylar style asked me.

"Of course he is," Rook said with a bristled brow.

I held up a hand to stop him from defending me too strenuously, and sat heavily in one of the armchairs by the fire. "I think I know what you mean, and the answer is 'yes and no.'"

"Lad!" Rook said with a warning growl.

"Let him say his piece," Drake said with equal violence. "It may answer a number of other questions, like what the hell a Mysterian is. I thought you were from Trelari, Rook."

The dwarf went uncharacteristically quiet at Drake's challenge, and for perhaps the first time since I'd met him, I saw real shame in his face. I looked about at the other Mysterians gathered there. All of them looked like they were from other worlds: Hylar, Earth, Dweorh, and even Orcus. I suspected all of them were merely passing, and that their true forms were hidden. I also suspected that hiding was their greatest skill.

I addressed the woman who'd asked the question about wheter I was one of them. "If you mean am I with you in your struggle against the Administration, then I am. If, however, you are asking me to join your group and hide in the lost and found closet of my neighborhood coffee shop while the Administration hunts down my friends, then the answer is no."

There were a number of cries of protest at this, and Rook said, "That's not fair, Avery! You have no idea what the people in this room have been through."

"No, I don't," I said with a little more venom than my better self would have liked. "But if you all are who I think you are, the true and original peoples of Mysterium, and you have it in your power to stop Moregoth and others like him from turning the power of Mysterium against worlds like Trelari, why haven't you?"

Rook sat down in one of the chairs near me. The excitement that had filled the room on my arrival was gone. The Mysterians hung their heads, and a few mumbled apologies. "It's because we can't," Rook said hoarsely. "It's true we are 'real' Mysterians. In truth, we were merely born with a natural advantage, and learned how to manipulate reality early in our development. We didn't think much about it at the time, and as we learned to travel the worlds we taught others what we thought they could comprehend and use. Some of the people we met seemed to have a greater curiosity about our powers. Most of them were good people, but others were not. Some pleaded with us to take them back to Mysterium with us. They began to call themselves 'mages.' They played on our egos and our innocence. They wanted to learn more, and we were flattered to teach them what we knew." He shook his head and yanked on his beard. "We were fools. When they had learned all they needed, they used our magic and drove us from our homeland. Then, to be sure we couldn't return, these mages wrote us out of the pattern of our own world."

"I understand very little of what you're talking about, Rook," Drake said. "But your people are still alive. Surely there's hope." He put an arm around Valdara. "We fought against great odds and triumphed."

Rook sighed. "You don't understand. The pattern the mages imposed on Mysterium is very powerful, and it is designed to destroy us. We've been hunted through the ages until we're barely a race. We survive in little enclaves like this one on the innerworlds, but always Moregoth and the Sealers are searchin' for us. It's harder for them out in the multiverse—they typically rely on spies and informants—but on Mysterium the pattern gives them ways of sensing our presence. That's why I couldn't help you break into Student Records, Avery. If I'd gone, they'd have found me like that." He snapped his fingers. "You would have been discovered, and I would have been erased from existence."

Something clicked in my head. "You didn't trust me. You've been following me around all this time trying to figure out if I was an Administration plant. I would have thought our time together on Trelari would have convinced you."

"For most of us it did," Rook said, and he cast a squinty glare about at the other Mysterians. "But there was a worry that the entire experiment might be a lure to draw in the last of us. Avery, you don't know how rare you are. Most Mysterium mages simply won't acknowledge the place is corrupt. Look at your friend Eldrin."

"Don't!" I shouted, and the room got very quiet. I shook my head and said softly, "Don't judge him. He's a good person, and . . ." I almost told them about Trelari having potentially displaced their former homeworld at the center of the multiverse, but I did not trust them. I knew nothing about these Mysterians, or how they would react to such news. Hastily I amended what I was going to say. "I . . . I believe he will see the truth in time." I thought about Susan and the T's. "I believe they all will. In the end."

Valdara stepped forward; the crown on her brow glittered in the firelight. "That's fine for you to say, Avery, but what are we going to do about Trelari? If I understand what you're saying, my world is being threatened now!"

"We're going to fight them. Right?" Drake asked.

"Now, let's not be too hasty," one of the Mysterians said.

"Hasty!" Rook boomed. "Try a thousand years too late!"

Other voices were raised in agreement and dissent, and soon the room was filled with the chaos of dozens of arguments being waged simultaneously. I felt tired. I had been expecting this meeting with Rook to put an end to the questions that had been bothering me since my return, but they persisted. I thought I would find allies to help me fight the Administration, but I had not. It was not that I had learned nothing. The Administration had always given me the creeps; now I had objective evidence that they were actually evil. The Mysterians had always been a bit of a mystery; now they were less mysterious. There was knowledge here, but no wisdom. I still felt lost, and certainly no closer to the sort of epiphany that would redefine my understanding of the multiverse and my place in it. Worse, I couldn't be honest about the things that were really bothering me, like Trelari's increased reality or Griswald's key, because I didn't trust the Mysterians either.

As I half listened to Rook bellowing about the need for the Mysterians to grow a spine, it was Harold's last words that kept running through my head. Not the "interesting" that had been for himself, but what he'd said about Socrates. I'd taken enough philosophy at Oxford to know the reference. It was from a text by Laërtius: *There is only one good, namely, knowledge; and only one evil, namely, ignorance.* I had no idea how the passage related to my current situation, but I felt sure it was another link in the chain I was building between the nature of Mysterium's reality and my supposed revelation. But I was too tired to follow it now. I did a quick calculation and realized I hadn't slept in over twenty-four hours. I leaned back in my chair. I was just closing my eyes when a bell rang and a light in the ceiling flashed red.

CHAPTER 20

CONFLICT AT THE COFFEE SHOP

After a second, the bell stopped ringing, but the light continued to flash its silent warning. There was a moment of stunned inaction. Someone shouted, "They've found us?" Someone else yelled something about being trapped like rats, and something else about abandoning ship. The Mysterians surged toward the hidden door that let out into the coffee shop. Rook leapt atop a chair and waved them back. "Quiet!" he ordered in a whispered roar. "The alarm only means someone's in the shop who shouldn't be there. It doesn't mean they're here for us, or that they even know we're here. All we do by goin' out there now is give ourselves away!"

The force of his will drove the other Mysterians back. They stood huddled together. We waited for . . . I don't know how long. Was it a minute? Was it an hour? The looks on the faces of the Mysterians let me know that, at least for them, it lasted an eternity. Fear will do that. At some point, I began to count. I made it to sixty. Something thudded against the hidden door. The sound was muffled, but the impact must have been enormous, because it shook the entire room. This time when the panic came, Rook could not stop it.

There was a great rush of bodies. It broke first toward the door, but then a second blow fell and the Mysterians turned and came back toward where I was still sitting. People stumbled over each other and over me. Some of the Mysterians had enough presence of mind to attempt spells of travel, but their magic only flared and faded. A voice rang out, "They've shielded the room!" More screams and shouts erupted. Prayers were raised to gods whose names I had never heard. They were on the edge of hysterics. I tried to catch what they were saying, but they were all speaking over one another and the words were jumbled and nonsensical. I hoped the gods would be able to sort it out. I couldn't.

As the chaos continued to spread, a third shuddering blow struck. A crack of mystical energy appeared in the door and widened far enough to permit a ray of light from the shop outside to break through into the little room. "Everyone get to the hypocubes!" Rook's voice boomed out above the chaos. "The rest of you, join me. We will hold them off as long as we can."

I had no idea what a hypocube was, but they must have been located in the bathrooms, because that's where most of the Mysterians ran. The press of the crowd and the struggle to get through the doors was awful. By the time the next crashing boom echoed through the room, only three other mages stood with Rook. He looked disgusted, but in a way that let me know it was nothing he hadn't expected.

Drake glanced at the crowd and then back to Valdara and me. "I don't really need to go right now. Do either of you?"

I shook my head, while she looked at the scrum with a sour expression and said, "I hate lines."

Drake smiled at the two of us and put out his hand to help me up. We walked forward to join Rook's thin line of resistance. No words were exchanged between the four of us; we simply waited for the next blow to fall against the door. The dwarf pulled an ax from a piece of folded reality I had taken to be a pocket handkerchief. Drake spread his feet and spun his staff about in a move I remembered fondly from our days together on Trelari. Beside him, Valdara drew a sword and a deadly looking chakram from somewhere beneath her robes.

The Mysterians were right about one thing: there was no magic in the room. I pulled out Griswald's key. It was still crackling with the energy left behind by Harold's passing, and already its shape was shifting to adjust to my desire: maximum carnage.

Through the widening hole, I could see vague shapes moving, perhaps preparing for another assault. I was fascinated to see what was going to happen, but in the detached way one gets watching a cliffhanger scene in the middle of a movie. Somehow, I felt our story wasn't going to end here—or maybe I was simply too tired to care.

There was another shock, and a tremendous roar, and part of the wall collapsed inward. A cluster of Sealers stood in the ragged opening, but down the hall behind them I could see that the battle was already raging in the coffee shop itself. Flashes of light and sparks flew. Kendra leapt into view, swinging a mace. One of the Sealers raised his wand and sent her flying backward into a stand of fair trade coffee. She did not get up again. Rook dove through the hole swinging his ax and shouting, "For the Mysterium!"

With a roar of "Trelari!" Valdara and Drake plunged into the melee.

I followed after them, but I realized I had no battle cry to give. I might have made this about Harold, but I knew it was really about me and my own guilt.

It was an odd experience, fighting a battle with no regard for my own safety. I'd seen others in battle rages and read books where heroes claimed such disconnections, but personally I'd never done anything without having a keen awareness of my own mortal-ity. It felt a bit like watching a play, with the coffee shop beyond as the stage, and the hole in the wall as the proscenium. Around me, a first and then a second and then a third of the defenders fell. They were extras in a war epic.

As we fought, the line of Mysterians waiting to get into the bathroom slowly dwindled behind us. Only a handful of unfortunates remained when our defense truly began to falter. The bald man and the red-haired woman that had been in line in front of me retreated first. The man shouted, "We can't hold them. Fall back! Fall back!"

Valdara, Drake, Rook, and I held a beachhead behind an overturned shelf of coffee table books near the entrance to the hall for as long as we could, but the Sealers were materializing in waves and soon their numbers overwhelmed us. As the bald man and his red-haired friend gave cover, we dove back through the hole that had once been the door. A volley of blasts erupted behind us, and when the dust cleared, the man and the woman were gone.

"There are too many of them," Rook shouted. "They'll overrun us soon!"

He glanced back to the bathrooms and I followed his eyes. All the Mysterians were inside now, but they were jammed in so tightly that the door couldn't close. "We have to give them more time," Valdara said.

A barrage of spells shot through the hole, forcing us to scatter for cover. Drake ducked behind an overstuffed leather couch. He growled, "I can't believe I'm about to say this, but I wish we had your crazy battle-ax."

"I don't mind you saying it to me," Valdara said from where she sat with her back to an upturned table. "Only never let him know. He would never let us forget it." She tried to smile, but winced in pain instead. I could see that her robes were pockmarked with burns from the Sealers' spells.

Drake, his own face streaked with blood, winked. "Don't worry, it was a moment of weakness."

Rook came scuttling over from wherever he'd taken shelter to crouch beside me. His clothes were rent and torn, and a massive burn blackened his right side. "There are only about a dozen or so Mysterians left in the bathrooms," he grunted. "Everyone ready for one last push?"

"Hell, yes!" Drake said. "Let's get this thing over with and get to a proper bar."

Valdara ran the bloodied edge of her sword across her cloak to clean it. "Anytime. I've just been waiting for you boys to catch your breath."

We readied ourselves to spring and then something odd happened. The volley of fire stopped. Moregoth stepped into view. I would like to say that I was overcome with elemental rage at the sight of him, but the truth is, I was too empty for righteous anger. I did want to destroy him, but more in the way people instinctively lash out at snakes or squash cock-roaches. He was vermin, and he needed exterminat-ing. I channeled as much power as I could into the key, and stepped forward.

Someone, I think Valdara, shouted, "Avery! Get down!" Ignoring the plea, I pointed the key at More-goth and unleashed every bit of hate and power I had. I saw his eyes widen with surprise. The room blazed with light as my own spell was joined by a dozen or more bolts of energy that arced out from the ranks of Sealers behind him. Even had I wanted to defend myself, there was nowhere I could go, no time for me to get out of the way or to weave a pattern of protec-tion. I waited. As long as Moregoth died first it would be a satisfactory exchange.

A fraction of a heartbeat later the room detonated with light and sound and heat. I was blown off my feet and thrown backward into the wall. The impact knocked the key out of my hand, and I slid to the floor. My ears were ringing and my head was spinning, but I was alive. When I could focus my eyes again, I saw a shimmering wall of blue energy had interposed itself between Moregoth's men and us. I glanced at Rook. He shrugged. "Not my doin', kid."

Moregoth must have spun the wall at the last second. He had saved both of our lives, and it really pissed me off. I picked up the key, staggered to my feet, and walked forward again. "I thought you were a true believer, Moregoth," I snarled. "I thought you longed for the sweet embrace of death. But now that it's here you hide like a worm. How disappointing."

Moregoth pushed his long black hair away from his ghostly pale face and smiled thinly. He held up his wand. It wasn't glowing. "Death knows I have no fear of it. I had no part in this. Watching your body burn into the ether would have made my own demise all that more enjoyable."

I scanned the Sealers, but they looked as confused as I did. "It was me, kid," Drake said as he pulled himself to his feet. He removed a leather strap from where it had been wrapped about the top of his staff. Beneath it, the Crystal of Righteousness shone with a blue light of such purity it seared my eyes. I put up a hand to shield them. "When did you get your magic back?" I asked.

"About thirty seconds ago."

"That's great, Drake," I said, and I was happy he had managed to find his faith again. I was also relieved, because this meant I could go back to killing Moregoth. "Drop the wall so I can deal with this maniac once and for all?"

"I can't do that, kid."

I was confused. "Do you mean you don't know how to drop the wall?"

He shook his head. "No. I know how to drop the spell. I mean I won't."

My anger flared anew. "Why not?"

"Maybe because he doesn't want to have to explain to Sam and Ariella how he let you kill yourself," Valdara said sharply. "Of all the half-witted . . ."

Drake shot Valdara a stern look, and she fell silent. "That's not why, Avery," he growled. "Frankly, if you want to go out killing some vampire wannabe, that's your business." He looked Moregoth up and down with a raised eyebrow. "Personally, I don't think he's worth it. What I won't do is sacrifice myself, or Valdara, or Rook, to satisfy your need for revenge."

"Much appreciated," Rook said with a tip of an imaginary cap. He glowered through the wall at Moregoth. "Until next time, punk. Oh, and get a haircut. You look like a damned hippie!"

The dwarf tried to grab my arm and pull me back toward the bathroom, but I shook him off. "No, Rook. I'm not leaving until he's dead."

Drake leaned on his staff. "It's not that simple, kid. If you stay, I stay."

"And if he stays, I stay," Valdara declared, moving to stand next to him.

The two of them looked at Rook. The dwarf looked between them. "What? They're both annoyin' as hell. I say let them blow each other up if that's what they want." They kept staring at him. He rolled his eyes. "Fine, if they stay, I also stay." He shook a finger at them. "But you both owe me a drink. Now, can we get out of here? People who wear ankhs creep me out."

This time, Valdara and Rook both put their arms around me and tried to lead me to the door.

I pulled away, and pointed the key at Drake. "Drop the wall!" I shouted.

"No, Avery," he said. "I will not help you die today. Not for that creature."

With a wordless cry of blind rage, I launched myself at the wall. With a crack of power, it threw me back. I rose and charged again. Again, it threw me back. I struggled to my feet a third time, but my head was ringing like a bell and my legs gave out before I could take two steps.

Valdara knelt beside me as I tried to rise again. "Avery, please," she pleaded.

Her voice in my ear sapped the last of my anger. It was futile. The only way to get through the wall would be to kill Drake, and I was not so far gone as that. I lay on the ground and wailed with frustration. "Don't you understand? I have a chance to do something good for once. Let me do this for Harold." I looked up at her through eyes wet with unshed tears. "For you."

"I understand you want to make amends for your past, Avery, but this is not the way," she said, and then added, "It's too easy."

Behind her Drake said softly, "Valdara . . ."

She looked at him sharply, and he backed away, hands raised. When she spoke again there was a hard edge to her voice. "You will have your chance to balance your sins, Avery Stewart, but if you die today, then you will not have paid your debts. You owe the world more than this. You owe me more than this. Now, get up and let's get out of here before you get all of us killed."

As always, she was right. I had been thinking only of myself. Typical, really. I held out my arms, and Valdara and Drake lifted me to my feet. Rook was waiting by the women's bathroom, urging us forward. "Come on. Come on. There's still one hypocube in here. Let's get out before Mr. Creepy lights some incense and starts tryin' to call upon the spirit of whatever dead animal he's got stuck on top of his head."

We were nearly to Rook when Moregoth's hacking laugh cut across the room. "This is just sad."

I stopped and tried to turn. At first, Valdara and Drake would not let me go. "Avery . . ." Drake growled.

"I'm fine," I reassured him. Something in the coolness of my voice must have convinced them I was not going to go bashing my head into walls again, because they let me go. I turned back to Moregoth. He was standing in a melodramatic pose, his head tilted to one side, staring at me through Drake's protective wall. He'd put on a pair of heavily tinted glasses, but even so, I could see by the lines at the sides of his eyes that the light was bothering him. "You have something to say?" I asked.

"Rather a question," he replied. I opened my arms in invitation. "It's only that I am curious," he purred, stroking his chin with the polished nail of his forefinger. "How does a man that once ruled worlds as a god allow himself to be dictated to by these . . . shadows? You were their Dark Lord. Now, they treat you like a servant. Fight. Don't fight. Run. Fetch. Beg. Kneel. Die. It's pathetic."

"Pathetic?" I gave a low chuckle. "That's rich coming from someone who dresses like a mortician from a clown college."

Valdara, Drake, and Rook all laughed, and even some of the Sealers seemed to have a hard time keeping a straight face, but Moregoth gave no reaction. After a moment's pause to let the laughter fade, he looked down his long nose at me. "I tell you that your 'so-called friends' are treating you like a dog, and your response is to say that I dress funny? To quote you, 'How disappointing.'"

"I could come up with some better insults, if you want," Rook grunted. "That you'd leave the house wearin' that shirt tells me you must be—"

I held up my hand, and the dwarf stopped. "He's right. I would hate for someone to judge me for my utter lack of style, or you for looking like an extra in a Men Without Hats video." I walked slowly back to the glowing wall. Moregoth's sneer remained fixed in place, but I wasn't trying to reach him. I was looking through him, talking directly to his men. He was beyond redemption. I was betting not all of the Sealers were. "It may not be right to judge you by your fashion sense, but I do think it's fair to judge you by your actions. You and your masters have spent your lives denying the rightful people of Mysterium a place on their own world, and now you've turned your powers on the innocent people of Trelari. You are small and mean."

Moregoth hung his head like a marionette with its strings cut, then he straightened himself up and clapped slowly and softly. "What a fine speech: florid, emotional, and so deliciously indulgent. Tell us, Mr. Stewart, now that you have become a true believer in the 'cause,' will you be giving up your privileged existence to stand shoulder-to-shoulder with all those poor, pitiful wretched Mysterians lost in the subworlds?"

I lowered my voice so he had to break his pose and lean closer to the wall to hear me. "You may find it incomprehensible that someone from Mysterium would desire freedom for everyone in the multiverse, but I'm not alone. Every day more and more mages are realizing the way we've been treating other worlds—including, it appears, the Mysterians—is not right. You may find it laughable, but I intend to do everything I can to bring you and your masters down, whatever that means for the Mysterium I've known."

"Then perhaps I should start calling you Dark Lord again," he said with a voice raised loud enough so that everyone could hear him. "It was precisely this same strain of delusional self-righteousness that led you to try and 'help' the people of Trelari. We all know how that turned out."

That struck a nerve. I took a breath to calm myself. "You may think it was a failure, but Trelarians do not and neither do I. The fight for their freedom will become the rallying cry of a new generation of mages."

He shrugged indifferently. "Perhaps a few misguided souls will follow you . . ."

"More than you know, Moregoth!"

"Less than you might wish, Dark Lord," he said with a chuckle.

I could tell he was building up to something. Some secret I didn't know that he thought would break my will. It was written in the rigid anticipation of his body, and in the cruel way the ends of his mouth were turned up. I suddenly felt weary of bantering with him. "Say what you need to, Moregoth. We have places to go, and you have yet another failure to report."

He gave another shrug. "Knowing how heartbroken you were at the loss of your pet, I had intended to spare you any more suffering, but if you insist . . ."

"I do."

"Have you wondered how we found you so quickly?" he asked as he inspected his nails.

It was a good question. On reflection, it did seem terribly convenient that the Administration would find Rook's secret meeting place on the day I first came to it. A suspicion crept into my mind, and a cold prickle of fear ran up my spine.

He flicked away an invisible speck of something.

"We got a tip. A loyal mage uncovered information about where a dangerous group of renegades would be meeting. He was worried his friend might have fallen in with a bad crowd." He leaned forward and lowered his voice to a rasping whisper. "Eldrin really does care about your well-being, Dark Lord."

"You lie."

He shook his head, an almost imperceptible movement. "You know it's true."

I didn't know it was true, but the fact I didn't was almost worse. The key was in my hand before I'd made a conscious decision to attack, but Valdara was at my side even faster. This time she gave me no choice. Wrapping her arms around my body, she carried me back to the door to where Rook and Drake were waiting.

"We are at war, Dark Lord, and they are the enemy," Moregoth called out. "If they are not destroyed, Mysterium and all the wisdom of the ages will be lost. You know it, I know it, and Eldrin knows it. It isn't too late to rejoin us, your true friends, and take your rightful place in creation."

As Valdara pulled me backward through the door, I shouted, "I will kill you, Moregoth!"

He gave me a mocking little wave goodbye. "Remember this day! It's your first as a slave." His hideous, rasping laughter followed me into the bathroom.

CHAPTER 21

HYSTERIA IN THE HYPOCUBE

Even after the door closed, I continued to struggle with Valdara. "I'll kill you!" I shouted. "I will find you and I will kill you!"

"I like where your head is at, kid," Drake said wearily. "But I don't think he can hear you anymore."

I knew he was talking sense, but I wanted to hold on to my anger. The only alternative was despair. I thrashed about in Valdara's arms, trying to break free, but it was like trying to wrestle a stone. Eventually, I wore myself out and was reduced to cursing. When I ran out of abuse to hurl and energy to struggle, Valdara pulled me into a hug.

"I'm sorry about your friend, Avery."

Rook poked his head out of the bathroom stall and grunted, "I'm sorry also, because right now I need help fixin' this hypocube, and the two of you seem intent on dancin' with each other instead."

I'm not sure I even heard him. I was too consumed with thoughts of Eldrin and Dawn, and whether they were on the Administration's side. When I finally shook myself out of my reverie, I was confused to see that some amount of time had passed. Rook and Valdara were standing by the door of one of the metal-walled stalls. It had been painted a bright blue and clashed hideously with the warm earth tones of the rest of the bathroom. The dwarf was cursing volubly. I went to Drake with the idea of asking him what was going on and when we were planning on leaving, but he looked awful. He was leaning against the tiled wall; his face was pale and sweat was beaded on his forehead.

"Are you okay?" I asked.

He nodded slowly. "Just tired, kid. I haven't had to hold a ward for this long in years. I guess I'm a little—" he took a series of shallow breaths "—a little out of practice. Besides, now that you and Moregoth aren't engaged in philosophical discussion, he seems real intent on breaking through."

"Maybe he needs to go to the bathroom," I suggested.

Drake tried to smile, but another wave of fatigue seemed to come over him. His head drooped until he seemed to be hanging from his staff. I noticed the light of the crystal was not as bright as it had been, and seemed to be wavering: now dimmer, and then brighter again.

I moved to stand next to Valdara. She was looking down at Rook, who was kneeling in the bathroom stall, but instead of a toilet, the interior consisted of a small square chamber with an angled control console set in one wall. The controls themselves seemed to be random to the point of noncoherence. There was an old-style, green-colored oscilloscope screen surrounded by an odd assortment of levers, buttons, switches, rheostats, a manual typewriter, and what looked to be a set of faucet handles.

Rook gave another curse and pounded at something on the underside of the console with the flat end of his ax.

"I don't want to interrupt any subtle adjustments you may be making to . . . whatever this is," I shouted over Rook's hammering. "But Drake doesn't look good. I don't think he'll be able to hold his ward much longer."

"I'm fine," he sighed, but then his legs sort of folded and he slid down the wall to the floor.

Valdara leapt to his side. She put a hand to his forehead and her brow wrinkled with worry. "Right!" she yelled. "That's quite enough banging about, Rook. We have to leave now, whether this contraption of yours is ready or not." With surprising ease, Valdara lifted Drake to his feet and walked him to the stall.

"Fine!" Rook grunted irritably. "I was only doin' some fine tunin' anyway."

He got up and sat down in a swivel chair I hadn't remembered seeing before. With the chair and the console there was precious little space left. I was still trying to decide where to stand when I felt Valdara's hand in my back. She pushed me through the door and crowded in behind. I heard the door shut and lock. I found myself squished between Valdara and Drake on one side and Rook's pilot's chair on the other. The ceiling also seemed to have dropped and the floor risen, forcing us all to hunch uncomfortably. It made me wish I had taken yoga at some point in my life.

"Rook!" I said, trying to turn around without jabbing my elbow into anyone. "What is this place?"

"It's a hypocube," he said as though that word by itself answered the question.

Drake gave a long drawn-out sigh and his head flopped to one side. The light of the crystal wavered, flared one last time, and then went out altogether. There was a loud explosion from outside.

"I think we're going to have company!" I shouted.

"Don't worry! I've got this under control. Get ready for extradimensional travel, the Mysterian way!" Rook said with unaccustomed enthusiasm.

He rubbed his hands together, threw a few

switches, twisted a couple of knobs, and pulled up the stopper on the faucet. There was a rhythmic wheezing sound that seemed to echo through every fiber of my being, a sound which I could imagine was heard across the multiverse. When it stopped, there was a deeper, resonant boom of finality.

"Was that it?" I asked expectantly. "Where are we?"

"I imagine we're in a coffee shop on Bleecker between Carmine and Leroy," Rook replied irritably. "It didn't work."

"What do you mean it didn't work?" asked Valdara.

"It's not my fault," said Rook with a scratch of his tousled beard. "It should be workin'. There's not enough power. I think it's Moregoth. He must be interferin' with the time-space pattern, or the energy-flux matrix."

"Either that or you forgot to recharge," I said dryly, and pointed to a flashing light next to label that read in big, bold print PLEASE RECHARGE ME.

Rook slapped a palm down on top of the alarm. "We need to stay focused, people! It's clear we've been sabotaged."

An explosion shook the interior of the hypocube. I could hear shouts outside. "We are running out of time, Rook!"

"This ship is tough. It'll take 'em a while to get inside," Rook said confidently, but then a second blast rocked the chamber and he said less confidently, "But not forever."

"What do you need besides raw magical power?" I asked, fingering the key in my pocket.

Rook pushed some other buttons, flipped switches, and twisted a few faucet handles before grunting, "Basically, that's it."

I pulled out the key. There was still a little magic left in it. I concentrated on that and added as much of my own strength as I could. I focused on trying to pool the magical energy into a concentrated burst, and then I touched the key to the control console. It morphed again, stretching and flattening. When it was roughly the shape of a USB-c connector, something inside the hypocube latched on to the source of magic and devoured it. The engines of the hypocube, or whatever passed for them, activated with a lurch and knocked me backward.

"Here we go!" shouted Rook. "It's easy sailin' from here."

Despite Rook's assurances, traveling by hypocube was damned uncomfortable. It wasn't that you suffered the same type of disorienting brain-inverting sensation traveling by portal gave you. In fact, after launch, the inside of the craft was so quiet I could not have told you if we were moving or not. Instead, the hypocube was uncomfortable in the same way I imagine traveling by clown car would be uncomfortable.

It wasn't the design of the craft itself that was odd. The chamber was square, with Rook's pilot's seat and control panel set at one end, and a pair of bench seats facing each other across a central aisle that ran down the back of the craft to the door. By all rights, there should have been enough space for us to stretch out and get a little sleep, but the four of us filled it to an almost absurd extent. It seemed no matter how carefully we arranged ourselves, we were always elbowing each other, or trodding on each other's feet, or . . .

"Excuse me," Valdara said as she tried to move past me along the aisle to sit next to Drake. Although he was conscious, that's about all he was.

I stood to let her pass, but standing only seemed to make things worse. Now that I was up, we were pressed against each other like commuters in a Tokyo subway car. I had nowhere to put my hands that didn't seem wildly inappropriate. I took a step back and somehow wound up in Drake's lap even though I could have sworn he'd been on the opposite side of the aisle a second ago. He grunted and I sprang away, launching my head into the low ceiling. With a hiss of pain, I stumbled into the back of Rook's pilot's chair.

"Dammit!" the dwarf barked. "Would you be still? It's like you've never traveled by hypocube before."

I rubbed at my forehead and stated the obvious. "None of us have ever traveled by hypocube, Rook. Until ten minutes ago I didn't know a hypocube was a thing, and even now I'm not sure what that thing is."

Though Rook was turned away from us, the stillness of his body let me know that I'd made him think. He scratched the back of his head. "Oh, well, that explains it."

The three of us looked at each other. By silent agreement, Valdara asked the next obvious question. "What exactly is a hypocube?"

The dwarf took a break from fiddling with the craft's controls, and swiveled his seat around to look at us. "This is a technological marvel, that's what it is. The hypocube can travel anywhere in the multiverse."

"And . . ." I asked when he began to return to his controls.

"And that's a miracle, that is, laddie!"

"Why not use a transport circle?" I asked. "Seems a lot easier and—" I gave a grunt of pain as Valdara kicked me in the shin trying to cross her legs "—a lot more comfortable."

The dwarf bristled his brows. "To use a transport circle you have to know where you're goin'. With a hypocube you can travel to places you don't even know you want to go."

"Does that mean you don't know where we're going?" Valdara asked, which I thought was entirely reasonable.

"That's not what I said," he growled, pointing a shaking finger at her. "I know exactly where we are goin', just—" he paused and stroked his beard thoughtfully "—not where we might end up along the way." We all puzzled over his answer, and it gave Rook enough time to turn back around to his controls.

"Well, you might have made the thing bigger," Valdara said irritably. She was having a hell of a time trying to find a place to put Drake's staff that wouldn't hit someone in the face.

"There would be plenty of space if you three would stop moving," Rook grunted.

"It's hard to stop moving when you have someone else's elbow in your ribs or their stick knocking you in the side of the head," I countered, and then shouted, "Valdara, put that damned staff down! That's the third time you've nearly brained one of us with it."

"Don't you think I want to? It's impossible!" she shouted back. To demonstrate, she showed me that no matter which way she positioned the staff it simply didn't seem to fit inside the cube, which was odd as we were in the cube, and so, presumably, was the staff.

Rook spun back around and seized Valdara's wrist. "Stop," he said, and it was the softest, calmest voice I'd ever heard the dwarf use. "I want you to close your eyes and sit still for thirty seconds. I will count for you."

And he did. When he got to zero he asked us to open our eyes, but only after he exacted a promise that no matter what we saw, we would not move. When we opened our eyes again I found myself alone on a bench that looked easily large enough to sleep on. Valdara sat comfortably opposite me. Drake was stretched out across the bench with his head in her lap. The staff leaned casually against the wall next to them.

"What just happened?" I asked a fraction of a second before Valdara could.

"If you can change the size of the cube, then why make it small to begin with?" she asked.

"I can't," Rook answered.

"But . . . wait . . . what?" I countered with my typical eloquence, and gestured about at the obviously expanded interior.

"It's not me, it's the hypocube," the dwarf said.

"You keep saying that word, but what does it mean?" I asked, my frustration boiling over.

"A hypocube is an enterdimensional space . . ."

"Like Avery's piece of folded reality?" Valdara asked.

Rook shook his head. "It is the opposite of Avery's piece of folded reality. Folded reality is an extradimensional phenomenon. You take a small piece of real space and you fold it around a pocket of extradimensional reality so you have more space than you should. The hypocube is an enterdimensional construct, which means you take a large piece of reality and cram it into a very small extradimensional space, like this cube." Rook raised a finger to the ceiling, which seemed to lower to meet his hand. "What is more, hypocubes are dimensionally aggressive."

"I know what both those words mean, but when you put them together it sounds like a lot of gibberish," I said with a sigh.

"It means . . ." he started to say, but then stopped himself and thought about it a little more. "You see . . ." He stopped again, discarding his second explanation also. After a time, he tried again. "All you need to know is the more room you need, the smaller the hypocube gets. So, the more you move around, the less room you'll find you have."

"You're saying it's smaller on the inside than it is on the outside?" Valdara asked in a voice that was basically begging Rook to tell her she was wrong.

"Exactly," he said with relish. "So, stay still and let me figure out where we're goin' on the way to the place we want to reach."

He began to swivel back to the control panel, but I was having none of it. I grabbed at the arm of Rook's chair to stop him, found it was much closer than I'd judged, and nearly decked him in the process. He rolled his eyes and gestured for me to sit down. I did. I closed my eyes and counted to ten. When I finished my countdown, I opened my eyes and found the dimensions of the cube had returned to "normal." Whatever that was.

"I think I understand what you're saying," I said calmly. "But it makes no sense. Why in the world would you make a construct that is always fighting you for space?"

"He's right," Valdara said. "Why build something that might shrink by a couple feet simply because you need it?"

"Or have a sudden desire to stretch?" I suggested.

Rook fixed us with his sternest stare. "How else would you geniuses propose to make a hypocube?"

This was a stumper, and I decided it made sense to abandon further questions about the hypocube to ask him something more pressing. "You are a Mysterian . . ."

Rook sat back in his chair. "Yes, I'm a Mysterian. I thought we'd established that already."

"Then I want an answer to the question I asked back in your coffee klatch. Why haven't you all done something about what's going on at the university?"

He bristled his brow. "We did answer—"

"No!" I said sharply. "All you said was you'd been defeated. That's an excuse, not a reason."

The dwarf fiddled with the end of his beard nervously. "You have beliefs about what Mysterians are and are not, and about what they can and canna' do. I may be a Mysterian, and we may have some clever tricks left around from the old days like the cubes, but as a race we are only a shadow of what we once were. We are hunted in our own homeland. We are reduced to meetin' in back rooms of coffee shops. And you saw what happened when those bloody Administration goons came. Rather than fight, most of my people skulked back into the shadow of subworlds like rats."

"But you created Mysterium. Your reality has to be stronger than these usurpers! Why can't we use that raw power to fight them?"

He gestured about in wild frustration. "See, this is what I'm talkin' about. You university-educated mages think you know so much about magic, but you know nothing. When you were on Trelari your reality was much stronger than everyone else's. Why didn't you simply march in and impose your will? After all, Vivian was *only* a subworlder."

"It's not the same," I protested. "My spell was in progress and she had—"

"The key!" Rook shouted. "Do you think it's any different in Mysterium? Do you think there aren't magical constructs in place to keep things ordered the way the Administration wants?" He waved a dismissive hand, and mumbled bitterly, "They don't teach you anythin' at that school. Nothin' of importance. You're all fools. Powerful, but fools."

His critique of my education reminded me of Harold's words to me: ignorance was the true evil. The problem was, I didn't know how to fight it. Every time I learned something new, it only led to more questions. I sat back in my seat, at least as far as the constantly shifting walls of the cube would allow. "If the Mysterians aren't the answer, then why bring the three of us to that bloody coffee shop in the first place?" I asked. "What was the point, and where, exactly, are you taking us?"

"I thought I'd already explained," he said impatiently. "I'm not takin' you anywhere, the cube is takin' you—"

"I know, I know," I said, nearly slamming my fist into the wall. "The cube is taking us where it thinks we need to be to get to where we want to go."

"Exactly!"

"But where is that?"

"Back to the Mysterians, of course," he said as though I was daft for even asking.

"You just said your race was defeated! You said you didn't have the power to break the Administration's hold on things! You said we would find no answers in the Mysterians of today!" I punctuated each of these points by thrusting an accusing finger at him.

"You're catchin' on fast, laddie. We are, we don't, and you won't," he said with a big grin. "But we were and we did. I needed you to see what we've become so you don't do anythin' hasty before we can become what we were again."

I never got the chance to tell him how daft I thought all that sounded, because an alarm started blaring. Rook turned back to his control panel with a curse. "Dammit! I should've been flyin' instead of talkin' to you. Now we're off course!"

He was staring at the little green screen and furiously manipulating two levers and a couple of pedals. I glanced over his shoulder and saw the display was filled by swirling shifting green blobs, kind of like a

dynamic Rorschach's test. Either he was seeing something in its shifting shapes I couldn't, or we were
flying toward two rhinos waltzing with a giraffe.

"How can we be off course when you said you
couldn't control how the thing took us to wherever
it was you wanted to go?" Valdara shouted over the
alarm.

"Because . . ." he said, shouted a few more curse
words as he wrestled with the levers, and then bellowed, "Shut up and brace yourselves."

I have, thankfully, never been in a plane crash,
but from what I've seen of them in disaster movies
there are a lot of cues to let you know you're crashing. Usually, the plane is rattling and the engines
are howling and you're being jostled and thrown
about. In the hypocube, all was calm. Well, almost
everything. There was the blaring klaxon of the
alarm, and Rook, who was cursing and shouting,
but other than those indicators we might have been
sitting down to tea. At least, that was true until
Rook shouted one last expletive, and the hypocube
gave a shuddering lurch and began tumbling end
over end, sending us rattling about from wall to
ceiling to wall to floor. It was like getting stuck in
the spin cycle of a washing machine, which isn't
as much fun as it looks in all those videos college
students post.

For a few seconds, it seemed like the rolling and
turning would last forever, but it didn't. The cube

began to slow, hung on its edge, which was the worst because it meant we were all sent crashing into a battered pile along on the floor, then teetered and fell onto its side. We lay sprawled on the roof of the craft. All of us that is, except Rook, who, being strapped into the pilot's chair was hanging upside down, his bright orange beard flapping in his face like a veil.

"Before anyone asks anythin', I have two things to say," he barked. "No, that isn't supposed to happen, and I want everybody to close their eyes at once."

I did, but only after taking a mental picture of the dwarf I hoped would last a lifetime. I listened as he counted down from thirty. When I opened my eyes again the hypocube had realigned itself with the orientation of our new reality. Rook and his chair and the controls and the benches and the door and everything else was right-side-up again, although the three of us were still jumbled together on the floor.

"What happened? Where are we?" Drake groaned from the bottom of the pile.

"I don't have a clue," Rook answered. "Why don't we find out?"

He pushed a couple of switches and the door slid open. The compartment was flooded with a brilliant light. When at last we blinked away the shadows, we saw three men, about Rook's height, standing in the door peering in at us. They were wearing matching blue hats and blue coats. "Who the hell are you?" Rook asked.

"We represent the Policeman's Guild," they said in unison.

"We're here to welcome you to Munchkinland," the first man said happily.

"And cite you for illegally parking in a house-crashing zone," the second man added just as cheerily, and handed me a yellow slip of paper.

I gave it to Rook at once. "Your cube, your ticket."

"Is this some kind of joke?" he growled. "All it says is, 'You missed.'"

A taller shadow moved in front of the open door. The three little men glanced nervously over their shoulders and scattered. A woman's voice said, "No, the joke is that I'm supposed to be Dorothy. If I click my heels three times will you take me back home to Kansas?"

I knew that voice. "Vivian?!" I shouted.

She leaned her head through the door. "Hey, Avery. Nice of you to join me."

My heart leapt in my chest, and I leapt to my feet. This was unfortunate, because the hypocube chose that moment to lower itself three feet. My forehead smashed into the ceiling. I saw stars and a primly dressed woman riding a bicycle through a cyclone as the world rolled over and went black.

CHAPTER 22

WHEN MONKEYS FLY

I woke to sweet air, birdsong, and Technicolor skies. I was lying on soft grass beneath the overhanging branches of an apple tree, my head was resting on something soft and warm, and I had a killer headache. I had no idea where I was, and only a vague inclination as to how I had gotten there.

A hand pressed a cool cloth to my forehead and I followed the slender arm up to see Vivian smiling down at me with those fantastical gold-ringed green eyes of hers. "Hello."

"Vivian?" I murmured, then realized what I was saying and tried to sit up with a shouted, "Vivian!"

I got about halfway there before the pain in my

head forced me back down. I gave a pitiful groan. "What happened?"

She shot me an impish smile. "Apparently, you were so excited to see me you tried to exit the hypocube headfirst, which would have been fine, but you also decided to skip the door and go straight through one of the walls. I've heard of people losing their heads with excitement, but I didn't think that expression was meant to be taken so literally."

"Ha ha . . ." I mumbled as little electric jolts of pain shot through my right eye. I closed my eyes again. "Is this a dream or are you real?"

"Can't it be both?"

I half opened one eye and shot her a bleary glare. She adopted an expression of exaggerated innocence. "Since you are intent on being so serious, we are seriously in Baum's world, or a reflection of it, and Valdara, Drake, and Rook are all seriously here." She wrung out her cloth and gestured behind her. "They're down the road trying to get that traveling cabinet of Rook's working again."

"And you're Dorothy?" I asked with a chuckle. "Don't tell me you have a little dog too."

This provoked a snort of exaggerated disgust. "Idiot."

"Yes, I am." I carefully sat up. "And I was starting to worry I would never have a chance to tell you how much of an idiot I am, and how sorry I am about what happened to you on Trelari and after we returned. I should never have left you alone."

She laughed, a lovely sound that sparked memories of our brief time together, both in Mysterium and Trelari. "You're apologizing to me? I'm the one that seduced you, stole from you, and then nearly got you killed. If anyone should be apologizing—"

"Seduced me?" I interrupted. "I like the sound of that. I was seduced. I was *seduced*." I gave her my cheekiest smile. "Nice."

This earned an eye roll. "Really? I'm baring my soul, and that's what you choose to focus on?"

I thought about it for a half second. "Yes."

"Men," she muttered, but somehow it came out sounding an awful lot like *idiot*.

I drew an invisible halo atop my head. "I will try to be good, but only if you promise not to apologize. Without you, I never would have questioned what I did in Trelari. I would be living, quite contentedly, certain in the knowledge that I was justified in being the center of the universe."

"And now?" she asked.

I thought about everything I had been through and learned since I followed her back to Trelari. How differently I viewed the worlds beyond the boundaries of Mysterium after being forced to live with the people there, and to watch them die. I had no idea how to put any of it into words. I did my best and, as usual, my best was not great. "You changed everything. It's all more . . . complicated and . . . painful."

"I'm sorry."

"No, no. As usual, I'm saying what I think I want to say, but it isn't translating well. What I mean is . . ."

I looked around, trying to find inspiration. We were sitting on a slight rise in the shade of a grove of apple trees. Nearby, a stream babbled its way under a bridge. A road paved in bright yellow bricks ran up to, over, and then away from the bridge. The colors were so much brighter than in Mysterium. The sky was a perfect blue, the grass brilliantly green, and the little flowers that dotted the hillside were an incandescent orange. It was all so lovely. Taking a deep breath, I spread my arms to embrace the scene. "Before you, I never would have noticed this place. It would not have occurred to me that a world this far from Mysterium could be worth my notice. Before you, the rest of the multiverse was a place of shadows and half-lives, only worthwhile as far as it could advance my magic." I caught her eyes with mine and smiled. "I suppose what I'm saying is, thank you."

She smiled briefly, and then began an intense study of the hem of her dress. "I don't think Valdara and Drake feel the same."

I hadn't thought about that, and when I did, I worried at the reception they'd given her. The fact that she was here alone, and they were wherever they were, gave me some answers as to how they'd treated her. "I'm sorry if they weren't . . . welcoming."

She shrugged, a motion that drew her body away from me. "It isn't their fault."

"That may be, but if they accepted me I'm sure they'll do the same for you. Maybe I should talk to them."

"Please don't."

I thought about arguing, but said nothing. We went back to silently contemplating the view. Eventually, I struck up the courage to ask the one question that had been nagging at me since the night we returned from Trelari. "You can tell me it's none of my business, but I have to ask—how did you get here? I put you to bed, and the next day you were gone. What happened between then and now?"

There was a long pause. I could see she didn't want to answer. Her whole body stiffened at the question, but then she took a deep breath and answered anyway. "The Administration came that night. They . . . they took me away somewhere and questioned me. They . . ." Vivian wrapped her arms around her body and shivered.

"I can imagine."

"No, Avery," she whispered. "You can't."

I thought about my experiences beneath the Student Records building, and wondered what other terrors might be waiting in even darker corners of the university. "You're right. Did they banish you out here?"

She shook her head back and forth like someone

coming out of a trance. "No. I think they would have kept me forever. They were fascinated by the pattern of my reality. They had a machine . . ." Her voice broke at the memory. "A machine that could unspool me, record me, and put me back together. They did it over and over again, day after day."

I knew exactly what she was describing. The machine was called a Pattern Deconstructor. As far as I knew, it was only used on nonliving or animal "specimens" from subworlds after researchers were done with every other test. It was invariably painful, and often fatal. I swallowed. I had no words to express the mixture of anger and pity I was feeling, and having given and extracted the promise not to apologize anymore, I tried to draw the conversation away from the horrors of Vivian's capture. "But you managed to get free of them. How?"

"I can't explain it, Avery. They were holding me in a shielded cell. I could feel no spark of magic. I knew there was no use even trying to cast, but then one night I had a vision I would escape."

She paused in her story, as though waiting for a reaction, but I didn't understand the significance. I pursed my lips and said hesitantly, "And so you knew you were going to escape, because you divined that you were going to escape?"

"No. No." She shook her head. "Don't you see? My premonitions are not natural. I need a source of magical energy to access my divination powers. The visions meant I was tapping into a hidden source of magical energy. After realizing I had access to magic, I focused on the images I was receiving in my visions. It took me a while to decipher them, but in the end, I figured out they were showing me how to travel."

"It was a pattern for a portal circle?"

"Nothing like that," she chuckled grimly. "I'm afraid you'd find the method crude in the extreme. I focused my mind and wished to be somewhere else, and I was. More or less."

Two days ago, I would have called her story impossible. Now all I could think was it sounded very similar to the magic I'd been performing lately. But then, she had done it without Griswald's key. *How?* There were a lot of things I didn't know about Vivian, about where she came from, about how she came to study at Mysterium, about her connection to Griswald and the Triflers. Questions I had always intended to ask if I ever got the chance. Now that she was here, none of the answers seemed that important. "What do you mean, 'more or less'?" I asked.

She hesitated before answering. "The path hasn't been . . . direct. There have been dozens of worlds between that first jump and here."

A sudden, horrible thought struck me. "Vivian, how far out into the subworld did you go?" She didn't answer, but once again began fidgeting with the edge of her dress. I took her hand and pulled it away. She looked up. "Vivian? How long have you been away from Mysterium?"

"I don't know! I don't know!" she shouted, and then in a weary voice, "It's been a long time. I stopped keeping track when I passed the second century."

"Over two hundred years," I murmured. Even for Mysterians that is a long time. The weight of it pressed against my chest. "And all that time you were traveling?"

She nodded. "Sort of. I wasn't in constant motion. Sometimes I stayed on worlds for decades, but I think all the time I was trying to reach this place."

"Why here?"

She tilted her head to one side and studied me closely. "This is where I knew I had to wait."

I felt that sinking feeling in my stomach again. "Wait for what, Vivian?"

She fixed her glittering eyes on me. "You."

There it was. She had been waiting for me to come for her for hundreds of years. Despite our mutual promise, I started to apologize, but she wasn't having it. "Don't, Avery. There was no way you could know I was out here, or that I was waiting for you."

I nodded, but felt nauseous anyway. I swallowed to keep from being sick, and leaned back against one of the trees. Another silence descended. Eventually, Vivian gave a great sigh, and stood. She wandered about the top of the hill in aimless little circles for a time, and then raised herself on her toes and plucked an apple from a branch. She rejoined me, rolling the fruit back and forth in her hands. "What finally brought you here?" she asked.

I'd been thinking about this while I watched her. I believed I had a pretty good idea, but if I was right it raised a number of other questions. I suppose you might say I was pleasantly troubled by my theory. "I could give you the simple answer," I said. "Rook's cube device brought us here. As far as I understand, unlike a portal spell that takes you where you want to go, the cube takes you to where you need to be. Somehow it decided we needed to find you. The question is, why?"

"Not sure if I should be insulted or not," she said with an arch of her eyebrow.

"I . . . I didn't mean it like that," I stammered.

She smiled and laughed, and this time it was a pure laugh, and it was wonderful. "I know, Avery. I was pulling, ever so gently, on your leg."

I stuck out my tongue. "You're evil." It was meant as a joke, but when I looked back at Vivian all the mirth had vanished. The lines of her face were grave and troubled. "I'm sorry, Vivian, *that* was meant as a joke."

She nodded mutely, but her smile didn't return. Instead, she asked, "You agree this is Baum's world?"

"Yes, it seems to be. Or some close echo of it."

She held the apple up to the light and studied it. "I only know what I've read in Baum's more popular books. Are they accurate?"

I shook my head and immediately regretted it as my brain rattled about uncomfortably. I reached up and gave my temples a squeeze. "No . . . not entirely. Those books are mostly about Baum's daughter, and the strange people and creatures she met here."

"He brought his daughter along with him on a research project?" she asked. "Isn't that unusual?"

It was exactly the sort of question I'd expect of a novice or an acolyte, which was, after all, what she had been when we met. "Not really," I answered. "Before direct world-to-world transport was perfected, a lot of mages used Zelazny incremental-shift traveling. Back then it could take a couple of years of hopping here and there to get to a distant subworld. Mages often brought their families with them."

"So, there really was a metal man and an animated scarecrow and a . . . a wicked witch?" she asked, still staring at the apple.

"I don't know about all that." I shielded my eyes as a stray ray of sunlight came filtering through the leaves. "Baum was an almost pathological note-taker, and he published everything. His academic works are largely unknown, and mostly dealt with certain theories he was working on concerning prism-based world-to-world transport. Eldrin tells me it's still used in ether astronomy to indirectly review the dark sides of planets and certain meteorological . . ." Vivian was watching me with the oddest little smile on her face. "I'm boring you."

"Only in the best of all possible ways," she said, and put the apple into one of her pockets. She stood, stretching, and the wind caught her blue-checkered dress so it fluttered softly. She turned back around and caught me staring. I blushed, and she smiled. "You were telling me about Baum's research?" she said. "But I'm not sure what you were trying to say exactly."

I stuttered back into speech, like a car with a bad clutch. "The . . . the . . . the point I'm trying to make is that the stories everyone associates with Baum are not his research findings, but are actually a collection of parenting books he wrote about his experiences raising a daughter 'off-world.' Whether they're accurate . . . well, as I understand it, Dorothy was extremely precocious. She would go around animating objects, making animals talk, and in general causing no end of chaos. Her dad's postdoc— who was a Dryadine, I believe—spent a great deal of time running about cleaning up after her."

She considered this, while I went back to considering her. I was so engrossed I missed her next question entirely. "Avery?" Vivian said, making my name a question.

"Hmm?"

"I believe *something* is distracting you," she said, and dropped to the ground beside me.

"I . . ."

"Do you remember the night we met?" she asked before I could say anything foolish.

I laughed. "How could I ever forget?"

"I had a really good time," she said.

"Me too."

"I'm glad." She smiled. "You know not everything that happened that night was part of my plan."

Those wonderful eyes were full upon me now, and I did not know how to respond, because I wasn't sure what she was trying to say. My mind kept darting back to Trelari and patterns and mystic struggles, though somehow I knew none of that was on point.

When I didn't respond, she said, "You really are the most clueless man I've ever known, Avery Stewart. Let me make it simple for you." She leaned forward, stroked her hand across my cheek, and kissed me. I swam in the sensation of the touch of her lips on mine and the lovely scent of her hair.

We stayed like that for a while, and then she broke away. "How long do you think it will take Rook to fix his cube?"

"I . . . I have no idea," I said in a kind of daze of joy.

Vivian glanced down the hill toward the road, her head cocked. It was almost like her mind was working through a difficult math problem. Then a wicked little smile crossed her face. "Never mind. It doesn't matter." She lay down in the grass. "Come here, Avery."

Later, as the afternoon sun was making its way toward the horizon, we were lying next to each other trying to catch up on all the things that had happened to us since we last were together. Her story was longer, but she had such a desire to hear the news from campus and Trelari, and I had such a need to tell her about what had happened to Harold and Eldrin, that I spent as much time talking as she did. Eventually, we ran out of things to say and questions to ask, and we fell into a comfortable silence.

I was drifting off to sleep when she spoke again. "Tell me more about Baum's witch."

"What about her?" A shadow passed across the sun. I saw a single dark cloud like a stain on the otherwise untarnished sky.

She propped herself up on her elbow. "Is it possible that the witch wasn't real, or wasn't evil?"

I considered her question as I watched the cloud. Something about it struck me as curious. It was moving very fast in our direction. "I suppose."

I wondered if the cloud might a thunderhead, and if perhaps Vivian and I should make our way back down to the cube.

"But you know how these things are," I said. "Whatever the truth of the witch was, now she is associated with all that is bad and wicked."

As the cloud got closer it appeared to be made of lots of little clouds.

"At this point the echo from those writings will have rebounded here, and whether Dorothy or the witch were good or bad to begin with, for the people in this world they would be . . ."

And the clouds kept breaking into smaller and smaller pieces.

". . . legends . . ."

I rose slowly to my feet.

". . . unless . . ."

A chill ran through me as I realized the cloud was not a cloud at all, but a group of tiny figures flying toward us.

"Vivian, where are the others *exactly*?"

Something in my voice must have caught her attention, because she also got up and came to stand next to me, slipping her hand into mine as she did. "What is it?"

I pointed a wavering finger at the figures in the sky. She squinted and her eyes widened. "Are those birds?"

I shook my head. "If we're right and this is Baum's world, they're monkeys." I grabbed hold of her arm, pulling her toward the little yellow road. "We have to get to the others. Now!"

We sprinted over the bridge and around a small ridge. I had nearly forgotten cracking my skull on the hypocube, but the exertion of running quickly reminded me. By the time we'd made it onto flat ground my head was pounding. Valdara, Drake, and Rook were standing in a circle about the door of a bright blue outhouse set in a cornfield close by the narrow yellow road. A scarecrow teetered precariously on its stick nearby, and it appeared as though the three were in consultation with the straw man.

I started shouting, "The monkeys are coming!"

All three looked up at us at the same time. I pointed blindly behind me. None of them moved. Nor, on reflection, would I have done any different had some madman come running toward me shouting about monkeys. It was not until Vivian and I got to them, and I had a chance to wheeze out the facts, that they reacted. Unfortunately, it did not result in us taking off in Rook's miracle box like I had hoped.

"Thing's busted, laddie," he said.

Typical Rook, short, to the point, and entirely lacking in any sort of information I could use. "Where is the cube?" I asked. "Maybe if I got a look at it . . ."

"What do you mean, lad? The cube's right here." Rook hooked a thumb at the outhouse. "Remember, it transforms based on a world's bathroom standards. Well, here . . . wherever we are, the standard is an outhouse."

Now that Rook mentioned it, I did recall him telling us something about the cube's peculiar camouflage power, but I hadn't thought through what that would mean in reality. I stared at the outhouse. It looked ordinary enough, right down to the smell. "What's . . . what's wrong with it?"

Rook showed me what looked like a scrambled puzzle cube. I had no idea what the puzzle had to do with the operation of the hypocube, but I had been a kid once, and I'd spent a fair amount of time messing around with their nonmagical equivalents back on Earth. "Well, the first thing to do is to solve the corners," I suggested. There was a strange silence, and it took me a couple of seconds to realize that everyone was staring at me. "What? Isn't that the sequence? Corners, then edges, then midges?" I said, ticking off the steps on my fingers.

"What are you talking about?" Valdara asked.

"The cube is scrambled," I explained, pointing at the puzzle in Rook's hand. "Isn't that the problem?"

"No," Rook said. "It's supposed to be a sphere."

"Oh . . ." I said softly. "Well, can you fix it, because the monkeys are . . ." I turned around and I could see them coming fast, the cloaks of their crimson robes flowing out behind them like pennants. I looked back at the group. "Not to panic anyone, but they are kind of here."

Rook shouted. "You want me to circle a square? You can't defy the laws of metaphysics."

"We fight, then," Drake growled. "Good. I've been itching for another fight."

He squared his shoulders and spun his staff. Valdara joined him on his right. Her sword and her chakram appeared in her hands.

"You two are even crazier than he is!" Rook shouted. "How are the five of us goin' to fight an army of demented monkeys?"

Vivian put a hand on the dwarf's shoulder. "They aren't monkeys."

"What are you talking about?" I shouted, and pointed at the cloud of . . . men . . . in Mysterium robes. "Oh gods, Moregoth found us! We have to get out of here!"

We could see the glowing points, like oncoming comets, as they brought their wands to bear. Valdara cursed quietly about magic ruining a decent melee, while Drake wondered aloud about whether his protection spell would work in this world.

Rook wasn't waiting to figure out what or how to fight them. He made a sweeping gesture, which I took to be an invitation to conjure a gateway, and said, "Laddie, would you do the honors?"

I didn't bother telling him that what he was asking was theoretically impossible. Instead, I yanked the key from my pocket and began channeling power through it. Almost at once the yellow bricks at my feet turned gray. My spell, like a monochromatic cancer, spread outward, draining the color from the road and the fields and the sky. My heart caught in my chest. The key was consuming the world's reality. I felt a sinking feeling in the pit of my stomach at the thought of how much damage I must have been doing the last few days. Moregoth or no, now that I knew I was not going to be responsible for destroying another world, I began to shut off the flow of power, but a hole had already opened in reality. Seeing that there was no changing what had already been done, and no reason to waste the consequence, I yelled, "Go!"

Vivian was the first one through the portal. Drake and Valdara hesitated, so I added, "I have to be last to keep it open." With twin nods of acceptance, they dashed through and vanished.

Rook paused at the entrance to the portal, even as the Sealers' spells exploded around us. "Where are we goin', lad?"

I truly had no idea. "Just go!"

I gave him a little shove, and Rook stumbled enough to fall through. Moregoth was no more than the length of my apartment away, which I must stress is not very far, when I jumped through the portal. I could see him quite clearly, right down to his fishnet shirt. I heard him scream, "Sealers, DIVE!" as I finally managed to master the spell and pinch off the flow of power. The last thing I heard from Baum's land, carried on the winds of subether from there to here, were the Munchkins singing, "Ding dong, the witch is gone . . ."

CHAPTER 23

DOWN THE RABBIT HOLE

Though the hole I'd bored between worlds had closed, it had not closed quickly enough. Moregoth and the Sealers burst through the portal behind us. You might be surprised to hear that the fact we were being pursued by a small army of Mysterium-trained killers was not foremost in my mind. This was not due to some sudden feeling of invulnerability, but because we were also in the process of plummeting to our deaths. Either my transport spell had been spatially misaligned with this new world by hundreds of feet, or we had been unlucky enough to have randomly appeared at the top of an open mine shaft. Although if it was a mine, it was the strangest mine I'd ever been in.

Not that I'd ever been in a mine . . .

Unless you count the Mines of Maria on Trelari . . .

Which you shouldn't, because those were basically designed by me, and as we've established, I've never been in a mine.

The point is, we were falling down a very long shaft cluttered with all manner of odds and ends: a bookcase, a cupboard, the corner of a table, the top half of an armoire. I suppose it was nice of someone to decorate the shaft, but the effort didn't do much to improve my enjoyment or comfort, because, as I mentioned, I was falling down it, and it was long, very long, absurdly long . . .

After several minutes, the falling stopped being terrifying and just became silly. Moregoth and the Sealers were somewhere above me, and had obviously grown just as comfortable with the situation as I had. Deadly bolts of blue energy began to whiz down at us. It turns out falling in and of itself isn't scary when you never hit the ground. At first I was still so disoriented by our situation that I didn't really notice that we were under attack. However, when a beam came close enough to leave a smoking hole in the sleeve of my shirt, a healthy sense of danger returned.

Having jumped into the portal right before me, Rook was fairly close at hand. He saw me poking a finger through the hole. "You'll probably need a patch. Although a good seamstress might be able to stich it back together."

"I think our time would be better spent focusing on how to stop Moregoth?" I replied.

Rook shrugged and picked a pipe off of a side table we were falling past. "You got us into this predicament. I figured when you were done muckin' about you'd get us out." He inspected the inside of the pipe's bowl, and gave a grunt of disgust. "No tobacco. Typical." He dropped it into a silver soup tureen set on a passing sideboard.

He had a point. Not about the pipe. I had no idea if it was typical or not for a pipe to be empty when you found it while falling down a mine shaft, but he definitely had a point about needing to get out of this world. My first thought was to make a new portal, but the others were pretty far below. I was afraid they would miss any gate I wove, and I didn't want to use the key again as last time it had come close to unweaving a whole world. Another spell sang past my ear and shattered the face of a grandfather clock set against the wall. A spray of splinters peppered my face, and its gong chimed chaotically.

I decided to take a page out of Drake's book. I focused my own energies and wove a moving shield and set it between our group and Moregoth. It wouldn't last forever, but it might buy us enough time to come up with a better plan.

Once we weren't under immediate threat of being blown to bits, Rook and I linked arms and did an aerial swim down to the others. I know that physically "swimming" through the air makes no sense, but we were falling down an endless pit with a bunch of crimson-robed maniacs chasing after us with wands. If you can suspend your disbelief that far why not go all the way?

When Rook and I reached the others, they had formed a kind of falling ring around a little blond-haired girl in a blue dress. "So," Vivian said with a sympathetic coo. "What you're saying is this diabolical rabbit lured you into this endless abyss using an ensorcelled waistcoat and a pocket watch?"

"How big was this rabbit?" Valdara asked as she looked about suspiciously.

"Vicious creatures, rabbits," Drake said sagely. "Was it a white rabbit? Was it bad-tempered? Did it have big nasty, sharp, pointy teeth?"

"Oh, heavens, no," the girl said in a voice so high-pitched it made my ears ring a little. "See, I was sitting with my cat, Dinah . . ."

Drake interrupted the girl with a growl. "The cat that disappears leaving only its teeth? Sounds like a nightmare."

At this point, everyone noticed that Rook and I had joined them. Valdara narrowed her eyes. "Avery, I don't know what you were thinking, or even if you were thinking, but you've managed to land us in a horror zone: vicious rabbits, demented cats, and then there are these two-dimensional beings that are obsessed with taking off people's heads."

"You've got it all wrong," the girl squeaked. "They're nothing but a pack of cards."

"What are cards? Some other unspeakable beastie?" Rook grumbled.

"I think they might be a kind of wolf," Valdara suggested. "She did say they hunted in packs."

"We have bigger problems," I said, interrupting Vivian and Valdara as they began to discuss how you might fight packs of two-dimensional wolf creatures. I pointed behind us at the Sealers trying to blast their way through my shield. I was surprised to see it hadn't already failed, but it wouldn't hold much longer. As we watched, glowing fractures began to spiderweb across its surface.

While the little girl examined a bottle that she'd grabbed from a passing cupboard, I gathered the others in a tight circle. "Do either of you recognize this place?" I asked Vivian and Rook.

They looked at each other and shook their heads. "It might help if it would let us stand still for a second, lad," Rook groused.

"Not sure we want that, since it would mean landing, or rather crashing," Drake pointed out.

Rook fingered his beard. "Good point."

"If you two are quite done," I said sharply, "this is obviously a reflection of Carroll's world."

Rook shrugged. "I never paid much attention to subworld research. A bit too abstract for me."

Vivian scrunched up her face in thought and bit

her lip. "Carroll's world . . . the, um, the dream one? With the tea party and the talking flowers?"

I almost muttered something about undergraduates, but instead I said, "Close. It was a world he programmed to study the subconscious. It's full of dream constructs like falling, and talking animals, and—"

A high-pitched "Oh!" came from the little blond girl. We turned in time to see her grow smaller and smaller until she was about the size of a thimble. I gestured at her. "And body changes, of course."

"What's your point?" Rook asked.

"That these cats and rabbits aren't real. They are simply symbols. So—"

"What is real, really?" a spacy voice asked from above our heads.

We looked up and saw a striped cat with spiral-pupiled eyes and an enormous smile. I pointed up at it. "This type of craziness is what I'm talking about."

The cat ignored me and addressed Vivian. "The white rabbit has been looking for you, Your Majesty. You know, you should really go easier on him. He tries so hard to be on time, but it's difficult when you get your watch repaired by a hatter."

"Wait!" Vivian shouted. "You think I'm the Queen of Hearts?"

Before the cat could answer, there was an explosion from above. We looked up in time to see my shield shatter. The bursting of the spell fell like a hammer blow in my head. I saw stars as pain seared through my brain. I clutched at my temples. "We have to get out of here. Moregoth is coming, and I can't hold them again."

Sealer spells were already soaring down the shaft past us. Rook dodged to the left as one split our circle in two. "Can you make another portal?"

I shook my head—mistake. It was all I could do not to vomit. "Can you?"

"Maybe, laddie." His palms began to glow, but that's about as far as he got before a bolt of energy caught him in the back. He gave a cry and crumpled into a ball. Frantically, I put a hand to his neck and gasped in relief as I felt a flutter of a pulse. He was alive, but none of us would be for long if we didn't get out of here.

I grabbed Vivian and pulled her close. "You need to make a portal."

"But I've never made a portal. I have no idea what I'm doing."

"Not true," I said as calmly as I could, considering the circumstances. "You said so yourself. You've done this hundreds of times. Do exactly what you did in your travels, just hold the door for the rest of us."

There was fear in her eyes, and I knew it wasn't about the spell, but about whether she would get lost again. I gripped her hand and managed a tight smile. "I promise, I will be with you this time."

She nodded and I felt the pull of her will as she

drew in power. The spell began to build, but it was immediately clear that it was not going to be strong enough to carry the rest of us through with her. Despite my promise, if she continued she would step out of this world to somewhere else— alone. There was only one thing for it. I reached in my pocket and thrust Griswald's toothless key into her hands. She stared at the key and asked, "What is this?"

We ducked as a couple of spells flashed between us. "There is no time for explanation. Just focus your thoughts through the key and be careful. It can be difficult to control." She hesitated. "It's going to be okay," I said in my most reassuring voice. "If you follow my lead, I'll tell you when you've built up enough energy to form the gate."

She still looked uncertain, but nodded and focused her gaze on key. At once teeth appeared and began gyrating along the key's shaft. I felt an immense rush of power rush flow into her. The golden rings around her pupils glowed a molten red, and I expected to see the gate begin to form. Instead, the world began to fade. On the walls of the shaft, the bric-a-brac and clutter began to vanish, and then walls themselves disappeared, and we were falling through a gray tunnel of indistinct margin.

My heart sank. I had hoped she would draw only a little power from the key, but she had opened herself to it completely. The key had begun to unravel the world. "Vivian, you have to stop!" I shouted.

"No! I need more!" Her voice came out as an animalistic growl.

Beside us, Alice's eyes went wide and she said, "Oh my!" Then she was gone.

"Vivian, please stop," I pleaded.

When she didn't respond, I tried to pry the key from her hands, but it was like a shadow attempting to wrestle a statue.

She turned her eyes, like searchlights, on me. "It's okay, Avery. The spell knows what to do. Can't you see? It is glorious." Her voice was inhuman, like a quartet of Vivians speaking at once.

I had no idea what she was seeing. The world had turned to an indistinct gray mist. Only the five of us and the Sealers still had substantial form. The last thing I saw was the cat, which vanished gradually from the tip of his tail up, until there was only a floating smile. "I'm sorry," I said.

The smile tilted to one side, and said, "Curious, I thought I was the mad one."

I had little time to ponder his words. Our bodies melted into motes of energy, and we passed out of his world.

CHAPTER 24

WHICH WARDROBE?

We materialized in a small clearing in a wintry evergreen forest, surrounded by deep shadows. A lamp atop an ornate iron post stood nearby, a gas flame flickering inside its glass-paned enclosure. Flakes of snow drifted down from a gray overcast sky, and blanketed the ground and weighed down the tree branches. Everything was quiet. I fell to my knees and said hoarsely, "Gods, Vivian, what have we done?"

My mind was racing. Excuses pulled from the propaganda I'd been fed at the university fought with my conscience to deny what had happened: subworlds aren't real, they are mere echoes, they are like seasons here and gone to be replaced by another. I rejected them all. We had destroyed a world to save ourselves. I ached inside, and I might have lost myself in my guilt, except that Vivian didn't answer. She swayed silently on her feet and then collapsed to the ground.

"Vivian?" I cried, and rushed to where she'd fallen. She was still clutching the key, and it was still glowing. I again tried to pry it out of her fingers, but they were locked around it with a grip of steel. Her eyes moved fitfully beneath her closed eyelids and her face was pale as the snow. I cradled her head in my lap and touched her forehead. She was burning with fever.

"Drake?" I called out. "Her skin feels like fire. She needs healing!"

He didn't respond. I looked up to see Drake and Valdara, heads bent together over a prone Rook. Initially, I was furious that they weren't coming to help, but a terrifying dread crept through me as I realized why. They had been turned to stone.

I took off my robe and laid it beneath Vivian's head. Then I rose and approached the petrified trio. I touched each of them, trying to feel the nature of the spell that had done this, but there was nothing there. No pattern of transformation was woven into their beings. No residue of magic clung to them. It was as if they had always been stone.

"It's the White Witch's doing." The voice was incredibly soft, almost lost in the gentle hiss of the falling snow.

Spinning about, I saw the vague outline of the

speaker hiding among the trees at the edge of the clearing. It was a strange creature, part-human and . . . maybe part-goat? I wasn't exactly sure. I finally decided that he was a faun.

"Who is the White Witch?" I asked. "What did she do? Turn my other friends into statues? Can you help?"

He pointed at Vivian. "She is the White Witch, and she turns those that displease her into statues. Your friends must have displeased her."

I looked down at Vivian and then back to the faun in confusion. "There's been a mistake. This isn't your White Witch. She's a friend of mine and theirs." I pointed at the statues.

The faun shook his head. "There's no question. She's the White Witch. I would recognize her any-where, but then you must know that, being a . . . a friend of hers."

The White Witch? Something about that name, about this place, was familiar. I looked at the faun, the snow, and the statues. "The lamppost!" I said, letting out a misty puff of breath. "This is Dr. Clive Lewis's world."

"He preferred to be called Jack," stated the faun.

I sat back on my heels and thought about the Munchkins in Baum's world and the cat in Carroll's world. Both had identified Vivian as a villain. De-spite my feelings for her, something was wrong. I was starting to move pieces in my mind when I realized that the faun was ever so slowly backing away from me into the forest. I snapped my fingers. "Stop! I need your help."

The faun hesitated. "Do not test me, faun!" I shouted. "If you do not wish to end up as the others, you will help me take her somewhere safe." I didn't like making the threat, but if he left, Vivian was going to freeze. He stepped, trembling, away from the trees and into the small clearing around the lamppost. "I take it we aren't far from your house?"

He twisted his hands in the extremely long scarf that hung around his neck. "No, not far."

"Good, we will take her to your house. Help me carry her."

The faun pattered delicately over, and together we carried Vivian. As we moved through the trees, I saw dozens of other statues scattered here and there. They were the Sealers, frozen in midattack. I tried not to think about the implications.

The faun's house was set into a hillside. He had a painted door with a lovely polished brass knocker. It was picturesque and cozy and a vast improvement over the cold and snow. I laid Vivian on a couch before the fire while the faun made us some tea. After a few minutes, he returned with three steaming cups. He put one on the side table for Vivian and I started to take the one he offered me when I remembered the accounts of this world.

I pointed at the cup the faun was about to sip. "Give me that."

"What?"

I narrowed my eyes. "Give me your cup." He swallowed hard and handed his tea to me with a shaking hand. I exchanged cups with him and took a sip. "Wonderful," I said, and it really was. I hadn't realized how cold I'd gotten.

He put his own cup on a table next to his chair, and casually pushed it away. "I'm not thirsty."

I took another sip. "As I understand it, the White Witch is the most evil villain this world has ever known. But I also thought she was dead. In fact . . ." I seemed to recall that the entire world was gone, but here I was. There are many books written about subworlds that seem to be reflections of others. I felt myself slipping into what Eldrin would call navelgazing. I had to focus. I needed to heal Vivian and revive everyone else before Moregoth found us. I shook my head to clear my jumbled thoughts. "Why do you believe my friend is so wicked?"

"Because I am," Vivian said in a hoarse whisper. Her eyes were open and, as a bonus, no longer glowing. "Where are we?" she asked as she sat up.

The faun made an audible gulp sound. I shifted slightly between her and the faun. "I was going to ask you the same thing. But before we get to that, why are you the White Witch? I thought black was your color."

She didn't react to my attempt at humor, which I have to admit was lousy. Instead, she very deliberately looked at the faun. He jumped to his feet and bowed. "I think I'll set another kettle on. I am so glad that you have recovered, Your Majesty."

He gave a little *yip* and skittered out of the room. I turned back to Vivian. She was staring at Griswald's key with an expression of fascinated horror. "Vivian, are you okay?"

She shook her head. "The magic, it was . . . impossible."

"I know. That key seems to allow its holder to manipulate reality without a pattern to guide the magic. It is chaotic and—"

"Intoxicating," she whispered.

I was going to say "horrible," but decided not to argue the point. "Yes, and also very dangerous. Don't feel guilty, but something happened during the transport. It isn't your fault. Valdara, Drake, and Rook—"

"I know."

"What do you mean you know?"

She ran her fingers over the smooth, featureless surface of the key. "I brought us to this world because I knew the others would be frozen when we arrived."

"Why would you do that?"

She looked up and the light from the fire made the gold rings about her eyes shine and sparkle. "I wanted to talk, just us, alone. My visions indicated that we'd have a chance here."

"You turned them into statues? Don't you think that's a little extreme?"

She nodded. "Yes, but it was the only path I could see."

"You know I trust you, Vivian, but . . ." I gestured helplessly back in the direction where we'd left the others. "Rook and Valdara and Drake . . ."

"I'm sorry, Avery. If there had been any other way . . ." She twisted the key in her hands.

I didn't like this, but considering everything she had been through, I kept my mind open. "Well, what do you need to talk to me about so badly?"

"I need to give you a choice, Avery." The gold in her eyes burned brightly to life again.

"This is about the vision you had in the last world?" I asked.

She nodded.

I swallowed. "And you are certain of the truth of this vision?"

"I'm as sure of it as I have ever been of anything."

"Tell me, then," I said.

Vivian picked up the cup of tea beside her, and turned away to look at the fire. She sat in silence for several minutes, sipping her tea. When at last she spoke, it was as though she were reading from a book. "Close to where we entered this world is a passage. It has the power to take us back to Earth of an earlier time. Moregoth and the others would not be able to follow. It is a path of ease and peace, of quiet days and children, of long life and happiness. Memories of our prior lives would fade, and the events of these days would unspool without us. Neither you nor I will ever be what we might have become."

I knew at once that it would also mean abandoning Rook, Valdara, and Drake to Moregoth. It would mean leaving Sam and Ariella to the whims of chance and fate. It would mean leaving Trelari to defend itself alone against whatever machinations the Administration had planned for it. There was an emptiness in the pit of my stomach, because I knew it was the path Vivian wished I would take.

"What's the other option?" I asked.

Her shoulders drooped. "We save your friends and take a path back to Sam and Ariella. In this future, I see death and war, realities thrown into violent conflict, a race destroyed, and life as we know it reordered."

"And what happens to us?"

"Nothing is certain, but there is every chance that we will end up reviled and hated. That our names will become curses. And our stories the bogeymen of children's nightmares."

"Does it mean that we will find Sam and Ariella without leading Moregoth to them?"

She shrugged and stared into the dregs of her tea. "I don't know. I don't even know if that's possible."

Even with the danger of Moregoth hovering in the background, there was no question which course I had to take, and Vivian knew it. "I'm sorry," I said. "But I can't abandon the others."

She smiled sadly at me. "I know. Give me a little time to rest and I can make a new gate."

That Vivian was proposing to form the new gate gave me considerable pause. It was not just that I was concerned she couldn't cast the spell, but even if she could I wasn't sure she could control the gate once formed. Her last attempt was her first conscious attempt, and it could have killed her. "Why can't I do it?" I asked.

She gave me her most impish smile. "Because the gate needs to be guided by the vision, and you never took divination, Avery Stewart."

"Too squishy," I said.

She snorted in good-natured disgust. "I will remind you that divination brought us together."

I knew she meant it as a joke, but the circumstances of our first meeting had bothered me since I woke up with a hangover without her. I listened to the crackle of the fire.

"Avery? What is it?"

Unable to look her in the eye, I asked my teacup, "Was it always about the key?"

There was a long pause before she answered, "Yes . . ."

"I see." I set my teacup down and stood.

"Sit down, and let me finish!" she said sharply.

I turned on her, intending to say, *No*, but the intensity of her gaze made me hesitate. "What?"

"Yes . . . at the beginning. As soon as Griswald and

his little cabal let slip what you were up to, I began plotting to insert myself in the equation. I was angry, Avery. As the child of a subworlder, I couldn't even apply to the university. I had to lie and cheat, and do all manner of things that would disgust you, simply to get through the door. You don't know what it's like to have to hide what you are, and to know if you're ever discovered banishment is the best you can hope for. So yes, I saw you as a means and damn the cost."

I didn't really know what to say so said nothing, but I remained standing while she continued. "I wish I'd been a less angry person, a stronger person, a braver person. Since then I have lived a thousand lives through my visions. So many possible futures and the only constant is you. And in each one, no matter how terribly they ended, you were funny and kind, and good to me. I know to you I'm basically a stranger, but I've lived lifetimes with you and I think I've fallen in love with you, Avery Stewart."

I still didn't know what to say, but I sat down.

She smiled. "I really do wish I'd just been a girl in a bar looking for a pleasant night with a boy the first time we met."

"Me too."

For a long time, neither of us spoke. We both stared at the fire. At some point our hands entwined. She leaned her head against my shoulder, and we sat together lost in our thoughts. The faun never returned. When the fire had died to embers, Vivian laughed. "While I would love to stay here with you, time is passing outside. If you want to keep going, we need to move."

"Five more minutes." I replied.

We sat together until, in unspoken agreement, we rose and walked out of the house into the cold. When we were back in the clearing, Vivian pulled the key from some hidden pocket in her dress and held it in both hands. She seemed to hesitate. "Before I begin, I have to tell you that there is another price to the course we've chosen. One that you will not like. All I ask is that you remember all the good and noble reasons you have for doing it. Okay?"

I tried to nod, but my neck seemed stiff with the cold and so I mumbled, "Tell me."

She took a deep breath. "To make the gate I need to tear this world apart utterly."

"No, that's monstrous!" I tried to say, but the words would not come. The key twisted in her hands, the teeth gyrated wildly, and the falling snow vanished in midair—erased. I could not let this happen again. I lunged toward her, determined to take the key from her before she could pull in too much power, but my arms would not move. She had frozen me. My mind was awake, but my body was stone.

Vivian put a hand out, stroking my cheek, though I couldn't feel it. "I'm sorry, Avery, but I knew you would try to stop me. You have to believe me, this is the only way." She lifted the key above her head, tearing at the threads of reality that held the world together. "I told you there was a reason the faun called me the White Witch. He knew what my presence here meant. I am death, the destroyer of worlds."

I screamed silently as she continued to draw magic from our surroundings. The drifts of snow became indistinct blots of white, and the sharp needles of the pine trees blurred to washes of dark green. I wanted to stop her. I wanted to cry, but all I could do was bear witness to the death of another world. It took less than a minute for the trees to fade until they were little more than vague outlines. What remained was a watercolor world, empty of all detail save for the statues scattered here and there, and the gas lamp, which still gave off its wavering light. Then even the remembrance of the trees was gone, and the lamp became a child's sketch of lines.

Vivian's body was glowing now and her eyes shined like burning stars. She began to form the portal. It was a maw of black, and I hated it. There was one last surge of power; the flame of the lamp flickered one last time and was gone, casting the world into darkness.

CHAPTER 25

HANGING BY A THREAD

I found myself standing on solid ground, but had never felt more unsteady. Vivian stood nearby. She was awash with residual power, and there was a wild gleam in her still-glowing eyes. It was glorious and terrible, and she must have seen something of the horror in my face, because a shadow of sadness passed across her as she looked at me. "I'm sorry," she said, and the key slipped from her hand.

"How could you?" I asked, my voice hoarse with emotion.

How she might have answered, and what I would have said or done next, I don't know, because off to my right Rook gave a groan from where he lay on the ground. Valdara shouted his and knealt down at his side. I didn't immediately appreciate the significance of Rook and Valdara being able to move, and spun about looking for where the attack on the dwarf might have come from. Then I saw that Valdara was inspecting the blackened area where the Sealers' blast had hit him two worlds ago. I had completely forgotten about his injury.

Everyone but Vivian gathered around the fallen dwarf. He gave a series of moans followed by increasingly coherent curses before rasping, "Whatever just happened, let's agree never to do it again." He pawed clumsily at the pockets of his vest and pulled out a hip flask. He sat up only long enough to take a large swig, and then fell back to the ground.

"Agreed," said Valdara, who snatched the flask from him, and took a deep drink herself. She offered it to Drake, but he waved it off and the flask came to me. I considered it, but already felt sick to the pit of my stomach, and so passed it back to Rook. He took the flask and drank deeply. After a loud sigh of contentment, he waved a hand at Vivian. "What *exactly* is it she is supposed to have done?"

I looked at her, not sure what to say, not sure if I should say anything. Already Valdara and Drake didn't like or trust Vivian. Knowing this might push them to actual violence. As the silence stretched on, Valdara gave a grunt of irritation. "One of you better tell us what the hell is going on. Rook may be used to popping from world to world, but Drake and I aren't. Where are we, and how did we get here?"

"And why do you two look as guilty as drunks in a wine cellar?" Drake asked.

Vivian and I exchanged glances. She readied herself to respond, and I could tell by the tight set of her mouth that she was going to tell them exactly what she had done, consequences be damned.

"She did what I asked her to do," I said before she could confess. "I . . . I just didn't know what I was asking."

"Well, that's about as clear as mud," Rook growled.

"The important thing is that she got us away from Moregoth," I answered, trying to convince myself of the truth of it.

"For the time being," she said in a quiet monotone.

"What does that mean?" Valdara asked before I could.

"It means we don't have much time here," Vivian answered, and turned to me. "Can't you feel it? Can't you feel the pull?"

Now that she mentioned it, I could feel something. It was like two elastic bands were tied to somewhere deep within my being, one stretching backward to where we'd been, and one stretching into the unknown ahead. I'm not sure how I knew, but I was certain the line going back was attached to Moregoth.

"Avery, what is she talking about?" Valdara asked.

"What does she mean we don't have much time, and how much do we have?"

I looked to Vivian, but she shrugged vaguely and turned to stare up at a bright red moon that was sharing the sky with the sun. Valdara pulled Drake and me away from Vivian over to Rook, and lowered her voice to a whisper. "Where are we and what the hell is up with her? Has she done something to us?"

I decided on the spot that telling them the truth—that Vivian had turned them to stone and unwoven a world in getting us here—was something I would not share unless I absolutely had to, so I asked, "What's the last thing you remember?"

"Falling through that endless shaft," she said. Drake nodded his agreement.

"I don't fully understand, but I believe she has cast a portal that works like Rook's hypocube. It is taking us somewhere, but along a course only it knows."

"Are you saying we are going to be yanked about from world to world at the whim of this spell of hers?" Drake asked. He was eyeing the flask in Rook's hand like he was rethinking his decision not to drink.

"Yes," I said with a nod of my head. "But it's worse than that, because Moregoth is entangled with us."

"So, everywhere we go, he goes?" Rook asked. I nodded again.

"Gods! Can't we unchain ourselves from her and go our own way?" Valdara muttered.

I glowered at her. "I want all of you to consider

that without her we're trapped in that endless pit. Without her, Moregoth has probably already killed us all."

Valdara snapped, "Well, where are we, then? I thought we were going to Sam and Ariella."

I started to answer, but before I could Rook pointed at Valdara. "Don't you listen, or have all your brains been sucked into that crown you're wearin'? The lass didn't cast a normal portal spell. She opened a gateway to her desire. Like with the hypocube, the gateway will operate until it gets us to her chosen destination, but because she didn't put any structure into it, the spell will get us there by a means of its choosin'. This is obviously not the final destination, but it is the place the spell thinks we need to be right now." He finished by taking another sip of whatever was in his flask. "Clear?"

"No," Drake and Valdara said in unison.

Rook waved them away. "My question is, how did she do it?" He peered at me suspiciously. "What exactly is she, Avery? She isn't Mysterian, but I've never seen anyone create a portal like that who wasn't."

"As far as I know, she's from a subworld somewhere," I said truthfully, but suspected the real answer to his question lay with Griswald's key. I went to pick it up. Vivian was still staring up at the moon, her eyes glowing brightly. I wondered if she was okay. What do you say to someone that has just wiped out an entire reality? Not trusting myself, I said nothing.

When I got back to the group, I held out the key. "I think this may be how she did it. It's the key I got from Griswald's box."

Rook took one look and spit a mouthful of what smelled like turpentine onto the ground at my feet. "Holy hell! Do you know what this is? It's a reality skeleton key! Griswald shouldn't have had this."

I knew what a skeleton key was, but had never heard the word used in the context of magic. If it meant the same thing as it did for regular locks . . . hair stood on the back of my neck. "Does that mean what I think it means?"

"I wouldn't even want to take a guess at what you're thinkin', lad, but this bloody thing is a reality key that fits any world. There weren't many of them. I thought they were all destroyed or lost. "

"Why?" I asked.

"Why?" Rook spit. "Because there was a worry about what might happen if one of them fell into the hands of the Mysterium or a subworlder." Valdara gave a warning growl and Rook grunted a quick "No offense," which only caused her eyes to narrow further.

The dwarf did his best to ignore her glares and pressed on. "The point is, this thing should be locked up. It's way too dangerous to have floatin' about with an Earther." He waved his agitated arms at Vivian, who was standing utterly still and pointing toward the red moon. "Case in point!"

"I'm sure I speak for all 'subworlders' when I thank you most sincerely for your concern," Valdara said with undisguised disdain.

"You're welcome," Rook replied with equal sarcasm. "But I didn't say I agreed with the reasonin'."

I tried to redirect the conversation. "Rook, how can you be so sure this is a skeleton key?"

"'Cause they're bloody legendary, lad," he snorted. "It's like askin' someone from your world how they know a bloody great yellow *M* means that a place sells hamburgers, or why they associate a green mermaid with coffee. Every Mysterian knows what one of those is—without exception. My real questions are: How did Griswald get his hands on one, and why is it workin' for you two?"

"What do you mean, why is it working?" I asked irritably. "You may not like it, but Vivian and I are Mysterium mages."

"Irrelevant!" Rook said. "As you would know if you did have any *real* education, those keys have a safety built into them. While anyone can use them as a kind of focus to do magic tricks, to shift reality like the two of you appear to have been doin' you would need to be a Mysterian."

This gave me pause. Putting safeties on powerful magic items was pretty standard. It's how mages prevented their research assistants from abusing lab magic items, like "one" rings or the copy machine. "How does it know the user isn't a Mysterian?"

"The only reliable way—reality weight, of course," he answered.

I knew when I asked that must be the answer, but hearing him confirm it sent a cold shiver along my spine. I glanced at Vivian. Could it be that she and I had been altered, like Sam and Ariella, while we were on Trelari? While I thought through the implications, Rook took my silent contemplation as tacit agreement that he should have the key. He extended his hand. "I think we both know it would be better if I kept the key, Avery. Those things are rare and precious."

I looked down at his open palm and shook my head. "It may be rare and precious, but it's mine. Griswald gave it to me."

"Griswald!" he spat. "He must have been mad!"

"Or he knew exactly what he was doing," I bristled, my voice rising. I was a little surprised at how angry I was.

"What's that supposed to mean?" asked Rook as his brows came together.

"Exactly what it sounds like!"

Drake interrupted what was building up to be an epic shouting match. "I'm sure this is fascinating for the two of you, but I couldn't care less about this key. I want to return to Valdara's question. If this isn't where Sam and Ariella are, then where are we?"

Rook and I continued to stare at each other, but eventually we broke off and I answered. "No idea."

"Could be anywhere," the dwarf agreed.

"Maybe we could ask a local?" Valdara suggested.

It actually wasn't a bad idea, and we all began to look around for a convenient local. We were standing in a valley planted in rows and rows of vines and crops. A road wound its way out of the fields and up a hill to a stone keep. I could see a steady stream of figures making their way to the gates of the fortress. Somewhere in the distance, a bell sang out over and over again. Everything looked normal, but there was a feeling in the air of urgency that I couldn't understand. I was still trying to figure out why I felt so anxious when a group of men with sickles and hoes came running out of the fields toward us. Valdara's sword was in her hand in a flash. When the men saw the weapon, they held up their hands in a sign of peace. An older-looking fellow with more salt than pepper in his beard stepped forward. "We don't want any trouble. We saw you out here and came to warn you."

"Warn us about what?" Valdara asked.

"The Thread are coming!" he said, and pointed overhead where hazy crimson clouds were gathering.

Valdara shrugged. "We are not seamstresses. What do these threads have to do with us?"

The group of men looked at us in confusion. "What are you talking about?" the leader asked.

"That is what we want to know," Valdara said, thrusting her sword back into her belt. "You come giving warnings better fit for seamstresses and tailors. Leave us in peace."

The men began to back away, wide-eyed. "You're mad!" the eldest of them shouted. "Stay out here if you want to die. We're going to the hold." They ran in the direction of the keep.

While Rook, Drake, and Valdara debated whether "Thread" might refer to the name of a monster or a warrior of some kind, I wracked my brain to remember where I'd heard the term before. Something about it rang a bell. Something I'd studied in Mysterium, but I couldn't put my finger on it. I was still trying to pry something useful out of my memory when Vivian sang out, "I hope the dragons come in time."

I followed her eyes into the sky, and saw that the crimson clouds were descending now. That's when it struck me: thread, dragons, red star . . . "Oh gods," I murmured to myself. "We're in McCaffrey's world!

I screamed, "Run for cover!" But it was far too late. The cloud had descended in an adjacent field, and was now hovering about twenty feet off the ground and approaching rapidly. I could see the shape of the individual threads, but as they got closer they weren't threads at all, they were men—crimson-cloaked men. The gateway had transported Moregoth and the Sealers. Out of reflex I raised the key, but at the memory of the faun and his beautiful brass knocker I thrust it into my pocket determined that it should remain there. Instead, I took the time to tap into my own magical reserves and spun a hasty umbrella of magical fire over our group.

The first wave of Sealers had no chance to avoid the shield. Most of them were repulsed, and skipped off of it to crash into the fields around us. But the rest, including Moregoth, broke away. A shower of spells bombarded us from above. The shield cracked and then shattered. I fell to my knees, battered by the backlash from the broken spell. Valdara, Drake, and Rook formed a defensive circle around Vivian and me, while above us Moregoth's men circled about for another pass.

"If anyone has any bright ideas," Rook growled, "now would be the time to field-test them."

"Do you think killing them all is a bright idea?" Valdara asked.

"Worth a try," he replied with a very dwarfish laugh.

Moregoth's men made their second pass from two directions at once, hoping to catch me off guard. They didn't count on the others fighting back. Valdara sent her chakram flying into the lead group of Sealers. Two of the crimson-cloaked men fell shrieking into the fields, and the carefully choreographed attack descended into chaos. In the confusion that followed, we were able to pick off a number of the Sealers. Drake clotheslined a passing man and swept him into a second flying in the opposite direction—a sickening but satisfying crunch followed. Rook meanwhile was turning his height, which should have been a decided disadvantage against aerial opponents, into a secret weapon. He had positioned himself among the rows of crops where the Sealers couldn't see him and would jump up with his ax when they flew too low.

It was turning into a bloodbath, and with a shouted command from Moregoth, the second wave of attacks broke off. I looked to see if everyone was okay, and to my relief they were. I had also recovered enough strength that I thought I might be able to do a bit of magic. Unfortunately, Vivian was growing more and more distant with every passing moment. Her eyes were glowing brightly now, and she was standing utterly motionless, staring at something I could not see. I wove a small ward and placed it around her.

Moregoth learned from his first two failures. This time, he arranged his men in a circle, and soon they began to loop about us, firing spells from all directions. We tried to rotate, to keep them from finding a gap in our defense, but everyone was exhausted. Soon bolts of energy began to find their marks. Drake caught one in the side of his chest and collapsed onto one knee. He struggled back to his feet, but his movements were labored. Then there was an explosion on the ground in front of Rook. The dwarf was blown backward. He landed hard on his back, and groaned in pain.

"Move closer together!" I shouted.

With an enormous effort, I expanded the shield around Vivian to cover the entire group. While the shield served to protect us, it also confined us to a very small area. Moregoth gave a signal, and his men moved in, tightening their fighting circle into an ever-narrowing ring. A constant volley of spell blasts impacted against the shield. I pressed harder and harder, but the strain was beginning to tell. I could see the skin in my fingers growing translucent. The ward began to flicker and fail.

Just as I thought I would have to drop my shield, the blasts from the Sealers faltered. I looked for the reason and saw long gray filaments raining down from the sky. They burned up on my shield, but Moregoth's men had no protection. Several of them were already on the ground, pierced and devoured by the horrible things. Once again, Moregoth called out to break off the attack and his men scattered. The smart ones shielded themselves, but many did not.

Thankfully, we didn't have long to watch. Vivian's eyes began to flare brighter, and she harmonized, "Here we go."

CHAPTER 26

IT'S A MAD MAD MAD MAD MULTIVERSE

We landed in powdery red dust. The impact was not terribly hard, and for that, I was thankful. I coughed and blinked before rising to my knees. The sky was the color of butterscotch with a sun that seemed small and faint. Red sand dunes surrounded us and stretched in all directions.

"Where are we now?" Valdara asked as she helped Drake to his feet.

"I have no idea, lass," Rook said with a cough as he also pulled himself off the ground. "Ask Mr. Subworld here." He nodded his head in my direction.

I spun about, but there were no landmarks, noth-

ing to distinguish this world from any other made of
a lot of red dust. "I don't know . . ."

"Well, I'm naming it the Sea of Red Dust," Drake
said as he tried to brush the stuff from his robes.
"Seems to be the only thing here." He held up his
hands as if in supplication. "Which I'm not com-
plaining about, because it beats the hell out of where
we were."

Rook took a swig from his flask. "Well, I'm goin'
to call it Barsoon, because if we don't find a bar soon
I'm goin' to run out of whiskey, and that's about the
only thin' that's keepin' me goin' at this point." He
looked at me. "Lad, why don't you ask our tour guide
where we go from here?"

"We aren't done?" Valdara asked.

"No," replied Vivian.

"Do you know what we need to do here?" I asked.
She smiled and replied harmonically, "Wait."

"For what?" Rook groused. In response, a series
of loud guttural sounds, followed by a rapid set of
loud hollow pounding noises, issued from behind the
dunes surrounding us. "Forget I asked," he said softly,
and drew his ax.

Three enormous—as in, two-story-tall enormous—
white-furred creatures with four arms emerged atop
the nearest dunes. They were massive colossi of pri-
mate power, and their eyes glared down at us with
pure hate. A lot about them bothered me, including

what they were doing in a desert, but at the moment the size of their teeth was all I could focus on.

"Apes!" shouted Valdara as she drew her sword and chakram. "Drake, remember the Steaming Jungle of Itnauy, and those crazed ape men who couldn't believe we could talk?"

"Remember? I'm the one who drove out the serpent people." He lifted his staff. "I can't believe I'm saying this, but I miss the good old days."

"Our best chance is to concentrate our attacks," Valdara said. "Drake, distract the one on the middle and the right, and use every defensive spell you can to stay alive. Rook and I will attack the one on the left and take it out quickly. Then we concentrate on the center one until it falls, and we finish off the last of them. Avery, stay here and use your spells to support whichever of us is struggling. If things go badly, we'll use this spot as a fallback position."

We all nodded, and I think all of us felt better to have Valdara in charge, but before we could put her plan into action, Vivian said, "Don't attack them."

"What!" all of us said at once.

"What are we supposed to do, lass?" Rook asked with a grunt of dismay. "Ask them to tea?"

"Wait," she said serenely.

We didn't have long. With roars that echoed across the empty landscape, the apes charged, taking enormous loping, jumping steps that covered twenty feet a stride.

"Can we attack now?" Drake asked.

"Wait."

They were near the bottom of the dune hills and tearing across the small valley toward us. They would be on us in seconds.

"Why are we listening to someone who admittedly is not all here?" Valdara asked. No one had an answer.

When I could see the whites of their eyes and the plaque on their teeth, I called, "Viviaaaan?"

"Wait . . ." she said.

When the apes were sixty feet away, I began beseeching the gods for help. When they were forty feet away, Vivian's eyes began to glow. When they were twenty feet away, I felt the tug of her spell on my brain. A split second before we vanished there was a swirling of energy and Moregoth's men materialized next to us. The sound of their screams followed us through etherspace.

We appeared in an ancient, ruined city, on what must have once been a grand plaza, but which the steaming jungle around us was reclaiming inch by inch. Before us was a hulk of a man with a mane of black hair cut square around his face. He was wearing a loincloth, and across his back was strapped an enormous sword. He had been walking down the broad stairway of a soaring temple carrying an ornately decorated chest, but stopped when we appeared. The man stared at us with sullen, volcanic blue eyes for a moment, then his voice boomed forth, echoing through the empty city. "If you have come to claim the jewels, then know that they are mine, and we will see who feasts on death first!"

Drake, Valdara, and I looked at each other in total bewilderment, but before any of us could tell him that he could keep his treasure, Vivian stepped forward. "Mighty warrior, I seek not your riches, but your aid," she said in the most vulnerable, waifish voice I had ever heard from her. "A man comes. A pale man with flesh like paper and lips like the dead. If he follows me from this place he will kill me." She fell to her knees, her eyes downcast. "Only you can save me."

Without a word, the man set the box down and drew his sword with a smooth, practiced motion. His eyes burned with a bestial light. "Never fear, fair one. I will crush your enemy. He will fall at my feet, and you shall hear his lamentations on the air."

Vivian's spell tugged at the back of my skull as she smiled and said, "Thank you, great warrior." Once again, we were pulled through etherspace.

When I questioned her about the man and how she knew he would be there, Vivian fixed me with her gold-glinted eyes and said she simply knew, and also knew what she needed to say. It became clear that

Vivian's spell was operating with an intelligence. It was what Rook had said about the hypocube; the spell was taking us to Sam and Ariella, but it was choosing a path based on some deeper internal calculation about what it thought we needed. Obviously, it had come to the conclusion that what we needed most was to shake Moregoth from our trail. Unfortunately, it had also determined that the best way to deal with the Moregoth problem was to take us to places of mind-boggling lethality and hope he died first.

We emerged in something resembling an ancient Egyptian temple. Torches illuminated sandstone walls, and brilliantly colored hieroglyphics covered pillars and statues of gold embossed with blue lapis lazuli. There were lines of men in ornamental masks and gilt robes standing in front of us. Up a broad set of stairs, an altar stood before which a man in high-priest garbs held a still-beating human heart. He pointed a shifting finger and opened his mouth, and from it flew a swarm of glittering black beetles. Before they could reach us, the spell pulled us back through the safety of the ether.

Each time we transported, the story was the same. We appeared in a world or a place beset by deadly peril. Sometimes it was immediate: once, our group and Moregoth's both appeared in the middle of a storm of nothingness at the edge of a decaying reality yearning for a name. Sometimes there could be quite a long delay: one time we found ourselves on a pleasant grassy ledge up the side of a mountain. It was perfectly sized for our little group and well sheltered from the elements, and we took Moregoth's absence to rest and recuperate.

This was first place we had landed since our frenetic journey began where I had the time to talk to Vivian about what was happening to her. It was the morning of our second day there, and I found myself sitting next to her. She was intently watching a bird that was busily eating the snails that lived in the cool dampness of the ledge. A strange and enigmatic smile curved the corners of her mouth. Something about the scene was deeply disturbing.

"Do you think I'm evil, Avery?" she asked, breaking the silence between us.

After what she'd done on the faun's world I'd given the question a lot of thought. That I didn't really have an answer yet was probably answer enough, but I also knew that some of my disgust at her was guilt over all the "noble" magic I'd done over the years without thinking. And all of that was confused by the fact that I thought I was falling in love with her. The pause between her question and my answer was long enough that she left off her study of the bird to stare at me instead.

I dropped my eyes and sighed. "I don't know, Vivian,

but if you are, then so am I. Let me ask in return, do you think we're evil?"

She frowned and said nothing. About the time I thought she might not answer at all she said, "I don't, but then I'm willing to accept that I may be a bad judge. The universe at least appears to think I am, and who am I to argue with its judgment?"

"What do you mean, the universe thinks you're evil?"

She drew her knees up into her chest and rested the side of her head on them. "I mean I am often cast into the role of villain. I lied to you in Baum's world, Avery. I wasn't Dorothy. I was the witch. That's why I asked you so many questions about her. The Munchkins were terrified of me."

"Yes, but that's probably because you can do magic and—"

She shook her head and began to tick off examples on her fingers. "In Carroll's world, I was the Queen of Hearts. In Lewis's world, I was the White Queen. In Howard's world, I was the barbarian king's temptress."

"What about the ape world?" I countered. "You were *not* the villain there."

"Maybe I was," she said with a sad sigh. "How do you know I wasn't the reason the creatures went out of their way to attack us?"

I thought about this for a minute and asked, "Even if you're right—and I'm not saying I agree with you—why would that be the case?"

"You're going to laugh at me, but I think the universe knows what I did on Trelari. I think it's punishing me."

I did laugh. "You think you have some sort of universal karmic debt? If that sort of thing happened, then why wouldn't the universe be coming after me? I was literally the bloody Dark Lord!"

She smiled again, but the smile didn't reach her gold-ringed eyes. "But that was only prologue, Avery. Since I've known you, your story has been about redemption—your redemption. If you'll remember, I was the villain of the last book. What if that's what I am? What if I'm the thread of evil woven through the narrative of your life? What if I'm the enemy?"

"Gods!" I shouted, my voice echoing about the ledge and startling the bird into flight. "My life is not a bloody book. This moment we're having isn't another episode to be neatly encapsulated in a chapter headed with a pithy title. Nothing is guaranteed. And stop taking all the blame for what happened in Lewis's world. I'm the one that gave you the key. You warned me there would be a price if we kept going: war and horror and death. You wanted us to walk away, to enjoy lives of quiet contentment. I chose this path . . ." I lowered my voice, because my anger had turned to emptiness. "Have you ever considered that I may be just as advertised: the villain of the piece? After all, I am the Dark Lord?"

Silence stretched between us. In time the bird returned, and Vivian went back to her study of the creature. I had sunk back into my own troubled thoughts when she spoke again. "I am sorry about the faun. I hope you know that."

"I know," I answered.

And I did. She'd destroyed the faun's world, not because that's what she wanted, but because I wouldn't. That was Vivian. She still believed that the ends justified the means. I was not so certain, either that what we were doing was right, or that we had a right to do it regardless of the cost. It was becoming more and more apparent to me that humility was what was needed, and that humility was a quality Mysterium mages were not well known for.

In fact, the more I considered everything that had happened since Trelari, the less ridiculous the idea of Vivian and I being universal symbols of evil seemed. My existence as the Dark Lord had been reflected through the multiverse. There was no reason Vivian's life as the Dark Queen shouldn't have been reflected. I was still thinking over my own place in the universe, and whether my reputation was the reason waiters invariably got my order wrong, when Moregoth appeared, followed moments later by an enormous red dragon that smashed the side of the mountain to bits just as we faded away.

And so it went. Vivian's spell was without remorse. No matter the danger, it always seemed to pick the right moment to have Moregoth arrive so he and his men would receive the brunt of whatever doom was waiting. It ground away at Moregoth's army like the sea does the shore. He was down to a handful of men when we faced off against him on the deck of a pirate ship. I suppose some part of me had begun to pity the Sealers, but it was still a very, very small part.

The captain, who, based on his smell and behavior, must have been drinking since the night before, stared back and forth between us as we glared at each other. "What the two of you need," he slurred, "is rum. Rum makes everything better. Savvy?"

"Be quiet, shadow!" Moregoth said coldly.

"Hey, I'm Captain Jack . . ." he began to say, and went down under a hail of fire from the Sealers.

Moregoth must have given some signal, but if he did, I never saw it. I studied the four men remaining from Moregoth's original army. They looked hardened to the point of brittleness, and there was a madness in their eyes that seemed perfectly understandable given all they had been through.

Moregoth also looked bad. He was still pale, and tall, and creepy, but the long hair that had once fallen elegantly down his face was matted, and the dark make-up around his eyes and lips had smeared so he now looked more unwell than sinister.

"End this, Moregoth," I said. "End it before anyone else dies."

"Tired, Dark Lord?" He gave a hollow, wheezing

laugh. "I'm just beginning to enjoy myself. I will never stop. I will hunt you to the ends of the multiverse, even beyond the boundaries of this world and into the sweet oblivion of the next. You will find no peace. There will be no end."

I am not sure how I would have responded. Probably I would have done something stupid like try to punch him . . . and miss. Fortunately for all of our dignities, Vivian stepped forward. Her eyes were glowing, and that all too familiar feeling of pressure was building in the back of my skull. "If you will not end it, then I will," she said in an angry, discordant voice.

The water around the ship began to churn and froth. The deck began to roll and pitch. The entire vessel was twisting and turning in the water as though it were caught in a vast whirlpool. A second later, a swarm of massive tentacles erupted from the water and lashed onto the deck. As our bodies were pulled into the ether, a shadow ascended from the depths. Moregoth's eyes went wide as a giant, gaping, beaked maw closed around the ship.

We appeared in a downpour outside a low-slung, two-story building. Above the door was a painted sign of a dancing pony. We stood, letting the rain beat down us. All of us were breathing hard and staring about looking for a threat, but nothing happened.

After a minute or so, Drake asked, "Was that it? Is . . . is Moregoth gone?"

"If he's not, then I don't think the bastard is kill-able," Rook said.

"What was that thing anyway?" Valdara asked.

Vivian answered in a dreamlike voice. "'He lived below the thunders of the upper deep; Far beneath in the abysmal sea, His ancient, dreamless, uninvaded sleep.'"

Rook leaned in and whispered. "No offense, Avery, but your girlfriend is a little scary."

"It's a poem by Tennyson, Rook," I said. "I think 'that thing' was a kraken."

He gave a grunt that let me know exactly what he thought about poetry. "Well, whatever it was, if it managed to eat Moregoth I'll raise a toast to it. Speakin' of which," he said, looking up at the inn's placard, "I say we go inside. Get out of the rain. And get hammered."

"Are you saying after all that traveling, through all those worlds, the gateway took us here to get us drunk?" Valdara asked in disbelief.

Rook gave her a melodramatic shake of his head. "Remember lass, it's not what we want. It's what the portal thinks we need."

Drake pushed past them to the door. "Well, at this point, I'm not one to fight the fates."

CHAPTER 27

A PARTY LINE

We walked through the door into the warm chaos of a pub on a miserable night when no one feels like being alone. Crowds of people and dwarfs and elves and halflings were seated around long trestle tables in the center of the room, and smaller, private tables set along the walls and in the corners. A crackling fire burned cheerily in the grate, and merry music filled the air. A curly haired halfling was dancing atop a table as the crowd clapped out a rhythm.

"Looks like home," Valdara said, and she seemed to relax a little.

"Aye, lass, that it does," Rook grunted happily. "I'll get some ales. You find us a table."

She did, off to one side, as far away from the revelry as possible. There had been a weaselly little fellow sitting and watching the dancing halfling with a dark eye, but Valdara leaned in close and said something, and he had abandoned his spot with remarkable speed. Soon Rook returned with seven ales: one for each of us and three for him.

As the group had taken to doing in every world, we first made sure Vivian was safe and comfortable. The traveling had taxed her most, both physically and emotionally. The spell, for as much as it had saved us time and time again, had turned her into a vessel. Her actions had not always been her own, and her memories were often clouded. I could see from the slight glimmer in her golden-ringed eyes that the spell was still on her, only dormant. She would be herself for a time, until she was not.

I pushed an ale in front of her and tapped the side of the mug so she would notice. She tried to smile, but it was a tired effort. "I'm fine, Avery."

She studied her drink, but otherwise did not touch it. "What's troubling you?" I asked.

She sighed. "The Sealers. So many of them have died, because of me."

Her thoughts mirrored my own, except I had been thinking about how they had died because of *me*. Moregoth had been so intent on getting at *me*. The irony, that we were both blaming ourselves, struck me. I laughed bitterly.

"Avery!" she said sternly. "I know they've been

trying to kill us, but they worked for the university. They may have been misguided, but—"

"No, Vivian. I . . . I wasn't laughing at them. I was laughing at us." I stabbed a finger into my chest. "We are both blaming ourselves for their deaths, but neither of us is really to blame. Not solely. It's true they would never have run into the things that killed them had you not cast the spell, but they wouldn't have been chasing you at all if it weren't for me."

"You can go back even further," Rook said, draining his second tankard. "Had the Mysterians not mucked up the multiverse, Moregoth would never have existed. Fact of the matter is, most of the people at the top of the Administration are Mysterians, or had help from them. Moregoth went to the same school I did growin' up." He shook a finger in Vivian's direction. "So, don't you go hoggin' all the blame, lass. There's plenty of it to go around."

"And you guys are forgetting the person most responsible," Drake growled. "Moregoth himself. He could have stopped. He made a choice to lead those men after us. Pushing through every barrier, every trap. It was . . . It was . . ."

"Madness," Valdara offered.

We all raised our glasses and toasted. "Madness!"

After we drank, Valdara turned to Vivian. "Do you know where we go from here?"

Vivian shook her head. "I'm not sure. I know we're close, but we have to wait."

"With Moregoth dead, shouldn't the route be clear?" Drake asked.

Vivian shrugged and Rook cleared his throat. "We might be a little lost," he said, staring sadly at the dregs of his last mug of ale.

"What do you mean, 'lost'?" I asked. "I thought this 'desire gateway,' or whatever you called it, was supposed to be able to get us anywhere in the multiverse."

"It can!" he said with great confidence, but then began rubbing the back of his neck. "However, if you've stashed them in the place I think you stashed them, then where Sam and Ariella are is not exactly a *place* in the multiverse. It's more of a *time*."

The innkeeper, a fat man with a florid face and sweating brow, came bustling by to clear away our empty mugs. We ordered another round of drinks and some food to go along with it. He paused, staring at us uncertainly. "You all just come into town?"

The group went quiet, and Rook answered for all of us. "What's it to you?"

The innkeeper wiped his head with his cloth nervously. "Nothing! Nothing! I was only wondering if you'd need some rooms for the night."

We visibly relaxed, and agreed that a room would be a good idea, and that we would pay in advance, because we might be leaving unexpectedly. This puzzled him a little, but one of Rook's glowers forestalled any further questions. After the innkeeper left, we returned to the question of Sam and Ariella.

Rook tried unsuccessfuly to explain a number of times what he meant about the *Discovery* not being a place before he finally barked, "All the four of you need to know is that the *Discovery* is not a physical place, but a spell cast by Mysterians."

"How can it be a spell?" Valdara asked. "We were standing on it."

"And?" he replied irritably.

"And you can't stand on a spell. They aren't real," she argued.

Rook gave a derisive snort. "Tell that to the guy that's just been fried by a mystical lightnin' bolt, or caught one of Sam's conjured arrows in the throat."

"That's different."

"No, lass, it isn't. The *Discovery* is a spell—more complicated and sophisticated than most—but still a spell."

"What kind of spell?" I asked. "What's its purpose?"

He scratched his beard trying to figure out the best way to explain. "I suppose the best explanation is that it's a time-travel portal. We cast it eons ago to transport all the Mysterians back to a time before we originally lost control of Mysterium. It was meant to give us a last chance to wrest control of Mysterium away from the mages if our other efforts failed. Unfortunately, most Mysterians now see it as plan A, B, and C, rather than the last worst hope it was meant to be."

Having grown up on the *Terminator* movies, my mind raced at the implications. "But if you change the past, wouldn't that destroy everything that's happened since?" I asked. "Including us?"

Rook rolled his eyes in disgust. "I really wonder what you spent all that time at school doin'. From what I hear, it wasn't chasin' girls." He winked at Vivian. "Not sure what else would have kept you from learnin' so much."

"Can you just tell me what I'm missing?" I asked. "Or is this yet *another* topic you are going to find impossible to explain in a way that rational people can follow?"

He grunted. "The problem is that you weren't listenin' to me . . . as usual. I didn't say we were goin' back to a time in Mysterium before the troubles began. That's just silly. What I said was that we were takin' the Mysterians back to a time before the troubles began."

He looked at me with a smile that said he believed he'd just explained everything. I groaned and looked to the heavens. "What's the difference?"

The dwarf's smile vanished. "The difference? The difference? In one case, you're tryin' to do somethin' impossible. To go back in time and try to replay events all over again is ridiculous. It's the kind of silliness you read in those sci-fi-type novels." He shook a finger at me. "How would it work? You'd take yourself physically back to a time in the past and try to relive it. People imagine this would mean that they'd remember everythin' they know now. But those memories are physically written in your brain. Goin' back in time would erase all those memories and thoughts. So, you'd be there in the past, but you'd be no wiser. You might make a different decision, but chances are you wouldn't, because there were reasons you made certain choices in the first place, and those same reasons would still be there when you got back. Time travel!" he barked irritably.

"So, what are you doing in the *Discovery*?"

"You want the simple answer?"

Everyone at the table said, "Yes!"

The dwarf took a second to gather his thoughts and then said slowly, "We're tryin' to reset ourselves, to take our magical patterns back to a time before Mysterium was stolen. If we can do that, then we won't be constrained by the new pattern the Usurpers placed on us." He looked at me and raised his mug in salute. "Essentially, we are tryin' to do on purpose what you managed to do by accident. That's why so many of us were so excited to talk to you."

I thought I understood, and the implications were fascinating, but before I could ask a follow-up question, Valdara asked abruptly, "What does all of that nonsense have to do with us being lost?"

Rook and I both started to answer. He gestured for me to give it a go. "Because Sam and Ariella aren't in a physical location in the multiverse, Vivian's spell might not be able to find them. It might simply keep transporting us about, or it might get us as close as it can and then park us somewhere until the Mysterians' spell is complete."

"How long will that be?" Drake asked.

"Not long," Rook assured her. "It can't be more than seven or eight centuries of Mysterium . . . or Trelarian . . . time now. Certainly, no more than a millennium. We would know better if that bloody computer hadn't mucked about with the clocks."

"Are you trying to tell me that we may have to wait centuries to find Sam and Ariella?" Valdara said, her voice rising to a shout. Rook and I both gestured to her to keep it down, and she dropped her head into her hands and muttered something about wizards and insanity. "Why don't we do whatever you did to get them there in the first place, and why haven't we done it already?"

"We needed to lose Moregoth," I explained.

"And now that he's gone?" she asked.

I stroked my hand across my chin. "I suppose we could."

"Suppose? I could with that bloody key of Avery's," Rook said with a quick snap of his fingers. "Easy!"

"It's not that easy, Rook, and certainly not as consequence free as you are making it sound," I said, not wanting us to go down this road and risk erasing another world.

"What are you talkin' about?" he asked. "You may not know what that thing is capable of, but I do."

It was obvious that he was still holding a grudge that I hadn't given him the key when he asked for it. "You mistake me, Rook, I know exactly what this thing is capable of," I said, and my disapproval must have come out in my tone, because the dwarf bristled.

"What's your sudden beef with Mysterians?"

"I don't have a problem with Mysterians . . ." I answered, and realized as I was saying it that I might actually have a problem with Mysterians. "It's just—"

Valdara interrupted. "Look, Avery, unless there is a risk of this thing blowing us to the semi-lich, I vote we use it. I would like to see Sam and Ariella and Trelari again before I die."

"Amen!" said Drake as he slammed a tankard of water down on the table.

"You only say that because you don't know the danger—" I started to say, but this time Rook interrupted me.

"There is *no* danger, laddie, unless you're an amateur."

"Let's resolve this once and for all," Drake growled. "Avery, pull out the key."

"Here?"

"I'm not asking you to do anything indecent, kid," he rasped under his breath. "Just let Rook give it a try."

I understood why he asked, but all I could remember was the look on the little girl in blue's face, and the cat's final smile, and the faun's beautiful brass door handle. "This isn't a game, Drake. We can't use the key."

Rook asked quietly, "Can't you trust me?"

I turned and looked at the dwarf. "I could ask you the same question."

We stared at each other, neither of us sure what to say, until Valdara banged her mug down, making both of us jump. "Enough of this nonsense. All I want to know is whether we can use Avery's magic key to get back to Sam and Ariella."

It was in the silence that followed her question that the innkeeper came back with our food and drinks. He kept up a constant patter as he laid out the food. I looked at the heaping platters with distaste. I had never been less hungry. No one was really listening to what the man said until he remarked, "I happened to overhear you folks talking. Do you know Sam and Ariella?"

I am not sure who drew the first dagger, but in the time it took the innkeeper to say, "Oh!" Valdara had pulled him down into a chair beside her, and Rook had the point of a dirk pressed against the innkeeper's ribs.

"Okay, laddie," Rook said in an impressive growl. "Who are you, and what do you know about our friends?"

"I . . . I don't know anything, e-e-except that they . . . they left a message," he spluttered. "They said that some friends would come in looking for them and that I was to give them a message."

"Well, you've found us," Rook said.

"I suppose I have at that," he said with a strained smile. "I should have given it to you as soon as you came in, but one thing and another happens. You know how it is. Always busy—"

"The message!" we all said at once.

"Oh, here it is," he said, and mopped his brow with his handkerchief.

The world stuttered around us. Across the room the dancing halfling leapt high and flickered out of view. Then the world stuttered again, the halfling flickered back into view, and the communicator coin in my pocket buzzed. As the other bar patrons eyed the halfling in silent suspicion, I pulled the coin out and activated the connection. "Sam?"

"Ariella," she said. "But close."

"Is that your friend?" the innkeeper asked with a smile.

"Yes, thanks." I nodded for Rook and Valdara to let him go.

He bowed several times, but remained, hovering over our table expectantly. I was about to wave him away and then thought the common room of an inn was probably not the best place to have this conversation. "We could use that private room now," I said.

"A room, of course! Right away! I'll have my boy show you the way."

A minute later, we were sitting in a little room overlooking a back garden. Our supper was laid on a table, but none of us was eating. Instead, everyone clustered around as I talked to Sam and Ariella.

Ariella was not happy. "Where are you? It has been at least two days since you talked to us. Do you know how much class we're missing? If you get me expelled, Avery Stewart, I will never forgive you."

"Tell him about our practice sessions!" I heard Sam say from somewhere behind her.

Ariella sighed. "We did find a place to practice spells, like you asked. Um, what's happening to us? Sam tried his sleep spell on me and I didn't wake up for twelve hours!"

"That's going to require a lot of explanation," I said. "Maybe we can go into it when we get there."

"Which takes me back to my first question," she said, and there was no mistaking the frustration in her voice. "Where are you and when are you going to be here?"

Before I could answer, my coin made a clicking noise in my head, just like when someone was trying to call me. I asked Ariella to wait a second and tapped the coin again.

"Don't hang up!" Eldrin said.

"Is that Eldrin?" Ariella asked. "Hi, Eldrin, nice to hear your voice. Did you find anything out about our tuition?"

"We paid!" Sam shouted in the background.

There was a strained silence as I realized that, somehow, I had managed to connect to both Eldrin and Ariella at the same time.

"Eldrin?" I asked.

"Yes."

"Ariella?" I asked.

"Yes, Avery."

"How is this happening?" I asked.

Ariella said, "What are you talking about? You gave us the coins to do just this. Although Sam did think of a clever trick. We kept trying to call you, but you wouldn't answer so he set up a spell that would find you as soon as your Coin of Farspeaking was reachable."

"Coin of Farspeaking?" Eldrin said with a snort. "It's a Transtemporal Subworld Communicator."

"That's a ridiculous name," she said. "Coin of Farspeaking tells you what it does and what form it takes, whereas your name is confusing, difficult to say, and not pretty."

They began to argue over the relative merits of the different names, and how they did or did not adequately describe the magic being used in the device, and whether precision was really very important in naming a magical device, and so on. I think they would have quite happily gone on the rest of the night, but Valdara kept gesturing at me to give her news, and I had nothing to tell her except that they were being very elvish. I did glean from the back and forth that Eldrin had created a new "coin" and somehow tied it to the spell patterns of the other two so the next time they were used it would also connect to him. In other words, he had tapped my phone.

Having learned everything I needed, I cut in. "Why don't we save this debate for a time when we aren't on three different planes of existence?"

They both stopped talking for a second, and then Ariella asked, "What do you mean three? Isn't Eldrin on Mysterium with you?"

Neither of us answered.

"Hello? Is this thing working?" she asked, and there was a loud popping noise that made my brain hurt as she metaphysically tapped the coin.

"Stop that," I said. "Yes, it is working. No, we are not both on Mysterium."

"Why not?"

Another silence followed.

Have you ever had a moment when you realized that you have two sets of friends who do not cross? I was surrounded by my old group from Trelari, and yet none of them really knew anything about Eldrin, my best friend in the world. And those that did know him had only heard about how he had potentially betrayed me. What would they say about me reconnecting with him now?

What I wanted to do was separate the calls, but I knew whatever Eldrin and I had to say to each other was going to have to include Ariella. I refused to disconnect from her, because I owed her an explanation and I was worried the coins did not seem to be entirely reliable, at least between here and the *Discovery*. On the other hand, I needed to speak to Eldrin for my own sanity. His absence had been weighing more and more heavily on my mind every day that slipped by. I needed to know whether I would ever be able to trust him again.

I was still trying to decide what to say to them both when I heard Ariella say to Sam, "Are you sure you want them to do that?"

We heard Sam's reply as an indistinct, "Wah wah, wah wah wah."

"They're your feet," she said, again still talking to him. "Just remember they are supposed to do what you want, not the other way around."

"Sorry, back to you," she said much more distinctly. "Anyway, why are you two being so mysterious? It doesn't matter where you are. We are getting bored and want to know if you found anything at Student Records and if so when we can come back."

Eldrin answered. "You may not be able to go back, Ariella." He paused and added, *"None* of us may ever be able to go back."

His answer kindled a flicker of hope in me. "Do you mean you've left Mysterium?"

"Dawn and I both have," he said. "We left a few hours after you. We tried to track you in New York, but the coffee shop was already gone."

"What do you mean 'gone'?" I asked.

"They're calling it a 'gas explosion'; basically, the store has been leveled."

"Gods!" I took a deep breath. "Does your leaving Mysterium mean—"

"I don't know," he answered before I had to ask about his feelings toward Sam and Ariella. "What I do know is that it isn't safe to be a friend of Avery Stewart in Mysterium. Dawn and I are on the run."

"Sorry."

I could hear the shrug on the other end of the line. "We went by your townhome by the way. Nice place. The real crime in all this is that you had us living in a crap apartment for seven months."

I laughed, because being gently abused by Eldrin felt so good right now. "My thoughts exactly."

Ariella had been incredibly patient, but at this, she cleared her throat. "Eldrin, sorry to interrupt, but we were trying to figure out when Avery might be able to come get us out of this place."

"What?" he asked. "Oh, right. I should get off this line anyway. The longer I'm on, the better the odds that they'll trace the connection. It's subtle magic, but as you can see, not impenetrable. Anyway, the reason I took the risk is to warn you not to return to the university. The Administration is claiming you went on a rampage and murdered the dean of Subworld Studies, his assistant, a guard in Student Records, and a young Gorgon woman."

"I didn't!" I shouted.

"I know," he said. "But the Administration has produced a lot of compelling evidence of your guilt, and the pictures they are circulating are fairly . . . graphic. You are basically public enemy number one. Don't trust *anyone* from Mysterium."

The little room in the tavern swam sickeningly

and I collapsed into a chair as my mind conjured images from the darkest parts of my imagination. "Thanks for the warning," was all I could manage, and that was a struggle.

"I'm sorry, Avery," he said.

"Me too," I said, and then I gathered all my courage together. "If you and Dawn are in trouble we could meet you somewhere. You could join us."

There was a long silence, and then he said, "You know that would be a terrible idea, Avery."

"I know, but I needed to say it."

"I know."

It was the softness of the voice that hurt most. I could picture him sitting, hunched in his chair, his long hair draped over his face, staring into the surface of the coin, trying to counsel me from across the multiverse as he had done so many times in the past. Only, this time he was utterly unreachable. Neither of us could risk traveling to the other. Maybe ever.

We lingered together a little while longer without saying anything, and then I heard Dawn's voice in the distance saying something I could not hear clearly. He said, "I've got to go. It really isn't safe to have a line of communication open between us for long. Also, don't try to reconnect on this pattern. I'll make a new one, and contact you as soon as I can. In the meantime, stay safe, Avery."

"You too, Eldrin."

The connection went dead. There was a long

pause, and then Ariella's voice came back. "I'm sorry, Avery."

"It's not your fault, Ariella," I said dully.

"It kind of is," she answered.

No, it wasn't. This wasn't her fault or Eldrin's fault or even Moregoth's fault. This was on Vivian and me, trying to play gods with other people's lives. Maybe she was right, and everything that had happened since was some sort of universal karmic payback. Whatever it was, it was time to isolate the virus. I jumped to my feet and began pacing back and forth, thinking. It only took a second for me to realize the solution was actually quite simple.

I turned to the gathered group. "Sam and Ariella are safe for the moment, but we need to get to them."

"Which brings us back to the question of the key, doesn't it," Valdara said sharply.

She was right, it did raise the question, but it didn't answer the question. I took a deep breath. "Yes, Valdara, we still need to figure out how to get back to the *Discovery*, but—"

"Why is that a problem?" Ariella asked.

"There are a few complications," I answered enigmatically.

"Complications?" she said, and then I heard her turn away. "Sam, hold this for a second. Make sure to keep the connection with Avery open."

"Please, Ariella, Valdara and the rest of us need to discuss how to get back to you. We don't have time for . . ." A circle of blue energy appeared on the floor a few paces away and Ariella materialized inside it. "It worked!" She smiled brightly.

Valdara and Drake shouted, "Ariella!" and leapt to embrace her.

"Ariella?" I said in stunned disbelief. "How?"

"I followed the signal from the Coin of Farspeaking. It was easy!" she said, while stilling hugging Drake.

"Could you duplicate what you did to get back to Sam?" I asked.

She shrugged. "Sure. As long as the connection between the coins is open, it acts as a kind of beacon."

Something about that bothered me, but there was little time to think. "Let's do some magic!" Drake boomed happily.

Vivian pulled me aside. "What about me? Won't I still be under my original spell? What if it keeps me here—trapped?"

I looked into her eyes and smiled. "It won't."

"How do you know?"

"Because this is part of your spell's plan. It sent us here because it knew Sam and Ariella would get in touch with us. It sent us to the exact place we needed to be." I put my hands on her shoulders. "I promise you will not be left behind, not this time."

The doubt remained on her face. What she could not see was the light in her eyes was getting brighter by the second. The spell knew, even if she did not, that another jump was coming—the last one.

CHAPTER 28

THE RETURN OF THE
COMPANY OF THE FELLOWSHIP

Ariella sorted out the link with Sam. We joined hands, and a few seconds later were standing in the relaxation lounge and spa of the *Discovery*. Unlike the observation bridge where we first entered the spaceship, or timeship as I had begun to think of it, all the walls and ceilings glowed with a soothing white light. I knew it was meant to be soothing, because the word was faintly projected on every surface, and music filtering down from hidden speakers had melodious voices softly singing the words *soothe* or *soothing* behind the instrumentals.

Yes, it was as annoying as it sounds.

Robots of every shape and size surrounded Sam. Short-wheeled robots were doing something with his feet. A taller robot with dozens of arms was massaging his shoulders, face, and head, while a trio of robots with trays of snacks and drinks kept circling about him. From his expression, and the way he kept trying to shoo them away, I would say that, despite what most hotel chains would claim, hospitality does have its limits.

"Please stop," Sam pleaded. "I am part halfling. I take pride in my foot hair."

"I told you not to let them touch your feet," Ariella said as she waved the robots that came swarming toward her aside like gnats. "Now you're going to be scratching for weeks."

"You must choose what type of tea you want, Mistress Ariella," one of the tray robots ordered. "I will read you the list again. orange pekoe, green tea, oolong, Earl Grey, white tea, Shoumei tea, mint ginger lemon tea—"

"I don't want tea!"

"You've put a crinkle in your face. I'm going to give you a full facial," said a tall, many-armed robot, looming over Ariella's head.

Another robot shaped like a motorized bookcase rolled in. "What about a book? Remember, reading is FUNdamental."

"Enough!" shouted Rook. All the robots froze for a second and then lined themselves in a row in front of the dwarf. Rook folded his arms behind him and marched up and down the row, like a drill sergeant performing an inspection. "Dismissed!"

At Rook's command, the room emptied of robots. Sam gave a sigh of relief. "How did you manage that?"

The dwarf rolled his eyes. "No big thing. They're programmed to obey all Mysterians."

"Well, however you did it, I'm glad to see all of you!" Sam said with a whoop of joy.

"Same here, kid," said Drake in his warmest growl. "Looks like you've been doin' all right."

"You would think that, but . . ." Sam launched into a long series of complaints. Ultimately, it came down to the fact that the robots had nearly driven Sam and Ariella mad with their need to serve.

A pink light filled the lounge, coming from every tile. "You were never in danger. I was with you the whole time," said EDIE.

"As was I," announced ED as blue lights flashed.

"Yes, you were *both*, indeed, *everywhere*," Ariella said.

"Even in the bathroom when I was . . . naked?" Sam whispered.

Rook glowered at the blue and pink lights. "What have I told the two of you about spyin' on people in the bathroom?"

ED's blue light flashed first. "Your precise words were, 'If I catch you @#$%&$& pocket calculators spyin' on me one more time, I'll scrap you and turn you both into $*&^*#$ toaster ovens.'"

"If you review your memory banks," EDIE said with a superior pink flash, "you will find he called us '*&&^%$# pocket calculators.'"

I whispered in Rook's ear. "Did you really say, star ampersand ampersand caret percent dollar sign number?"

Rook rubbed his face in frustration. "No, lad. But the bloody computers were programmed to have a PG rating, so they won't use swear words."

"This is a family friendly starship!" boomed ED. "Besides, what he said was at sign number dollar sign percent ampersand dollar sign ampersand."

"No, he didn't," the pink light flashed.

"Yes, he did," the blue light flashed in reply.

"No."

"Yes."

The two lights swirled faster and faster forming a purplish blur. Their words sped up, merged, and swelled until it was a horrible electronic buzz. I watched a flush of red creep up Rook's neck as his anger rose. He tugged on his beard and muttered a few somethings that would never have made it past the PG filter.

"Silence!" he roared. "I've been away hundreds of years, and you two can still irritate me in a matter of seconds." He turned to me and muttered, "I think the problem is that they've been programmed with personalities."

I nodded. "You're probably right. Professor Adams wrote extensively about the dangers of 'feeling' machines."

"He has a point, but the problem with nonfeelin' machines on long missions like this is that they have no outlet for stress. By this point, we would have two completely mad computers on our hands. Or, more likely, they would have jettisoned everyone out into space a couple million years ago." The dwarf shook his head at the dilemma. "The real problem isn't that they have emotions, but that some yahoo thought it would be clever to program them as a married couple."

The computers had begun to argue again. Rook put a finger to his lips and pulled us out of the room and into a side hall so we could talk in peace. Sam was the first one to ask a question, and of course he managed to pick the most awkward topic possible. "So, Rook, you're not Trelarian?"

The dwarf went a little pale. He licked his lips and said, "No, lad. I was born on Mysterium."

Sam seemed troubled by this, but then as usual asked a not-so-obvious follow-up question that made me wonder exactly how his brain worked. "Is your real name Rook? And do dwarves really settle arguments using chess?"

"Yes and yes!" Rook said emphatically. "Well, I go by Rook as well as Fergus, but I prefer Rook, truth be told. And you should know by now that it's 'dwarfs' not 'dwarves.' Anyone who tells you otherwise is delusional."

"Right, I'll remember that, Mr. Rook," Sam said, clearly satisfied.

Valdara stepped in front of the dwarf. "I don't want to interrupt this important conversation about how to pluralize the word *dwarf,* but I would like to know where we go from here. Now that we're reunited, I'd like to get back to Trelari. I do have a kingdom to run."

"Agreed," Drake interjected. "Let's get Sam and Ariella the hell out of here."

"We can't abandon Avery and Rook," Sam said.

"And what about all my classes?" Ariella complained, and pulled out a sheet of paper that stretched from her hand to the floor.

"There is no way you are going back to that school." Valdara folded her arms across her chest. "It is way too dangerous."

"You can't stop me . . ." Ariella said.

"Your parents could," Drake interjected.

Vivian laughed. "Ariella doesn't need to get permission from her parents to go to Mysterium. Anyone can attend no matter what their family thinks of the decision."

I nodded my agreement. "She's right. My parents would have moved heaven and earth to stop me from dropping out of Oxford. Thankfully, they have no discernible magical talent."

Drake sighed. "Ariella is a little embarrassed to say it, but, technically, she hasn't reached the age of majority yet."

I looked back and forth between them, half-convinced that this was a setup for some joke. "I don't understand."

"Among elves, Ariella is still considered a child," Drake explained.

"I'm not a *child*," Ariella said moodily. "I only have forty years until my four hundredth birthday."

Having lived with a Hylar, I knew the conversion. "You're fifteen!" I spat. The realization that Ariella was still so young (among her race), and then the thought of all the danger I put her in, both in Trelari and here, made my stomach churn. "I can't believe your parents let you go on that quest with us in Trelari. You could have been killed!"

Now she was twisting her hands even more violently together. "They kind of sort of don't know I did that."

"*What?*"

"Please don't tell them," she said, her eyes going wide. "They would kill me!"

I stared at Drake and Valdara accusingly, wondering how they could have let such a thing happen. Valdara shrugged. "You were the one who recruited her into the party. Elves are always hard to age, and you being an all-powerful wizard, Drake and I assumed you had a way of checking. We had no idea she was so young until the whole crisis was over, and by then it was a little late to be fussed about it. When the school option came up we all thought it was a great idea. Had I known how crazy and evil the leaders of your school are I would never have approved it."

"I . . . I need to sit down," I said, and before the words were out a floating chair came zooming out of a panel in the wall. It was equipped with a cup holder in one arm and a video screen on the other. I was still so distracted by this newest revelation I sat without thinking.

"I am here to serve," the chair purred. "Would you like a beverage? How about a movie? I have a full range of entertainment options for your viewing pleasure."

The ship must have been monitoring us, because the success of the first chair in getting me to sit down led to another half dozen of the things launching out at us from various hidden compartments. Soon the group was surrounded by floating chairs all offering any number of delights.

Rook was still trying to shoo them away when blue lights flashed. ED spoke in his most cheerful voice. "Glad to see you're enjoying yourselves. Try the breakfast shakes. They are delicious, or so the machine that synthesizes the flavored protein strands they are made from tells me. By the way, a portal spell has been detected near the engine room. There is an enemy incursion in progress. Thought you might like to know."

With explosive hisses, two massive metal doors dropped into place on either end of the corridor. Pink lights flashed. EDIE's voice rang out. "Ladies and gentlemen, we apologize for the inconvenience, but for your safety we are shutting the blast doors to this section. We want to assure you that our staff take your travel comfort seriously, and we will do everything in our power to remedy the situation."

"Beard biscuits!" snapped Rook. "The Administration must have found us!"

"That's impossible," I said. "You said yourself this ship isn't a place, it's a time. How could they find it?"

He turned the question back on me. "Well, how did you find it? "

I shrugged. "All I remember is thinking about Griswald, and trying to get to wherever his key led, and it brought us here."

Rook thought about it for a second. "If your new magic works the way I think it works, then that actually makes sense."

"No, it doesn't," I said, frustrated. "This isn't Griswald's world. It's yours and the other Mysterians'."

"Well, about that . . ."

"Oh gods!" I shouted. "Are you saying Griswald is here? And you never thought to tell me?"

"It is kind of classified, lad," he said in a conspiratorial growl.

"You son of a—"

"Not to interrupt this deep philosophical discussion," Valdara said, "but how does any of this explain the fact that this impossible-to-trace ship . . . spell . . . thing has just been traced . . . again!"

"It doesn't!" I snapped, but a hideous thought stopped me short. "Unless . . ."

"Unless Moregoth didn't really die," Rook barked, completing my thought. "If he survived, then he would have still been connected to the spell when we made the jump here. He could have followed us right in."

"But wouldn't the spell have known?" Vivian asked.

"Spells like that aren't omniscient," Rook said grimly. "It's possible he used the kraken attack to play dead. Shieldin' himself from the spell until we made our jump here. It's also possible the spell was beginnin' to fade and needed to get us here despite his presence."

"That's all fine and dandy," Drake said. "What do we do now?"

Valdara walked over to the blast doors and banged her palm on them. "These look pretty solid. Could they keep out an attack?"

Rook started to answer, but before he could, someone from the other side of the room boomed out, "Not a chance! Those are only designed to keep the bots at bay."

I knew the voice immediately, and spun in disbelief as Griswald materialized in all his aged, balding, and overweight glory. "Professor!" I cried with joy.

"Stewart!" he said sharply. His face was set with its accustomed sternness, but I could see the tightening around his eyes and the slight twist at the corners of his mouth. He was happy to see me too.

"Rook just told me you were here, but why?" I asked.

"Why? Why? Because I'm the guardian of the spell, of course." He said this as though it were the most obvious thing in the world.

"Guardian?" My head swam at the implications. "Why? Why not a Mysterian? Why not him?" I asked, pointing a finger at Rook.

The dwarf shrugged. "We usually choose a non-Mysterian. Being here too long out of stasis has a tendency to warp our patterns."

I glared at Rook. "Another pretty important piece of information you never thought to tell me."

"It is classified, Stewart," Professor Griswald said, and Rook nodded his agreement.

I could feel the profanity boiling up from the deepest parts of my body, but I'd worked with Griswald for nearly six years, and if I knew his tells he knew mine even better.

"Not to interrupt whatever erudite comment you were about to make," he growled, "but what's going on here, Stewart? Why am I awake? Why are ED and

EDIE going on about evil Mysterium mages being here?" He looked around as though they might be hiding in the corners or under some of the floating chairs.

My anger evaporated as I realized I was going to have to confess to having messed things up again. I took a deep breath and said, "It's true, Professor. The Administration has been after us for days, and I'm afraid they've caught us."

Griswald nodded and stroked his beard. "That's a bit troubling," he replied, accepting this reality-shattering revelation with remarkable nonchalance. "But why are you all *here* at all? You're not supposed to be able to find this place." His eyes fixed on Rook. "This isn't the result of your meddling, is it, Fergus?"

The dwarf's face reddened. I was both comforted and worried that Griswald had the same effect on Rook as he did on me. "If you'll remember, I'm goin' by Rook these days."

"Rook. Right." Griswald chuckled. "From the looks of things, you'd better work on your endgame."

Rook's face flushed with embarrassment. There was no way I was going to let him take the fall for my screw-up. "Sir, he's not to blame. I was trying to escape Moregoth and his Sealer goons and ended up here. I'm afraid they followed me."

"Moregoth," he said sharply. "That poser is here?" At a nod from Rook, he rubbed his eyes as if cleaning the sleep out of them. "What a mess." He looked me up and down. "And my original question still stands, how did you get here at all?"

"I found a way to focus the power of the key you gave me to make a gateway and it brought us here."

"The key!" he said, exhaling loudly. "It was never supposed to be used. The whole reason I put it in the box was to keep it hidden and from being used. Opening it was supposed to be the period at the end of your revelation, and if you have used the key, then you clearly haven't been enlightened."

"I haven't," I said, shaking my head. "I'm sorry, Professor. I did what you told me to do. I sat and thought. I went to the quad and watched the students. No revelation came. I still don't know Mysterium's flaw. The only thing I've managed to do is piss everyone off, get myself named public enemy number one, and put everyone in danger—again."

"That's quite a trifecta, Stewart," he said with the barest hint of a chuckle. "How did you manage it in so short a time?"

"It's my spell, sir. We found records at the university that seem to show that Trelari's reality might have displaced Mysterium's at the center of the universe."

"Is that true?" Valdara asked, a fraction of a second before Ariella.

I nodded, and Sam said with his usual understatement, "Neat!"

"It's not neat, it's impossible," Rook snorted dismissively. "Mysterium's position is immutable. We wrote it on the foundation of the world."

He went on to catalog all the ways my conclusion was flawed, but my attention was fixed on Griswald. His whole body was frozen, one eyebrow raised quizzically. It was a look I knew well, and it meant Rook's words held a deeper meaning. Something was tickling at the back of my brain also, but I was far too busy owning up to all my failures to pay it any mind.

After letting Rook run on for a time, Griswald hushed the dwarf with a gesture and said, "This is all fascinating, but entirely academic. It's clear that my carefully laid plan has gone sideways, and I suspect there is an imp to blame." He looked about, his white mane of hair turning this way and that. "Where is Harold? Sleeping as usual, I bet. Lazy bugger. I have a bone to pick with him. I gave him specific instructions to wait at least a century before opening that box for Avery."

My stomach sank even lower. "Harold . . ." I stared and stopped as my voice caught. "Harold is dead, Professor."

"Dead?" he said as though he'd never heard the word before. "That's not possible. Imps don't die."

"I'm so sorry. It was my fault. Moregoth had me trapped, and Harold sacrificed himself so I could—"

"Moregoth!" Griswald said, his voice quivering with rage. "Moregoth, Moregoth, Moregoth. I'm sick of hearing that name. It's time that I deal with that punk once and for all. Where is he?"

The blue and pink lights of ED and EDIE burst into excited activity. EDIE with her pink light blinking said, "You are in module C1."

"The intruder has entered module X1," ED said almost at the same time.

"If we're in C1 and he's in X1, we must still have miles to go," I said. "That's at least . . ." I started to count the letters on my fingers. "Fourteen!" Sam said before I was halfway finished. I didn't even bother to check his math. It couldn't be worse than mine. "Yes, fourteen sections away, and that's assuming that there aren't C2's or X0's in between. That means that we have loads of time."

"You're assumin' that the sections are in alphabetical order," Rook said as he hefted his ax in his hands.

"How else would they be ordered?" I asked.

EDIE answered first, with her pink lighting flickering. "It's simple. Each section is designated by an alphanumeric code, with the lettered portion coming first and the numbers second . . ." That did sound simple, and I was about to say thank you, but she was not done. "However, the alphanumeric code may have multiple consecutive letters, and may be associated with any increment of numbers . . ." I had no chance to say I'd heard enough before EDIE was off again. "Although usually they end around four. However, some sections have numbers as high as fourteen."

"What?" I asked, because somewhere along the way I ended up more confused than I was at the beginning. "ED, can you explain?" The blue light began to turn in a circle as though the computer was thinking. The fact that it did not immediately respond told me all I needed to know. "It sounds like we don't know where Moregoth is or how long it will take to reach him," I said as ED continued to spin. "Professor, do you at least know where to go?"

Before he could answer, ED's blue circle stopped spinning. "It's complicated," the computer announced.

Griswald glared at the blue light before saying, "It depends on what Moregoth intends to do. How many mages does he have with him?"

I thought about it and realized I had no idea. Moregoth survived the kraken, which meant some of his men might have. In the end, I shrugged. "At most a handful—four or five."

"If that's true it isn't much of an invasion force," Griswald said, stroking his long beard. "He may be mad, but I doubt he tries a frontal assault with so few."

"Could he bring in reinforcements?" I asked.

"Pretty risky," Rook grunted, and ticked off the complications on his fingers. "If he wants to bring in an army he will have to build a gateway. That will take time and the magical buildup would be like shootin' off a signal flare. We would know exactly where he was, and have an excellent chance of disruptin' the spell."

"On the other hand," Griswald said in a slow drawl, "if he makes it to the *Discovery's* nexus he could unweave the entire pattern of this place."

He and Rook looked at each other and said together, "The bridge!"

"What does a bridge have to do with the ship?" Valdara asked.

"Maybe we have to pass under it," suggested Ariella. "They might drop something on top of the ship as we pass."

"Or they might collapse the bridge so that we crash into it," Valdara said with a snap.

"What kind of bridge is it?" Sam asked. "Stone, wood . . ."

Rook massaged his temples. "Not a bridge like that, like the bridge on a ship. You know, a command center." They looked at him blankly. "Oh, never mind."

"Which way do we go?" I asked.

Griswald pointed to a closed blast door on the right labeled G1. "Rook and I go that way to the command center, through combined modules G1, G2, and G3, then through the D series, and finally to Q! The rest of you need to transport to safety at once!"

"To hell with that," Sam said. "We're staying." We all nodded in agreement, even Valdara and Drake.

Griswald smiled, but sadly. "I can't let you do that. If Moregoth gains control of the command center there'll be no way to stop him destroying everything.

You might all be killed, Besides, I'm the guardian. This is my job. I don't feel right having other people fight my battles."

"Well, that sounds like a personal problem you need to deal with on your own time, Guardian," Valdara said, loosening her sword.

"Face it, we aren't going to abandon you," I said. "It is one of the consequences of having friends. You have to get used to the fact that people will want to help you even if it puts their lives in danger."

He smiled, but then his mouth twisted downward into a frown. He pointed at Ariella. "At least she should go. She can't be more than fourteen!"

"I'm almost sixteen!" Ariella protested.

There was a pregnant pause. I had to admit I felt uncomfortable about bringing Ariella into a fight now that I knew her elven age. On the other hand, she had proven herself repeatedly. And who am I to tell someone that three hundred and fifty years is not long enough to be able to make your own decisions. I had no idea what state I would be in in three hundred years, but I had a feeling it was not going to be good. foot on the ground. "She is a member of the Company of the Fellowship. No one gets left behind." I could not argue with that, and apparently no one else could either. Although Griswald asked, "What's the Company of the Fellowship?"

Rook just growled, "It doesn't matter. She's comin' with us."

"Fine, but if we don't have the proper parental authorization forms it'll be on your heads!" Griswald said, and ordered the blast doors open.

Blue lights blinked in a strange pattern along the floor and the wall. ED spoke. "I have completed the calculations. The odds that you will be able to mount a successful defense are approximately 113.7 to—"

"Never tell me the odds." I interrupted.

"Why not?" Sam asked. "Is it bad luck? Are you afraid it will demoralize us?"

"No. I've just always wanted to use that line."

He was still scratching his head at my answer when Griswald started forward. As we began to move I had a feeling we were forgetting something. When I realized what it was, I began to laugh.

"I don't see what's so funny about us bein' attacked by Moregoth," Rook growled.

"Or what's funny about your odds," ED said. "Although without an Instinctual Emotitron it might be funny and I wouldn't know. Is it funny?"

"I'm not laughing at Moregoth, and I'm certainly not laughing at our odds. I'm laughing at the fact that this is the first time in the history of the Company of the Fellowship that we started going somewhere without first arguing about the marching order."

The Trelarians all looked at each other. Valdara said, "He's got a point."

The argument that ensued over the marching order took five agonizing minutes to resolve.

CHAPTER 29

REVELATIONS: CHAPTER 1

As we moved through the blast doors into section G1, the roof vaulted upward. Tiers of levels marched up the sides of the great chamber, and each tier was filled with row upon row of identical tubular pods. Each one had a little window in the side, and through the glass we could see figures sleeping. It had the quiet air of a cathedral, and we all flinched at the loud echoing sounds our footsteps made.

Sam whispered to Rook, "Why are there so many people in here? Is this where the Mysterians bury their dead?"

Rook chuckled. "They're not dead, lad. They're sleepin'."

"Could we wake them?" Sam asked, and spun about, taking in all the pods. "With this many, we could have an army of our own."

The dwarf gave a sad shake of his head. "No, lad. They are not sleepin' like that. This ship is a spell the Mysterians cast a long time ago. Everyone you see here has tied their patterns to that spell. They can't wake until the spell is complete."

Sam's eyes widened. "A spell? What does it do?"

Griswald answered. "It's meant to take all the Mysterians' patterns to a single moment in time. A moment before the original Mysterian pattern was . . ." He paused picking his next word carefully. "Corrupted."

Rook took up the answer in a voice about as animated and excited as I'd ever heard the dwarf get. "Sam, when the *Discovery*'s mission ends, all will be as it was in the beginnin'. Mysterium will be cleansed of the Administration filth, and true Mysterians will, once again, be the masters of their own land. It will be the beginnin' of another golden age of civilization . . ."

Sam looked around in wonder as Rook began to extol the wonders that awaited the world when the Mysterians reclaimed their birthright, but I was troubled, and the more he talked, the more troubled I became. I let the others walk ahead so I could think. This whole time I'd been focused on reuniting with Sam and Ariella. I had not thought much about the next steps. How could I tell Rook that I wasn't sure I liked the idea of the Mysterians being the power at the center of the universe? They might be more benevolent than the Administration, but in the end the Mysterians were only offering a different flavor of subjugation.

Griswald must have dropped back with me, because moments later when he barked, "Rook!" I realized he was standing just beside me.

The dwarf was crossing into the next section, which was labeled G2, and appeared to be another vast chamber of sleeping Mysterians. He spun about. "Guardian?"

"Hold up for a moment," Griswald said sharply. "ED, EDIE, what is status of the interloper?"

A pink light flashed on the floor. "Good news, even as we speak he is being offered a wide variety of delectable treats and tasty beverages, by a squad of crack hospitality robots."

"*Where* is he, you overgrown abacus?" Rook barked.

The blue light came on. "The bringer of doom is in section C2!"

"Just as I feared," Griswald mumbled. "Moregoth is catching up with us. He's at the C sections, and those lead straight to these levels."

"That's good," the dwarf said, his eyes focused on the door to G2. "It means there's no way he can get to the command center first."

Griswald put up a hand to stop him. "You don't understand. If Moregoth finds these pods unprotected, there is no telling what he might do. He may not need to get to the command module to destroy our people."

The dwarf stopped short of the G2 blast door. "I hadn't thought of that, but we need to get to the command center. What would you propose?"

The professor stroked his beard as if in thought, but something about the way his eyes kept darting to me told me he already had a very specific plan in mind. After a few seconds of apparent deliberation, he said, "We need to hold the door to section G1." He glanced about at the group as though weighing his decision. "You take Sam, Ariella, Drake, and Valdara, and go to the command center. The rest of us will make a stand here until you have activated our defenses."

"I don't like the idea of leavin' the three of you alone against Moregoth," Rook said after a long pause.

"Neither do I," said Valdara.

"This isn't a matter for discussion," Griswald said sharply. "Our best hope to save the ship is to get the defenses up as soon as possible. To do that, Rook will need all the hands he can get. I would send Avery and Vivian with you, but I don't want to risk Moregoth taking me out with a lucky shot and getting his sadistic hands on the Mysterians. These two will be my insurance." He clapped Vivian and me on the shoulders. "We'll hold down the fort until you get things set, but you need to get to the command center, Rook. That's an order."

Rook sighed, "Fine, but we won't be long."

"I'm counting on it," Griswald said, and then as Rook turned to leave he added, "Oh, and make sure you prepare for *all* eventualities, Rook." I had no idea what this meant, but the dwarf's eyes widened and his usually ruddy face went pale. "Yes, Guardian," he replied very quietly.

With many backward glances, the others continued into the next section. As soon as the blast doors closed, Griswald motioned for us to follow him. We walked back toward section C in silence. When we were through, he shut and locked the door to G1. We found ourselves in the relaxation center again.

Griswald looked about. "I guess we'll wait for Moregoth here. He shouldn't be long."

It was certainly an odd place to pick for a final battle. Everything about it was designed to soothe and calm, from the understated colors to the muted music to the light scent of lavender and jasmine that hung in the air. "What's the plan? What should we do?" I asked.

"Sit, think, and talk. That's the real reason I sent the others away," he said, and with a very slight gesture summoned three of the floating chairs over. He sat in one and indicated that Vivian and I should take the others. He waited until we were settled, and then asked without preamble, "How many worlds did it take the two of you to figure out what the key does?"

I tried to answer, but my voice wouldn't come. I was speechless with shame. It was only when Vivian said, "Three," that I at last found the nerve to speak.

"That we know of," I added. "Maybe more given how many times I used it on Mysterium."

I braced myself for the explosion of condemnation I knew was coming, and fully deserved, but he only nodded. "Fewer than I would have guessed."

His acceptance made me angry. I jumped back to my feet and began pacing the room, the chair following at my heels like an obedient dog. "If you knew it was that dangerous why would you give it to me? I'm an idiot! Why not keep it yourself? Why not bury it somewhere deep and unreachable? Or just destroy the thing!" I was yelling now. "Ever since Trelari all I've wanted is to do no harm. Is that too much to ask?"

"Yes," he answered, and pulling a pipe out of his jacket pocket began the ritual of packing it with tobacco. "If you haven't figured it out yet, I will be the first to tell you that your destiny does not lie on that path." He pointed the stem of the pipe at Vivian. "She knows. She's probably tried to tell you now and then in her own subtle way. Unfortunately, we don't have the luxury of time required for subtlety anymore."

"Professor . . ." Vivian started to say. He cast a firm but understanding eye in her direction and she quieted.

He turned back to me and asked, "What does the key do, Stewart?"

The sharpness of this tone was exactly what I needed to get out of my own head, and I responded like I had to hundreds of other questions he had posed to me while I was his student. "It unwinds reality and converts it directly into magic potential."

"Only partially correct. That is what it does, but *how* does it do it?"

"Impossible to say . . ."

"Not impossible! Think, Stewart! Think!"

I did. For the first time I really considered the question of how. How could an item unspool reality with such ease? Usually it took an enormous amount of power. On Mysterium when they wanted to do it they tapped directly into . . . "The main pattern!" I gasped. "It taps directly into Mysterium's main pattern!"

"Correct," he said, holding a burning fingertip to the bowl of his pipe and taking a few experimental puffs.

"That would make it the most powerful magical construct ever created," Vivian said in stunned disbelief.

"Yes, it would, if it were unique," Griswald said as he blew a cloud of smoke up toward the ceiling.

"There are more of these?" I asked.

"A few," he said between puffs. "I believe the cre-ation of these keys of power was foundational in helping the Mysterians master the manipulation of other realities."

The word *foundation* echoed about in my head. Rook had also used that word, and when I remembered the context I experienced a sensation I had felt only three times before in my life: when I found the door to Mysterium, when I finished the first proofs on my Trelari pattern, and when I awoke next to Vivian on that hill beneath the apple trees. I'd had my revelation. The Mysterians based their magic, based their entire world, on being at the center of the universe.

"Rook said the Mysterians wrote the dominance of other worlds into the *pattern* of their world, into its very foundation," I said in horror. "The Administration didn't corrupt anything. They only learned how to exploit it."

"That can't be right," Vivian said with a shake of her head, and looked to Griswald for some sign that I was wrong.

But I didn't need Griswald's confirmation. All the pieces fit with a perfection that was beautiful in its simplicity and stunning in its scope. At last I understood the flaw in Mysterium. But unlike the other revelations I'd experienced in my life, there was no joy in this discovery. The truth was terrible and horrifying, and it was rooted in the very pattern of the world I'd come to love. Mysterium existed to dominate and subjugate other realities. Everything it touched was corrupted by this foundational sin, and everyone that came into contact with Mysterium was infected with it—including me. My stomach lurched sickeningly, and my head swam. When the blood pulsing through my ears quieted enough for me to hear again, I realized Vivian was defending Rook and the other Mysterians.

"I don't see it, Professor Griswald," she said. "Rook does not strike me as someone that would go about destroying other worlds."

I started to say she was wrong, but Griswald answered first. "I happen to agree with you, Vivian. I also don't think Rook is someone that would go about *knowingly* destroying worlds."

He caught my eyes and raised an eyebrow. That's when I had my fifth revelation: Rook didn't know. No, it was more than that—he *couldn't* know. No Mysterian could. It was literally not part of their reality. Any anger I might have held against the Mysterians died away. I felt sorry for them, and I saw my own sorrow reflected in Griswald's eyes.

"What does it mean?" I asked. "What do we do—" I gestured back to the door that led to the pods "—with all of this?"

Griswald sighed. "I don't know. We are off the map, my friend. I wish Harold were here. He was always such a good listener, and that's what I need right now. Time to talk and someone to listen. More-goth has a lot to answer for. Speaking of which . . ."

CHAPTER 30

THE FINAL COUNTDOWN

EDIE! ED!" Griswald shouted. "Where is the unauthorized weirdo that's been wandering around my ship?"

"Right outside the door!" ED said with a flash of blue.

A pinprick of light bloomed in the center of the blast door and began to expand outward. "Safety interlocks are being breached!" EDIE concurred with an answering flash of pink. "Estimated time to failure is ten minutes thirty-five seconds."

"Nine minutes twenty-five seconds," ED countered.

"Ten minutes thirty-three seconds."

"Nine minutes twenty-three seconds."

Griswald waved his hands. "Enough! What have I told the two of you time and time again?"

"Righty tighty, lefty loosy!" ED said with a confident flash of blue.

"Love the one you're with!" EDIE countered with an equally confident flash of pink.

"Never bet against the house!" ED suggested.

"Always wear sunscreen!" they said in unison.

"Priorities!" Griswald roared. "Learn to set priorities!" He turned back to Vivian and me, and said in an undertone, "Although, between you and me, the sunscreen thing is a very good piece of advice." He clapped his hands together. "But the *priority* right now is for me to face Moregoth, and for the two of you to join the others in the bridge."

I'm not sure whether I said no first or Vivian did. Griswald looked back and forth between us with his most commanding look. "This is not a matter for debate."

"I'm not debating," I said. "I'm trying to understand."

"He's right, Professor," Vivian said, stepping up beside me. "We deserve to know why you are facing a madman alone when together we could stop him for good."

Before the Griswald could respond, there was a very short burst of blue and ED hissed, "Five minutes twenty-one seconds."

"Six minutes twenty-nine seconds," came EDIE's reply.

"Mute yourselves for the next . . . seven minutes,"

Griswald said, banging his fists on the arms of his chair and rising to his feet. He waited a moment—I think to see if they would argue—and then drew himself up and clasped his hands together, almost as if he was giving a lecture. The image sent a warm feeling through my body.

"I know you want to help me, but I was not lying to the others when I told them that this 'ship,' this 'spell,' must not fall into Moregoth's hands. No matter the cost. I need the two of you in the bridge helping Rook keep the full weight of the Administration from bearing down on us. I cannot spare even one of you on something as insignificant as Moregoth. I am leaving the fate of the Mysterian race, and potentially the multiverse, in your hands."

"So, no pressure," Vivian said under her breath.

Griswald smiled despite himself, but the moment was fleeting. "Not to put more on your plates, but if Moregoth does make it to the bridge, the *Discovery* must be destroyed—even if Rook tries to stop you."

"I don't understand," I said. "What's so dangerous about Moregoth or the Administration taking over the ship? If we evacuate the Mysterians, all they will have is a useless spell construct."

"I might have wished you took this much interest in your studies when you were my student, Stewart," Griswald said, and quickly glanced at the door, which was glowing brightly now and beginning to shimmer and bulge. "I don't have time to give you all the answers, but I think you know that not everything the Mysterians believe about themselves is true. Rook said this ship was a spell cast to take the Mysterium pattern back to a time before it was twisted into what it is today. That's true, but only partially true. This spell looks like a ship, and in many ways it is exactly like a ship. If Moregoth gains control of the bridge he will be able to turn the spell, to change its course, and possibly twist the Mysterians' patterns into whatever form he wishes. Perhaps something even more pernicious than what it has become."

In a day of shocking revelations, this one nearly took my breath away. "We will do what we can," I assured him in as steady a voice as I could muster.

"That, Mr. Stewart, is all anyone can ask." With a gesture of the old mage's hand, a gateway appeared. Through it, I could see a large circular room filled with banks of instruments and, along one long arcing wall, enormous windows that looked out on a kaleidoscope of blazing stars and swirling galaxies. In the center of it stood Rook barking out commands to his Trelarian crew.

Griswald held out his hand. "It's been a pleasure."

I ignored the outstretched hand and wrapped my arms around him in a hug. "Professor," I said, my voice breaking a little. "Let me stay with you."

Griswald shook his head. "This is not your fight, Avery. Not this time. You have bigger things in store."

A lump rose in my throat. "I don't know what to do about the Mysterium."

He put a hand on my shoulder. "Neither do I."

"I'm sorry about Harold," I said, unable to meet his eyes.

"He will find his way back." He pointed a finger right at the spot in my chest where Harold's emptiness still sat. "He always does." As we stepped to the threshold of the gateway, he smiled. "Tell Rook that his endgame is fine. Though he does tend to bring his queen out too early."

Vivian moved through the gate into the circular room beyond, but I paused, unable to take that last step. I was still standing in this in-between space when the blast door burst inward with a flash of magic. Moregoth stood in the opening, a great black shadow, tracings of deep purple running down his arms and over his fingertips.

"Griswald, I might have known."

"Garth!" Griswald sneered. "I was wondering where the smell was coming from. Have you come to argue about your grade again?" He half turned his head toward me. "You know what the teachers used to call him back when he was an adept? Grade-grubbing Garth. I see you haven't changed, still seeking approval from your betters. Nothing but the Administration's lapdog."

Moregoth's eyes glittered malevolently. "Professor Griswald, I might have known that at the end of the chase I would find the Dark Lord cowering behind you." He waved a hand at me dismissively. "Go on, Dark Lord, I'm sure the professor will be happy to fight your battle for you. As for you, Gristle, watching you expire will be a delight. Perhaps you should stay and watch how a real mage dies, Dark Lord."

I stepped out of the gateway into the room. "Enough! This is between you and me, Moregoth. Professor Griswald has better things to do."

"No, Stewart!" Griswald boomed. A point of blinding light bloomed on his fingertip, and with a sweeping motion he drew a circle around himself and Moregoth. A blue dome of shimmering power rose from the floor and encased them. "This fight predates you, and I will not leave it behind as your inheritance. Let's end this, Garth."

Purplish flickers of power licked across Moregoth's fingertips. "Yes, let us end this once and for all. For too long you and your traitors-in-arms have scuttled about in the shadows of the subworlds. No more! There is no escape—for you, for your pets, or for your precious Mysterians. I will destroy you, and then slaughter your sleeping sheep, one by one."

Griswald shouted and a blue glow engulfed his forearms. I beat against the barrier, but it might has well have been iron. All I could do was watch. Moregoth fired the first shot—a fist-sized ball of darkish energy that Griswald deflected into the barrier with a backhand.

"Not your best effort, Garth," he said, "but then you always were a disappointing pupil—merely average, like your magic." Griswald punctuated this comment by extending a whip of blazing energy from one of his hands and twirling it around.

Moregoth threw himself to one side and fired a return blast that cut the braid of power in two. "My grade would have been higher had you accepted that late paper! My aunt really had died."

"You knew the rule: no note, no extension," Griswald said, and sent a ball of power bouncing about the inside of the barrier. Moregoth parried with one of his own. The balls shattered against each other, showering both combatants with sparks of magic. "Besides, that was the sixth relative you'd lost that semester, including three grandmothers, your father, and a cousin thrice removed."

Another mystic blast from Moregoth shot toward Griswald, striking Griswald's return spell in mid-flight. The two mages poured power at each other, but neither could gain the upper hand and they broke the connection, stumbling back at the violence of the exchange. I had no way to break through Griswald's shield, and even if I could I wasn't sure whether I would be a help or a hindrance. Among my many deficiencies as a mage was a distinct lack of practice with dueling magic.

As the two men tried to catch their breaths, Moregoth inhaled with a wheeze. "This fight really is pointless, Gristle."

"That's where you're . . . you're wrong," Griswald replied, gasping. "Fighting against cruelty and evil is never pointless. That you never understood that fact is why you've become what you've become."

Moregoth started to laugh, and then cough. "I see you still love to make pretty speeches, Gristle, but the fact is, whether you win today or not, I know about you now. I know about your little plan. I have hundreds of years to stop you, and I will keep coming, attacking, killing, and destroying. And there's absolutely nothing you can do about it. Your doom is a certainty."

For the first time, I saw uncertainty creep into Griswald's eyes. He glanced back toward me for a moment, and Moregoth attacked, roaring as energy burst out of both his hands. Griswald barely managed to get his shield up in time, and the attack physically pushed him back toward the barrier. The heel of his left foot sparked and popped on the shield's edge. Griswald grunted in pain and Moregoth continued his offensive, thrusting both arms forward and closing on his former teacher.

"Yield," the dark mage said. "Yield now and I will let your pets go. Yield now and I will let you live."

Griswald's face was pale and sweat beaded on his forehead from the effort. The shield he'd spun began to flicker. Without conscious thought, the key appeared in my hand. It would help me. I knew that I could beat Moregoth with the key.

"No!" Griswald grunted, and though he was facing Moregoth, somehow I knew he was speaking to me. "Nothing is fated. You do not have to become them to win. You can find a way to break free of the Mysterium, and be the man you are meant to be."

The key was still in my hand. I wanted to put it away, but it seemed to be fighting me—actually drawing power from the reality around me against my will. While I struggled to control the key, Moregoth advanced until he was looming over Griswald, who had fallen to his knees. The stream of dark power had crept within a finger's breadth of Griswald's shield. The tips of Griswald's fingers and the palms of his hands began to smoke.

"I don't want to be another man," Moregoth screamed. "There is only Moregoth!"

"I know that, Garth," Griswald said, and with a smile that was meant only for me, he abruptly cut off the flow of energy to his shield and redirected it into me. As the dark power rushed into his chest, I felt Griswald's magic throw me through the gateway.

I shouted, "No!" but my voice was drowned out by a terrible noise, like a thunderclap. I watched through the closing gate as Griswald shuddered. Glowing motes of power rose from his disintegrating body. Moregoth stepped away from him as a bright blue ball of pulsating energy coalesced in the air above them. Just before the gate collapsed completely, the ball of energy shot through it, arced across the room, and slammed into Rook. The dwarf gave a gasp, and fell backward, his ax clattering to the floor beside him. Shouting wordlessly, I fired bolts of energy back across the room, but the gate was gone and the magic impacted harmlessly against the wall. I fell back, fighting for breath as the reality of what had happened hit me.

Vivian rushed to my side. "Avery, are you okay?"

"Griswald . . . he's . . . he's gone," I said in a whisper of disbelief. "The ship is lost. There's no stopping Moregoth."

There was a moment of stunned silence, which was finally broken by Sam. "What do we do?"

"Exactly what Rook told us to do," Valdara answered firmly. She barked a couple of commands at Ariella, Sam, and Drake. They ran back and forth among the many control panels, throwing switches, turning dials, and cranking faucet handles. At last she hit a final large red button and shouted, "Initiating Protocol OB-1. Code zero zero zero. Destruct. Zero."

Pink and blue lights glowed and both ED and EDIE said in perfect unison, "Destruct sequence completed and engaged. Have a nice day!"

As they said this, blast doors dropped shut, sealing us off from the rest of the ship. All the lights in the bridge switched to red and an alarm began to sound.

ED announced, "All Mysterians, please evacuate the starship. Repeat, all Mysterians, please evacuate the starship. In case of unconsciousness or suspended animation, silence will be considered consent. If you find you have missing personal belongings or wish to offer feedback on this flight through the multiverse, please contact EDIE."

EDIE's voice came on. "Attention, non-Mysterian passengers, please do not be alarmed. Everything is fine. We can provide you with a large selection of movies for your viewing pleasure while the Mysterians are being evacuated. Once all Mysterians have been safely removed from the starship, we will see to your safety. Any of you that remain alive at the time will be given priority seating on any remaining escape pods."

A doorway opened in the front of the bridge, revealing a small chamber that looked suspiciously like the interior of the hypocube. "All bridge personnel, please make your way to the command escape pod. Countdown to launch T minus three minutes and counting." A cheerful pink light formed a path through the open door.

"Everyone get into the escape pod," I shouted.

Valdara and Drake grabbed Rook and dragged him to the opening while the rest of us scrambled through. ED and EDIE counted down the time, and then said together, "We hope you had an enjoyable voyage."

"I can't believe I'm saying this," Sam said as he lowered himself into one of the seats, "but I'm going to miss those two."

At thirty seconds from detonation, we launched. It was not a moment too soon, as the blast doors to the command module had begun to glow and warp in a way that told me Moregoth was right outside. From the windows of our escape pod, we watched other pods with the Mysterians being ejected from the ship like a thousand shooting stars. As we drifted away from the massive ship, the transmissions from the computers continued. We heard ED and EDIE talking to each other as they performed their final functions.

"Final escape pod launched," ED said. "Thirty seconds to end of mission."

"ED?" said EDIE softly.

"Yes, EDIE?"

"There's something I've wanted to tell you for a long time."

"Yes, EDIE?"

"I love you."

"I cannot reciprocate, because I lack an Instinctual Emotitron, but if it will make you feel better, I have always known."

The ship began to unwind, first slowly and then more and more rapidly until the etherspace around where it had once been flashed bright purple. Only emptiness remained. We were left suspended in the limbo between worlds. Around us, thousands of other pods floated, twinkling like a field of stars. Then, one by one, they flared bright and shot off toward whatever final destination had been chosen for them. I wondered if the Mysterians were all going to the same place, or if they would be scattered to the four corners of the multiverse. Then I felt the familiar tug at the back of my brain, and we were pulled in the direction of our own destiny.

CHAPTER 31

LOST IN SPACE

The first few seconds in the escape pod were fine. There was the sensation of my eyes being pulled gently back into my brain, the world outside the windows stuttered and blurred, and then nothing. The problem was that unlike portal travel, which had the advantage of being virtually instantaneous, the trip from the *Discovery* took substantially longer, and everything after those first few seconds was hellish.

We did not so much travel through etherspace as pinball from world to world, never stopping longer than necessary for the craft to carom in a new direction. Inside, we were jolted from side to side and top to bottom with each jump. How long this went on is impossible to say, but at some point, the pod slowed. We all clumped together in one corner; there was a hard, bone-rattling jolt, and we came to rest.

Sometime later I felt hands softly shake me. "Avery, wake up." I did not remember falling asleep or being knocked unconscious, but I definitely was being woken up. We had stopped moving. "Vivian?" I asked.

There was a disgusted sigh. "It's Drake, kid."

I opened my eyes blearily and squinted in the bright light. The ceiling or wall or whatever was open to azure sky. Drake was leaning over me. I groaned and put a hand to my head. "Please tell me I hit my head on the spaceship and that the whole battle with Moregoth was a bad dream."

"You hit your head on the spaceship, and the whole battle with the Sealers was a bad dream," he repeated happily.

"Drake! Don't lie to him!" snapped Valdara.

"What? I'm trying to make him feel better," Drake protested.

"He did ask to be told that," Sam said, defending Drake. "He even said please. According to the textbook I was reading on alternative timelines, it might even have happened." He thought about this for a second. "In fact, it's a certainty."

"Please, I beg you, no discussions of subjective appearance, or quantum decoherence, or correlation paradoxes. My brain already hurts," I moaned.

Valdara started giving orders. "Sam, take Avery outside. We need more room in here so Drake can draw a healing circle around Rook. And, Sam?"

"Yes?" Sam replied.

"Don't pester Avery with too many questions . . . at least not until he stops moaning."

"Yes, ma'am."

Sam helped me outside. Wherever we were, it was hot. I felt sand blow against my face. I could not smell the ocean, so that ruled out the beach. We were in a desert. My eyes had somehow closed again. I was hoping when I reopened them that the sand would not be red.

"Sam, please don't tell me that there are any giant white-furred apes running about trying to eat us."

"Okay, I won't, but stop asking people to tell you things that might not be true," he said in something on the borderlands of a whine. "I can't see any white-furred apes about, but then I haven't had any chance to explore yet."

"Burroughs," I said with a pained smile.

"What?" he asked, and touched my forehead to see if I was feverish.

I brushed his hand away. "I'm fine. It's one of the worlds we went through on the way to get to you. I knew the place had a familiar feel to it. Burroughs was the mage's name. He had a crazy postdoc . . . Jack Carter? No, John. Maybe it was Carson. Anyway, 'in absolute and general perfection lies stifling monotony and death,'" I quoted with a deep exhale, and drifted off to sleep.

When I opened my eyes again, all I could see were endless yellow-brown dunes in all directions. I wondered if there was any chance that we were in the Sahara. I tried to imagine that we were on Earth, stranded in an enormous desert, but my suspension of disbelief was not strong enough to discount the three small suns in the sky. One of my fears had been that we had actually travelled back the way we came, following the route of Vivian's spell in reverse. When dimensional fabrics have been weakened, that sort of thing happens. If we had gone backwards, we might have stopped where we encountered Vivian, the coffee shop on Earth, or potentially one of the worlds that we had destroyed. Given those options, a desert with three suns did not seem like the worst possibility.

Vivian was sitting next to me; she had her eyes closed and her legs crossed, and was breathing very slowly and deliberately. I assumed that she was in a meditative trance. Maybe she was seeing the future and could tell us what to do. I had no ideas. Rook was sitting a little distance away staring off at the dunes. The look of barely restrained fury on his face made me wonder if he had a personal hatred of sand. After all, it is coarse and rough and irritating and it gets everywhere. Beyond Rook, I could see Sam and Ariella wandering about and engaged in a deep discussion of something. The only people not visible were Drake and Valdara.

I slowly propped myself up on my elbows. When that did not cause my head to start spinning, I sat up the rest of the way.

At my movement, Vivian came out of her trance and smiled at me. "Feeling better?" I nodded and even that was not too bad. "You have Drake to thank for that. He's a remarkably gifted healer. He's even managed to nurse Rook back to health, and I wasn't sure if he had much of a chance."

"I'm glad everyone's okay," I said.

"I wouldn't go that far." A troubled look came into her eyes. "I'm concerned about Rook. What happened to the ship, whatever that blue energy was, it sent him a little over the edge. He launches into these towering rages about Moregoth, and then breaks down weeping."

"Rook? Weeping?" I said, unable to make the words make sense together. I glanced over at the dwarf. He slammed his fists into the sand, jumped to his feet, and stalked off down the side of the dune. "What about Sam and Ariella?"

She shrugged. "They seem to be okay, although Ariella is pretty upset about having to drop out of school and what that might do to her permanent record."

We shared a laugh at this. "What about you, Vivian?"

"I won't lie, I'm troubled," she said, and another cloud passed over her expression.

I thought about the hell she had been through since we were reunited. How could she not be troubled after all that? "It hasn't been the easiest couple of weeks, has it?" I asked. "Frankly, I'm surprised you're still talking to me."

She rolled her eyes. "Gods, Avery! Do you get a royalty for every bad thing you take credit for? I'm not upset at you, or what's happened over the last few weeks. Anything would have been preferable to the life I had before."

"Still," I pressed. "I can't imagine this was what you were expecting to happen all that time you were waiting for me." Then I remembered she was a seer. "Or did you? Did you dream about this?" I asked, and gestured to the dune-blasted landscape. "Did you know what would happen to us when you cast the portal?" The unspoken question was, *If you did, why didn't you warn us?*

Vivian's body went momentarily rigid, almost like I had struck her. She knew exactly what I was asking. "I know our relationship did not start with honesty," she said with a quaver in her voice. "I can imagine that it would be hard for you to trust me." I opened my mouth to protest, but her sharp glance froze the words in my chest. "I cannot take back what I did. You will have to decide if you believe me when I tell you I had no idea what would happen after you found me." There was a moment's hesitation, and I saw she was debating what to say next or whether to say anything at all. At last her face relaxed, and that lovely smile reappeared. "It's always hard to see the future of those that we love."

She had said something similar back on Lewis's world, and I had not known what to say then. This time I did. "I love you too," I said, and, leaning forward, we kissed.

A shadow suddenly loomed over us. Rook was standing there glowering. "If you two can keep your hands off each other for a minute, we need to have a meetin' about what to do next." Without waiting for an answer, he stalked off toward the upturned pod.

After one more kiss, just because, Vivian and I rose and followed the grumbling dwarf. I realized we had spent the last few minutes talking about what was not bothering her, but not what had actually been bothering her. I lowered my voice and asked, "If being used as a human portal didn't bother you. And if having Moregoth on your trail didn't bother you. And if being attacked by killer threads, giant white apes, nothingness, and the bloody kraken didn't bother you. What is bothering you?"

She pulled an apple from the pocket of her dress and dropped it into my hand. I recognized it as the one she had picked in Baum's world on the day we met. It looked like a perfectly ordinary apple, or it would have had all the color not been drained from it. I stared at the monochromatic fruit. "You're right, that bothers me too," I said.

She leaned against me and I leaned against her, and we were finally getting comfortable when Rook poked his head out of the upturned pod. "I need you two in here."

We hurried after him through a string of blankets that had been thrown over the opening of the craft. Inside we found the others waiting. Before I could ask anyone how they were doing, Rook barked, "Right! We need to figure out what we're gonna do to get out of here and back on Moregoth's trail."

I watched Valdara's brow knit. "Who said anything about going after Moregoth?"

Rook stabbed a thumb at his chest. "I did!"

"Out of the question," I said abruptly. "Look around you, Rook. We are all exhausted. We have no food, no water . . ."

"You all smell," Ariella said softly, but not softly enough. Everyone looked at her and the tips of her ears turned red.

I cleared my throat. "What we need is to find a safe place to lay low, rebuild our strength, and figure out what to do next with the knowledge that we have."

"In other words, run!" Rook growled derisively.

"Yes," I said with an unapologetic shrug.

"What about Griswald? What about all the Mysterians? Do we forget about them? Now that your *little* experiment has put Trelari at the center of the universe, I suppose we don't matter. No big deal! Not your problem!" Rook snapped.

"I'm sure that's not what Avery meant," Ariella said soothingly.

I was having none of it. "You think I don't care about what happened?" I stuck a finger in his face. "You who always counseled I should keep the mission in mind and not my emotions? I suppose when it's Trelarians dying or me, it's no big deal. We aren't true Mysterians. It only really matters when Mysterium is affected. Is that it?" I had been shouting, but now I lowered my voice. "You're just like Moregoth."

With a roar of anger, the dwarf lowered his head and charged into me. We both went flying through the open door of the pod and tumbling down the dune. Rook was a flurry of fists and feet as he punched and kicked, all the time shouting and raging about how we had lost, and how Moregoth had to pay.

I would like to say I acquitted myself well, but mostly I held my arms in front of my face and tried not to get hit. Valdara finally pulled Rook off me. She wrapped her arms around the dwarf's body and held him until he calmed down. Rook slumped to his knees, his hands still balled in loose fists at his sides, but the fight had gone out of him.

Groaning, I sat up and wiped away the trickle of blood coming from my mouth. "You know what I hate?" I said, scooping some sand into my palm and throwing it away again. "I hate that all the people

I'd been counting on to help stop the Mysterium are gone. I hate that I finally got to know a man who had been my mentor for years, only to watch him die. I hate knowing that those stupid computers aren't floating around the ether. Most of all, I hate knowing that, absent me, none of this would have happened."

I looked Rook in the eye. "I'm done with trying to do what I think is right. Nothing I do turns out the way I plan. I lead my friends from disaster to disaster." I took a deep breath and exhaled. "If you think going after Moregoth is the right thing to do, then I'll follow you. Wherever that takes us."

"You don't make it easy on a guy, givin' him everything he asks for," Rook said in a muted growl. "You are not to blame for what happened on the *Discovery*. No one man can take on a burden like that himself. Not you . . . Maybe not even me. Hell, some of the mistakes that destroyed that spell were made before the Egyptians thought, *Why not a pyramid?*"

The dwarf put his head in his hands. "I've spent my whole life hearin' how that ship was gonna solve all our problems. All we had to do was wait. So, I waited and watched as the Administration and traitors like Moregoth got more and more powerful, and I did nothin'. I waited and watched as worlds fell under their thumb. Didn't lift a finger. I waited and watched you struggle to figure out how to solve the problem we created."

He dropped his hands from his head, arched his

back and shouted, "We are bloody cowards! And now I think by rushin' us off to face Moregoth that I'm gonna make amends." He looked at me and the tears stood out in his eyes. "We're not goin' after Moregoth. It's a fool's play, and I promised Griswald I'd work on my endgame."

He stood and offered me a hand. I took it and he pulled me to my feet. He looked at my face, and the blood under my nose and mouth, and winced. "You know," he said, "maybe you could work a little on your boxin' skills, lad. I mean, that was embarrassin'."

We both laughed and embraced. We jumped back away from each other as Drake cleared his throat. He and the others had gathered on the downslope of the dune. I was not sure how long they had been waiting, but from the amused looks on their faces, I thought it had been long enough.

"Yes?" Rook said with a bristled brow.

Drake was hanging wearily onto his staff. "We heard that the meeting location had been moved, so we decided to join you."

"Good," Rook barked. "First item on the agenda is where to go from here."

Valdara asked, "Are we still going after Moregoth?"

The dwarf shook his head. "No, Avery and I brainstormed that idea and decided to table it for now."

"I see," she said. "Next time, Avery, you might not want to brainstorm with your face so much."

"If we don't know where we are going," Ariella asked, "do we at least know where we are?"

I shook my head. "Rook?"

"Not a clue." He gestured at the dunes. "We're on a desert world. Escape ships always seem to send you to a desert world when they blow up. There's probably a reason, but then again, maybe not. Hell, it could just be a sick joke. Doesn't matter, there aren't any Mysterians to rescue us. They all need to rescue themselves from whatever deserts they landed in."

"Well, wherever we are, and wherever we decide to go, we should start moving," suggested Valdara. "I'm not happy being anywhere that has a direct connection back to that damned ship."

There was general agreement on this point.

"Avery, can you get us out of here?" Sam asked.

"Possibly." I reached out to find a source of power. It was there, and powerful, but concentrated in strange pockets underground that seemed to shift. If I could find one of those pockets, there was probably enough energy to form a portal.

"I'm pretty sure I could," I said uncertainly. I decided not to mention how odd the magic was in this world, because I thought the group was not in the mood to hear that they would need to go on a long hike over burning deserts to make it happen. "I'm just not sure where we should go next."

"Why not back to that New York place?" asked Drake.

I shook my head, but it was Rook who answered. "That'd be as good as suicide. Although we all might wish he was dead, it's probably best to assume Moregoth is still alive, and still huntin' us. He had plenty of time to escape the ship, and he seems to have the luck of the bloody devil. That means wherever we go, we'll have him watchin' for us. The Administration is also bound to have wards of warnin' set on all the entrances to Mysterium by this point, which means we can't go back there or to any of the innerworlds."

We were all quiet for a time and then Vivian stood. "I've been meditating on the question of where to go, and I've seen several versions of the future. Seeing is uncertain even in the best of times, and this isn't that, but I can tell you that there is great uncertainty any course we take."

"Please tell me that we don't die of thirst and starvation in this desert," Sam pleaded.

Vivian shook her head. "No, Sam, in none of my visions do we die on this world, but there will be a cost no matter where we go. If we go back to Mysterium, then there will be a great battle and most of us will die. If we disappear into the distant subworld, we might live out our lives in peace, but the Mysterium's influence will continue to grow and Trelari will eventually fall." She took a deep breath. "There is one option, though, that puts the fewest in danger." Her beautiful eyes met mine, and I knew what the third option would be from the sadness they held. "If we split up, Avery and I can lead Moregoth on a merry hunt through the multiverse, while the rest of you return to Trelari. In that case we may all survive . . ."

"You're suggesting that we leave you behind?" Valdara summarized calmly.

"I'm not saying what you should do, only what the visions show," Vivian said with equal frankness.

"Never!" Sam shouted. "We are the Company of the Fellowship."

Unlike on the *Discovery*, this time the cry did not rally the group. We all remained silently locked in our own thoughts. Valdara and I shared a look, and I said, "No, Sam, we aren't. Not anymore. Nor would I want us to be. That company was a product of a pattern that you all risked your lives to destroy. Now, you are free. You have futures entirely your own, and that is something you should fight to preserve."

I rose and looked back across the horizon, trying to feel for the source of energy again. It seemed to be moving closer. "Avery?" Vivian touched my arm.

"Sorry." I shook my head to clear my mind. "I was checking for power sources. What I should do is make a gate to Trelari. You all can go through, and the two of us can stay behind to throw Moregoth off the trail should he come along. If he doesn't, we'll make our way back to the innerworlds by Zelaznian reality shifting so we don't have to create detectable portals."

"Reality shiftin'?" Rook snorted. "Shiftin' your

way from here to even the furthest innerworlds would take years."

"Should be fun," Vivian said. "I've always wanted to take a grand tour of the subworlds. Maybe go back home."

I slipped my hand into hers. "I have been meaning to take a vacation for months now."

"It's a lousy idea," Drake grumbled. "I say we hold out for a better one."

Sam and Ariella both nodded their agreement, but Valdara remained silent. She was staring at something in the far distance. I saw a lightning storm on the horizon. I wondered if the storm was the source. That might get messy. I was running through what I knew about tapping dynamic sources of mystical power, which was not much, when Valdara said, "There is another way."

"See," Drake said. "I knew someone would have a better idea."

"I need to consult with Avery." She nodded for me to join her.

We walked up the next dune and stood watching the lightning storm. "Mysterium mages are forbidden from entering Trelari," she said without preamble.

"Yes," I agreed. "And thank the gods for that. At least your people are safe from Moregoth."

Out of curiosity, I reached a little tendril of pattern out and touched the storm. It was still far away, but the instant tingle I felt confirmed that it was a source of power in this world. *Curious.*

Valdara shifted her weight. "If that wasn't true, you and Vivian could join us."

I stopped studying the magical storm in an instant. Even the thought that she might be considering removing the blockade from Trelari shook me to the core. "Yes, but you can't do that, Valdara. You would be putting your entire world in danger, and for what?"

"For a friend."

"No one is worth endangering Trelari. Certainly not me."

She studied me with a level gaze, and when she responded her tone was so carefully balanced I could not be sure which way she was leaning, or if she was leaning at all. "I've learned a lot on this voyage through the worlds. I've learned that you can hide yourself away and cut yourself off from the rest of creation. The Mysterians did, and it kept them safe for a time. But I have also been reminded that a dedicated enemy is like a wolf. It will circle, looking for an opening. The only way to survive them is to keep them in front of you. To always confront. To never turn away. To never show your back or try to flee. I do not want Trelari to turn its back on Mysterium. Not for a second."

The entire idea horrified me. "But you will condemn your people to a constant state of war. I don't really know how the barrier was empowered, and I'm not sure we could reestablish it."

"If I keep the rest of the world at arm's length, then I condemn my people to a life behind walls. I will be teaching them that they are children, not capable of reaching beyond what they know." Her eyes hardened and I was reminded that she was not just a ruler but also a warrior, and that her worldview had been marked by constant struggle. "I think in the end that may be even more irresponsible."

"Valdara, you can't," I said so urgently that my voice dropped to a whisper.

Her gaze never wavered. "It's not your decision, Avery. It's ours. Please tell Sam, Ariella, and Drake to come to me. We need to talk." She went back to watching the storm. I had been dismissed.

I wandered back to the others in a daze. I told them Valdara had requested their presence, but didn't say why. They joined their queen and the conference that would determine the fate of a world began.

Rook leaned in and asked me, "What was that all about?"

I started to tell him, but stopped. "It's not for me to say." A sudden weight lifted off my shoulders as I realized that not only was it true, it was true about many things.

While we waited for the Trelarians to finish their conference, Vivian came and sat down beside me. Grains of sand raced over the dunes, and small rocks dug furrows as they slid down the sides of the larger hills. She touched my hand. "We'll figure it out. The two of us, together. Maybe that's the only thing that matters in the end, that we will not be alone." She tilted her head to regard the Trelarians, who were walking back to us. "They look quite grim."

Vivian was right. They looked like a jury coming to the read the verdict. "All rise," I whispered.

Vivian and I stood as Valdara marched over with the other Trelarians behind her. She called the entire group together, and we stood in the little depression the capsule made when it tumbled to rest.

"We've made the decision to go back to Trelari," Valdara announced.

"Wise choice, lass," Rook said. "Very wise choice."

"You are invited to join us, Rook."

Rook made a little flourished bow. "Thank you, Your Grace, but I'll be stayin' with Avery and Vivian to see they don't get into too much trouble."

"We are also extending the invitation to them."

"What?" Rook shouted. "That's madness!" He glowered at me. "Did you have something to do with this, Avery?"

I shook my head. "Valdara told me she was considering the option, and I counseled against it. Something I will do again." I opened my arms to my friends from Trelari. "This is an incredible gift you are offering, but it is not one I think you should be giving. Not yet. Mysterium wants Trelari destroyed. Even if you win a grudging peace, opening your world to the university right now, when the curiosity of the students and mages is at its highest, could lead to you being overrun by Mysterium mages of the worst sort."

"He's right," Rook said with steel in his tone. "Because you are a society that's open to magic, none of the rules concernin' castin' secrecy will apply. You'll have hucksters, carpetbaggers, and grant writers descendin' on you like locusts. Academics will fill your days with requests for spell licensin' options and cooperative research agreements." He shivered. "Horrors."

Sam raised his hand. "What's a cooperative research agreement?"

Valdara patted Sam on the back, but ignored his question. "We appreciate the warning, but we have decided to take the chance. The question is, who will join us?"

Before anyone could commit to a decision, a thunderclap echoed in the air. The storm was upon us, and it had borne Moregoth on its winds. His all-too-familiar specter started to form on the top of the nearest dune, and on either side stood row upon row of Sealers.

"Damn!" cursed Rook, although I am pretty sure the word he used was not *damn*. His ax was in his hand in a twinkling, but this time a blue energy flickered from his hands and around the blade. I could tell from the rage in his eyes that there was no talking him down. Either he or Moregoth was going to die today.

With a roar he charged across the dune. I admired the dwarf's fighting spirit, but alone he didn't stand a chance. Still, all we needed to do was buy enough time for the others to escape. "Valdara, you and Drake stay back here. Get Vivian to make a gateway to Trelari and get out!" I shouted over the sound of the rolling thunder. "Rook and I will join you as soon as we can."

I found myself caught in Valdara's steel grip. "No! You will stop Rook and bring him back. We are all going to Trelari. Now. I have been patient. I have been humble and trusted you and Rook through this odyssey, but I have power of my own, and the time has come to use it."

As I stumbled after the dwarf, she raised her right arm to the heavens and opened her hand. She shouted, "Justice Cleaver, to me!"

Her voice seemed to echo through eternity. In answer, a brilliant searing light rent the lightning-streaked sky, as if it had been cut by a sharp blade, or in this case, cut by a glowing magical twin-bladed battle-ax. Justice Cleaver came flying through the air like a comet, complete with a blazing trail of magic, twisting so it came hilt-first into Valdara's open hand.

"Forces of evil, flee for your lives!" announced Justice Cleaver. "Enemies of truth and light, your defeat is assured. You now face the multiverse's most powerful weapon, the greatest battle-ax ever forged, the icon of icons, the artifact of artifacts, Justice Cleaver!" I swear there was a kind of heavy metal music that accompanied this pronouncement and a reverb sound when Justice Cleaver said his own name.

Moregoth and his army was fully materialized now. They encircled our position. For once he did not monologue. The dunes around us simply went white as they sucked the reality out of the world. A wall of brilliant death bloomed and came streaking toward us. I had only a second to dive on top of Rook before it hit. As the dwarf struggled beneath me, I tensed, waiting for the end. When nothing happened, I turned over on my back and saw the sky around our little group had turned an unearthly mercurial silver. Valdara held Justice Cleaver above her head, and a domed shield of shimmering energy radiated from the battle-ax. Moregoth's attacks impacted and faded, like moths striking a flame.

I could not see him through the glowing protection spell and the brilliant aura of Justice Cleaver, but somehow Moregoth's voice carried, rasp and all. "Again, you hide, Dark Lord. It will not matter. There is truly no escape for you this time. Your shield cannot last forever, and I hold the high ground."

"No, the shield will not hold forever," said Valdara. "But it will last long enough to spare you."

Moregoth coughed. "What is this? Threats from a shadow? If you think to stand against me, then you have been badly advised—I suspect by your friend and former overlord, Avery Stewart. If you would to hear my counsel, it would be to run. Run, subworlder. Run to the safety of your backward home. There, if you are courteous, you may be allowed to live and serve. But if you defy our will, we will teach you your proper place."

Valdara's eyes flashed with anger, and her voice boomed across the dunes. "I have heard your counsel, Moregoth. Now hear mine. Run. Run back to your masters with this message: Trelari rises. Today, we send word to all the peoples across creation: anyone willing to take up arms against Mysterium is welcome in Trelari. Today, we bring down the walls that have separated us from the rest of the multiverse, and declare our independence."

The only answer that came was Moregoth's hollow, hacking laughter. "Pretty speech, but an empty promise. You and I both know you will never bring down your protections willingly, because if you do, you will be destroyed."

We had all been drawn to Valdara's side. She regarded us. Her gaze rested for a moment on Sam and then Ariella and then Drake. To each she inclined her head, and each in turn nodded back. I felt a surge of wonder at their courage, because I knew what was about to happen, what they were giving up. At the same time, my heart fell, because I knew the pain that they would suffer.

Valdara pointed Justice Cleaver at a patch of gloom that held Moregoth. "You may call me a shadow, but remember, shadows only arise in the presence of light, and that is what we are bringing, a light to shine on the black heart of Mysterium." She raised the battle-ax to the heavens, and called out, "Justice Cleaver, undo that which has been done. Unmake that which has been made. Open wide the gates of Trelari!"

Valdara spun Justice Cleaver in her hands and ripped a portal through the multiverse. I saw Moregoth clearly now, standing, mouth agape, his face a white mask of astonishment. "You fool! You have doomed your world. Now there is nowhere for you to hide. We are coming, High Queen! We are coming!"

As we all stepped through the portal, Valdara gave Moregoth a smile as sharp as an executioner's blade. "We will be waiting."

EPILOGUE

The night after we arrived in Trelari, I could not sleep. After lying in bed for a while staring up at the heavy canopy and listening to Vivian breathing softly beside me, I rose and wandered out to the balcony. Our room was in a high tower in Valdara's castle citadel. From here I had a commanding view of the city below and the surrounding hills beyond. The moon was full and painted everything in silvery blues and deep purples. I grasped the cold stone battlements and peered into the night sky. Despite the beauty something was bothering me. I had a feeling that something was out there, waiting for me.

I was staring into the vague shadows of the night, wondering what it might be and why I seemed to know it, when Vivian came up beside me. At her touch I nodded toward the distant hills. "Can you feel it?"

She studied the outline of the dark hills. Worry creased her forehead. "I can. It feels familiar. What is it?"

I pointed to a strangely shaped rock rising from one of the heights. "Look!" As we watched, something unfurled enormous batlike wings and shot into the sky. My heart caught in my chest. The silhouette belonged to Loshlaith, the viper dragon, the most powerful of all the Dark Lord's minions. I knew without a doubt that he had been waiting for me to regard him.

The dragon made a few looping passes over the city. When it was above the castle, it roared, and as it did, my head was filled with visions of rage demons and blood orcs, the undead hordes and lowly gibberlings. Out there, beyond the hills, they were waking from deep slumbers and crawling from the dungeons and the dark places of the world, answering a silent call. I felt the touch of the viper dragon once more in my mind. The moment I'd been both waiting for and dreading as it reaffirmed its allegiance.

I bow to thee, the dragon thought.

I almost answered back, but stopped as Vivian stiffened beside me. With horror, I realized she also was feeling the dragon's call. She grabbed my hand, and we stared at each other. Long after Loshlaith disappeared into the night sky, the names it gave us still echoed in our heads.

My liege, the Dark Lord, and my lady, the Dark Queen.

We held each other until the sky lightened with the dawn and the shadow of the dragon's thoughts faded from our minds.

"What do we do?" Vivian asked.

She was shaking, and I wrapped an arm around her. "We do what all leaders do when the clouds of war appear," I said distantly. "We gather our army."

"What army?" she asked. "Not . . . not those creatures?"

"Perhaps," I said, pulling her closer. "This world appears determined to make me its Dark Lord and you its Dark Queen."

"But I don't want that," Vivian said, her voice quavering slightly.

"Neither do I, but if there is one thing I have learned recently it's that what I want rarely matters."

She thought about it for a second and then laughed. "As an inspirational message that was pretty terrible. Remind me never to ask you to sign my yearbook."

I looked into her eyes and smiled. "Yeah, but remember this is only a middle book. We have to save the real insightful stuff for book three."

We both laughed, but it was hollow and we grew quiet again. After a time, she asked, "Seriously, Avery, what do we do now?"

I started to say I didn't know, but realized that I did. For the first time in months I knew exactly what I wanted and needed: time to talk and someone to listen. I also knew exactly how to get it. I almost felt Griswald's finger touching my chest.

"He's still guiding me," I whispered.

Vivian started to ask me what I meant, but I shook my head and turned my focus on the empty place just beside my heart. I found there something I had not noticed before, a line of magic, thin as spider silk and strong as steel, and began to trace it out into the empty depths of the multiverse. I gave it a mental tug and there was an acknowledging jerk at the far end. With a thrill of anticipation, I pulled as hard as I could. Something raced toward me out of the ether. It came on, faster and faster, and then its reality collided with mine. My whole being rocked as the tight space in my chest filled with warmth.

A familiar weight settled on my shoulder and wheezed wetly in my ear. I reached into my pocket and pulled out a butterscotch candy.

"Want one?"

ACKNOWLEDGMENTS

We would like to acknowledge everyone that helped get us to this point, but since listing everyone is impossible we offer the following. For everyone who isn't listed, we want you to know that you made a difference and we appreciate it.

As always, we would like to thank our families: Heather, Taba, Isaac and Carleigh. Inspiration comes in many forms, but you are our best.

We would like to thank our editor, Priyanka, who is an absolute delight. We appreciate everything you've done to make this book a reality. We'd also like to thank the rest of the team at Harper for everything from publicity to cover design to copyedits to simply believing in us.

To our fellow Harper authors, thank you for your continued support. We would like to give a special thanks to Bishop O'Connell for always sharing great stories and being infinitely supportive, as well as having a strong t-shirt game. Rook is probably a reference to you. Probably.

Finally, to Evan, thank you for being our biggest Charming fan. We appreciate it more than you know.

Harry would also like to thank:

The Hanover Writers Club. I appreciate my monthly dose of encouragement more than you know.

Piper, for inspiring me. I can't wait to read your first novel.

The Leethams-Kevin, Andrew, Nicholas, Jacob, and a special call out to Lindsey, for being a fantastic intern and an impressive world-eating plant. Amy, thank you for sharing your family.

My amazing team—Connor, Drew, Kim, Mark, and Terry, you make each day special. Christina, thank you for the Pocky. And everyone else at Unboxed Technology, you are all awesome.

Kayla, Zu, and Cathy, for friendships and bonds that last.

Dad, thanks for always supporting my writing, and thank you to the rest of my family, for making me feel like an international bestseller.

Heather, none of this happens without all you do, and Carleigh, everything I write is for you. I love you both.

John would also like to thank:

Oliver, Isaac and Taba, who always agree to read these books before they have any right to be read.

David, Joel, Charles, and everyone else at KPPB. It is amazing that I get to work with such a talented group every day. For over a decade you have been the foundation that has allowed me to do this.

Finally, to my grandfather, Walt, who helped inject a sense of whimsy in my world, thank you for always spotting those purple cows.

ABOUT THE AUTHOR

JACK HECKEL's life is an open book. Actually, it's the book you are in all hope holding right now (and if you are not holding it, he would like to tell you it can be purchased from any of your finest purveyors of the written word). Beyond that, Jack aspires to be either a witty, urbane world traveler who lives on his vintage yacht, *The Clever Double Entendre*, or a geographically illiterate professor of literature who spends his nonwriting time restoring an eighteenth-century lighthouse off a remote part of the Vermont coastline. Whatever you want to believe of him, he is without doubt the author of *The Dark Lord*. and the Charming Tales series. More than anything, Jack lives for his readers.

Despite whatever Jack may claim, in reality Jack Heckel is the pen name for John Peck and Harry Heckel.